ACKNOWLEDGEMENTS

I thank all my sisters, especially Jenny Valentour, who showed me the better life, and Dr. Gail Gibson, who pushed me to finish the novel when I was ready to give up. Gail and Jenny know the sorrow and rejoicing that went into it, as does Sam, my husband, best friend, and right hand.

Members of my immediate family, especially my daughter, Heidi Klein, and son, Gary Solomon, were my backbone. I could not have published without them. Thank you, my dear ones.

I thank Jasmine Williams, a loyal typist and best friend. Thanks also to Henry Hurt, a successful writer and Editor-at-Large for the earlier *Reader's Digest*. I must also mention Amy Abbott and Linda Lemery from my River City Writers' group; they are great readers, writers, and friends. I appreciate those good friends like Collette Polsky who understood my absence from too much of the fun.

Last, I thank Joyce Wilburn, loyal friend and editor of *Evince* magazine in Danville, Virginia, who helped craft the book to the point of publication.

Abe Siler survived the explosion at Cordel-Lewis Number One coal mine. Survived it without so much as a scratch while ten others weren't so lucky. He'd experienced far worse explosions. Compared to most, this was merely a mishap. Still a part of him died that summer afternoon in Harlan County, Kentucky, there among a hundred or so other miners, namely *Uncle* Kromer Root and a greenie known simply as *Kid*.

It was the summer of 1955, blazing hot outside but underground temperature in the sixties. For months the miners had been carving into a six-foot coal face in one of the area's deepest and most dangerous seams. They had left coal pillars to hold up the million-ton ceiling and now returned to rob the last of those pillars, every second increasing the chance of a roof fall or gas explosion, or both.

Abe—tall, muscular, with silky black curls and rugged good looks—was the man in charge of cutting and drilling the coal before setting explosives. Today he yelled, "Fire in the pit!" three times, detonated the black powder, and ran like hell with the others. Blasting was one of the leading causes of mine fatalities, but Abe was a pro. Though his hands shook and his heart pounded in his ears, fear of a misfire was the least of his worries.

The coal landed safely, and the miners stooped through the tunnel and back to the working face. Along the way Uncle teased a rat and chuckled as it skittered through lunch crumbs and old wrappers. Abe joined in the fun.

But the new kid had no such sense of humor. He was a tall, lanky fellow with blonde hair, blue eyes, a nose turned-up to resemble an electrical outlet, and a wide-eyed look of innocence and naïveté. He, like Uncle, had the dangerous job of hand shoveling the stray coals onto the electric conveyor belt while avoiding a spark.

"Them rats is drivin' me nuts!" the kid complained. "Cain't they poison 'em or somethin', them nasty, ugly rats? They give me the creeps!"

"Listen, kid," Abe warned, "Them rats is a miner's best friend." He pushed toward the cutting machine and his next section. "If the earth shifts, they'll be the first ones to run and you'd be smart to follow!" He took his seat on the machine and glanced over his shoulder to see the kid's legs trembling under his coveralls. Abe had a green-behind-the-ears kid of his own, one of the lucky ones, hell-bent on college. "How long you been in?" he asked with more interest than usual, and pictured a jailhouse.

"A month. I got a girl, Elsie, and we got a eight-month-old baby. Come Sunday we're gettin' hitched—provided I live that long!"

"You're not drunk enough is what your problem is," Uncle teased and slapped his thigh with such delight that you could see his missing molars.

"I don't drink," the kid said. "Had a drinker daddy. Damn near kilt my ma. Me, I'm gonna do better." He studied the live wires running down the tunnel walls and stuttered, "It's a bad thing to die in a mine and nobody can find you."

Abe tapped a shovel against the coal ceiling and frowned at the shrill, warning sound of a soft top and possible rooffall.

The walls were fuzzy with ignitable dust and in bad need of a water dusting to keep down the fire risk.

"You'll be okay," he said.

"Elsie calls this place a hellhole," the kid volunteered. "Satan's furnace."

"Kid, you'd be smart not to think so much. Thinkin' can get a man into...trouble." Abe coughed and spit black on black. "Into deep shit," he'd meant to say before eyeing an old, neglected pile of coal scraps and dust at the kid's feet, too close to the conveyor tailpipe and a possible spark.

"But what if somethin' bad was to happen and Elsie, she ain't got nobody to look after her and the baby?"

"Just you keep a eye on them rats." The light on Abe's hard hat danced ahead to the foreman, the man with the gas gauge, in charge of safety but owned by the bastard Company.

He, a big fat man with a short neck, glared at Abe and blew on a whistle.

"Keep that coal movin'!" he yelled.

"You sure?" The kid sleeved his runny nose. "You sure it's safe?"

"In this hole, *sure* turned tail and run. But the Company has safety standards to meet, so if I was you, I think I'd be more scared of a shotgun wedding." Abe placed a hand on the kid's shoulder, dropped it a second later, and mounted his machine. Down here the name of the game was survival. Down here fear turned men into the stuff laid to rest in closed coffins or under rocks. Down here was no place for pity.

"Don't forget. The wedding's on Sunday," the kid called.

"Happy humpin'!" Uncle said and winked.

"Yeah, congratulations." Abe had slammed the gear into reverse and was moving toward his next section when he tasted sweat and realized a ventilation fan at the surface had stopped pumping cold, clean air. "Dammit to hell!" he cursed and delivered a bone-on-steel blow before lunging off the machine and toward a hundred or so unsuspecting miners, working on as usual.

"Run!" he shouted, his arms prodding, slapping, funneling men deeper in the mine toward the escape portal and shutting off sections.

"Run!" he shouted while helping to carry out gassed miners.

"Run!" he was shouting when the place exploded in fire and rock, and he hit the outside ground just seconds before going back for the kid.

CHAPTER ONE

At the time of the explosion, Lily, Abe's wife and the unofficial camp nurse, toiled over a galvanized-tin washboard and tub in a drab little kitchen equipped with a cook stove. The mining camp, Lewellyn, was one of a hundred or so such camps on Clover Fork, a branch of the Cumberland River. It was the home of Cordel-Lewis No. 1 mine and some five hundred mine employees—three hundred working the pit and two hundred the surface.

Lily was a sensible woman, more handsome than beautiful, and as unaffected as nature. Her Hershey-brown hair drawn back from her face, her light splay of caramel-colored freckles, and her loose-fitting clothes gave off an air of modesty and self-containment. Although she was not a woman given to dreaming, her tub sat on a board-and-block table under a window, where she would sometimes watch the sun rise and set over the dusty, mountainous region known as Appalachia. But this day there was rain.

Lily and Abe had what was considered a good marriage and six fine children, their ages ranging from six to eighteen. Their youngest, Rosy, stricken by rheumatoid arthritis and mostly home schooled, lolled on a nearby rollaway bed in a mound of Little Golden flea-market books and make-believe toys, notably an old fur collar that passed for a teddy bear or nose tickler when she sucked her thumb. The house, a three-room shack owned by the Company, appeared to face backwards. It had a railed front porch under a lean-to, two splintered plank steps stacked on field stones, and gray clapboard siding with six single windows. The inside was hard swept and lean. In the living room, pictures of Franklin Delano Roosevelt and "The Last Supper" hung over a navy mohair couch with a matching armchair and ottoman. A line of rain buckets stared up at yellow and brown rings on the kitchen side of the ceiling.

The wind and rain started slow but mushroomed into a storm. Within minutes, thunder rattled the windowpanes. Lightning shot through a lace curtain, and a wall lamp over the loft staircase flickered off and on. Rosy clung to Hairy, the fake fur collar, and screamed for her mama.

"Read me a book," Lily called as she lit a coal-oil lamp in case they lost power and then ran to calm her.

"It's ghosts from the mine! They're rattling the windows trying to get in!" Rosy cried.

"There's no such thing as ghosts, and you know it. Hopefully the storm will blow over."

"What if it blows our house down?"

"It won't."

"But it could."

"Then we'll hold on to…"

"God," Lily was about to say when the mountain roared and a vibration rocked the house like a marauding tornado. Cabinet doors flew open. Glass dishes and doodads slid off shelves and tables, crying as they crashed. Fiberboard tables sailed across warped linoleum floors, slick with Johnson wax.

Above all the commotion Rosy recognized the blood-curdling screech of the mine whistle. A look of torture shot across her face, and she flew off the bed, her arthritic joints popping.

"The mine alarm!" she announced with a sob. "Daddy's hurt!"

"It's probably a mistake. I'll go in case I'm needed, and you stay here and wait for your sisters and brother. Tell them I said I'll send word, and they're not to leave the house, hear!" Lily kept her voice level and her hug playful. She tossed aside her bibbed apron, grabbed her nurse's kit, and headed toward the door and ultimately the mine.

Rosy threw on her hand-me-down clothes and shoes and was reaching for her leg splint.

"I'm going too."

"No, it's too far and too wet. You stay home and pray."

"But Daddy might be hurt...or something."

"Daddy's smart. He can take care of himself." Lily could not bear to look back at the child's spray of red freckles, her snaggle-toothed mouth set in an O, her short brown hair that spiked after nights of battling with leg pain and sleep. She sprang for the door as Rosy clicked the last buckle on her splint, threw herself forward, and launched at Lily's hemline. Refusing to let go, she teetered and fell on her stomach while Lily tore free and ran.

Outside, Lily heard Rosy screaming and tearing at the door she had locked behind her, and she yearned to turn back. Her mind flicked to the past and her own ma tying her squalling younguns to bedposts so they wouldn't follow her toward the *devil's laugh* mine whistle. Her ma's overall principle—"You do what you gotta do!"—was like a wind at her back.

That and the fact that her bigger-than-life husband could be maimed or dead like the others.

Abe woke up in a stupor, spotting the wreckage and crying out for his son, Will, who he confused with the new kid. On a naked hillside above him, coughing miners from every shift stood with their hats in their hands, grieving and swearing at the sonovabitching Company.

"Will's safe," Uncle said. "He's home with the girls."

"He is? Are you sure?"

Uncle tugged on an ear.

"Sure."

"What happened?" he asked but didn't wait for an answer. He blinked at the ominous black cloud above the mine, re-claimed most of his memory, and pushed up with his hands only to fall back down. The doctor ordered everybody to move back and give the man air.

"The new kid?" he asked.

"There was a explosion and cave-in," Uncle said. "Thanks to you, most got out in time. The portal's blocked now with ten men trapped inside. The rescue team's on its way."

Abe cringed. "Who?" he snapped and pulled back the tears while Uncle accounted for nine.

"The kid? Where's the kid?"

In the silence, Abe sought out Uncle's eyes. Wet, brooding eyes, in spite of his usual bullshit.

"Let's go git 'em!" he cried, and squirmed to get up.

Uncle threw out a hand to stop him.

"Buddy, you know we're not allowed back inside."

"Says who? The Company what sent a kid to do a man's job? I good as promised I'd watch over him. He trusted me."

"Let the rescue team save 'em. They're safety equipped."

"Hell, we can dig!"

Abe pushed up on legs weak as cornstalks, and staggered toward a pickaxe and shovel. Uncle, shaking his head, followed with the others.

A mob of neighbors swarmed Lily in a fog of umbrellas and arms. They stomped through gardens and garbage, and through puddles of runoff from high surface privies. Barefoot, snotty-nosed children jerked along by a mother screamed at the lightning, thunder, and barking dogs dragging their chains.

Lily ran a distance of two miles, all the while dodging speeding pickups, their beds packed with welded tool boxes, caged dogs, and mining families from outside the camp. At the tracks she squeezed between gondola cars and entered the mine yard—a maze of old railroad ties, junked parts, and trashed rocks and slate. Twice she fell and got up, a swoop of rain licking the blood.

"Please, Lord, please let me find Abe okay!" she was praying when she spotted Luke Myers, the camp doctor.

"Luke!" she cried. "What happened? Where's Abe?"

"Don't know much. They're saying the conveyor belt most likely overheated and ignited the coal dust. Ten men still inside. The rescue team's here now and waiting for the gas to clear so they can go in."

"Oh, dear Lord!" she whispered as if praying. "Abe? Have you seen Abe?"

Dr. Myers pointed toward an arc of pink lights over the mine's entrance.

"He was fighting to get back inside when I last saw him. The rescue team stopped him, of course, and now I hear he's organized his own team and is breaking rocks at the surface, hoping to clear an air pocket which is not likely, but..."

By then Lily was well beyond hearing range. The rain came down hard, then soft. Twenty or so feet beyond the mine entrance, in a knot of bare-backed miners swinging sledge hammers, pickaxes, and shovels, she spotted Abe's muscular shoulders and back, and his mouth snarled with curses. She threw out her arms and ran like a girl.

"Abe!"

"Lily!"

He hurled aside his tool, and they gripped each other so tight his mud and dust smeared her housedress. She held his head in her hands and kissed him with such passion that the other miners might have blushed under their blackness.

"Oh, Abe! I was so worried! Thank God you're safe!" She dusted the grit from his eyebrows and teeth. "What happened?"

"Explosion and cave-in due to gas and faulty ventilation. Nine men and the kid trapped inside." He hacked up some mucus and tucked his tongue against the roof of his mouth for an angry spit.

Smoking slag heaps gave off the stench of sulphur and smoke, commonly known as the devil's bad breath. Ambulances and fire trucks shrieked as their engines roared and their wheels crunched over broken scraps of coal. Women rattled the chain-link fence and howled like coyotes. They waved fists and damned the no-good company.

"Go home," Abe told Lily. "See to the kids."

"Any idea how long?"

"Hours. Days. Go on now. Tell 'em their ole man's safe and got ever'thing under control. Not to worry."

"If you're sure, I'll go and come back."

"And tell Will I said soon as we shore up here, him and me'll go fishin'."

"I love you!" Lily shouted as she turned and ran without looking back.

"Yo!" he yelped, and in spite of it all—his pathetic urge and puny chance—she threw back her head and let out a laugh.

CHAPTER TWO

A rescue team worked through the rubble and carried ten men from the pit to the surface some nineteen hours later. Dr. Myers pronounced seven dead on the scene. The kid had burned to death and was identified by a circular brass tag clutched in a hand. An ambulance rushed three others to the hospital in Harlan town, the county seat, a high and rugged spot in the Cumberland Plateau, not far from Virginia.

Bleary-eyed wives passed out sandwiches and hot coffee in the mine yard. The *Louisville Courier-Journal* and *Knoxville News Sentinel* snapped photos of the wrecked tipple hillside. Abe searched the yard for families of the victims. He made a point of breaking the news to Elsie, the kid's girlfriend, and left her, limp and muddled, in the care of older, more grief-experienced women.

It was Saturday then, and still raining. Under street lights installed to discourage violence in case of a strike, Lily plodded the muddy trail home. The air smelled charred, tinted with the odors of outrage and fear.

Once there, she went straight to the loft, where four daughters spooned in an iron bed, its frame painted brown to match a gutted Victrola cabinet used as a clothes chest. A quilt, made from squares of old dresses, lay on the floor. With light from a dormer window, she checked it for spiders, centipedes, cockroaches, maybe a rat. In spite of the crawling creatures, she had always cherished nighttime. Growing up on a farm, she had loved it for its stars and moon, its promise of tranquility. Now she loved it for its power to disguise gloom.

When sure that each girl was fast asleep, she felt her way toward a little bed inside an arched closet, where she found Rosy cuddled to her brother, 18-year-old John William, *Will* to his daddy and *Sweet William* to the females of the family. She reached to feel the child's forehead for fever and brushed away her tears.

"Why aren't you sleeping?" Lily asked softly.

"I was afraid. Is Daddy okay?"

"Didn't Ceola tell you?"

"Yes, but I thought she just didn't want me to worry."

"Daddy's fine. You go back to sleep, and I promise he'll be here when you wake up in the morning."

Rosy gripped Lily's hands.

"Why not tonight?"

"Because some families were less fortunate. He wants to go comfort them."

"Who?"

"We'll have to ask your daddy."

"Should I wake up Hairy and tell him?"

"Why not let him and Sweet William sleep?"

"But Hairy had the *mopsies* like me."

"Then by all means, wake him," Lily whispered as she tiptoed toward the girls' room, threw kisses, and turned to go down.

While waiting at the hospital for news of the three injured miners, Abe silently prayed to the Man Upstairs and dropped his head to hide more tears. Thirst hit him like hunger for food, and he craved the silky smooth taste of sweet liquor.

Liquor, he thought, the universal switch for turning darkness into light. Too bad he'd promised Lily he was done with the stuff.

In his thirty-three years of mining coal he reckoned he'd seen it all. He'd seen miners with short-handled shovels and coal picks crawl through seams on their bellies. He'd seen men run down by trams, drowned by floods from underground springs, crushed to death under fallen rocks, electrocuted by live wires, and burned to the bone. He'd heard the shrill cries of miners scratching through rocks, looking for a hand or a foot. He'd seen legs and arms fall from a stretcher, and the jam-like guts of those scooped up in a shovel.

Yep, he'd seen it all with nerves made of steel because you had to. Because grieve and leave was the motto. But this time was different. This time they'd been the brutal, all-for-nothing death of a innocent kid the likes of your own. A fearful kid that takes you back to your own first descent into silence so queer it rings in your head, and so black you know you've reached hell.

"Damn the Company! Damn their sorry asses!" he said to himself and prayed the doctor would come with good news.

He left the Harlan hospital somewhat relieved and drove through Golden Ash and Blackjoe, through rain so heavy his Studebaker crawled like some gutless road animal circled by vultures. His head throbbed. His joints ached with a bone-on-bone soreness. His mind couldn't let go of the kid he'd helped kill, and the six other brothers he'd failed to save. *Brothers* at this moment, nameless and faceless, he thought, because such made them seem not so real and their deaths easier to take.

He turned on the radio and lit a Camel, and still his mind drifted. He'd not always wanted to be a coal miner, he recalled. As a boy he'd loved going to school and reading books. But when Prohibition came and the war with revenuers got too bloody, his daddy'd forced him to drop out of fourth grade and work in a coal mine as his *chalkeye* apprentice. Chalkeyes did jobs like separating waste slate from coal, opening and closing trap doors to keep the gas out, and bailing water from underground streams. As a lonely kid scared to death of the dark, he'd calmed his nerves by making chalk drawings on black walls. It beat going nuts.

He'd survived the Depression of the 1930s and the days of Bloody Harlan, with its picket line confrontations and gun thugs licensed to kill United Mine Workers of America sympathizers. He'd lived to see the time when men were paid by the day and not by the pound; when coal was cut by a machine and not by a auger and pick; when motors and shelly cars moved the coal, not ponies and donkeys; when men wore battery-powered lamps on their hats in the place of open carbide torches. But the overall character of a coal company—its greed and more greed—hadn't changed. Otherwise seven dead miners would still be alive.

Before reaching his home in Lewellyn, he passed some twenty miles of vacant ghost camps with only gas pumps and a post office to prove they'd existed. Near midnight, he parked on a hillside before his house and spotted his good buddy, Dog Brackin, rain-soaked and flagging.

Dog was a stout, level-eyed man with a handlebar mustache, paunchy jowls, and a possum-gray ring of hair. He was the son of *Bull Dog* and daddy to *Pup,* his only child, a third-generation miner electrocuted in a flood from an underground stream. Foreman of the hoot-owl shift, Dog lived on privileged Silk Stocking Row and was in charge of mostly cleanup and repair, but with too few workers and broken-down equipment.

"Howdy," Abe said and threw out a hand.

Dog caught both the hand and the sarcasm.

"Get in out of the storm," he said.

"It ain't storming."

"It will be. What's the word?"

"Seven brothers dead, as you know, God rest their souls. The new kid must've panicked and got lost in the flames. Tub and Stormy are being treated for smoke and gas inhalation. Josh has a concussion and some cracked ribs."

Dog removed his cap and ran a hand over his head as if plowing through a feather duster of hair.

"Damn shame, especially about the kid, only a boy. You can bet your bottom dollar the Company'll blame it on lightning."

"I guarandamntee it." Abe eased out of the Studebaker. He'd been sweating as if still on the job, and the drizzle felt good. It helped keep his eyes open.

"Filthy hot mine. That dust so damn thick you could plow it. The men's threatenin' to strike and you cain't blame 'em," Dog said.

"Hell, no, you cain't!"

Dog glanced down the hillside toward his house.

"The wife's a nervous wreck. She's afraid some hothead will get drunk and fire at one of us foremen." He faked a laugh. "You know how women are."

Abe eyed the line of empty gondola cars on tracks under the slide tipple. It was the perfect place for a sniper to hide and aim at a row house.

"You got a gun?" he asked.

Dog shrugged his shoulders. "Somewhere, I guess."

"Find it."

Lily heard the slow, tired thud of Abe's boots on the back porch and ran to the door. Her long hair was brush-shined and her cheeks pinched the color of primrose. Not that she'd expected him to notice, but primping had helped her stay busy. It had given her a place to put her quivering hands.

"Oh, Abe, bless your heart!" She led him inside, had him sit down at the kitchen table, brought his ashtray, and served him coffee.

Rain plopped into buckets. The sad sound of Hank Snow singing "Let Me Go, Lover!" spilled from the radio. The dress she had worn to the mine lay soaking in a tub of increasingly black water.

"You should get out of those wet clothes. I'll help you," she said.

"I'm good," he answered. She stooped to remove his kneepads and cuff bands and heavy, hobnailed boots. "What a mell of a hess!" he said, and she knew he was not referring to the mud and dust on his clothes. Careful to sound cheerful, so he would consider himself pampered but not nursed, she cleaned his cuts with antiseptics, dabbing rather than rubbing and blowing the sting. Then she served him bacon and eggs with biscuits and white sawmill gravy and sat down with her own cup of coffee to study him over its rim.

"Lily, I don't feel like eatin'," he said.

"Try." She reached to check his forehead for fever. He dodged her hand and pushed away the plate.

"The dodos?" he asked.

THE TIME TO RUN · 23

"The children are fine." She returned the plate. "The poor little things had a tough night so I had them sleep in. Rosy said she had the mopsies. I'm sure she's awake. Should I have her come down? Should I wake the others?"

"The mopsies again, eh? Did you tell her I said there wadn't no cause to worry?" He yawned into his hand and leaned across the table. "Lily, there was this kid about the same age as Will I been tellin' you about. He's dead and it was my fault."

"I heard. Edgar Jarvis. It was not your fault but the Company's!"

"He was countin' on me to save him. I good as told him I would."

"You did your best."

"Like hell I did!" He slammed down a fist that left flakes of dirt on the table. "Damn me. I knew he wadn't ready. I should've had Uncle keep a eye out."

"You weren't the one who hired him."

"He had a baby and was all set to get married. Blond and lean like Will he was but not near as smart. I know times is tough, Lily, but I was thinkin' we might could give Elsie, his girl, a little somethin' to help out."

"Of course, and the girls and I can knit baby clothes." She took in the stench of sweat and bad breath, of anger and yearning. In an ashtray his cigarette shrank into a rope of gray ash.

"I looked that kid square in the eye and made like he'd be okay. A stupid thing it was, and I damn well knew it. You cain't make promises in a hole run by the devil. Not where rights to that black gold are concerned, you cain't." He swiped half a biscuit over the gravy and downed it in one bite. "You say the dodos are okay?"

"Proud to a fault."

"Prou...?" His hoarse voice gave out. He coughed and spit, nabbed a breath of air and asked again, "Proud?"

"Proud of their daddy's courage. Everybody's talking about it. They say the Company tampered with the foreman's gas gauge to make it read lower. Hon, you're a hero!"

"A hero, huh?" His eyes softened, then fired up again. "Hell, I ain't no hero. It's just that I know the place, see? I went to work in that pit when I wadn't knee-high to a grasshopper. Ole Beelzebub and me, we rubbed sleeves. Hell, the two of us, we're damn near family!"

Lily threw a glance toward the loft. Satisfied that no one, not even Rosy, was listening, she went to stand behind him, rolling the skin toward his shoulders and massaging the swollen places. Back and forth her hands worked, like a bride over-kneading her first loaf of bread.

"Lily, I ain't kiddin'. The devil, he's there in that pit— guardin' what's his, claimin' a pound of flesh for every ton of coal mined."

"Hon, maybe what you're describing is the pressure you feel when you're down there. The pressure of knowing the mine's unsafe and everybody's life depends on you and not the foreman."

"Pressure, hell! What pressure?"

"Well, anyway, everybody's grateful that you knew when to run."

"A good miner always knows when to run."

Again and again Lily had rehearsed this moment of Abe's homecoming. She had planned to delight him with food and affection, to make him feel like the next best thing to God Himself. But her intentions, however sincere, were overcome by a nagging sense of duty.

"Hon, maybe you need to quit them mines now, while you still can," she suggested.

"Lily, that mine's the tune I dance to. Why sit it out when you can dance to it?"

"Because your mother's right. You're digging your own grave in that pit."

He guzzled down what was left of his coffee and thrust out the mug.

"Be a good girl," he said.

She brought him a fresh cup but didn't sit down. He stirred in a Goody's Powder and watched it dissolve.

"You worry too much."

"But next time you may not be so lucky."

"Luck? Luck, hell! Luck ain't got nary a thing to do with it. We outsmarted the ole rascal is what we done. Smarts, that's the ticket!"

"But your lungs…"

"Not now, Lily."

"You need to go see a doctor."

"I said not now."

Lily was not one to backtalk, but today she had assumed the role of a nurse, a professional, and felt stronger as a result.

"Then when?"

Abe gritted his teeth, slammed down the coffee mug, and screeched back his chair, and she ran to go fill his tub with hot water. Along the way she grabbed Deep Heat and the faded black towel that hid stains; then she came back to help him undress. He limped toward the water and inched down on his back, leaving his legs dangling. When he'd squirmed into a position of bearable pain, he hummed "Ah-h-h" and reached for her hand.

CHAPTER THREE

Like the patients she'd seen take a bad turn and die, Lily watched Abe's personality change after the explosion. When they made love, it was not the slow, gentle, made-to-order kind he'd always taken pride in, but a manhandling rush of choppy movements and hard breaths, as if he were angry or drunk. Now, the best part of loving was falling asleep afterwards, her head on his shoulder and her legs entwined in his.

Two weeks after the explosion came even more bad news—a hen-scratched letter from Maude, Abe's overly zealous mother, complaining that she had taken to her bed after hearing of the awful mine explosion but hoped to be well enough to visit by the weekend. Nothing agitated Abe more than her fanatic lectures against mining coal and her unreasonable insistence that the coal pit and Satan's pit were one in the same.

Lily fretted over the bad timing. In spite of her dread, she managed a smile before gathering the children to share the news and assign duties.

"Let's make this place so clean Maude will forget it's a row house," she said as she covered the dust mop with a pair of old rayon panties and set up a utility ladder for Verni, sixteen and the oldest daughter. Then she put Iris, fifteen and sick with asthma, in charge of washing windows with Daisy and Tansy, junior high students, sometimes referred to as *the twinsies*, as her helpers. Sweet William, eighteen, was to do the yard work.

"What about me?" Rosy, six, curled her fingers around a lacquered broom handle with straggly gray straw. "Don't I get a job?"

"You can sweep the porch," Lily said.

"Why does Grandmother have to come here? Why can't we go there instead?" Verni—radiant with ruby cheeks and bright, fleshy lips—blew away a strand of curly black hair.

"You know your daddy has to stay here to shore up the mine section and clear away rubble." Lily wiped flour fingerprints from a rusty-rimmed canister and measured the last of the cornmeal, hoping to stretch it into enough fritters for supper.

"We could go without him if you'd learn to drive," Verni said.

Lily threw up her hands, palms outward to ward off the thought.

"Why, law, your daddy would have a conniption."

Verni shrugged her shoulders. "So what?"

"Is Grandmother coming to scold Daddy again?" Rosy asked. "Will she say he'll die and burn in hellfire?"

"Sure she will. She bores me to death with all that God crap," Verni said.

"Verni!" Lily scolded. "Trust me, Verni, you will not die of boredom. When you've lived through as many ups and downs as I have, you will realize that boredom is beautiful, the absence of conflict. Oh, how I wish I could be bored for just one single day."

"You're welcome to mine!"

"Verni, mind your tongue!"

"Okay, so long as we don't have to mind Grandmother. She thinks everything we do is catching our death."

"Mind your parents and respect your grandparents," Lily said. "Love all four."

"Yeah, well, that's easy for you to say," Verni snapped, and Lily was tempted to say that when it came to Abe's mother, nothing was easy.

Maude and General Sherman Siler, Abe's parents, journeyed close to a hundred miles over hairpin mountain roads enclosed by sandstone-limestone bluffs and dense stands of rhododendron and mountain laurel. As their Ford pickup truck approached the mining camp, Maude took out her starched handkerchief and sobbed into a bouquet of embroidered roses.

To her, a stern Pentecostal Holiness Christian, the trip was a mission; more than a mission, it was an obsession, a chance to save her son, body and soul, from the devil's underground pit.

The couple arrived as the girls were putting away the dinner dishes, turning them upside-down so they wouldn't collect coal dust. At the time there happened to be sunshine, so rare in a mining camp people said it was piped in.

Maude, sixteen years younger than General Sherman, was in her mid-fifties. Dressed in a long navy dress with a white lace collar and thick, high-heeled tie shoes, she wore her usual eagle frown, justified, she believed, by the fact that there is not one shred of evidence in the Bible that Jesus Christ ever smiled. General Sherman, never a soldier, wore a plaid flannel shirt and droopy overalls. Next to Maude, he looked like the short end of a chicken wishbone. He, too, was a Christian, a deacon in the church. But before his conversion fifteen years earlier, he'd sold whiskey for a living, the safer kind, run through clean copper tubing.

Abe met his parents on the front porch.

"How do?" he said, and edged behind Lily.

"Son Boy!" Maude cried. She hugged him so tight he pretended to choke and then planted a kiss on his face that he boyishly wiped off. Sherman hugged Lily as he would a real daughter, and she gave him an extra squeeze to say he was loved. Abe and his mother walked ahead, and Lily waited while Sherman gave each of the children a stick of Beech-Nut chewing gum and an Indian Head penny. The older three made themselves scarce while the younger ones stayed behind for company treats.

Inside, Abe pointed to a couch with sunken seats and squealing springs.

"Take a load off, why don'tchy," he said and turned to Lily. "Be a good girl and bring 'em some coffee."

The three sat down while Lily hurried to the kitchen. Knowing what was coming, she shooed the children outside, left the coffee brewing, and returned to support Abe.

Maude wasted no time. She snatched the mine-explosion article from her purse and flicked it at Abe.

"I ain't slept a wink since it happened," she said. "I had to come see for myself that you ain't kilt or maimed like them others!"

"Well, now you see I'm fine and dandy."

"Not for long you ain't. *I cast them down to hell with them that descend into the pit!* the Bible says. "That includes you, Son Boy."

"Take it easy, Maude." Sherman removed his old straw hat and worked its rim with his fingers.

"Mother, things are different now." Lying made Abe nervous. He chewed his upper lip and raked a hand through his hair. "Today there's more mine safety regulations. Better ventilation and housekeepin', more rock dustin'. Nobody could've predicted lightnin' would take out a ventilation fan. Freak things like that happen."

"Don't you lie to me. Everybody knows the Company don't put equipment down until it breaks down."

Abe coughed and fumbled his guitar belt buckle.

"Mother, work's scarce. I got a wife and kids what have to be fed."

As they spoke, the afternoon sun meandered behind a peak, and a shadow fell over the window, turning day to dust.

"The valley of the shadow of death!" Maude wailed. "It's the Lord telling you, Son Boy, that unless you leave this here mining camp, there will be no green pastures and no still waters. Your family will bear the suffering of what you've brung on."

Abe's breaths rose and fell, calling attention to his swollen lungs and chest.

"Dammit, Mother!" he yelled.

Lily ran to the kitchen and rushed back with a tray of coffee, vanilla wafers, and cherry Kool-Aid. She placed it on the coffee table and deliberately sent Abe and Sherman outside to bring in the younger children. She was expecting Maude to be her usual anxious self and was surprised by the new, kind look on her face.

"Lily! Sweet Lily! I been looking forward to our own chance to talk. Shame on Abe that he don't bring you to visit me more." Maude yanked Lily onto the couch and squeezed her hands until they hurt. "Us women have got to stick together and I need you to help me convince Abe to leave that pit and Satan behind while he still can. He thinks I'm just a foolish old woman but you, he'll listen to."

"I've tried, Maude, honestly, but he won't budge. Bless you for caring, but we both know coal is his life's blood."

"Threaten to take these younguns and leave if he don't and I guarantee he'll come to his senses."

Lily pulled back her hands. She turned away from the wild look of Maude's eyes and the whistling urgency of her breath.

"Oh, no, no I couldn't. Not now. Not while he's still grieving. See, for some weird reason, he holds himself responsible for the...accident."

"He'll grieve a whole lot more if you don't!"

"You know he's got a bad temper, especially now. If I upset him, he might take it out on the children."

"The children need a daddy, temper or no, who's gonna put food on the table and a roof over their heads." Maude got up and fell to her knees. "Please, Lily, please. He's all I got. Think as if it was Sweet William, *your* only son. Would you just stand by and let Sweet William die a devil death?"

"I'll try again when it's safe," Lily said.

Maude put out a snicker. Her hands made fists in her lap.

"Safe? Safe and him in that pit? No, we got to do it now! Today! The boy's cursed, I tell you. Not just his body but his soul is at stake!"

"Maude, Pa's a preacher, and he feels Abe's soul is safe. He says Abe shows his faith by his good works."

"Bull. Abe needs to repent and be forgive of his sins before his personal Lord and Savior."

Lily adjusted her face to hide the irritation.

"What sins, Maude? Why do you dwell on Abe's sins? Did something bad happen in the past that I don't know about? Is there a family secret I'm not aware of? Tell me, please. What makes you so convinced Abe's doomed to damnation? Tell me, and maybe I can help."

Maude hopped up and grabbed her pocketbook.

"You'll help by doing what you're told."

"They're back!" Lily called and ran outside to join Abe and Sherman as they returned with the younger children. To avoid another Maude scene, the family—joined by Iris, Vernie, and Sweet William—said their loving goodbyes outside. Then Sherman climbed inside his pickup and honked for Maude.

Maude came in time, dabbed her eyes, hugged Abe and the children, and blew kisses. She shot Lily a glaring look, and Lily, the peacemaker, answered with a helpless expression of apology. All five girls followed Sherman's pickup toward the school playground, and Sweet William pedaled off on his bike.

"Make sure she exercises her legs," Lily called to Verni, who had hoisted arthritic Rosy onto a hip and was toting her like a heavy sack of potatoes. Daisy and Tansy skipped ahead. Iris trailed behind, her hands in her pockets, her eyes on the ground.

When alone, Lily noticed Abe holding his chest.

"Come lay down, and I'll fix you a cold compress," she said.

"Naw." He lit a cigarette, took a slow drag, and stared toward the mine tipple, the only place he knew where a man was judged by how much coal he mined, and women, considered bad luck, were not allowed past the supply yard. In time he flicked the flame from the cigarette, saved the butt in his shirt pocket, lumbered inside, swallowed a Goody's Powder, and sat down to stare at the newspaper.

Lily had bathed and washed her hair and changed into her housecoat. When she had prettied herself, she went into the kitchen and returned with two cups of coffee.

"John L. Lewis! Doesn't anybody bother to write about anything but John L. and his Union?" she asked from over his shoulders. She placed the tray on a table and squatted on the floor before him. He set aside the newspaper, and she placed her arms and chin on his knees, her sweet-smelling hair within easy reach of his fingers.

"Lily, I wish Mother wouldn't leave here in such a tizzy," he said. He coughed and winced from the pain. "If the ole gal would put aside the Jesus crap, she might see I ain't so bad a fellow. I'm a mason, ain't I?"

Lily looked on him as one would a small child with an *ouchy* to be kissed.

"She would indeed," she said, and planted a kiss on each knee. "The children are gone, and we have the house all to ourselves. Can you believe it?"

He slurped down his coffee.

"Sometimes she stares at me like mine's the face of the devil. Masons stand for good and right."

"It's only because she wants you out of the coal mines and into the church. We all do."

"It's like she sees me as some freak of nature."

"She hates the danger you're in, is all. Especially now, after the explosion."

"Well, she's barking up the wrong damn tree if she thinks I'm quittin'."

"You're tired," she said. "Why don't we go lie down? We can talk about it there."

"I'm a good family man, ain't I, Lily? Ain't that what counts?"

"Why, sure, you are. You're a good, hard-working man. The very best when you're not exhausted." She pulled back the collar of her robe and placed his hand on her chest.

"Why cain't she get it through her thick skull that I'm a believer like everybody else? At least part of the time."

"Try not to worry," she said weakly, and waited before heading toward the kitchen. The evening service was coming up, and everyone would need to be fed.

"Did I say I was worried? Hell, I ain't worried. It bugs me, is all. It bugs the livin' crap outa me, if you care to know the truth of the matter!"

CHAPTER FOUR

The girls returned from the school playground, and Rosy hopped onto Abe's lap, crushing his newspaper. "Daddy!" she cried.

"Hey, Squirt." *Squirt* he'd nicknamed her because she was small and quick. "My rose among the thorns," he sometimes said when no one else was listening.

"Can we play the make-up-words game? P-l-e-a-s-e?" She dropped her chin and pretended to pout in case he said no.

"Rosy, stop wallowing on your daddy," Lily called from the kitchen. "Verni, I need you to come bake the cornbread. Iris, you set the table."

"Yes, ma'am," they said since their daddy was there and wearing his miner's belt.

When Sweet William returned, the family sat down to a supper of cooked cabbage with leftover ham chips, sliced tomatoes and green onions fresh from the garden, and Verni's cornbread.

"Children, your daddy has a big surprise for you!" Lily said with cheer in her voice. She smiled so that her white teeth sparkled under the ceiling lightbulb. "While we were at church this morning and the other miners were having their Sunday snooze, he was out buying you treats."

"Snooze?" Verni said with a sneer. "You mean the other miners were soused on rot gut and sleeping it off. It's Sunday. Miners always break bad on Sundays."

Lily kicked Verni under the table.

"Tell them, hon," she told Abe.

"It's ice cream. I couldn't remember which flavor you each one like so I got vanilla and your mama here cooked up some strawberries."

"I wanted chocolate!"

"Vanilla ice cream with strawberries? Oh, boy! Can we have it now?"

"Please? Pretty please with sugar on it?"

"You girls know better. Now hush," Lily fussed, but with a proud curve of smile. "And bow your heads, please. I believe it's Iris' turn to say grace. Let's not forget to pray for the poor miners' families."

"Remember the kiss formula. Keep it simple, stupid," Sweet William teased.

"*Kiss*, formula? Oh, please! Like you would know!" Verni snipped.

"Children, please! Is this any way to thank your daddy?"

"Let 'em be, Lily. They ain't no harm in havin' fun."

Heads had bowed, and hands were reaching for hands when car horns beeped from the hillside. The smell of liquor and cigarette smoke drifted through screened windows.

"What on earth?" Lily shot from the table and to the front window. "Abe! It's the mine bunch!"

Abe was wearing socks, loose trousers, and a ribbed cotton undershirt. He grabbed a real shirt and shoes, and Lily followed him outside.

"What is it, Abe? What's going on?"

"It's nothin'. Eat and give them the ice cream."

"We'll hold supper."

"No. Feed them now and keep them in the kitchen, away from the windows."

Lily grabbed his arm, reconsidered, and let go.

"Abe, let the foreman handle it!"

"The foreman, hell! It's me they'll listen to."

"It's not your place."

"Go inside, Lily. And bolt the door."

Cars, trucks, and motorcycles lined up on Checkerboard Hill, midway up the mountain. Stubble-bearded miners carrying glass fruit jars and stoneware jugs tacked a sign to a sycamore tree pocked with bullet holes from the days of the Great Depression and Bloody Harlan. It read:

We ain't asking for a lot.

Just bread, milk, some beans in a pot.

Dog heard the commotion and came running. Sweet William also showed up, grinning as if the miners were pals from his high school in Evarts. Moving from vehicle to vehicle, he invited them to have coffee and a slice of his mama's lemon ice-box pies.

"Pie?" Abe asked with a grunt, and Sweet William winked.

"Thank ye just the same, Will, but we're here on business," Floyd Bowes called out.

"But Mama's already put the coffee on," he continued the charade.

"Another time, Will."

"Hush, Son! Go home b'fore your mama has a hissy fit."

Sweet William smiled again, showing good teeth like Lily's. A tall and lanky boy resembling Wade Eakins, his mama's pa, and the handsomest boy in his class, he had bright blue eyes and hair the color of young acorn squash.

"Anybody here hungry for a slice of lemon ice-box pie?" he called as he turned from his daddy but stopped short of going inside. "It's Mama's Sunday special. Made fresh this morning."

"You take it easy, Will, hear?" Josh Payne leaned a foot on the running board of his Oldsmobile sedan. "Tell your mama I said, no, but thank ye all the same."

Abe flashed his own toothy smile. Yellowed by nicotine, it still lit up his face and made him all the more handsome.

"What can you do for me, boys?" The muscles in his face moved under his skin.

"We ain't come to see Dog. He's a Company man!" somebody shouted from a pickup truck with oversized wheels. "He don't belong here!"

"Yeah, what's Dog doin' here?"

"Dog here's a team player and you boys all know it," Abe said. "He's riskin' his neck to try and help us."

Lance Porter, a squat man with a blemished face and peroxided hair, stepped forward, a rolled cigarette clinched between his front teeth and a revolver protruding from his left hip pocket.

"I reckon you boys all read today's paper," he shouted. "The Company got eighty citations for safety violations that should've been 180 and it's still blamin' the explosion on lightnin'! Seven miners dead and another three maimed and their goods put out on the street. No offense, Dog, but we've come to see if Abe here is interested in evenin' the score."

Coon dogs barked from their cages in pickups. Across the tracks on Colored Row, eyes peered out the edges of dark windows. Shades scrambled from their rods, doors slammed, and lights went out. Folks on Colored Row knew their place and didn't take chances.

One of Lance Porter's chums got out and slammed his car door so loud Lily heard it at the kitchen table. He wore cowboy boots and rolled-up short sleeves to show off his muscles.

"Rescuers that went in said the fire suppression system was down to a trickle. I've heard said the ventilation fans needed junkin' years back. Ain't nothin' about to change around here 'lessen us miners git rough and tough."

"Yeah, and don't forget the self-rescuers was mostly out of air!"

"We slave in the devil's pit and all we get is pink slips. Them that stay on get cut to three days a week. Some days we show up and get sent right back home!"

"You tell 'em, buddy!"

"Damn straight!"

"The Company promises the Safety Commission it'll make all sorts of changes but the two of 'em's in cahoots and you boys all know it!"

Lance Porter had worked his way up the hill. He took a final drag from his cigarette and flicked the butt at Abe's feet.

"I say it's time for a wildcat strike and Abe here should lead it. How about it, Abe? Are you with us, or are you suckin' up to management? B'cause if you ain't, John L. Lewis will be only too glad to step in!"

"Yeah, John L! He's the man!"

"He's the onliest friend miners got!"

"Thank God for John L!"

Dog's face turned the color of flowers on pole beans. He wiped the sweat from his brow and blew out a breath.

"You wanta discuss the Union and its leader, Lance? I'll be only too glad to. I'll tell you straight out what John L. Lewis has done for you boys. He's done bled the companies dry is what he's done. Why, with the slack in demand and the price hikes on haulin' and miners everywhere strikin' for higher wages and better benefits, little coal companies cain't no longer afford to keep operatin'. The bottom's fallin' outa the bucket, boys, and not just here in Harlan County, but north to Pennsylvania. If I was you, I'd go home and come back when you're sober and had time to think."

"You criticize John L. in these parts and you better be armed!" Lance Porter jabbed a finger in Dog's face and grinned at the commotion it stirred.

Abe stepped around him and stopped to clear his throat. His voice was calm, and so low men eager to hear made hushing sounds to the crowd.

"I hear you ever'one and I couldn't agree with you more but Dog here's right. Look around you, boys. Times is changin'. First there's surface mines to compete with. Too, the larger mines are mechanized now and don't need the manpower they once did. I hear that new continuous miner can dig and load ten tons of coal in less than a minute and that's the work of fifty men. The technology's out there, boys. It's just a matter of time til it reaches Cordel-Lewis, provided we're still here. Why pay men when you have machines that'll do the work cheaper and a whole helluva lot faster? I tell you, boys, hard times is coming and the onliest way we're gonna beat the odds is to mine more and better coal faster and at a much lower cost."

"Still I won't rest til we get even with the bastard Company!" Lance Porter pitched the words as if hurling stones.

"Hell, yes! But do it right, boys. Write your governor and senators. Go to Frankfort with me and speak out. Demand they send us fair inspectors that won't measure the mine's air quality from outside the mine."

"He's telling it like it is, boys!" Uncle spoke up. "Only the Company'll most likely get to government first with their bribes, and money talks. My daddy, he always said the only honest politician is a dead one!"

"I'm with Abe!" Josh Payne, known to be an honest man, turned and walked toward his truck, followed by others.

"Now hold on a sec!" Lance Porter said with a snort. He grabbed Josh's shoulders to turn him around, and a bystander quietly stepped between them. "Fools! Pack of cowards!" he continued. "This thang ain't over. We'll be back. You can bet your bottom dollar!"

"Yeah, count on it!" came from one of his sidekicks.

"Come on back, boys. The door's always open," Abe said.

"Yeah! And next time be sure and save room for Mama's lemon ice-box pie!"

Abe stopped to smoke before going inside and sitting down to eat. At the table, he coughed and choked and finally pushed away his plate.

"Children, go upstairs," Lily said, "and let your daddy and me talk."

"Are we in some kind of danger?" Verni asked.

"Let's go, Verni." Sweet William clamped his hands over her shoulders and gave her a slight shove. The other girls followed.

"No wait!" Abe called. "Verni's right. The onliest way you're gonna learn is to ask questions." He took out a Camel and tapped it against the table, but didn't light up because of Iris' asthma. "There's always high tension at a mine after a explosion and I won't say there ain't. But there's a rotten apple in every crowd. What you saw here tonight was mostly the work of one rotten apple and he left here disgraced. Trouble takes time to brew. If'n I thought you was in immediate danger, I'd leave and take you to Saxton tonight. So you go on like your mama said and don't you be worryin'."

Will and the girls vanished, and Lily placed an ashtray near Abe to say he was free to smoke. The Company, even doctors and Santa Claus, claimed cigarettes were good for one's health, but Lily knew better.

"Now the truth," she said when seated beside him.

"Lance Porter's kind thrives on trouble. The men's down all right but they ain't 'bout to leave a sinkin' ship. It's me they'll listen to."

"A sinking ship?"

"Times is tough, Lily. The boys need a boost in morale."

Lily squinted. "Like what?"

"Well, Dog's asked, and the U.S. Bureau of Mines has agreed to come here and offer a course in mine safety and first aid to license and safety equip any miner interested in going inside a mine in a emergency. Think, Lily, think how good it would've been if'n I could've got back in the mine after the explosion without having to wait for a safety crew what don't know their asses from a hole in the ground. Think how I could've saved the new kid and the six others."

"No, Abe, no. You don't know that for sure. It's too dangerous. Think of your family!"

He picked up a biscuit and broke it in two.

"Be a good girl, will ya, and pass me the butter."

Maude was glancing over the *Knoxville News Sentinel,* reading what words she could, when she spotted an article and photograph featuring Abe, Dog Bracken, and Josh Payne, Cordel-Lewis miners who were taking the course in mine safety and first aid that qualified them to enter not only their own mine but any region's mine in case of an emergency. She clawed at her pinned-up hair and screamed until she was hoarse. When she'd stopped screaming, she threw down the newspaper, found her Bible and prayer shawl, and set out for her special praying place in a cave in the woods.

The familiar trek carried her back to a time before Sherman and Abe, when she'd been pretty and pleasant and giggled like normal girls. She'd been fourteen then and in love with her first and only sweetheart, Caleb Cash, a handome boy with thick black hair, bushy eyebrows, and skin as smooth as the leathery leaves of a rhododendron. She pictured him then at age sixteen, sprawling in the grass with his head in her lap, a straw between his teeth, squinting at the sunlight.

Caleb was a coal miner, but the two had met while working as field hands, first stealing glances and then hidden moments in a nearby woods. He worked two jobs and had little time to court her, but they arranged short walks. One day they stumbled upon a hidden cave, once a family's hand-dug coal mine, big enough to hold a coal wagon. They dubbed it *their* place. They wove a rug out of straw, and Caleb brought candles he'd stolen from a neighbor's wedding. He even built a little altar of coal and spoke of worshipping her, of pleasuring her with the purest form of union between a man and a woman. She accepted a ring made of clover and floated into lovemaking as naturally as a stream flows into a river. The cave became her first home.

Sunshine and shadows now mingled on the trees, mostly pines, maples, and oaks. She followed a path strewn with sycamore balls and animal droppings and arrived at the pond where they had gone swimming and napped in the sun. On one occasion they had fallen asleep on a high, flat-top rock while admiring a bald eagle, and she had unconsciously spooned him the way she had spooned Blessie, her one sister, to keep warm in an unheated attic.

A breeze now ruffled the hem of her long black dress. She drew in the skirt and crawled under a barbed-wire fence bordering a pasture and a creek. She remembered that she and Caleb had held hands as they crossed this creek on a log. Later that day he'd strummed his banjo and sung her love songs. He'd laced sweet-scented wildflowers through her swoop of red hair. His own black hair smelled of coal and Camels.

That same bed of wildflowers waved on the gently sloped hillside she climbed and descended until she reached the cave. There she cleared the opening they had hidden with field stones and stooped inside to the altar, where she lit two sooty candles and took up her Bible. After reading and praying herself into a Pentecostal-Holiness spell, she reached for a clump of old switches and an animal bone shaped like a stick. Wailing, she flailed her back and arms until they oozed blood, then recovered on a mattress of fresh-smelling quilts.

Here in this cave she had departed from God's word and conceived a child cursed by the sins of the fathers, or in this case, mother. Here she had bought forty-two years of suffering and shame, and here she had paid the price a hundred times over.

An hour passed. When Maude felt certain God had shown her the path to reclaiming her son's soul, she left the cave in a hurry. Once home, she stripped off her stained clothes and bathed in a tub of Epson-salt water. Then she dressed and whistled for Sherman in the sweet potato field by the creek bed.

"We're going to see Abe," she said when he came. "Get cleaned up and I'll explain on the way."

Sherman took in her red swollen eyes and bent back. He heard the hoarseness in her voice and knew she'd been crying.

"Maude, don't tell me you've gone back to that cave?"

"Sherman, I have finally found a way to save him. *They shall lie with the uncircumcised, and with them that go down to the pit,* the Bible says. I can get him out."

"Please, Maude, give up this craziness. You ain't as young as you once was. What good has torturing yourself done?"

"God tests our faith, Sherman. I passed that test and today I'll get my reward."

Sherman mumbled under his breath and stalked off in a huff. As if pitying the wife he sometimes thought he'd long ago driven to madness, he turned and came back.

"Maude, please. Sand clenched in a fist slips through the fingers. I'm beggin' you to leave the children alone. Abe's sick to death of your preaching and so is Lily. Can't you see all this fuss is driving 'em away?"

"On the contrary." Maude's steely eyes softened. Her lips framed the gentlest of smiles. "I'm bringing him *home.*"

Maude and General Sherman arrived at the Lewellyn camp as Lily's four-o'clocks shriveled into tiny yellow and red trumpets. Sherman looked peaked. Verni hugged him and persuaded him to go rest a spell in her parents' bedroom. As a rule, hard-working folks like Sherman didn't believe in taking naps, swinging, rocking, or loitering at the country store, but they would occasionally *rest a spell*, or nod off in their tweed recliners.

"Where is everybody?" Maude asked Verni, who had been left in charge of the four younger girls.

"Mama's at Ceola's getting her hair cut."

Maude drew in her lips and rolled her eyes.

"At this hour of day?"

"She'll be right back. Supper's warming in the oven. Daddy's bath water's on the stove and I'm watching both."

Daisy and Tansy, followed by Rosy, came with hugs. Iris remained in the loft, hunched over her Dear Diary.

A line of denim-clad miners tromped home in a rhythm, swirls of cigarette smoke trailing behind them. Abe caught sight of his daddy's Ford pickup, said goodbye to the other miners, and angled toward the front porch, where Maude and the girls stood waving.

"Howdy, Mother." He bypassed Maude's hug and chucked Rosy's chin. Rosy had just come from playing on a coal pile and was more black than white.

"Weighed in at sixteen tons, did you?" he teased her.

"Hello, Abraham." Maude frowned at his blackness. From the beginning she'd known her bastard child would face trials, and so she had named him after Abraham, the Bible man of faith. Only God knew what misery she had suffered from knowing he was Satan's.

"What brings you here unexpected?" Abe said and reached for the doorknob.

"I've come with a plan to get you out of them mines."

"Cut me some slack, will ya, Mother? Coal's a sure bet. Somethin' I can count on."

"Count on nothing and nobody of this world, Son Boy. That way you won't be disappointed."

"Yeah, yeah. Only Jesus, right?"

"Close."

Inside, he tossed aside his hardhat and hobnailed boots and eased into his wooden corner chair with no padding. In Lily's absence, he lit a Camel and looked toward the bedroom.

"What's wrong with Daddy? How's come he's in bed?"

"Son Boy, you need to give up them smokes. Think of your lungs. Think of poor Iris."

"Dammit, Mother, is Daddy ailin' or what? Should I challenge him to a game of checkers?

"Hay fever is all." She turned up the heat under the bath water and brought him a mug of instant coffee.

"Lily will fix him right up. Where is she anyway?"

"Let's get straight to the point, Son Boy." She pulled up a side chair and thumped down, not believing her good luck of having him all to herself, with the exception of Rosy, who she sent to go wash.

He gulped down the coffee, the hotter the better to clear his clogged throat.

"Muchas gracias," he said.

"Now listen here," she stated. "Sherman and me've decided to give you the farm, all twenty-three acres, house and all. Not one red cent will you pay. But it's a now-or-never offer."

"So good, so far. Go on."

"He's grown old and can't no longer keep the place up. It ain't worth a lot of money but the soil's a plenty good for growing tobacco. Lily could make a garden, keep cows and some chickens. They's sawmills nearby for part-time work if you want it. Sherman and me'll start turning the tractor barn into a simple house just as soon as you give us the nod and then we'll try and stay outa your way, except when you need us."

Abe raked a hand through his hair and finger-combed it over his right ear and birthmark.

"What's the catch?"

"There ain't no catch."

"You're pullin' my leg, right?"

"I didn't come all the way here to pull on no leg!"

"You're sayin' the land and house would be mine? All mine?"

"I am indeed."

"And Daddy would take a backseat?"

"He'd be at your beck and call."

"And you'd try and zip up your mouth?"

"The good Lord willing, I would."

He finished the coffee, took a final draw from his cigarette, and dunked the butt in the mug. The new kid came to mind. Here was his chance to get even with the sonovabitchin' Company for the kid's sake. Without him there to keep up morale and watch out for dangers, the mine could hit rock bottom like all them others. Then the crooked officials would get a taste of their own medicine. A eye for a eye, tooth for a tooth.

"I don't know, Mother. Me, I'm a underground man. Right green when it comes to farmin'. And Daddy and me, we've never been ones to see eye-to-eye."

"That was then. This is now and a chance to do better. Think of your children, Abraham. Think how they'll love you for lettin' them live near their cousins and aunts and both sets of grandparents. Just think how happy Lily will be living on a farm again. You know she and your younguns are suffocating to death in this filthy, nasty camp."

Abe bit his lower lip and hummed with indecision.

"Did she say that?"

"More or less she did. She's a schooled nurse. Too educated for the likes of poor folks. Sooner or later she'll pick up your younguns and go where the grass is greener."

His right thumb worked the fullness of his cheek.

"Funny she didn't mention it to me."

"She was counting on me to do it."

"And like I said, your daddy will teach you everything he knows provided you ask and then leave you all to yourself. He's ashamed of his old ways. Will do anything within his power to try and make amends."

Abe's face lit up. He clapped his knees together.

"I'm a hellova fast learner!"

"Why sure you are."

"We could raise a patch of burley tobacco. We'd sell it in the fall, just in time to buy Christmas presents. Lily could have a Maytag."

"A Maytag? What does she need with a Maytag? What's wrong with a wash tub and stir stick?"

"Yes, sir-e-e. Them dodo kids of mine could ride a school bus and have that set of encyclopedias I been promisin'. Iris could shake off the asthma."

"Iris would get well in no time atall and Rosy would have space to exercise her poor leg." Maude reached out a hand. "Come on, Son Boy. Let's go tell Sherman."

Abe dropped his hands onto his knees and was pushing to get up when he suddenly sank back down.

"I should tell Lily."

"We'll tell her soon enough."

He bit down on his lip and raked a hand through his hair.

"I don't know, Mother. Movin's a big deal and I need time to think."

Maude tilted her head and squinted her eyes.

"This is no time to be dragging your feet, Son Boy. Opportunity may not knock twice."

"Tell you what. They's good men dependin' on me and that mine for their livelihood. Give me a year. A year and I'll have it back on its feet and high rankin' on the production charts. Then you and me'll get down to business."

Maude took off her glasses, blew on the lenses, and polished them with her skirt hem.

"But poor little Iris may not hold out a year. The longer she breathes this coal filth, the sicker she'll get. I tell you, Abraham, asthma ain't something to be took lightly. They's people dying of it left and right." She shook her head and clicked *naughty boy* with her tongue, then searched his face as if waiting for his reaction to what was to follow. "You know, Lily would hate you for life if something was to happen to one of these younguns on account of you and that mine."

He coughed long and hard and cringed at the pain.

"Ah, hell, Mother."

CHAPTER FIVE

From Ceola's beauty-shop window, Lily had spotted Sherman's pickup truck meandering up Checkerboard Hill and flinched at the thought of going home to face Maude.

"Peace comes with a price," she had told herself to the point that she sometimes felt like putty in Maude's hands, a mere shadow of her old, spunky self. Now, while Ceola swept up hair and set up her station, she consoled herself by thinking back to a time when she was ten and a new Christian. Hands on hips, mouth in a pout, and eyes set to cry, she had insisted—wouldn't take no for an answer—that her unruly miner pa accompany her to a tent revival. Amused by her sass, he had given in, and while there he had found the Lord, sobbed like a baby, and traded in his shovel for a Bible.

Then later she had shown her spunk by quitting teaching, the most highly respected profession for a woman, to become a nurse—a Jezebel and a whore of Babylon in his eyes and the eyes of his church. And hadn't she shrugged her shoulders when he threatened to disown her for marrying a coal miner and the son of a bootlegger?

"I'll be back in a jiffy!" Ceola said. She bounced toward the kitchen and returned with a plate of her special chocolate-chip cookies and coffee. A short, squinty-eyed woman, so round it took two boards parked side-by-side to iron her blue jeans, Ceola could curse like a man and out-drink her husband, Dog. Lily overlooked her shortcomings and envied her oomph, spunk, don't-give-a-durn resilience, in some ways like Vi's.

"So what do you think of my art?" Ceola asked while pointing toward a flaming pink ceiling designed for women with their heads in a shampoo bowl.

Lily stared up at posters of Johnny Weissmuller's loin-clothed torso, Jeff Chandler's gray-brown chest, and Hank Snow's slim rhinestone hips.

"How could I have missed them?" She chuckled, the first good laugh she'd had since her last visit. "It's a thousand wonders OWLS hasn't come and shut this place down!"

Ceola burst into her own laugh—the hardy, husky, gut-splitting roar of a coal miner. She lit a Lucky Strike, leaving lipstick stains the color of eggplant.

"Older Women Loving Saints ain't about to mess with Mother Hen and Chicks!" she boasted. I know too many of their secrets!"

Indeed, Ceola's beauty shop was every bit as popular as the camp commissary, where women went to buy groceries and worn miners scrambled for seats on porch rocking chairs or benches.

"And speaking of secrets, what's going on at the mine?" Lily asked. "Abe won't tell me a thing."

"Things have settled down for a while, knock on wood, but Lance Porter and his cronies ain't about to stay quiet for long. He's got a corn cob up his ass that one does. He's so full of shit his burps come out farts."

Lily blushed. "My word!"

"I reckon you heard Palatia Porter, Lance's dumb wife, got herself a poodle." Ceola puffed on her cigarette and blew out a fury of smoke.

"A curly hairdo, you mean?"

"I mean a poodle dog. A *miniature*, she called it. Named it Fifi."

"Fifi? You don't say?"

"Indeed she did. Marched right up to my front door with it in her pocket and said it needed grooming."

Lily's mouth flew open.

"Why, you don't say. Grooming? A dog?"

"Swear to *Wod*!" Ceola, leading soprano in the church choir, considered taking the Lord's name in vain a sin, perhaps an unpardonable one, but the words felt bold and colorful and far too suited to her personality, her style, to give up entirely. "Well, anyway, Hell, no, I said. I don't do bitches, human or otherwise. She got my drift and stomped off mad as a hornet! Then she come back the next day wanting to know if I could recommend something for the bags under her eyes and I said Preparation H."

"Preparation H! If that ain't a hoot?"

"*Hore* is more like it! She's hot to trot that one is!"

"Really?" Lily said.

Ceola dampened Lily's hair and tapped her knee with a rattail comb to remind her to uncross her legs if she wanted a straight cut. Then she combed as she snipped.

"The Porters are trash. The very thought of them raises my blood pressure, which is already too high."

"Maybe you and Dog should consider changing your diet."

"For starters, they've got no pride."

Lily's jaw dropped. "Don't tell me they'll beg!" According to her pa, there were burglars and there were beglars. In his eyes, there was not one whit of difference.

"Ye damn tootin' they'll beg. Beg you right out of house and home if you ain't careful."

Only they call it *borrowing*. The oldest boy, Bill Fred, I reckon you heard he's a Peeping Tom!"

Lily's mouth flew open. She thought of her five girls, especially Verni, already endowed like a woman.

"Can't somebody call the law or something?"

"Sugar, you ever heard of *Bloody Harlan*?"

"Sure, everybody has."

"Well, *Bloody Harlan* got its name in the 30s when the asshole companies deputized gun thugs to kill off Union sympathizers and the fightin' ain't never stopped. The sheriff is scared to death to come poking his nose into these coal patches, and with plenty good reason!"

"Why, law..."

"No! No law! Not in *Bloody Harlan* there ain't."

Ceola cut the last of Lily's ends and flicked a velvety-soft brush over her face to scatter the loose hairs.

"Seriously now, you tell Abe to watch his step, hear? Lance Porter has been passed over for foreman twice that I know of and he's bitter and mean and set on ruining anybody what makes him look bad. Dog says he packs a .22."

"Oh, my," Lily said. "He's the drunk one Sweet William told me about. Some miners, mostly nice, came complaining to Abe about mine injustice. Lance had a pistol."

"You got it! Dog wadn't about to leave Abe alone, not even to go have a piece of your lemon ice-box pie."

Ceola snickered, and Lily smiled as if amused.

"I heard. Shame on my boy for fibbing," she said.

"Shame nothin'! That boy saved us from a revolution."

Ceola finished the cut and reached for a broom and dustpan. Lily shook out her lap and held out some money. As usual, Ceola pushed it away and motioned for a hug.

"Stay for more coffee," she said.

"I best go. Maude and Sherman are here, and I don't want to be rude. Let me know when you need another enema, and next time don't wait so long."

"It ain't right you seeing my fat butt laid out like a stuffed turkey," Ceola said.

"Then eat more greens."

Ceola squinted with disgust.

"It ain't too late for a style. I know a hundred women that'd simply die to have your thick head of hair. How about some curl?"

"Oh, no, no." Lily took the hair ribbon from around her wrist. Ceola had finally broken her of using rubber bands, which she said caused split ends. "Maude's faith teaches that cut and curled hair on a woman is a sign of worldliness. I don't want to offend her."

"Piss on that. I say in your own house you do what you want to."

"I suppose. But I keep hoping we'll be friends someday. For the family's sake."

The cuckoo on the wall gave five calls, and Lily couldn't believe how fast time had flown. She opened the front door, and a blast of wind whipped her back inside. Black clouds moved in from the west. Some hunkered low to the ground.

She could smell a storm coming.

Heavy rains came and went for a week. They washed away crops, bridges, roads, and hopes. They nibbled at low wooden porches like seas do wharves. Tipple doors swung open as usual, spilling coal into gondola cars on the tracks. But schools closed, and church services, interrupted by the coughing, sneezing, rattling sounds of sick children, were poorly attended.

Abe's miner's asthma, like Iris', grew worse by the day. It worked on his already low spirits. At night he lay awake thinking about his responsibility to keep his family healthy and safe and about Lily's hatred for the life he'd forced on them all. He struggled with the poor state of things at the mine and his duty to miners. He tried to pray over these and Maude's offer, but ended up feeling like a hypocrite taking the easy way out by using the Man Upstairs to tote away troubles. Would anybody believe him, he asked himself, if he said his heart now hurt worse than his lungs?

One night, he and Lily were awakened by the sound of Iris coughing and wheezing. Lily ran to Rosy's little bed in the living room, where asthmatic Iris was temporarily sleeping.

"Don't panic, honey!" She flipped on a light and saw Iris' lips had turned purple. Her eyes were glazy and weak, her speech a child's stutter. Instantly Lily put water on to boil to make steam and grabbed a sheet to use for a tent. While waiting for the water, she collected the child in her arms and rocked as she prayed.

"Is she okay, Lily?" Abe asked. He paced the floor with bare feet, recalling the time Iris had attempted to write in her diary at the supper table. At the time he considered her puny and lazy. The two had never been ones to see eye-to-eye, and he'd assumed she was making him look bad.

"Instead of takin' ideas from your head and puttin' them inside that blank book, you should be takin' ideas from a real book and puttin' them inside your blank head!" he'd yelled. He'd gone as far as to slap the diary from her hands, scattering the pages. Then he'd hated his rotten soul while he stood watching her on her knees on the floor, wheezing and sobbing, fitting the pages back together like they were living parts of her own broken self.

"Tell me what to do, Lily. Does she need water? A blanket?" he begged.

"Just get dressed in case we need to take her for oxygen."

For some moments he felt frozen. Bumbling words came to mind.

"The Studebaker's broke down," he finally stammered.

"Still?" Lily cast him a hard look. "I asked you days ago to have it fixed for this very reason."

She had asked, yes, but pride had kept him from saying he couldn't afford to replace the dead battery, even with one from the junkyard.

"I'm sorry. I really am."

"Forget it."

"Maybe I should go get Dog's pickup." He darted off, his throat screaming for hot coffee and the liquor he hadn't touched in over twelve years.

"I said forget it."

The other kids heard the noise and tumbled downstairs. Lily asked Verni to go make coffee. She sent Daisy and Tansy for a paper bag for Iris to blow into. She had Sweet William help her place Iris under the tent with steam from the boiled water. Abe dressed and hurried back into the room, hoping Lily would have an assignment for him, too.

"Tell me how I can help," he urged and reached for Iris' hand. It felt cool and clammy, like a slice of Cheddar cheese. "Huh, Lily?"

"Go outside and smoke. I'll call if we need you," she said.

He wished she had said *when* instead of *if—when* we need you.

"You sure?"

"I am."

"You'll let me know when things change?"

"I will, yes."

Her flat voice said she was pissed, and he couldn't blame her. After all, she'd trusted him to be the head of the family, and he'd fallen down on the job. While his family hung in mid air, he'd let go of the rope. Might as well go, he thought. Might as well drop off the face of the earth.

"I'll be right back, honey. Now you get better," he told Iris. At the door he turned to add, "And that's the boss talkin'!"

Outside he lit a Camel and tried to pray again, but still he, a sinner, felt like a phony, a user. In time he heard chitchat and made out Iris' voice. The other kids were laughing.

Lily had promised to call him when Iris got better and she had forgot. He was tempted to go inside anyway and join in the celebration. To hold his frailest daughter to his chest like Lily would and say, "This is your daddy come to say he loves you better than a Sunday sunset and is sorry for all those times he lost his temper."

But Lily had not bothered to call him. Even Rosy, his rose among the thorns, hadn't noticed he was missing.

"No sweat! To hell with 'em!" he told himself. He dropped down on the swing and stared through the window.

September approached, and school was just around the corner. Lily had prayed Abe could afford to pay for the car battery and still have enough money left for the children's school clothes and supplies. Her hopes were dashed when he left home on foot early one Sunday morning and returned after noon behind the wheel of a 1942 Plymouth Roadking. Like him, the 13-year-old car sputtered but had a strikingly bold and handsome appearance.

"The deal of a lifetime! A whoppertunity too good to turn down! Low-priced beauty with a luxury ride!" he told the children while caressing the car as a man might a woman's silky trail of hair. "You alls be good and your ole man just might take you to Saxton." Saxton meant Buck Creek, home to Lily's parents, and Mud Creek, home to Abe's.

"Whoopee!" The girls jumped inside and toyed with the knobs. They inspected the glove box and looked for pocket change trapped in the seats. Sweet William slipped behind the wheel and started the engine. He said it purred like a kitten.

"Where on earth did you get it?" Lily asked, her face stiff with fear.

"I bought it off Josh Payne. Josh knows cars. He ain't one to do you wrong."

"However did you pay for it?"

"He's gonna take the Studebaker in trade."

"A clean trade?"

"Not exactly."

"I wish you'd had June look at it first." June was Lily's oldest brother. He and his wife, Eula, lived nearby on land that had belonged to Wade Eakins, Lily's pa.

"No sweat. If'n it breaks down I'll take it back."

Lily considered the nearly empty Aunt Jemima cookie jar that held what little money she'd earned from selling her walnut-stained baskets and canned goods at the commissary. She envisioned the newspaper liners staring up from her bare pantry shelves. She felt the pressure of tears behind her eyes, a pounding in her head. But like her part-Cherokee ma, she had never been one to rant or cry openly. She had sometimes imagined her tears trickling into some inner box, something like what catches coins inside a machine that dispenses soda pops.

"You coal miners think you can eat ham on sow-belly wages!" she was dying to scream. She ached to set her face in a scowl and give Abe the tongue lashing Maude so often gave Sherman. But then she considered the mine explosion and his already low spirits.

"Well, it's a fact we needed it," she said in spite of her worry, and gave him a child's pat on the back.

Lily packed coffee, water, and bananas, and the family set out for Saxton, eighty or so miles away, the following Sunday. Fellow travelers were mostly sightseers following the bright leaves of autumn and the rural scenery of quaint farmhouses with clean fields of baled hay. Supporting a population of less than a hundred people, the area had no stop signs or traffic lights, just the option of honking horns around curves or corners.

"So what do you dodos think of the ride?" Abe asked with a boy's excitement.

"Smooth, real smooth. Easy on the rumps," Sweet William answered. Abe smiled and the girls giggled.

"Smooth as silk, right?"

"You got it!"

As usual, Abe drove too fast, and Lily braked from her side of the car.

Rosy sat between them, holding Hairy and Abe's Cincinnati RedLegs baseball cap; the team had temporarily changed its name from Cincinnati Reds in order not to be associated with Communists. The four other girls lolled in the back seat, complaining of heat and exhaust fumes and Sweet William, sprawled across their feet. On the radio, Hank Snow sang "I'm Movin' On," and everybody hooted the Siler version: *"This rattletrap ain't good as new / But hello, Buck Creek, we're comin' to you / We're movin' on!"*

Lily loved to look. She pointed out waterfalls and the ballerina blossoms of pink mimosas. She called attention to white-water creeks and purple and blue mountains, their colors changing according to the sun.

"Do you think Uncle John Mason might be at Granny's?" Rosy asked. "Of all my uncles I like him the best!"

"Yeah, he's cool," Verni said. "Not a stick in the mud like Uncle June."

"Let's hope he will," Lily said and smiled with hope. John Mason, her baby brother, had always been her favorite.

They were Christian fellows, her brothers, family men with good heads on their shoulders. She often speculated that if Abe had gone off to World War II like them, instead of staying home to help supply the growing need for coal, he may have returned more confident and less attached to his mother. He may have had the money to buy a reliable automobile and known how to repair it.

As if Abe had read her thoughts, he suddenly pulled off the road, cut the engine, and twisted around in his seat.

"Okay, dodos, now listen up," he said.

"Abe, hon, I do wish you wouldn't be calling them names. They're every one as smart as can be. I'm afraid they'll take you for serious," Lily whispered.

"Hell, Lily, you think I don't know Abe Siler's bunch has got *the know*—what it takes to be somebody big in this world? This here is called psychology. If'n they don't like the insults, they'll work all the harder to prove me wrong, get my drift?"

Lily twisted a strand of hair around a finger.

"Okay, you dodos, this here's the deal," he continued. "But it's a secret til I say it ain't, see?"

Everybody agreed, and Abe breathed in a mouthful of air.

"Well, seems your granddaddy, he's tired of farmin' and feelin' puny and Mother, she's asked me to come take over the farm—house and all. I figure we can grow a patch of burley tobacco and earn enough money to help with college. You girls will have the chance to work in the field and earn some of your own college money. So in a nutshell, I've decided to quit the mine and move us to Mud Creek. How's about that, sports fans? Does your ole man do good by his family, or what?"

Lily's first expression said the last place on earth she wanted to live was near Abe's mother. The girls seemed too shocked to reply. Thinking of their other Saxton relatives, especially the cousins, they recovered with grins and all sorts of questions.

"But where will they live?" Sweet William asked.

"Mother and Daddy are converting the barn into a house as we speak and they'll live there where it's all new and cozy."

"Way to go, Boss! You've been holding out on us!" Sweet William launched forward and tapped his daddy's big right shoulder. Just a tap because of his sore joints. "Even Mama looks surprised."

Lily's face showed the discomfort of some small, cactus-like wound. But feeling eyes on her, she managed a smile for the sake of the children and Abe's temper.

"How come you and Maude didn't tell me?" she asked.

"I knew how bad you pined for the country and your family and hated the nasty mine and so I wanted it to be a big surprise." He broke into a chuckle, the happy kind. "Growing tobacco could be our big chance, Lily! If it works out, hell, Abe Siler's family will be healthy and done with scrimpin' forever!"

"And you're sure there was no chance of a misunderstanding?"

"Like I said, Daddy plans to teach me the tobacco business and butt out. I tell you, Lily, this time I put my foot down. I said there'd be no meddlin' and Mother, she agreed. I said I only want what's best for my family and you be good to 'em, I said, or else we'll leave."

"That's good to hear," she said with a questionable optimism, but allowed herself to dream. "Now I can help Vi see to Ma and Pa's health. Pa's eyes have got so bad of late he uses a magnifying glass at home to read by. And Ma's blood pressure's running high. Vi says she got hot in the field last week and nearly passed out." She paused to consider. "And, Abe, now we'll be able to keep an eye on your daddy. He's not been well for some time now. It wasn't like him to pass on this year's tobacco."

"And Mother. She was limpin' the last time we saw her. Don't forget the ole gal ain't no spring chicken."

"We'll finally have a house outside a mining camp! I can't wait to polish the windows til they squeak like clean hair. Then I'll make some pretty yellow curtains from that roll of organdy Iris won at bingo. If this works, we should all give God the glory."

"Hell, yes, you can have curtains!" Abe's eyes twinkled. "You want a Maytag? Just you say the word, and I'll by-godly buy you a Maytag! The whole shebang will be yours for the askin'!"

"All-l-l right!" Verni cheered while Iris stared at him with a blank face.

"Hooray!" the twinsies shouted.

"Golly Jees Moses!"

"We can finally join Pa's church! It's high time you were rededicating your life to the Lord, Abe. It's been more than a year, you know."

"Maybe I'll rededicate, but no more baptisms, thank you muchly. Hell, I've been baptized so many times, the damn fish all know me by name!"

"And little good it did you!" Sweet William teased.

"Boy, you're achin' for a breakin'!" Abe answered and smiled at his face in the rearview mirror. He reached over Rosy to pat Lily's shoulder, and his voice fell to a whisper.

"So what do you think, Lily? Has your ole man lived up to your expectations? Ain't you glad you hung in for the long haul?"

Lily glanced out the window. A falcon and its mate sailed into a canyon, where they swooped high and low, playing like happy young lovers with no cares and no sorrows. They reminded her of herself and Abe, once upon a time.

"Why sure, I'm glad!" she said with animation, and her thoughts returned to those rose-colored days of youth and passion, without Maude and before the start of the long haul.

Memories of those good times were like a tonic for Lily's soul, and she thought of them often. The two had met in 1929, the same year President Hoover and Wall Street went bust. It was at the Middlesboro Hospital in Bell County, Kentucky, where she trained. Abe, eighteen, had undergone an operation to repair a crushed ankle and awakened in a panic, thinking his buddies were still trapped inside the coal mine. Lily, twenty and a student nurse, was wrestling with his flailing arms and legs and his feverish resolve to go save lives when he woke up staring into her eyes. Big brown eyes, he said later, like the seed pods of sunflowers.

At the time he was leader of a Bluegrass band called "The Cumberland Fox Chasers". He read Zane Grey books and wrote country-western songs while confined to bed. But the minute he was able to maneuver a wheelchair, he followed her up and down halls, strumming his guitar and singing an improvised version of "Thinking Today of My *Brown* Eyes" and "*Brown* Eyes Crying in the Rain."

He was the handsomest man she had ever seen outside the movies, with teeth made for laughing and a body built for love and hard work, and the other nurses seemed to hold that same high opinion. He became everybody's favorite patient, and she was at first flattered by his special attention. But bad is good that has been carried too far, her pa had taught her, and Abe's pumped-up personality and appeal for attention soon began to grate on her nerves. When he left the hospital five days later, asking to see *Brown Eyes*, she placed a shush finger against her mouth and hid behind a curtain.

Life without him seemed calm and peaceful at first, the way a hospital should be. She enjoyed the old predictability, the dignity of once again feeling like a professional. But calm could be tedious, and sick patients could be demanding and depressing. Before long she found herself missing his impish sense of humor and overall good nature. When a memory of him crossed her mind, she would find herself smiling and wishing she had not been so quick to dismiss him.

She and her suitemates, Beulah Lee and Bunny, attended a hospital fund-raising jamboree three weeks later, knowing Abe's band would be performing. They had helped her choose a simple white blouse with a gathered skirt and a patent-leather belt that made her feel prissy, and she had curled her hair to look full and bounce with her movements. She even wore lipstick and a slight touch of rouge.

"Maybe it's true. Maybe absence really does make the heart grow fonder," she told her suitemates, and laughed to show she was joking.

"Must be the weather," answered Beulah Lee, large boned and freckled. She winked at Bunny, a cute little blonde with a pageboy haircut. Lily hadn't the slightest notion the two had conspired with Abe to arrange the meeting.

Abe's new look—a rhinestone shirt accenting his broad shoulders and tight-fitting jeans with a side seam open to accommodate his leg cast—made her heart pound. In his Western attire he was shiny, slick, sexy—a man designed for the limelight. At the hospital, where he dressed in pajamas and mostly lay in bed, she had held herself above him. Now, on the lit stage, he sang down at her:

There is many a man I have seen in my day
Who lived just to labor his whole life away.
Like the fiend with his drops and the drunkard his wine
A man will have lust for the lure of the mine.

Lily recognized the song, "Dark as a Dungeon" by Merle Travis, as well as the professional quality of Abe's voice. He crooned more lyrics, and for the first time she noticed that his face had the tarnished look of an old mirror that needs re-silvering. She had often seen this same look on the faces of patients hearing bad news or on family members' faces when doctors advised them to call in the preacher. She couldn't help but wonder what pain, what fright, what tragedy had hit him so early. Why did he need to perform when on stage, and off? At what age had he mastered his art of deception?

He finished the song, tipped his cowboy hat, and hobbled on one crutch into Beulah Lee's and Bunny's wide-open arms. Signatures in lipstick and nail polish stared up from his festive ankle cast.

"Care to dance?" he asked Lily.

"May I sign the cast first?" she couldn't resist teasing.

Beulah Lee and Bunny detected the immediate chemistry between her and Abe and made themselves scarce. The band played on.

"Follow me, will ya? I gotta little somethin' I wanta show you," he said.

Lily held back until Beulah Lee and Bunny urged her outside the reach of her pa's rules and toward her own spirited self. Abe, as if full of confidence, took her hand and led her into a cluster of red, yellow, and orange maples, gleaming like Japanese lanterns in the sunlight. He fumbled inside his jeans pocket and dug out a ring wrapped in white net with a little red ribbon. Then he hobbled down on his one good ankle and reached again for her hand.

"Marry me?" he said, his old eyes shining, too dear to re-sist.

CHAPTER SIX

Abe stopped for gas before reaching Saxton and bought each kid a bottle of soda pop to celebrate the occasion. Lily bit her lip to keep from reminding him that poor people can't afford the luxury of store sweets.

"Drink fast so we can leave the bottles," she told the kids. "Otherwise we'll have to pay a deposit."

"You dodos take your time," he contradicted her. "Enjoy every drop like it was your last. Eat, drink, and be merry— hell, that's the ticket!"

Their first visit was to Buck Creek, where Lily waved to neighbors, one cutting back her bearded irises and another carrying canned jars from the cellar. The Plymouth Roadking crawled around a sharp bend and climbed uphill to a white salt-box house that Wade Eakins, Lily's pa, had built for his wife, Sarah, at the turn of the century. Lime-green shutters with wrought-iron hinges dressed the long windows; a forest-green tin roof covered a spectacle of white paint. In the garden, a spool table with four cushioned chairs encouraged company to sit and take in the view—a lovely landscape of flowers, shrubs, and trees planted by Sarah to look natural, as if put there by God, Himself.

Abe parked the car and got out. A breeze stirred the pop-cap wind chimes Lily had made as a child at Vacation Bible School. Her pa had restrung and re-varnished them so conscientiously that she could still make out the different flavors.

"Okay, you dodos, now listen up," he said. "I told you a secret, right? The idiot that lets the cat out of the bag gets beat to a pulp, you read me?"

"Yes, sir," each answered.

Lily was laughing extra loud to say he was only kidding when Fairy Enlow, a ragged girl from the backwoods, stepped outside a wall of tall cedars. Her blonde hair fell over her face in a tangle, and she crossed her ankles in an attempt to hide her bare feet. Although Lily was not usually one to criticize, the Enlow family was to her what Lance and Palatia Porter were to Ceola—trash. The kind who disregarded cleanliness and spread germs.

"Now go say hello to your grandparents, and don't forget to be on your best behavior," Lily said. She pointed all six children away from Fairy and toward the front door. Every girl but Verni followed her finger. Sweet William took a detour.

"Hey, Fairy," Verni said at the cedars. "Whatcha up to?"

"Hi, Verni," Fairy answered and stepped into the light. Her long brown legs descended from a pair of cropped denim shorts. A t-shirt revealed child arms but full breasts. Nature had favored her with a nearly perfect figure and a pretty face like Verni's, but paler and softer.

"I've come to invite you all to a picnic in the woods," she said with a quivering voice and a lisp when pronouncing the *l* sound. Fairy's home, that she was no doubt ashamed of, was a leaning shack yellowed by mud daubers' nests and rain rot. It sat behind a wall of kudzu planted by neighbors like Jake Creech, sister Peony's husband, too cowardly to burn out the shack families but hopeful that a cigarette butt or stove pipe would.

"Thank you Fairy, but..."

"It won't be nothing fancy, just some Kool-Aid and pea-nut-butter cookies I baked myself but I'd sure *wove* it if you all could come and bring Sweet William. My *wittle* brothers will be there and they're all dying to ask him what will become of his bicycle when he goes off to college. Oh, and, don't even think of bringing presents."

"Verni!" Lily called.

"I'd love to, Fairy, honestly, but we've got other grandparents to see and we're rushed to get back home in time for evening worship."

"It won't take long. I can bring the treats here if you want me to."

"I'm sorry but I think we'll be busy. Granny, she's got old people's sickness. Mama likes us to help her cook and clean up and such. The same goes for Grandmother."

"Then can Will come to talk to my brothers?"

"I'll tell him you asked. But Papaw, he's sick, too. Daddy and Sweet William have come to help with the farm work."

"On a Sunday?"

"Yep. That's daddy's only day off. Mama says God understands about taking care of old people. We gotta go now. You be good, Fairy."

Verni waved goodbye and headed toward Lily, who shooed the other girls inside.

"Next time you mind what I say, young lady," Lily said.

"I couldn't help it. She's so pitiful. They say at school her evil stepmother once locked her in the cellar overnight and Fairy screamed and cried til she damaged her vocal cords or something. Sometimes she talks funny."

Lily paused, her eyes sharp with interest.

"Tell me, how do you think Fairy knew Sweet William is about to go off to college?"

Verni shrugged her shoulders, slightly lifted her eyebrows, and smiled like somebody with a secret.

"I'd suggest you ask Sweet William."

They had reached the front porch when Lily's pretty younger sister, Vi, short for Violet, came running from her sunning blanket on a side lawn. She wore a dotted Swiss cover-up and a skimpy two-piece bathing suit ordered from the magazine, "True Confessions". Rings of bleached hair branched over her head, resembling the finger-like roots of a Johnny-house lily. Her makeup was mostly fresh, in spite of the sun, and her red fingernails were long and sharp like the talons of a baby owl. Judging by her dolled-up appearance, Lily assumed she was expecting her boyfriend, Clyde Turnblazer, a wrestler from nearby Indian Mountain.

"I was listening to the radio and didn't hear you pull up!" Vi hugged Lily and the girls and wiggled one of Sweet William's big Wade Eakins' ears. Ice tinkled in her glass of sugar tea. "Where's Abe?"

Lily checked out Vi's Sunday outfit and fought off the urge to show disapproval. She thought of her poor parents and the humiliation Vi had brought them through the years, especially after they gave her land for a mobile home for the sake of their grandchildren.

"Where's Abe?" Vi asked again.

"He's going to see June."

"I wanted to tell him how sorry I was to hear about the mine explosion. I'm sure glad most everybody got out alive."

"We're all thankful, yes."

"It must've been hard on him, poor darling."

"It was, but he's better now."

Abe was smoking nearby. He ground out his cigarette and stopped by to be polite. He'd been Vi's dead husband Brody's best friend, and Vi tended to look on him as a keepsake, a pal, the next best thing to Brody himself.

"Hey, handsome, stop and chat a while," she said, wrapped her braceleted arms around his neck, and giggled at the jingle. "Tell me something, will ya? How come all the good men like you are already taken?"

"Dunno," Abe answered, and looked off toward Vanderpool Mountain.

As if to reaffirm ownership, Lily took his arm and pulled him slightly to the side.

"Don't you want to come say hello to Ma and Pa first?"

"Later. Me and June's got important business to attend to."

Her face lit up. She gave his arm a little squeeze and lowered her voice.

"Are you by any chance asking June for a job?"

"I'm givin' him a opportunity. The ole scratch-back plan."

"Scratch back?"

"We help each other. I'll hear what he has to offer and see if I'm interested."

"I see." Light poured from her eyes, and she gave him a slight hug. Her brother June, a contractor, managed a construction company owned by her pa. She had told him Abe would need a job, but had been careful not to come out and ask.

"Don't be gone long," Vi called out.

"Good luck!" Lily said as he swaggered away, his once white rabbit's foot bulging in his pocket.

Sarah, Lily's ma and a Four Star mother, gave the children hugs, sweet words of love, and warm molasses cookies, and they went looking for the pleasures they'd come expecting. The twinsies seated themselves on opposite ends of a board-and-block seesaw. Verni dashed off with Minnie Mo, Vi's teenage daughter, and Sweet William caught up with her brother, Buddy, also called *Buddy the Beast*. The four cousins had grown up together. They had napped in the same playpen and teethed on the same rings and rattles.

Lily's middle sister, Peony, also lived on the farm with her philandering husband and their six duplicate sons, known as *the Creech boys,* or *those lazy Creech Brothers.* Brother June, or Junior, and his barren wife, Eula, farmed a piece of land Wade Eakins had once offered to Lily and Abe. June acquired the land after Abe turned it down.

"Where's Pa?" Lily looked around before asking, and Sarah explained that he'd gone to the creek to think out his evening sermon. "I promised him I'd whistle when everybody got here."

"We were hoping to see John Mason."

"He left directly after lunch. Said to give you his love but had a important deacons' meeting and couldn't stay."

Dressed in a floral cotton dress of her own making, Sarah was tall and trim like Lily, with Lily's big eyes, dark hair now mostly gray, and high cheekbones. One side of her face had been partially paralyzed by a stroke, and she had little dandelion-petal teeth stained by snuff. Lily had often compared her loveliness to seedpods fit for bouquets, even when seedless and dried up.

"Ma, can we talk?" Lily asked when the greetings had died down, and she'd encouraged Rosy toward the board-and-block seesaw.

Sarah removed her apron.

"Let me turn dinner down and we'll go get Wade."

"Why can't I go with you and Granny?" Rosy begged.

"Give Rosy a turn, hear?" Lily called to Daisy and Tansy as she and Sarah walked toward a patch of woods, alive with the sounds of birds and ground creepers. Soft trilliums nested in the grass, their colors changing from white to varying shades of yellow and purple,

"She's too little. She won't balance," Daisy complained.

"Then find her a rock."

"I'll help her," Iris volunteered, and Lily shot her a promise of a reward, no doubt something chocolate.

"Ma, you'd better sit down for this one!" Lily said as the two approached a realm of stately ferns and a bench made of hewn wood. "Abe says it has to be a secret for now, but I know I can trust you. You won't believe it, but he's agreed to give up mining and come take over his parents' farm. He's gone right now to ask June for a job until tobacco season starts." Lily let out a joyful laugh. "Oh, Ma, it's what I've prayed for all these years, that we'll finally leave those awful mining camps and come back to the country. Just think what this will mean for Abe's and the children's health, and I can finally be near my family!"

Sarah scratched above an eye.

"I was of the notion that Abe wouldn't never leave them coal mines. Whatever changed his mind?"

"Maude wants to give us the land—house and all. I know she has her own selfish reasons, and believe you me, I'm not comfortable with the idea, but you've got to admit it's an offer too good to turn down."

Sarah swallowed and the muscles in her neck wiggled.

"Maude? What about Sherman?"

"With Sherman's approval, of course."

"But you've always said Maude brings out Abe's dark side."

"They have a strange relationship, yes, but they love each other, and I plan to be a peacemaker. That's the least I can do. If Abe, love his heart, is willing to give up that mine, then I can, with God's help, overcome petty grievances."

"That's sweet, Lily."

"The girls are ecstatic about raising tobacco. They can't wait to have their own spending money, plus money for college."

Sarah nodded. "Still, it's a big undertaking."

"Normally it would be, but Maude and Sherman will remodel the barn and live there while they teach us. I'm hoping Buddy and Peony's boys will pitch in to help. Lord knows we'll need all the help we can get."

"Abe's a proud man. It's not like him to take orders...from his daddy."

"True, they've had their misgivings, but Abe is all set to try." Lily paused to wait for a reply that didn't come. "Ma, think of Abe's bad lungs. This move might save his life!"

"Well, it sounds like a plan. Your pa will be happy to hear it."

"And you? Aren't you happy?"

Sarah's face wrinkled. She slowed her gait.

"There's nothing on earth I'd love better than to have my family near and healthy. But, Lily, don't you think it's a lot to ask of a man—to give up what he knows and loves best for something as uncertain as raising tobacco?"

"Pa did it. He gave up mining coal to be a preacher. My brothers did it when they left the farm for the city."

"No, Lily, no. Your pa was at heart a farmer and builder. Mining coal to him was nothing more than sure money during hard times. He hated the mines and if he'd loved them like Abe does, he'd no doubt still be a miner."

Lily sighed and let go of Sarah's hand.

"Ma, something tells me you're about to rain on my parade."

"All I'm saying is, don't compare Abe to your pa and brothers. Abe's a different breed. Your brothers served in a war while Abe's manhood was in mining coal."

"So you think we should turn down the farm and stay in that filthy camp?" Lily said with some degree of irritation.

"I think you should do whatever it takes to keep the family together."

"That's not as simple as you make it sound."

Sarah landed a spit of snuff outside some heads of ruffled iceberg lettuce.

"Nothing worthwhile ever is."

Abe was a coal miner, heart-and-soul. He knew practically nothing about house construction, and he knew even less about growing tobacco. Moreover, he wasn't interested in learning. He recognized that the wages June offered weren't good, even for an apprentice. He recognized, too, that in order to support his family and help with the cost of renovating his parents' barn, he would have to find part-time work as a railroader or logger. But at Sarah's table with the whole family present, he swallowed a Goody's Powder and proceeded to make the big announcement.

"Daddy, he's been peaked of late and needin' a rest. Him and Mother has asked Lily and me to come take over the house and farm. So I reckon we'll be moving to Saxton to try our luck at growin' burley tobacco," he said with a false air of confidence and contentment.

"How soon?...When?...What can we do to help?" some asked while cheering and toasting, and he stumbled through answer after answer. His head and lungs and joints ached, but the real problem was his stomach, and his sickening urge to puke, not vomit or throw up or regurgitate, as Lily would say, but out-and-out *puke*.

Because Abe's parents on Mud Creek expected their own visit, the occasion broke up early. Abe waited in the Plymouth while Lily and the girls helped clean up the kitchen and said their goodbyes. Then Lily whispered her usual good-behavior reminders while hurrying everyone outside.

"Okay, all right, let's play a game. Which one of you do-dos can name me the most presidents?" Abe asked when they were seated and the sun visor adjusted. Quietly, he steered around curves that wandered as if lost and looking for a way out. "Got any takers?" he resumed, but without his earlier enthusiasm.

Lily placed a hand on his knee.

"I'll give it a try!" Sweet William spoke up. The boy gave the impression that he'd been born smiling and would die that same way. "A chip off the old block," miners said of his gifted wit and humor. His recitation of presidents had reached number sixteen, Abe Lincoln, when Abe interrupted.

"Good ole Abe Lincoln, now that guy was a player! The man I was named after, I reckon you all know. A man with smarts, he was. Who here can tell me how he got educated?"

"I thought you were named after Abraham in the Bible," Sweat William said.

"Walked ten miles to school in freezing cold weather with no coat and shoes," Verni volunteered with her usual sarcasm.

"Close enough. And just look where it got him. United States President, that's what! Education, that's the ticket!"

He turned his head back and forth to give his usual lecture on the importance of college, and the Plymouth Roadking swerved toward a wooden guardrail and gorge.

"Abe!" Lily slammed on her imaginary brakes.

"Dammit, woman, ain't I said you're in good hands?" He coughed and spit into a sparkling white handkerchief. How Lily kept those handkerchiefs so damn white without using Clorox that stopped up his head he would never understand. "Now where was I? Oh, yes, what I was just about to say when I was rudely interrupted is that they ain't no tellin' what your ole man might've made of hisself if'n he'd had the chance to earn that college piece of paper like did your mama. But I didn't, see? Had to quit school when I won't but a kid to go work in them pitch-black coal mines. There with ole Satan smackin' me with boulders ever damn chance he got and that poisonous gas so thick you could box it. But no whimperin', see? I done what I had to and I ain't never been sorry. The hotter the war, the sweeter the peace, right?"

"You tell 'em, boss!" Sweet William said.

"But times is changed now and I guarandamntee you, ain't a one of Abe Siler's kids gonna be made to crawl for a livin'. No, sir-e-e, not so long as I got a back what will bend. We'll make good at this here tobacco and you'll all six go off to college and come out a somebody big, hear? If'n I hafta knock you down and drag you there myself, you'll all six go to college!"

"Yeah, and Will's gonna be a doctor!" Rosy spoke up.

"You damn tootin' he is. Will here has got *the know*. He'll show 'em who's big and who ain't. He'll knock the socks right off their feet!"

"And Uncle June is loaning him some mon...!" Rosy was about to say when Lily slammed a hand over her mouth.

As if cued, Sweet William took up his harmonica and let out a toot.

"This rattletrap ain't good as new / But hello, Mud Creek, we're comin' to you / We're movin' on!" the girls sang.

"Yeah, buddy!" Abe hooted. He beat time on the steering wheel and dug into his pocket for a toothpick to twirl.

CHAPTER SEVEN

Abe turned onto Crab Orchard Lane at a flea market stocked with patchwork quilts and animal tapestries and eventually paused before the small stucco house where he was born. He sat for a moment and breathed hard, as if working up the courage to go inside. The kids, used to his tense mood when at Mud Creek, flooded him with questions.

"Daddy, can we have running water?"…"Who gets the big bedroom?"…"Can we raise watermelons?"…"Do we get a dog?"

"Okay, children, that's enough," Lily said.

"Hell, Lily, how they gonna learn if they cain't ask questions? You dodos want a dog? What kind of dog?"

"I want a cocker spaniel!" Rosy spoke up.

"A collie," Daisy and Tansy said.

"Please, Abe, remember Iris' asthma," Lily whispered.

"You cain't shelter the girls forever, Lily. What Iris needs is to build up a tolerance, like with me and my silicosis and ever other damn thing I got from either coal or rock dust. Fight back, hell, that's the ticket!"

He pulled into the grassy gravel driveway and cut the engine. Maude flew down the porch steps, her fleshy arms waving.

"I'm so happy I don't know what!" she said and threw her hands around his neck. He unlocked them and took a step backward.

"Howdy, Mother."

Maude whisked everyone inside her immaculately clean kitchen. She brought out a plate of hand-pulled taffy candy, still warm and as white as her milk-glass candy dishes.

"Maude, how kind of you!" Lily said, noticing Maude's palms, still red from the heat.

"Thank you," the children said, and grabbed ample portions.

In the living room, sheets covered the blocky furniture. Half-drawn shades, perfectly lined up, blocked light from the windows. Sherman again rested in his easy chair, under one of Maude's quilts, a perfect eight-to-ten stitches per inch. Without getting up, he hugged each child but forgot to give them their usual Indian Head penny and stick of Beech-Nut.

"Sherman, are you sick?" Lily reached to feel his head.

"Just lazy." One hand covered his mouth; the other fumbled the table for his missing upper denture.

"We've come to take you up on your farm offer," Abe spouted off as if afraid he might change his mind if he waited. "And to say thank you muchly."

"Golly Jees Moses!" Rosy exclaimed. She squeezed Hairy and coughed from the dust.

"Praise Jesus! Sweet, sweet Jesus! I knew He would work us a miracle!" Maude thrust her hands into the air and shook her head like a woman who has just removed the pins from her hair. As if moved by some higher power, alone but for Him, she mumbled in an unknown tongue and shuffled her feet to its rhythm.

Abe shot her a look of disgust mixed with mockery and turned to Sherman.

"Daddy, you ailin'?" he asked, and Sherman shook his head no. With Lily's help Abe made small talk about weather and crops, but soon ran out of both words and breath. When the old man lapsed into a stream of dry coughs, Abe excused himself and went outside for a smoke. His fingers quivered when he lit up. He took a few desperate puffs, saved the rest, and hit the ground running. It was not too late to change his mind and go home to the camp, he told himself. But then Lily would be heartbroken and Iris all the sicker.

The familiar path through the woods took him back to his boyhood and his drunk daddy. He remembered fleeing here with his mother, her babbling in tongues like she did when she was either real happy or real sad.

At church one Sunday, he'd watched her wave her arms and sway her hips like as if boogie-woogieing to the sound of honky-tonk music in some sleazy roadside joint. He was five at the time but could still make the connection between his daddy slapping her down and the Lord lifting her up. He'd crouched in the pew and sobbed into a gold cushion until some worshippers pounced on him and yanked him from his pew to the altar. They took his tears as a sign of repentance and cried, "Sweet Jesus!" Not a one of them, not even the preacher, suspected that it was General Sherman Siler, so drunk the night before that he'd chased his wife with a red-hot poker that made her cry even now. That General Sherman Siler and not the Lord it was who'd brought on this most sacred occasion.

Abe sat down on a stump for a short rest and smoke, then pressed on. He had come to Mud Creek expecting a sermon and he had promised Lily and the Man Upstairs he would be tolerant. But today his mother's jibber-jabber had made his nerves jump like gnats on a rotten banana. Today, when he had just signed his life over to June and a job he already hated, he found the above ground unbearable, even for a fighter.

He cleared a lump from his throat and trudged on, hearing squalls and buzzes so shrill they seemed to be inside his head.

"Abe!...Abe!" Lily cried from somewhere behind him, and he was glad of the distance between them. Not that he had anything against her, not much, except that today she was one of them, the enemy, all in cahoots to drive him out of the coal mines and into some scarier pit like the uncertain life of a farmer. Why was it they couldn't understand? The underground—alongside men like Josh Payne, Kromer Root, Floyd Bowes—was a place where he could go and be hisself, and not ever lonely. Up here clouds and wind came and went according to sunshine and rain and night turned to day. But the underground was dependable—always cool as a witch's tit and black as hell's soot. It was the one place where he felt safe and sure.

Lily was not fooled when Abe returned with a smile, saying he'd been checking out the soil and the lay of the land. They left soon for Lewellyn, using evening worship as an excuse. As if his black moods had a distinctly telling odor, the children quietly flipped through comic books and buried their heads in each other's shoulders.

But children will be children, especially when tense.

"Ouch! Get off me!" one cried.

"I'm not on you!"

"You're sitting on my leg."

"Am not!"

"Children!" Lily exclaimed as she noticed the annoyed look on Abe's face. It was also his look of impatience, not quite anger, not yet.

"And speakin' of books," he announced, "Rosy's goin' back to school."

Lily shot him a distressed look. Rosy was running a fever. The joints in her legs were swollen, and she still cried from the pain. Come winter, the walk to the bus would take up to ten minutes, plus the time Rosy would spend waiting. Didn't he of all people know that people with arthritis, especially children, cannot tolerate cold and wet weather? The thought of Rosy with stiff and aching joints cooped behind a desk in a cold classroom filled her with pity, and even anger. Sometimes it amazed her that men of reasonable intelligence could be so downright dumb when it came to matters of the heart.

"We'll see," she said and poured him fresh, hot coffee from his thermos. "It all depends on the weather and how she's feeling."

"Bull! The girl's tough. Ain't nothin' she cain't weather, ain't that right, kiddo?"

"Right!"

"Well, maybe," Lily said.

"Maybe my foot! Bedamned if I'll have her put back a grade like Vi's and Peony's bunch!"

"No, no, she's keeping up." *Mostly*, Lily thought, for Rosy was at best a fair student. "Daisy and Tansy bring home her assignments, and Miss Lucy comes every week to test her."

"I hate Miss Lucy! She calls me a daydreamer. She says I left my head at home on the coatrack!" Rosy spewed.

"I'm countin' on you to see that she don't slack off," Abe said.

"Oh, yes, yes, I will."

Lily had been expecting this matter to come up. Earlier that week she had overheard him and Rosy chatting. He had pulled a double shift, and Rosy had waited up for him to come chuck her chin and call her his rose among the thorns.

"You 'bout ready to go back to school, Squirt?" he'd asked her.

"Yep!" Rosy was the only one of his kids who wasn't required to say, "Yes, sir."

"And if that mountain's too high to climb?"

"Then I'll find a way around it!"

"Atta girl!" he'd said and limped away smiling.

Back home in Lewellyn, Lily took the children to evening worship while Abe washed the Plymouth under the moonlight. Lily had made him chuckle when she suggested that he wait until daylight, as if light made a difference. He soaped the roof and was about to rinse when he glanced across the tracks to Colored Row and the mostly toppled line of bricks from old coke ovens. The church's parking lot was almost empty, its congregation most likely afraid of a renegade's random bullets. The grit in the air made him thirsty. He licked his lips and imagined a swig of Kentucky bourbon or rot gut. Just a splash like coal oil to get the fire going and ease his jumpy nerves.

He reckoned he'd been bothered by the liquor allergy, as Lily called it, since those times when his daddy toted him on his shoulders to the still, then stood him on a wooden crate to help stir the mash. His daddy's four brothers had sneaked him the drink. Afterwards, they'd spun him around like a toy top, then slapped their thighs and held their sides laughing when he staggered and fell. By age nine, he was hooked on the stuff.

He lit a cigarette and glanced down at his dirty shoes. In the tiny, flickering flame of a matchstick, he saw that everything around him—houses, cars, even the moonlight—looked dusty and gritty and in need of a rinse, just like himself. A baptism of sorts, to wash away his fear of leaving the coal mine and moving to Mud Creek to grow burley tobacco. Liquor might be a solution, he told himself, but it never lasted. Even the religion fix lasted longer than the buzz got from liquor.

"Dammit to hell!" he kicked the wash bucket as he yelled, and he felt better until he felt worse. Then he felt better again because Lily, thank goodness, had not been here to scold him for blaspheming on the Sabbath.

He had finished the roof and was soaping a door when Ceola waddled up the hillside in her uniform black shift and dusty gold slippers. She sipped liquor from a coffee mug as if thinking she could fool him, ha ha. Over and over he'd tried to tell people he was not the least bit tempted to go back on booze. Now he reckoned they all knew he was one lousy liar.

Ceola panted as she pushed. Her strong perfume made his eyes water and set off a strangle of coughs.

"I wanted to tell you before you heard it at the mine," she blurted out. "This morning four men threw a tarp over Dog's head when he was leaving the mine yard."

Abe balled and pitched his sponge at the soapy bucket.

"Why the hell for?"

"They drove him to the river and tossed him in. We assume it was because he was heard criticizing John L."

"Lance Porter! The sonsovbitches could've kilt him! Everybody at that mine knows Dog's got a heart condition." Abe threw down his sponge and was swinging open his car door when Ceola thrust out her big, bullying arm.

"And just where do you think you're going, Mr. Hot Shot?"

"To find Lance Porter. You think I don't know him or one of his drunk cronies is who's been firin' into the colored church? And now it's Dog! Hell, they won't stop at nothin', that bunch, 'lessen we stop 'em ourselves." He ducked inside the Plymouth, and the big stone-and-silver rings on Ceola's right hand clanked against his guitar belt buckle as she reached for the belt.

"You stop right where you are, mister! Dog's convinced when mine tension's high, it's best to keep shit like this under wraps. Nobody's been hurt or killed, knock on wood, and he says if word of this was to get out, we gotta treat it like a joke, else things will get worse. He made me swear not to tell a soul, you in particular, which I reckon gives you some insight as to my sorry character."

"Maybe Dog's right about not makin' a fuss." Abe got out of the Plymouth. "That's just what Lance wants. But, there's other ways to skin a cat."

Ceola shook her head. "I've considered them all. I thought about poisoning their damn poodle myself. But if Dog was to find out, he'd have a heart attack for sure. What goes around comes around. Lance Porter will get his and don't you doubt it!"

"I guarandamntee it!" Abe coughed and took a deep breath. "Okay if I go see Dog?"

"Sure, but you run your mouth, and I swear to Wod I'll come sit on you, hear?"

"I'll say I'm fresh out of cigs. That I've come to bum one."

"That'll be the day! Lily would leave you for bumming and we both of us know it!"

"She's proud, all right."

"Proud like her husband."

"Proud like her pa, you mean."

"I mean proud like her husband."

CHAPTER EIGHT

Abe's arm seemed to have shrunk when he reached for the mine manager's doorknob. He went inside, facing a bulletin board with the smudged fingerprints of miners he could almost put a name to, including some of his own prints on a PTA notice he'd posted for Lily.

"Great timing. You must've read my mind," the manager exclaimed as he jumped up from his swivel chair and threw out a hand. He was a stout, gray-haired man in his late fifties, with a swarthy complexion and scary bloodshot eyes. "Have a seat!" he said.

"I come to uh…"

"I been meanin' to ask you about the foreman position comin' up. You interested?"

"Well, I…." Abe fumbled his rabbit's-foot keychain.

"A lot of coal can be mined in the time it takes to clean up a accidental-on-purpose spill or repair a booby-trapped machine. To obey Company rules, miners have to love the man giving orders. Everybody knows that's you."

Abe nodded his head as if to say he appreciated the compliment.

"Well?" the manager asked. "Can I take the nod for a yes?"

"Who's up for grabs?"

"Just you and Dog Brackin. Two good men to choose from. One a man born to mine coal. The other, a old-timer with a bad heart."

Abe breathed easier. "Only two? You're kiddin'! What about Lance Porter?"

"What about him?" To quench any doubt, the manager took out a cigarette and match and struck the match against his jeans so that it cracked like a tiny whip. "Do us a favor, Abe," he said. "Stay and keep her from playing out."

Abe steadied his legs. Smothered coughs rallied in his chest.

"Well, I sorta promised the missus I'd give up minin' altogether. She's all set on keepin' the kids healthy in Whitley County, and, truth bein', I come to resign. But Dog, he's a helluva good miner. So's Josh Payne."

The manager dropped onto his desk.

"Don't tell me you're serious?"

"Dead serious."

"But you're the man for the job."

"Dog's been here a lot longer. He knows these mines backwards and forwards. The boys, they trust him."

"Off the record, say the word and the job's yours. Any shift you want. All the work you can handle. No questions asked."

"No can do." Abe ran a hand through his hair. His thumb pressed the birthmark.

"I can't believe what I'm hearin'. Didn't think I'd ever see the day Abe Siler would leave Cordel-Lewis for good, much less turn down the chance to be foreman." The manager paused. "Tell you what. Don't make no rash decisions. Take a couple of weeks. Think it over. See if you cain't change the wife's mind."

"Not likely," Abe said, and the two shook hands. Before leaving the office, he ripped the PTA notice from the bulletin board, aimed for the garbage can, and made a perfect shot.

Lily had planned to tell Ceola about the move to Saxton just as soon as Abe officially resigned. But after hearing about Dog's misfortune at the river, she went calling the next morning. Dew glistened on scattered patches of grass. The roots of a walnut tree branched from the dust like the arms of a giant octopus. She moved slowly, careful not to trip and break the gift in her hands, two of her prettiest jars of home-canned tomatoes.

Ceola answered the front door in a scanty nightie and open housecoat. Her face was plastered in oatmeal, her hair stuck to her head like the fur of an otter. On the kitchen counter, stacks of dirty dishes gave off the smell of pig slop. A stalk of celery marked her place in a *Glamour* magazine, one of many spread out on the table.

"I'm sorry to wake you," Lily said. "I expected you'd be at the shop."

"I took some time off." Ceola nabbed a handful of newspapers so Lily could sit down. A Roseville vase of peacock feathers and a big-skirted doll dressed a wagon-wheel coffee table, the glass so thick with dust that Lily might have printed her name there.

"I came to see how you and Dog are doing." Lily crossed her knees, making a stand for her shaky hands and the tomatoes. "Abe came home so upset after he saw you last night, I made him tell me what happened. I hope you don't mind."

"Then I reckon you know what they done to Dog."

"I know and I'm sorry as can be. How is he?"

"Fine I s'pose. He won't talk except to lie and say it was all in good fun. I doubt I'd of knowed if it wadn't for Josh Payne who found him and brought him home soaked. All Dog ever thinks about is the camp women and children that'd go hungry if a strike was to come."

"Honestly, I could kill that Lance Porter!" Lily said. "What with Dog's weak heart!"

"You and me both!" Ceola's eyes hardened. "But I know for a fact Lance wadn't acting alone. There's trouble brewing here, Lily. The air's so thick with it people are afraid to go outside. The thought of dolling up one of them creeps' wives is driving me nuts. I tell you, I'll quit hair first. I swear to Wod I will!"

"Abe says the most of 'em's loyal," Lily said.

"One bad pea can spoil the pod!"

"Especially with morale so low now."

"Let's drop it b'fore he wakes up and hears us." Ceola sipped from an RC Cola with a straw to keep the syrup from staining her white teeth. At the same time, she rummaged through mostly empty wrappers inside a box of Whitman's Chocolates. "What's new with you?" she said and held out the box.

Lily declined. Her fingers made their way to her chest.

"Not much."

"How's Sweet William and the girls?"

"Good."

"Them sweet things are like my very own."

Lily winced. She had another of her long pauses.

"Ceola, maybe now's not a good time to say it, but you're my best friend, and I want you to be the first one to know." She looked down at the jars of tomatoes and took a deep

breath. "What with all the mine danger, Abe and I are afraid
for the children's safety. Maude and Sherman offered to give
us their farm, house and all, and, well, it's just too good an
offer to turn down. It won't be easy, but we've decided to
move back to Saxton and take over the tobacco."

To Lily's surprise, Ceola smiled as she huffed. She lit a
Lucky Strike with a jeweled lighter and snapped the lid shut.

"Sweetie, you know good as me Abe ain't about to leave
here." She turned down the television so they could talk better. "Hear all that rain?" she said. "Who'd have thought it'd
come up so sudden?"

"It was the hardest decision we've ever had to make."

"I'm telling you straight out that you're fooling yourself,
Lily. There ain't no way in hell Abe Siler would turn down
the chance to be mine foreman and not regret it later. Why,
this mine's his and Dog's baby. They'd die before they'd
leave it to Lance Porter's kind!"

Lily shuddered. "Foreman?"

"You mean you ain't heard? Fred Andrews got fired after
all the citations. I ain't s'pose to tell but they're about to
choose a new day foreman and Dog says everybody knows
Abe's the man for the job. Why else do you think Lance Porter was goading him and Dog like he did? He wants Abe to
screw up so's he can step in. He's a devil, that one is!"

Lily walked to the window. The rain gave off a thick,
thudding sound. On a side yard, a boy in wet clothes, mud
oozing between his toes, drove a hoop with a stick.

"And Abe knows about this?"

"Dog told him hisself but they's been no public announcement. Sweetie, that man of yours is a hero. Ain't

nobody but Lance and his jerks what don't love him to pieces."

Lily reached a hand to her right eye. That Abe had possibly known about the foreman offer and kept it to himself
when he agreed to move his family to Saxton filled her with
such affection that she felt like the young Lily again, wild
with love and lust and the freedom to be herself. She took a
moment to recover from the shock and resumed the conversation.

"But why Abe? He's been here only two years. There's so
many others. It's no wonder Lance resents him."

"Like I say, the other men love him to pieces."

"But what about Dog?"

"That coal dust has done screwed up his heart and the
Company knows it. I doubt he'd take the job if it was offered,
which it won't be."

"Josh Payne?"

"Dog says he's good but without enough experience."

"But Ceola, understand that we're all set to go. Abe's got a
job in construction. He gave Maude and Sherman his solemn
word that we'd help look after the farm. The children are
overjoyed."

"Set to go ain't the same as set on goin, Sweetie."

"But I tell you he's already put in his notice."

"They'd tear it up in a second."

"Ceola?" Lily whimpered what amounted to a plea for for-
giveness and pushed up to go.

Ceola looked her deep in the eyes.

"Sweetie, I'm telling you this for your own good. You
leave here and you'll be back. Once that coal dust gets in his
blood, a miner feeds on it." She sighed and shook her head.

"Abe won't last out there, Lily. Dog's gonna die soon of this place and I don't even bother to ask him to leave. Men like Abe and Dog got their ways from moles and voles that squint at the sunlight. They ain't equipped for up here."

"I'll help him. I won't leave his side."

Ceola dropped her massive arms on Lily's shoulders.

"Stop this, Lily. Stop it for your sake and ours. Your husband's crawled all his life. He deserves this chance to stand like a man. To be somebody important like his wife!"

Lily pulled away and backed toward the door, forgetting she was still holding the pretty tomatoes.

"He'll be fine once we settle in," she said. "It'll be hard at first, but once we get settled, I know he'll be fine."

There was no lovemaking that night, and little sleep. Lily grappled with her conscience, and Abe wrestled with the lady-in-black ghost, said to be the only woman to ever enter a coal mine. Legend claimed she was a dead miner's wife who came during the Great Depression to claim the soul of her husband buried under rocks, and never left. Some said she was simply the mine's mascot. Others saw her as warped miner psyche. To Abe she was not only real, but personal.

"What did she want this time?" Lily asked as she settled in to his arms.

"She said she wants my heart."

"Who could blame her?" she said lighthearted. "You're quite the catch."

"No, I think there's more to it. Funny thing. I think it might've had somethin' to do with me leavin' the mine. I think maybe she's tellin' me to stay on."

"Hm-m-m," Lily said, safely.

"Be damned if she didn't have hands warm as toast."

"Speaking of warm hands, roll over and I'll rub your back. Then you'll sleep better."

"Maybe she's nuts. Maybe she has a knife and really means to cut my heart out. She's a worriation that one is."

"Roll over," Lily said again and breathed in and out to calm herself as she rubbed. She had promised herself that come morning she would tell Abe that Ceola said he'd been chosen as the new foreman. She would say she had changed her mind about leaving and wanted him to stay and fulfill his life's dream. She would not take no for an answer.

By daybreak, however, she had obsessed the matter to the point of changing her mind. How could she, a nurse, stand by and let her husband risk his life and jeopardize their children's health for a cause people said was already lost? Hadn't most of the area mines already shut down? With all its safety citations after the explosion, how could Cordel-Lewis possibly make the mandated changes and still afford to operate? And what would his staying on do to his mother? Wouldn't she be wise to say nothing at all, under the circumstances?

For days she prayed God would forgive her sin of omission, and she usually arose from her knees feeling that He recognized her good intentions and even approved. When Abe officially resigned, she called her ma and pa at June's house to tell them the good news. Then she handed each girl a cardboard box with instructions to either pack up or throw away. She herself gave what wasn't needed to neighbors and friends. She had dared to hope the liquidation might include Rosy's Hairy, but might as well have asked for a snowstorm in July.

Otherwise, the move went as planned. June arrived early on Saturday in his Ford pickup, pulling a trailer built for horses. Lily and the girls waged a final war on dust while the men loaded furniture and cardboard boxes.

"We're tired...pooped...tuckered out!" the girls complained. "The place was filthy when we got here. Why does it have to be so clean now that we're moving?"

"Because I aim to see that you don't leave any part of yourselves behind," Lily felt like saying. "Do unto others...," she said instead.

CHAPTER NINE

"All right! Let's get this road on the show!" Abe announced as he shoved down the last of a baloney and tomato sandwich and licked the mayonnaise from his fingers and mouth. "Hustle your muscle!"

They were outside, crowded around a wooden picnic table, wobbly with rot. Quickly they cleaned up the mess and piled into two vehicles, with June and Sweet William pulling the trailer behind June's pickup, and Abe, Lily, and the girls following in the Plymouth.

"This rattletrap ain't good as new / But, hello, Mud Creek, we're comin' to you / We're movin' on!" the girls sang as Abe drove down US-38 toward Cumberland Gap, where Daniel Boone had led settlers. Near Evarts, he rounded a bend, and the sun fell back like a dog giving up chase. At Baxter he pointed to an obelisk-shaped mine monument built out of coal. His intention was to relax and make the trip fun for everyone. But he had just finished reading a book on raising burley tobacco, the kind housed by stalk and not leaf. Trying to recall the techniques for sowing seeds, setting plants, cultivating, topping, cutting, housing, and so forth had rattled his brain to the point that he felt panicky, no doubt like the new kid on the day of the mine explosion. The new kid, he thought, who'd opened his eyes and shut them at the same time. Good that he remembered the kid's awful death and the killer mine at this time, just as he was sorta considering changing his mind.

Outside Harlan County, the landscape changed from gray to green. Farm animals, mostly cattle, stared toward stacks of baled hay. Barns replaced privies, and silos gave off the welcome smell of fodder and forage.

"Daddy, tell a Little Moron joke!" Rosy held on to his cap and two books, one on construction and the other on raising tobacco.

"No, tell us about the mine ghost!" Daisy said.

"Yeah, the lady-in-black ghost with hands warm as toast," Tansy agreed.

"Let's not be silly," Lily said.

Abe squinted.

"Well, let's see. There was that time she followed me out of the mine but stopped just short of reachin' Cane Creek b'cause ghosts, you know, won't cross water and..."

"Why don't we leave the ghosts behind and look to a brighter future," Lily suggested.

Abe didn't appreciate being interrupted by a woman.

"The future! Hip, hip hurray! Bring on the band!" he exclaimed, and she turned to see he wasn't smiling.

"The construction job's only til spring, hon. Then we'll sow the plant bed."

"Yeah, sure."

"Maude says there's plenty of part-time work to be had if you want it."

"Righto."

"The tobacco will be a family affair," she said and switched to her rural vernacular. "Us all pitching in to help will be fun."

"You got it."

"We'll work hard and be successful, I just know it. The Lord, you know, helps them that help themselves."

Abe huffed and rolled out a breath.

"Why come you hafta bring God into ever'thing? Don't my sacrifices count for somethin'?" He'd fixed a fist to bang hell out of the dashboard when he suddenly parked the Plymouth, got out to stretch, and climbed back inside before anyone stirred. His breathing was labored. Lily passed him a clean handkerchief and placed a hand on his knee.

"The children," she whispered. "Think of the children."

"No pain no gain!" he whooped as he cut a right onto U.S. 25 and steered east to Pineville. At Barbourville, he saw signs leading to Union College. "Who here is interested in seein' a college?" he turned around to ask, and was disappointed when no one answered. Even Lily had leaned her head against the car door and closed her eyes. He was overcome with the old loneliness of childhood and considered jiggling her shoulder.

"No takers? Fine then!"

At Gray he spotted a white plank church with a tin steeple shaped like a cross. The windows were painted blue to look like stained glass. Nearby gravestones sank into thickets of bramble and chickweed. The place reminded him of Mud Creek Pentecostal House of Worship, his mother, and his always absent daddy.

"Why don't Daddy have to go to church?" he'd complained there, and he'd watched his mother's eyes go small and dead.

"Because he don't profess the faith."

"I wanta be like him. I wanta be like my daddy."

"God the Father is your daddy. Go to church and be like Him."

"But what about my real daddy?"

"You ain't got no daddy!"

Doubt struck Lily's conscience like one of nature's unforeseeable traumas. What if she had selfishly put her passion for farm life over Abe's love for mining coal? she asked herself. What if Satan and not God had led her to the decision she'd made? What if Abe had not known he'd been appointed foreman and would have changed his mind about moving if he'd found out in time?

They passed a field of groomed tobacco. She sat up in her seat to admire the blue-green leaves and ivory-colored stems of the plants, and to imagine what her own family's tobacco would look like. In one season the plants can grow as tall as a horse's belly, Pop had told her, and she entertained the vision while wishing that human beings could be as unfettered.

"Children, just look at this pretty tobacco!" she exclaimed. "Ours will be even prettier, won't it Abe?"

"Might," he said.

"Oh, Abe, you do think the tractor barn will be finished and the homeplace ours by the time the children start school in September, don't you? Change is hard. I need them to be settled in and at their absolute best when they take on the challenge."

"I guess we'll find out."

"I confess I had serious doubts about your mother at first, but now all that's gone. I figure she and Pop are every bit as eager to have a new home as we are. With just the two of them, Maude don't need a house and yard to keep up, and now the girls and I will be there to help."

"Fantastical."

"I mean, if the barn's not a house when we get there, I know Pa and June will be glad to pitch in and help. It's already wired for electricity, and there's water at the creek. Once the floors and walls are intact, why, they could practically move in."

Abe chuckled and coughed.

"Whoa, Nellie! Not so quick. We can't just move into their house and throw the old folks out."

"No, but you said your mother said they would start the renovation the very minute you gave them the word. I assumed you'd told them already."

"These things take time and money."

"But we don't have time. The children are due to start school soon."

"All I'm sayin' is, I don't want you to be disappointed."

"Disappointed? Why would I be disappointed?"

They arrived at Buck Creek that afternoon, and Lily perked up when she saw Vi and her 19-year-old son, Buddy, waiting. Buddy, who had dropped out of school to join June's construction team, nodded instead of smiling to hide his bad teeth.

Sarah and Wade Eakins had rearranged a shed and back porch to accommodate Lily's goods, and Lily temporarily stored everything but what would fit in June's truck. Then Sarah killed, dressed, and fried two chickens, and everyone sat down to enjoy the meal their hard work had earned them.

" 'T ain't much, folks, just enough to wetchy bread," Sarah said as she put down a pot of russet potatoes cooked in white gravy. Wade Eakins delivered a blessing so heartfelt it almost stirred Lily to tears. The sun was bright on the windows, and the laughter was loud. Lily prayed silently and sensed God's lingering presence.

Time flew, and the children complained when Abe said it was time to get a move on. On the way to his parents' home, Lily imagined the luxury of having her own well instead of standing in line at a community pump, then lugging the water home to strain through a cheesecloth. With fresh eyes she noticed filling stations, grocery stores, tractor dealerships, and mobile home lots that seemed to have cropped up overnight. In her head she planned cookouts and sleepovers, picnics and hayrides for the children. She envisioned croquet, badminton, swings, flower gardens. She even dreamed of piping water from the creek to the house and adding a bathroom.

The girls hugged as they chatted, and Verni, hands in air, was about to direct the theme song when Abe turned onto Crab Orchard Lane, and the glee fell like a bird shot in flight.

"What happened? The place looks dead!" Verni spewed.

The four-room cottage plus attic, hopefully their new home, appeared dark and abandoned. Shades hung low, hiding the curtains. Privet hedges grew over windows, and weeds smothered out grass.

"Maybe they've moved already!" Lily cried.

The girls and Sweet William were pushing to get outside the car when Maude appeared on the porch and flew down the steps.

"Praise the Lord!" she exclaimed as she hugged Abe off his feet. She put her hands on his cheeks and smiled into his eyes. "You've left that pit and come home at last!"

Since Sherman was nowhere in sight, Lily excused herself as if going to the outhouse but went directly to the barn. The path was a tangle of Johnson grass and wild periwinkle, and she kicked before she stepped to scare away snakes. Her hopes were dashed when she arrived and saw no signs of construction, only the usual Ford tractor occupying its old space. The presence of God she had felt at dinner turned into a knot in her stomach, and a sinking fear of Maude's betrayal made her long for the mining camp instead.

CHAPTER TEN

Lily took one look at Sherman, slouched in his recliner, with socked toes sprouting from under his afghan, and she understood why the place appeared so neglected. Recognizing the gaunt, pasty look of a man who won't or can't eat, she put out a hand to keep him from getting up.

"Gotta go help Abe," he said in a hoarse voice, his lips barely parting.

"That's what we have kids for," Abe said at the door and looked down at his arms. "Just show me where this stuff goes."

"I've cleared you a space in the kitchen," Maude said and ran ahead, and Lily reached to check Sherman's forehead for fever.

"Pop, how long have you been ailing?" she asked him.

"Old age is all."

She put a hand on his forehead.

"No, you're running a fever. Pop, you've simply got to go see a doctor!" Her eyes clouded over with regret. "I should've insisted. We should've made it a condition of our moving here."

Maude returned to the room, her warm voice now chilly.

"He's seen a doctor and little good it done him. What Sherman needs now is *faith.*"

"What doctor did he see? When? What was the diagnosis? Did he prescribe medication?" Lily questioned.

"When Sherman first complained of a sore throat, we went to see somebody in Williamsburg and he said to keep coming back and Sherman, he refused. We had laying on of hands at prayer meeting and the Lord, He promised to heal him, but only if Sherman holds firm to his faith. That means no doctors."

"Maude, please try to remember the doctor's name."

"I cain't seem to."

"Was it by any chance Dr. Humfleet?"

"The name don't ring a bell."

Lily gave up and went outside to help unload. By then it was dusk. Angled roof shadows snoozed on the front lawn. A gray and orange sunset measured its minutes.

"I can't wait to see the barn!" someone exclaimed.

"Me too!"

"Wonder why they've not moved in yet?"

"Maybe they changed their minds."

"Maybe they don't want us anymore."

Sweet William, Verni, and Iris finished their work and stole away to the barn. Slender arms swinging, hair fluttering on foreheads, faces beaming with laughter, they reminded Lily of children from a Winslow Homer painting. She followed them and arrived in time to see the three standing frozen, staring as if they were looking on the devastation of a road wreck or burning house. She understood their disappointment all too well.

"I'm so sorry, she said. A hundred times it seemed she'd uttered these same words to patients or patients' families. From the very depths of her heart she had felt them, but never as she did now.

"I don't get it!" Verni howled. She led everyone inside to climb the ladder to the loft, where they had stolen as children in spite of the threat of a *whoopin'*. Lily wondered if they were revisiting their old rebellion.

"I thought it would be ready for Grandmother and Grand-daddy to move in," Sweet William said as his foot hooked the last wrung. "I thought I would see everybody settled in and happy before I left for college."

"Pop's been sick," Lily explained from below as the three sat down on the same bale of hay. "It's a big responsibility. I guess he didn't want to undertake something this big until he got better. We'll just have to be patient. When he's better, we'll all pitch in and work twice as fast."

Sweet William questioned her with raised eyebrows, and Iris burst into tears. Verni smirked and railed in the often angry tone of her daddy.

"Here's what I think. I think Grandmother plotted all this just so she could use us to get her Son Boy out of the coal mines and all to herself. I bet she never had the slightest intention of giving us a home. Thought we'd all live happily ever after, all cooped up like sardines."

"Verni!" Lily cried.

"Well, it's true, ain't it?"

"Of course it's not true. I will never let you be used."

"Oh, yeah, and can you also see that we get our own house?"

Lily's throat felt blocked, and she forced a desert swallow. She thought of Abe, and how he would explode if he thought she was taking the matter of the house into her own hands.

Everyone was waiting for her answer, and she was floundering for words when she felt a sudden pop of memory. Had she not as a child, led her powerful pa out of a coal mine and into a church? Had she not become a registered nurse in spite

of her pa's threat to disown her? Had she not managed to finish her training early so she and Abe could marry at a time
when wives were not allowed to attend school?

"Can you?" Verni said. "Can you promise us a house?

Imitating her child pose, the one that tickled her pa until it
didn't, she placed her hands on her hips and said with an air of
defiance:

"I can, yes."

That night Lily and Abe slipped a quilt outside and spread it
under a sky with stars like little tacks holding up a black sheet
of night. They lay facing one another, smiling, making their
eyes speak of love.

"I'm worried sick about Pop." Well aware of Sherman's
sinful past, Lily now thought of him as the man who had during hard times slipped money into her apron pocket or fed
Aunt Jemima dollar bills when no one was looking. From the
beginning, she had found him as warm as Maude was cold.

"He's probably just missin' growin' tobacco. Daddy's
never been one to sit around doin' nothin'. It's natural he'd be
a little down in the dumps."

"No, I checked and he's running a fever. He hasn't been
himself for months now. I should have done more. I should
have insisted that he go see a doctor."

"Daddy's tough. He'll fight it off."

"Spoken like a true man. He used to be tough, but right
now he's frail and too pale."

"He's frail because he's give up the sun."

"But what if he's too sick to help us grow tobacco?" Lily
hadn't finished the words before she felt guilty, as if Sherman's usefulness was all that mattered.

"Ain't likely. But if you think he needs lookin' after, I'll call a doctor."

"I just don't understand why your mother's not doing more to help him get better. It's hard to go against her while we're guests in her house, but, Abe, sometimes I get the impression that she simply doesn't care."

She felt nervous, halfway expecting him to take up for his mother when he surprised her by nodding.

"We'll outsmart her. I'll have the doc come while she's at prayer meeting."

Lily's face lit up. She worked a hand through his curls. His hair was clean, soft, sweet smelling—enticing. His sweet, mischievous smile made him the handsomest, sexiest man on earth, and now, this moment of understanding between them, seemed like foreplay for love at its best.

"Oh, Abe, what a smart idea! If Dr. Humfleet would give me instructions, I could be Pop's private-duty nurse."

"Of course it'll work. They don't call me Albert Einstein for nothin'."

She slipped a finger between the buttons on his pajamas and drew curlicues in the thick hair on his chest.

"Albert Einstein?" she teased. "I thought it was Abe Lincoln."

"Tonight it's Don Juan at your service." He reached to kiss her and to lift her like a feather onto his big manly form, and at last she felt safe in the fortress of his arms.

A week into the living arrangement, Abe got up humming. He shaved, bathed, and put on his old poplin suit, dark striped tie, and shirt with a turned collar. Then he stood before the wardrobe mirror, slicking back his hair and showing his complete set of teeth. He turned sideways to examine his perfect shoulders and chest, his trim waist and flat stomach. Then he proceeded into the kitchen, to the mirror over the washstand.

"Guess who's goin' to church today!" he announced proudly.

"Sweet, sweet Jesus!" Maude exclaimed. "It's about time you come and meet our new preacher."

"Not today. Today I'm goin' with Lily to Little Wolf Creek. Sarah's got a solo."

"Come away from the mirror and eat your breakfast while it's still hot," Lily said to change the subject.

"So what do you think? Does your ole man scrub down good or what?" He buttoned and unbuttoned his jacket and loosened his tie. Everyone but Maude vouched that he'd never looked finer.

"I'm graying about the ears," he said.

"You're maturing is all," Lily said. "Like Roy Rogers."

"Mining coal naturally ages a man." Maude readjusted his tie. He pretended to cough and loosened it again.

Sweet William slid down the banister from the loft. The other girls showed up in their Sunday attire—lacy dresses with matching slips made by Sarah. They joined Sherman at the table.

"We were talking about church," Maude said. "I think we should agree to take turns. It ain't fair everybody going with Lily's family and Sherman and me not getting a chance to show off our grandyounguns."

Abe sat down, arms riding the table, fingers drumming.

"Now don't you all be gettin' no bright ideas about me and church just b'cause I'm goin' this one time." He passed out nickels for the children's offering, and Lily counted out the family's ten percent tithe. "The Man Upstairs and me, we got a understandin', see? He don't nag me and vice versa. Besides, why would I let some blabbermouth preacherman peddle me the goods when I can go straight to the maker?"

"Son Boy, that's blasphemy. You oughta be ashamed of yourself."

"He's just joking, aren't you, Abe?" Lily put a hand on his shoulder.

The girls giggled, and Maude clicked her tongue. She adjusted the hat on her head and grabbed her pocketbook and gloves.

"Hell's bells, Mother. Knock it off, will ya? You want my dodo kids thinkin' they got a damn heathen for a daddy?"

"I'm sorry, Son Boy, but Sherman and me simply will not tolerate cussin' in this house and most 'specially on the Sabbath. Now you go straight to the back porch and wash your mouth out with soap b'fore I do it for you!"

Abe skidded his chair from the table and stopped himself before charging.

"And where do you s'pose I learned them cussin' words, Mother?...At church, by-godly, that's where I learned 'em!"

"So now it's *by-godly*, is it? Like glossing over the Lord's name in vain makes you a decent follow!"

His angry eyes shot past her to his old escape route, a linoleum rug with liver-colored smudges leading to the back door and freedom.

"Abe," Lily said, and pointed to the children.

"Lay off, Maude," Sherman said.

"It's for his own good," Maude said.

"Gees, Mother, show this mason a little respect, why don't you? What is it you want from me anyway?" He raked his fingers through his hair and chewed on his bottom lip. "My soul?"

"I don't want it, no, Son Boy. But I suggest you give it to the Lord, where it belongs."

"Let's go, Maude." Sherman stood up and reached for his hat. Then he leaned into the wall for support.

"*Jesus wept!*" Abe cried out. "Surprised to see your sinner son knows scripture like the next guy, are you? You want I quote John 3:16?"

"I'm losing patience, hear? One would think at least on a Sabbath you could put Satan behind you and look to the Lord."

"Hell-o, Mother! I'm goin' to church, ain't I?"

Maude gathered up her Bible and Sunday school booklet and charged out the door.

"Well, ain't I?"

CHAPTER ELEVEN

Lily woke up one morning to see orange strips of sunlight on the wall facing her. Maude knocked at the door to announce breakfast. Lily jumped up, threw on her housecoat, and was relieved to see that Maude had gone, leaving behind a tray with two cups of coffee.

"See what fresh, clean air will do for you? You slept like a log!" she said, and brought Abe the coffee with an assortment of vitamins and pain pills. Then she raised the window shade and welcomed the light. Abe buried his head in the goose-down pillow and grumbled. She lowered the shade and switched on a dresser lamp instead.

"I feel dizzy," he said when sitting up. "Like the earth's upside down."

"You're used to the dark, hon. You'll get used to the light. Just give it some time." She dressed quickly and laid out his clothes.

"It's like I'm here above ground but not really here," he said and fell down on his stomach, his closed eyes enjoying the dark.

"Maybe getting only four hours of sleep a night is finally catching up." She noticed his sunburned back, reached for an ointment, and sat down to rub.

"Hon, did you by any chance remember to call Dr. Humfleet for Pop?"

"I tried but the nurse said he's on vacation. I'm thinkin' we should get somebody else."

"Oh, no, he's the best. I'm sure of it. I don't want to wait either, but I think we should." She worked in more ointment and continued to rub. "I was hoping we could talk about the barn," she said, her voice soft like her fingers.

He sat up, lit a Camel, and watched the flame lick the nail of his nicotine-yellow thumb. Yesterday he'd taken a half-day off to go look for part-time work as a logger or railroader. And he'd been told of layoffs and thick piles of applications.

"What about the barn?"

"I wish we could get started, is all. You're gone all day long, hon, and don't know how hard it is, two families trying to live under the same roof. Sleeping on the floor makes the children tired and grumpy. They fight like cats and dogs!" She considered mentioning her own discomfort when with Maude, but thought better of it.

"It won't be forever. Let them learn patience. It's a virtue, ain't it? Ain't that Bible?"

"But why not now like we planned, before they start school?"

"Now is too uncertain."

She shuddered as she recalled Ceola's warning about miners with coal dust in their blood. Was Ceola right? Was Abe considering going back to the pit?

"How come?" she asked, trying her best to sound casual.

"Well, for starters, Mother and Daddy ain't transferred the deed yet."

"Have you asked them to?"

"Not exactly."

"Why not?"

"It just don't seem right to me, Lily, takin' somethin' for nothin'. I think we should have the money to pitch in first. I've tried to find work and the jobs, they just ain't out there."

"But you're looking after the farm."

Maude knocked again. Abe took a drag from the Camel and polished off the coffee.

"Comin'!" he yelled. A fly whizzed by, and he watched it check out the grim bedroom possibilities before landing on the ceiling.

"What about the construction job you have now? Surely you'll get a raise once you're more experienced."

"It's a great job. *Trainin'*, June calls it. If'n I keep up the good work, pretty soon I'll of earned enough money to pay for my tools." He fell back, placed his ashtray on his chest and continued to stare at the fly on the ceiling.

"Now, hon, you said you wanted June to treat you like everybody else. No family favors, you told him."

"June don't bither me a bot."

"Abe!" His mother knocked a third time.

"Hell, Mother, hold your damn horses!" He stood up in his white boxer shorts and stretched into his trousers. The fly checked out the window and buzzed back to the ceiling.

"The job's only til spring. Then you'll quit to grow tobacco." Lily made up the bed and plumped the pillows.

"Righto."

"The children and I will sow the plant bed. That will save us the cost of buying plants."

"Damn tootin'."

"Your daddy will be well by then and able to teach us."

"Uh huh."

She reached to touch his face, gently because of the sun-
burn.

"Everything's gonna work out, hon, you'll see. Then we
can pay your parents."

"Yo." He backed away and pointed to the fly on the ceiling.

"Reckon what the trick is?"

"The trick?"

"That upside-down fly. What keeps it from fallin'?"

"I don't know. Maybe he's got little hooks on his feet that
help him hold on."

"Hooks that help him hold on, eh?"

"I think so."

"Lucky guy."

Lily arrived in the kitchen to find Maude had cooked Abe's
breakfast and placed an ashtray nearby, even though she dis-
approved of his smoking. She had even lit a small bees' wax
candle, a yield from one of Sherman's three healthy hives.

Lily looked around for Sherman.

"Where's Pop?"

"Slept in." Maude pointed to some small jelly-jar glasses
and handed Lily a pitcher of milk for the children.

"I hope he's okay. Did you think to check him?"

"What's keeping Abe?" Maude asked.

"He'll be along directly."

Maude poured Abe's coffee and Lily poured some buttermilk for Sherman. She always looked forward to meeting him
at the table, where he took her hand and called her "the
daughter I never had" or "Abe's better half." She had loved
him from that day Abe first brought her to this table to an-

nounce their engagement, she remembered. She'd been wearing a starched sailor dress and patent-leather pumps. Her hair curled in a flip on her shoulders. Maude wore a long black dress with pleats, and buttoned high at the collar. Her chestnut hair was primly braided in the same Brillo-like bun she now wore. Still in her thirties, she'd had the appearance of someone old and stooped.

"What should I call you once Abe and I are married?" she had asked Sherman, a glass of water quaking in her hand.

"Let's not rush things," Maude answered for him. "The marriage is still a long way off. Who knows what could happen between now and then?"

"Pop!" Sherman spouted off, his eyes shining and buttermilk crowning his thin upper lip. "I'd be honored if you'd call me *Pop.*"

Lily cleared her head and proceeded to set the table. She put the forks to the left, the knives and spoons to the right. As she moved, she felt Maude's eyes measuring her as she had on that first occasion.

"Is there anything else I can do? Can I wake Pop?" She had anguished over a home and considered coming right out and asking him to sign over the deed. Abe would resent her for going over his head, yes, but she had recently observed a mother bird and her babies in the vicinity of a black snake. The viciously flapping bird had confirmed her theory that nature's dwellers are uncompromising when it comes to the protection of their young.

Abe walked into the kitchen, flashing a grin and heading toward his mother.

"Mornin', Mother. How's the world treatin' ya? Them Itis boys behavin' theirselves, are they? Arthur and Burs ain't up to their old tricks, are they?"

"Well, if you ain't chipper!" Maude claimed a hug before serving him fried eggs and biscuits. One biscuit was already buttered, the other spread with his favorite strawberry jam. "Must be the new job."

"Must be." Never one to sip coffee, Abe gulped it down and handed Lily the cup.

"Be a good girl, will ya?" he said.

Lily poured her coffee after his and added cream. She sat down at the table and prayed somebody would bring up the subject of renovation. But Maude had clipped an obituary from the newspaper, and she and Abe entered into a lively discussion about the deceased—a man in his eighties, somebody who had once poached rabbits on their land, married a negro, grown a hermit's beard, and so on.

"Excuse me," Lily said, and got up unnoticed. She prepared a mayonnaise and Cheddar-cheese sandwich, wrapped it in wax paper, and sealed it with toothpicks. She packed it and two coconut-macaroon cookies inside Abe's lunch bucket and filled his thermos bottle with hot coffee. It was Saturday, no school, so she left Sweet William and the girls sleeping. "Today is wash hair day. Think I'll go check the rain barrel," she said, and lit out for the barnyard.

The morning air was warm, and she held up her hair to feel the breeze on her neck. She stopped to admire some trellised morning glories, red to attract humming birds, and some potted pink petunias, the perennial kind. They were blooming nicely, and she felt the soil before giving them water. *Tur-dle, tur-dle* came from the vicinity of low woodland, and she recognized the singing of a shy Kentucky warbler.

"I hear you, my friend," she teased. "And if you want your breakfast today, then we should meet face-to-face." Her certainty that she was being courted by the yellow-breasted bird reminded her of her pa claiming to hear the corn growing, and of Abe smelling the odorless methane gas.

Methane gas took her back to the mine, her sin of omission, and Abe's sometimes bad moods, and she wondered if a trip back to the camp might revive his old spirit. Then she considered the pain of saying goodbye again to old friends like Ceola and Dog. What if Abe made the trip and returned in an even worse mood? What if he didn't want to come back at all?

Abe finished his breakfast and headed outside to the Plymouth. She saw him and followed.

"Gotta go," he said when she reached for the usual hit-and-run kiss. "Tell the dodos their ole man said to be good and work hard and Sunday he might buy 'em a watermelon."

"They'll be ecstatic." She placed her arm through his and practically ran to keep up. "Hon, I'm counting the days til I can have the kitchen all to myself and be the one to cook your breakfast. Remember how this used to be our favorite time of day, before the children woke up? When we would lie in the dark sipping coffee and listening to the roosters crow before dawn? How you would let me feel your muscles one at a time, working down?"

Abe smiled. "Them was good times."

"Oh, Abe, they'll be good again once we have a place of our own. Pa and June will be happy to help with the barn if you'll just set a time. Get Pop to sign over the deed, and I can take things from there. In no time we can be settled in."

Blood rushed to his face. He put out a cough that triggered others.

"Like hell you will!"

She removed her arm and felt pressure building behind her eyes.

"I only meant I'd save you the trouble. Honestly, some responsibility more challenging than simple house and farm chores would do me good."

"Stay out of it, Lily!" he scolded, and she might have agreed had it not been for the promise she'd made to her children.

"But June promised. He said he'd help with the barn in exchange for me looking after Ma and Pa. Eula's a diabetic, and he wants me to be responsible for her insulin shots." She yearned to say that moving ahead with the barn project was as much for his sake as for hers and the children's because she had seen how his mother's needling was wearing him down, sucking his energy like aphids on plants. "It's been over a month now, and the children are still sleeping on the floor. I thought you wanted them to do good at school. They can't if..."

"I said to lay off!"

She toyed with her dress collar. She pictured arthritic Rosy sleeping on a quilt on a hard floor, and her droopy, drowsy eyes as she set out for school the next morning. She saw the teenagers with no place to groom and primp.

"I will, I promise, but will you at least try to call Dr. Humfleet's office again? This time, be sure and say it's Lily *Eakins* and not *Siler* who needs him. Back then, I had my maiden name. He won't remember me if you don't say *Eakins!*" She was sensitive to his lack of education and avoided using words like *college* and *degree,* although she sometimes wished he would take into account that she had a mind of her own. A particularly good one, in fact.

"Will do," he said.

"Leave June's number if Dr. Humfleet's not there!" she called as he turned the key in the ignition.

"You got it."

"Be sure to say *Lily Eakins!*" she cried breathlessly.

"Yes, ma'am," he said and tipped his ball cap.

Hoping to please Abe, Lily slaved on the farm like a hired hand and saw that the children did their own share of chores. Often she encouraged Maude to go to her bedroom to quilt or read the Bible or simply rest while she herself attended to the work. Sometimes Maude chose to spend that time walking in the woods. Lily always wondered what happened on those trips to make her return with such frantic eyes and movements so disoriented that the girls giggled and rolled their eyes. A time or two they even suggested following her, an idea Lily fiercely nipped in the bud.

"Where did you go on your walk?" Lily had once asked in a chirpy but insistent tone.

She'd noticed a trickle of blood on Maude's hand and attributed it to briars.

"To the Lord."

"You mean you worshipped God through nature?"

"I mean I went to the Lord."

Lily loved her time without Maude and the chance to pretend the house was all hers. She moved and then returned furniture with the enthusiasm of someone shaping a bouquet or getting dressed for a prom. She swept and mopped and polished the Victor Junior cookstove until it sparkled. "To God Be the Glory" she sometimes sang as she defrosted the refrigerator or rearranged items in the cabinets.

She liked working outside under the sunlight even better. When she milked Freda, the old Jersey cow, she pictured her own ma working her cow's udders, feeling them blindly as though knitting or kneading bread. Sometimes her ma skimmed off the cream and made round pats of butter. Rosy loved to help churn while the two sang: "Churn butter churn / Churn butter churn / Rosy's at the garden gate / Waiting for the birthday cake / Churn butter churn!" Afterwards Rosy ate the bubbles off the dasher stick with the excitement of someone licking meringue from a beater.

Working outside was not without its drawbacks. Lily sometimes felt so sweaty and exhausted at the end of the day that she looked upon the afternoon sun as a beating from God, a rod to punish her for misleading Abe. But on other days she felt she ran the risk of going blind while admiring its yellow splendor. Her skin had turned golden, and Maude suggested wearing a bonnet. She agreed that the precaution might preserve her youth and possibly her life, but couldn't bring herself to wall out the very source of her energy.

By far her happiest time of day was just after supper, when she turned the dishes over to the girls and declared herself officially off duty. Then she bathed, put on her blue cotton dress with a lace collar, prettied her face, pinned a flower or leaf in her hair, and stepped out on the mountain to meet Abe at Bryce's Cove.

Heart in a flutter, she sometimes ran in anticipation of some sweet laurel thicket, a hideaway behind twilight's gauze curtain.

CHAPTER TWELVE

Lily's pa, Wade Eakins, made a surprise trip to Mud Creek at a time when Lily and Vi had gone to buy groceries. His mission, inspired by pity for Lily and his grandchildren, was to discuss the barn's renovation with Maude and Sherman, volunteer his service, and make a list of the needed materials. The meeting went well, and afterwards he drove to Perkins' Lumber Yard in Williamsburg, where he purchased a substantial part of the supplies, hauling some and having the others delivered. The following Sunday he returned as unexpectedly as before with tools and workers, claiming Lily's sheep were stuck in a ditch, a Biblical excuse for tending them on the Sabbath.

A cool breeze blessed the air with the spirit of tent revivals and luncheons on the ground. Lily greeted everyone with enthusiasm while Abe charged over to his father-in-law, a look of contempt on his face, his words stinging. Wade Eakins finagled a handshake, slapped Abe's back, and steered the forthcoming argument down a knoll some seventy feet away.

Lily's heart pounded as she watched the two leave, and she slipped away to follow. A part of her longed to go stand with her husband; another part celebrated her pa for his grit and good intentions. If Abe wouldn't think of his wife and children, he should at least let somebody else try, she told herself. She even wondered if he had avoided the barn project to put off separating from his mother.

Abe and Wade Eakins stood under the shade of an old oak, saplings sprouting from its base and acorns crunching under their feet. Wade Eakins respectfully removed his old felt hat with sweat stains along the band and fumbled the rim. Abe lost no time. He accused Wade of meddling, and ordered him to return every last scrap of the lumber. The white-haired preacher, solid and handsome in a frontier way, smiled kindly, not once interrupting. But when his turn came, he drew a picture of pitiful and patient Lily, deprived of the home she'd been promised. He spoke of the poor children, forced to start school while living out of banana boxes and orange crates.

"God love their hearts!" he said like a true preacher, stretching the syllables to the next hollow and back. "If you won't consider Lily, then at least think of the children!"

Abe's face turned a crimson red. He took off his cap, planning to slap it at something.

"Think of the children? Think of the children? Ha, that's a good one! How the hell do you think I got myself in this scrape to begin with?"

"No doubt you did it for the sake of your family."

"You damn right I did."

"You gave up a lot."

"Hell, who's countin'?"

"Lily is. She wants to move forward as planned."

"Well, tell her to hold her damn horses."

"You know as well as me I've never been one to tell that girl a bless-ed thing. You might recall I once warned you to beware of the cornered coon?"

"You'd do well to save your warnings for the sinners and leave Lily to me."

The preacher, who had made a weak attempt at humor, nodded his head.

"Perhaps, so."

They argued on, Abe's temper rising, his breaths short and loud, and Wade's patience adding to his anger.

"You're a good man, Abe, try and do the right thing." Wade Eakins put on his hat and turned toward the house. "I'm sorry if I overstepped my boundaries."

"*If?*" Abe said with a snort.

"I'm sorry. Truly sorry."

Alone, Abe kicked the tree trunk. He glanced up to see Lily and assumed she had come to stand up for her husband, which would be only right. He dropped under the oak, rolled a Sunday cigarette, and waited. When he looked up to find out what was keeping her, he saw her walking arm-in-arm with her pa, the two heading back to the house and workers. Though lying down, a fatigue rode his bones like nothing he'd ever experienced in a coal mine. He leaned his back into the tree, eased out his legs, and chuckled at the irony: The man who had once carried a mountain on his shoulders was now ankle deep in debt and as broke as a false promise.

"Abe!" he heard, and jumped up, praying Lily had come to her senses. "Abe, is that you?"

Maude appeared from a shortcut. He grunted and threw himself back down on the ground.

"No, it's me," he answered sarcastically.

"Now you pull yourself together and come help with that barn, hear?" she scolded.

"Ain't you heard it's against the good book to work on the Sabbath?" he retorted.

"This ain't no way to treat company."

"Stop bellyaching, will ya? It ain't my company. Hell, I was the last one to know they was comin'. At least Lily could've give me a warnin'."

"Lily didn't know and I didn't tell her 'cause I knew she'd tell you and you'd try and stop us."

"You damn right I would've!" He took a drag from the cigarette and coughed. "What about me, Mother? What about the promises you made me? Ain't I at least due a opinion?"

"On your own home you are but this barn-house is mine and Sherman's."

"My own home? Ha, that's a joke! A real kicker! In case you ain't noticed, I ain't got a home. I ain't got a wife either, thanks to meddlin' Wade Eakins."

"Uh huh, and whose fault is that? All it'd take to clear this thing up is a trip to the courthouse so Sherman could sign over the deed."

"Now's not the time. It's gotta wait."

"Wait? Wait for what?"

Wait for June to pay me fair wages, he considered saying. "Wait til I have money to pitch in and help cover the cost," he said instead.

"But that weren't the deal."

"To me it was."

"Now you looky here. Lily and me maybe don't always see eye-to-eye but this time we do. Her and these younguns deserve a home."

"And they'll get it just as soon as I can raise the money."

"But I told you everything is free. Yours for the taking."

"Ain't nothing free, Mother. Ain't you learned that by now. A man's gotta pay his own way, else he'll be forever beholdin'."

"Not when it's family."

"Especially when it's family."

"And speaking of family, your wife's waiting with your company. So get yourself up and go be a gentleman."

"Like I say, they ain't my company."

"Maybe they ain't coal miners but they still count as humans."

"Get off my back, Mother."

"I ain't moving a muscle, Son Boy, til you gather your wits about you and get going."

He threw her a killer look and patted the ground.

"Then you'd better have a seat."

Wade Eakins departed with his crew when Abe failed to return, and Lily was sad but also relieved. They had not cleared the driveway when she raced off to find Abe and explain why she had appeared to choose her pa over him. When she couldn't find him at the oak tree or on the trail he'd used earlier, she returned to the house. He'd thought of something he needed at the store, she reasoned. Or maybe he'd left to pout and would come home in time for his Sunday supper with the family. Rarely would he miss spending Sunday with his children.

Hours passed. She made tapioca pudding and helped Maude prepare a beans-and-potatoes supper. They waited for him until just before church service and then ate quickly. While the girls washed dishes, Lily sponge bathed and debated as she dressed. Should she miss church to wait? Should she go? Could she afford to make two mistakes in one day?

There had been no sign of him when June and his wife, Eula, arrived in a two-door Nomad station wagon to collect their passengers. She went along, wishing she'd thought to leave a note beside his bathtub filled with hot water. At one point she almost asked June to take her back home.

The sermon, though Bible smart and certainly well rendered, failed to hold her attention. She watched dusk darken the stained-glass windows and admired her ma's bouquet at the altar; it was an arrangement of peppermint camellias with slightly frost-bitten edges, like cookies the moment they're ready to be snatched from the oven. She even outlined a tormented letter to Ceola, one she probably wouldn't write, in the margins of her morning bulletin. And throughout the hour, she dwelled on Abe.

"You're quiet tonight," June said on the way home.

"Am I?"

"Are you sure you're all right?"

"I couldn't be better."

They arrived home, and Lily spotted the Plymouth in the driveway. Except for a loft light, the house was mostly dark and quiet when she went inside. She made excuses to the girls and went to bed early, leaving Verni in charge of everyone's homework and grooming. She hoped by now Abe would be reasonably awake and willing to talk. She was prepared to use praise, flattery, seduction—every womanly gift the Lord had bestowed on her, including some He hadn't—to raise his spirits and convince him to give her a chance.

"Please, God, shield him from anger," she whispered as she undressed, brushed her hair, and cold creamed her face in the dark. Slats rumbled when she slipped into bed to whiff sawdust and sweat, and the usual tobacco.

"Hon," she whispered. "Hon, are you awake?" She sat up on an elbow, combed her fingers down his back, and felt his muscles tighten. "I'm sorry about Pa showing up here today. I know he wouldn't have interfered without a reason, and I guess I unknowingly gave him one, but honestly, I had no idea he'd get so involved." She slid her feet to his side of the bed, hoping he would reach out his own for the usual warming.

And still he played possum.

"I only left with Pa because he said to give you a chance to cool off. He said he'd take everyone away after I said goodbye, and then I should come back to you and make peace. I raced back but you'd gone."

The silence that followed, the severity of her punishment, made her shudder. So many times she had watched him spiral out of control, and her job had been to soothe him back to normal. What a shame that women are expected to mother their husbands along with their children, she thought. What a shame that men have so much ego and so little sensitivity.

"Please," she said. "I promise to do better."

A minute or so later she drew in her feet and turned toward the outside wall, where she listened to the lonely sounds of crickets and frogs. Waiting for morning and freedom from Abe's black mood seemed unbearable. She prayed for sleep and, without it, found herself sweeping up old hurts like morning's warm ashes.

There was the matter of him and Vi, for instance, on that night of Vi's husband's funeral. Vi and Abe had gone outside to smoke, no doubt drink, and escape from the clinging mourners. She had stood in a window and watched him and the poor grieving widow waltz in the moonlight. They had disappeared briefly behind the corn crib, and she had borne the pain of not knowing what happened between them every hour of every day for the past twelve years. Abe had sworn off liquor but she had struggled for months before finally forgiving them, or pretending to.

At least she had managed to maintain a silence.

Abe was gone from the bed when Lily woke up at dawn. She dressed quickly and hurried to the kitchen, where Maude sat at the table, sipping Hadacol from the bottle. Abe's plate of eggs and mug of coffee were untouched. His work boots leaned into a corner.

"Did you see Abe?" she asked Maude.

"He was mad as fire and dressed in his Sundays. Not headed to work, I can tell you." Maude set down the Hadacol and wrung her big hands. "Oh, Lily, tell me he's not gone back to them coal mines!"

"He was mad at Pa and June for coming here yesterday." Lily consciously removed herself from the list of offenders. "He probably just needed a breather."

"But to leave in the dark and not say where he was going."

"Now, Maude, you know Abe has his black moods. Give him some time to cool off. In the end he always finds his way home, right?" Her voice was more accommodating than usual, her way of thanking Maude for trying to bring Abe back to her pa and the company.

"But what about his job? What if June fires him and he can't pay back your pa? He hates that job, you know. Fall seven times, I tell him, and get up eight."

"Maybe he's called June already." Lily slipped away to count the change in the Aunt Jemima cookie jar and breathed easier, seeing that there was enough money to buy the usual staples.

"He was all spruced up and sweet smelling," Maude said with a moan.

"He didn't take a bath last night. Maybe he was trying to hide a smell."

"Like a man looking for a job, he was." Maude pursed her lips. "Or maybe a woman."

Lily thought of Vi that night of Brody's death.

"That's hardly likely," she said, and managed a laugh. She hurried outside to draw water, left it to boil, pulled the washing machine into the center of the floor, and dumped out a bin of dirty clothes. All the while she fussed at the balled-up socks and small items like Jack rocks or pennies carelessly left in pockets.

While she hung out the white wash an hour later, she stared into ghostly Vanderpool Mountain. She saw along the ridge the profile of a reclining man with a flat forehead, cone-shaped nose, and angular chin. He reminded everybody of somebody, and to her he was ailing Sherman.

A mental picture of the younger, healthy Pop brought a smile to her face. "Trotty little horsey going to town. Better watch out you might fall down!" she heard him chant while swinging one of the children on his ankle or knee. "Hey, Jim, how many tons of coal you loaded today?" he sometimes teased the younger girls at the end of a day, after they played in coal piles or rolled down hillsides made black or orange by mine waste.

Last evening she had served him crushed beets and a spread made of ground chicken livers with boiled eggs and fine chopped celery. He had eaten only a little and held his throat when he swallowed. Time was running out, and she knew if he couldn't see Dr. Humfleet soon, she would be forced to find another doctor.

Reaching for a bed sheet, she shook it so hard it flapped back at her. She doubled it and pinned up the corners, then hung two more sheets and raised the clothesline with a wooden prop. Abe would come home apologetic, and she would ask him to replace it, she thought. Or maybe she'd do better by asking her pa.

"Mama, come help us shuck the last of the corn!" Daisy and Tansy called from the porch. Their tender voices reached her like the rumble of coal leaving the Cordel-Lewis tipple. Like the coal, they invaded her rare chance for a rendezvous with self.

"Where's Iris?" she asked at the porch.

"She's inside with her diary," Daisy said.

Lily had hoped Iris would go to the picture show with Verni and Minnie Mo, chaperoned by Vi. But she had chosen to be alone.

"Tell her I said to come outside to the sunshine, will you?"

"I already asked her and she won't come," Daisy replied.

"Then I better check on her." Lily had taken hold of the door handle when she saw Sweet William round a corner of the house on his bicycle. It was lunchtime, and he'd just come from his summer job in tobacco. After Labor Day, the tobacco generally went to market, and the children went back to school.

"Mama, come watch us!" Rosy cried from the handlebars. White Leghorn chickens cackled as they scattered. Iris heard the noise and slipped to the back door, her figure dark behind the shaded porch and screen wiring.

"How come you're not shucking corn with your sisters?" Lily asked Rosy.

"Daisy and Tansy said to get lost."

Lily frowned at them, and the two raised their eyebrows to say they knew nothing of the matter.

"Come let me fix you a sandwich," she called to Sweet William.

"I ate already."

"Then I'll pack you some water. Remember to drink often. Not fast, but often."

"Can we take a real ride later?" Rosy cried when she and Sweet William sailed to a safe landing.

"Why sure we can."

"Watch out for her legs!" Lily said as if she needed to remind her perfect son to be gentle. She had always looked on his kind nature and determination to be a doctor as a document of sorts, proof that she and Abe were right for each other. She had often thanked God for him not turning out to be loud and stormy like his daddy; then afterwards she had felt her usual guilt. For Abe is a good man, she had reminded herself. Spoiled, stubborn as a mule, and prone to black moods, but good to the core. He is somebody I wouldn't consider trading for all the world! she had told herself to the point of believing.

She went into the kitchen where she coerced Iris outside and returned with a fruit jar of water inside a bag with woven plastic threads and a plastic handle. Sweet William attached it to his bicycle and adjusted the handlebars without looking up.

"Mama," he said, and paused.

"Yes?"

"I...I was thinking I might ride to Buck Creek tomorrow, after I leave work. See if I can help Papaw do chores or something. Maybe go fishing with Buddy."

Lily fought off the urge to warn him of the hair-pin turns and crazy mountain drivers who resent bikers' rights to the road. She resisted saying he should stay away from the Enlow family and why. After all, he was a man now, soon to attend the University of Kentucky.

"Just be home before dark," she said.

"I will."

"Can I go, too?" Rosy cried.

"Rosy, it's time for you to rest. Iris wants you to read her a story, don't you, Iris?"

Iris shrugged her shoulders, suggesting a yes.

"Can I read your diary instead?" Rosy pleaded.

"You stay outa my diary!" Iris turned to Lily. "Mama, tell her to stop trying to get inside my diary! No matter where I hide it, she snoops til she finds it."

Rosy crossed her fingers behind her back and made a pitiful face.

"I haven't, honest."

"Pants on fire!"

"Girls, please," Lily said.

"Okay, you can read me *Huckleberry Finn*," Iris said. "I brought it home from school so you could practice."

"Golly Jees Moses! Will you read me the part where Huck pretends to be a girl?"

"You read it to me."

"You read!"

Rosy scampered inside, followed by Iris, and Lily passed Maude going out for a walk. The sky had clouded over, and she was wearing her plastic rain scarf and carrying the usual prayer shawl.

"He's not home yet," Maude said, shooing away the last of the summer flies.

"It's early," Lily said. "Give him time."

"Then what?"

"Abe's a grown man, Maude. He'll come home when he's ready." Lily noticed Daisy and Tansy had stopped shucking to listen. "It's possible he went on to work," she added for their sake.

"Dressed in his Sundays?"

"Sometimes he carries extra clothes." Lily dropped a shucked ear of corn into a tub and moved toward the porch and kitchen door. The potted petunias were spindly, and she pinched the stems close to the dirt. Then she fed them some manure tea and hoped they would perk.

CHAPTER THIRTEEN

Abe returned home in the early afternoon and changed into his work duds. Lily was ironing clothes. She stopped to serve him a plate of vinegary mustard greens, pinto beans, and flat cakes with onions, but said nothing. In case he would work late, she packed him some jelly biscuits and coffee.

"I'm sorry, Lily," he said. "And I'll apologize to Wade and June if you want me to."

"Where were you?" she asked, cautious as usual.

"Frankfort."

"Frankfort? Why Frankfort?"

"There was no sawmill or railroad jobs to be had here so I went to test for my mine foreman's papers."

"Your mine foreman's papers? Why, whatever for?"

"Now don't get all bent out of shape. It ain't nothin' but a safety precaution. In case the construction job don't work out, I'd feel a lot better knowin' I had a backup. Six months til spring is a long time. A man needs to know he can put food on the table."

"But why wouldn't it work out? I talked to June, and he says you're a real hard worker."

"So that's what he says, does he?" He curled his tongue over his upper lip and paused to ask himself if he should tell her he'd recently hurled a hammer through a windowpane and kicked hell out of a sawhorse. That June had tossed him a math book and said to go home and learn how to count. That it would be only a matter of time til June would give him the ax, in spite of his sister. Instead he grabbed his lunch box, scrambled toward the door, and opened it a crack.

"Yes. That's what he says."

"Look, Lily, I wadn't cut out to be a construction worker is all."

"But you might come to like it."

His hand gripped the doorknob.

"I told you I wouldn't drag you and the kids back to Cordel-Lewis and Abe Siler is a man of his word. There's little truck mines all around here I can commute to if I have to."

"You mean those illegal mines with no safety precautions?"

"They pay money like all the rest."

"They're death traps. Why, the Union wouldn't touch them with a 10-foot pole."

"I know mines, Lily, even the hot ones. Like a piece of fruit, I can smell 'em, feel 'em, taste 'em. Ain't nothin' gonna happen to me in them mines. I'm too damn smart."

"Promise me you'll try and keep the construction job until spring."

"And then what?"

"Then we'll plant the tobacco."

"And just what are we supposed to live on between planting and harvest? The sawmills? Railroads?"

"Why, I guess I thought construction."

"But think, Lily. You just said I could quit construction come spring. Two and two don't make four here and you and me both knows it."

"I'll get a part-time job," Lily said. "Dr. Humfleet..."

"Like hell you will!"

Lily took a man's dark shirt from the ironing basket and was pressing the sleeves when Rosy stumbled into the kitchen, only minutes behind Abe.

"Mama, why did Daddy leave mad this morning?"

"Why, who said he was mad?"

"He was grumpy, I heard him, and Grandmother said the ole devil was on his back again."

"I'll have a word with your grandmother for putting such silly notions into your head."

"She won't switch me for telling, will she?" Rosy nestled Hairy under her chin. "Mama, did Hairy or me do something to make Daddy mad? Did we cause him to leave?"

"Why, Rosy, of course not. He was tired, is all. And a little peeved at your papaw and me for pushing him into the barn work before he was ready. But now he's fine, really."

"Well, will you ask Papaw if we can have a revival when Daddy comes home?"

"Daddy's come home already. He just left for work."

Rosy ran to the window. A scarf of dust was settling on the driveway.

"How come I didn't see him?"

"You were helping Daisy and Tansy pick tomatoes, and he was in a hurry."

"Well, will you ask Papaw if we can have a revival anyways?"

"A revival?" The tense look on Rosy's face told Lily to choose her words carefully. "Rosy, remember the song about how Jesus loves the little children? You're too young to be worrying about salvation. Twelve is the age of accountability for sin, and you're only six."

"It's not for me. It's Daddy I'm worried about. Grandmother says he's lost and in danger of hellfire and brimstone. She says the Lord won't be patient forever. I want Papaw to help me save him."

Lily thumped down the iron and took a calming breath.

"Your daddy has already been saved. *Once in grace, always in grace.*" The doctrine darted from her lips like "good night" at bedtime and "good morning" at breakfast. Since marrying Abe, she had embraced the words as if they were scripture. There were times when she had considered discussing the state of Abe's soul with her pa, but backed down. Possibly because she was afraid of what she might learn.

"What does *in grace* mean?" Rosy asked.

"It means once saved, you're saved forever."

Rosy's eyes lit up. She tossed Hairy into the air and caught him coming down.

"Golly Jees Moses! Then Grandmother's all wrong about Daddy?"

"She is, yes. Now go tell your sisters I said to come in from the rain."

Lily was creasing the legs of a pair of khaki pants when Maude entered into the kitchen from her walk in the woods. She moved in a stupor, and Lily could see she'd been crying. Something stirred the nurse spirit in her.

"Was that Abe I saw?" Maude asked, and Lily nodded.

"And he didn't want to see me?"

"He did. He wanted to come find you, but he had to get to work."

"Shame I missed him. Did he say where he'd been?" She wrung her handkerchief through her fingers, and Lily noticed her inside-out smock.

"He went for a ride."

"A ride?"

"A long ride to clear his mind. He's fine now and gone to work."

"Let's just hope June will take him back."

"I'll talk to June. He'll understand."

"Oh, Lily, would you?"

"Of course, I will. Just don't tell Abe."

"Well, looky there!" Maude perked up and pointed out the window, to where Daisy and Tansy came dragging half a bushel of German Johnson tomatoes. "When I told them to go pick, I didn't dream we'd have enough to put up."

Lily draped the pants over a tubed hanger, turned off the iron, and ran outside to help.

"Thank you, they look wonderful," she said, and slid the basket into the kitchen. "Now go wash and get out of those damp clothes."

"We should can them now." Maude grabbed some blue Mason jars from the pantry and put a pot of water on to boil. Then she handed both Daisy and Tansy a penny from her smock pocket.

"Good girls. Tell Sherman I said to take you to the store for a stick of hard candy," she said.

"I helped, too," Rosy whined. "Can I go?"

"You stay here and rest that leg," Lily said, fearing that three quarreling girls might be too much for Sherman to handle. "Tell them what kind you want, and they'll bring it back."

"But I hate that stupid bed! I want to go and get Blo Bubble!"

"She don't get nothin'!" Daisy and Tansy fussed. "We did all the work!"

"Did not!"

"Did too!"

"She'll get her penny's worth like the rest." Maude plunked a hand on Rosy's head. "But no bubble gum. You accidentally swallow that rubbery stuff and your insides will stick together. Sadie Eubanks knows a poor youngun what died of that very thing."

"Then I want licorice."

"No licorice. Anything that black is got to be of the devil. You'll have a stick of peppermint and be grateful." She fished out three more pennies and handed them to Daisy. "While you're at it, get Sherman some horehound."

"Yuk! I hate peppermint!" Rosy squawked, and Lily, suspecting that damp weather and joint pain accounted for her bad behavior, didn't bother to scold her.

Maude wasted no time once they had gone.

"I'm so disappointed in that boy of mine I could just sock his jaws!"

Blowing at her stubborn wisp of hair, Lily felt some of the old tension returning. She was tempted to remind her mother-in-law that her *boy* was forty-two years of age, a grown man with a family. "For God's sake, let him grow up!" she wanted to squawk.

"He'll be all right," she said instead.

"Pray tell, when is he gonna take some interest in Sherman and me's house. These younguns done slept on the floor long enough, I tell him. They need their own beds!"

The words were music to Lily's ears. Without thinking, she placed a hand on Maude's shoulder and let it slide to her elbow. Maude winced and sprang back.

"Is your shoulder hurt?" Lily asked. "Can I make you a cold compress?"

"Nothing a little witch hazel won't cure."

"Maybe I should take a look."

"No!"

Lily puzzled over the tension.

"I was going to say you don't know how happy I am to hear you've urged Abe to get on with the barn-house. I was afraid you'd maybe changed your mind."

"Lawsy mercy, no! I've told him time and time again we need to go to the courthouse and change over the deed."

"To tell you the truth, I was under the impression that the renovation would be well underway when we got here. I promised the children they'd have a home of their own, and, Maude, it's critically important that I keep my word."

"Absolutely."

"What do you think got in the way?"

"It was on account of Sherman not feeling like doing the work hisself and fretting over hiring somebody. And now Abe claims he's got no time to help. I tell you, Lily, I've had it up to here with that boy dragging his feet!"

"I think Abe has the notion that he needs to trade Sherman a house for a house. You know he's never been one to take something for nothing."

"Sherman wouldn't accept a dime of his money and you know it."

"I do."

Maude washed the tomatoes and lapsed into a cry.

"That mine's done messed with his head, I tell you, and he's having second thoughts. I got a feelin' he's at this very moment trying to go back."

"Oh, no! He wouldn't. I'll talk to him again. I'll remind him of his promise."

"Talk? Talking takes time we ain't got. Me, I say let's get on with it."

"Exactly," Lily said. "Soon Sweet William goes away to college. Without him, there's no counting on Buddy and Peony's boys to pitch in and help. Don't tell Abe I told you, but I talked to June, and he says they're pressed to get four more houses under roof before winter sets in, plus finish the ones they've already started. He says they're gonna have to string lights and work well into the night."

"You don't say!" Maude spilled boiling water over the tomatoes, and the two began the job of peeling and quartering. "Why, with Abe working nights, he'll be no help atall!"

"And with Pop ailing…"

"Thank the good Lord we can still count on your pa and brother!"

"Oh, no, no. You remember how furious Abe got when they showed up here last Sunday."

Maude put down her knife in order to think better. The gloomy woman from the woods had revived, and Lily's heart warmed from the sight.

"So maybe Abe made us promises he can't keep," Maude said. "Me, I've said before it's time us women take matters into our own hands."

Lily glanced up, her eyes big with surprise.

"Oh, no, no, we can't! Now of all times Abe needs to feel he's in charge."

"Why sure he does. And he will. The barn won't take all that much work. With a little help, the younguns and us could near do it ourselves. Why, the man should be proud!" Specks of light glinted on her glasses. "You said yourself Abe'll be off working. What he don't know can't hurt him, now can it? And besides, the barn is for Sherman and me and none of his business and I'll be only too glad to tell him so."

"But we've never kept secrets from one another." Lily looked around for Rosy. Not really, she thought. Not big ones, at least.

"But then your husband didn't break his word and go running off like some hired hand with a paycheck." Maude reached over and whispered into Lily's ear. "I take it you two made up."

"We did, yes, and he had no intention of running off. I completely understood his reason for being hurt. He plans to apologize to Pa."

"The boy needs roots, Lily. He needs a house to repair and a farm he can tend and be proud of." Maude put the tomatoes on to boil and dropped a teaspoon of salt into each of the scalded jars. "Sherman and me could have a new home to enjoy and you and Abe could get reacquainted, if you know what I mean. All in the world you two love birds needs is some time to yourselves."

Lily blushed. She scraped the froth from the boiling tomatoes and lined up the jars. Maude dipped the tomatoes through a handmade funnel, and Lily sealed each with a lid. She couldn't wait for the click that said the tomatoes were airtight and wouldn't spoil.

"They're pretty, if I do say so myself," she said.

Maude cackled. Her eyebrows arched over the rim of her glasses.

"Like I was just saying, a man's gotta have what a man's gotta have. If not at home, then he will roam."

Lily pictured the three-quarter moon. She saw Vi's hand in Abe's curls, her head against his shoulder. Feet almost still, hips swaying, Abe no doubt humming.

"Just say I did agree, where would we get the money?" she asked with a sigh.

"Don't you worry your pretty head about money. I've got a little nest egg what's burning a hole in my pocket." Maude sat down and placed her elbows on the table. "Now let me see. First we'll pay back your pa. There won't be much left over but we won't need much considering we'll be doing most all the work ourselves. Us and the younguns. Just think how good this could be for their character. Idleness is the devil's workshop, you know."

Lily had another of her long pauses.

"It sounds good. But I'll need time to think."

"You take your time, honey child. Pray on it. Seek out God's will. And remember—if anything should go wrong and it won't, the blame will be mine and I'll take ever last smidgen of it. I'm too old now to be ascared of anything, most especially my own son."

"Oh, no, I couldn't let you."

"Pshaw!" Maude waved a hand. "It's my plan, ain't it? With or without you. All you gotta do is ask your pa for the name of somebody reliable who wouldn't charge us a arm and a leg."

"Pa knows everybody in the trade. If I ask him for a recommendation but don't say who it's for, then Abe can't accuse him of interfering."

Maude tee-heed. "Atta girl!"

Maude and Lily walked to the barn after an early supper and light rain. They took measurements, discussed colors, and speculated on which piece of Maude's furniture would fit where and which didn't belong. As the two ambled home, shadows mixed with sunshine. Clouds moved toward the timberline.

"Has the Lord spoke about our plan?" Maude asked when at the end of the trail.

"Not yet. But I'm still praying on it."

"Like I said, you take your time. I wouldn't want it any other way." Maude waited out the seconds. "But time, you know, don't stand still."

Inside, they found the children sitting around the radio and listening to Minnie Pearl cluck, "How-Dee! I'm jes' so proud to be here." The two sat down at the kitchen table to chat and ended up piecing some of a Double Wedding Rings quilt Maude had just begun. Maude appeared kind and gracious, and the camaraderie they shared gave Lily hope that at last they were friends.

Maude encouraged Lily to talk about her brothers and sisters, especially John Mason, her favorite, and she took delight in hearing of the children's most recent triumphs at school. She herself revealed heartbreaking details about her mother's death from tuberculosis—the strangling coughs and the dots of blood on her bedclothes that turned into splotches and then splatters. She told how her daddy had beaten her and her sister, Blessie, with thorned canes of wild rose and later run off, leaving them alone with their mother. Practically penniless, they had taken turns begging on the streets.

"You poor darling," Lily said, and in spite of her nurse's discipline, she thought she would cry.

"Her death sent us to live with grudging relatives who hated we had no money to give them and left me to look after Blessie and my little baby brother, Clinton, only seven years old at the time." Maude took out her handkerchief. "They separated us after a year, once I finished all the washing and ironing shoved into a closet. Clinton, poor baby, ran away when he was eight and I never seen hide nor hair of him again. I figured he got a job logging on the Kentucky River and stole away on a barge to Ohio. Oh, how I did miss him! I married Sherman and he promised to find him but the trail, it just run out."

"And your sister?" Lily asked.

"Gone too."

"What a shame!"

Lily thought about the closeness between her own girls and Sweet William, and she pictured how pathetic each would be if any one of them were taken away. What a tragic life Maude had lived! No wonder the poor woman is peculiar, she thought, and slid her chair closer.

"Blessie and me, we met up later at a camp revival on Patterson Mountain and kept in touch til she married and settled in a place called Toccoa, Georgia. She had children but was soon a widow and we consoled each other. Then Sherman was so bad to drink, I was ashamed to death of what I might say and left off answering her letters altogether."

"But you're not ashamed now. I'm betting she's still in Toccoa. Maybe Abe could find her."

"Bless you, child."

Maude managed a tense smile and patted Lily's hand, and Lily looked on that smile as a precious gift, a healing of sorts, one family under God. She was so struck by their closeness that she forgot time and place and failed to show up at Bryce's Cove just before dark to meet Abe. She panicked at first but told herself there was a chance he wouldn't be there anyway, considering the new work hours. When she explained that she had felt needed like a nurse, he would surely understand and be grateful. After all, Maude *was* his mother, and he should be overjoyed that wife and mother were now such good friends.

But when Abe stormed inside less than an hour later, Lily took one look at his contorted face and ran to calm him at the door before he could upset the children. She put her arms on his shoulders and tried to give him a kiss. Maude rushed into the kitchen to warm his supper.

"Hon, your mother was telling me about her awful past and crying her heart out. She was so upset, well, considering how down she's been, I thought you'd want me to stay and look after her."

Abe coughed. "You two've got all day long to do nothin' but chitchat. Why now?"

"I know, but the opportunity came all of a sudden, and I thought this might be a chance to bring us together as a family. You know how important family is to me. I thought you'd be pleased."

"Maybe you and your husband had some mendin' of their own to do. You ever stopped to think he may have feelin's too?"

In spite of the tension, she felt flattered that he had missed her to the point of being angry.

"I'm so sorry, hon. You know I live for those times when we can be together. I was careless. I promise it won't happen again."

"Forget it." He pushed the pads of his fingers against his forehead, leveled his eyes on Lily, and lowered his voice. "And you say the ole gal unloaded everything?"

"She did, yes."

"Did she by any chance mention another man, maybe somebody before Daddy?"

"Just her own daddy and brother."

"Right," he said, and hesitated before moving toward the kitchen.

"Wait, Abe. Why would she? Who do you have in mind?"

"Nobody. Just askin'."

The next morning Maude stayed in her room, giving Lily a chance to cook Abe's breakfast, the usual eggs but with ham and red-eye gravy to make him feel special. Before sending him off to work, she made him promise to meet her that evening at Bryce's Cove, where the sweet air whispered the cries of nature and hidden lovers.

At the back door she undid the sashes of her housecoat, exposing, slightly strutting, her sheer gown and sensuous body. Her eyes sparkled, and her face held the Pond's cold-cream shine that made her look younger.

"You're teasin' me," he said as he explored her with a shiny-eyed grin and big roving hands.

"Do we have time?" she teased back, and pointed toward the curtained pantry.

"Waitin' makes it better." He placed his muscled arm around her shoulder, bringing her close for a real goodbye kiss, and left the house smiling.

Between chores, Lily washed her hair and dried it in sunlight. She bathed with Ivory soap and avoided other scents that affected his allergies. Then she dressed in her Sunday clothes and applied herself to working on her hair and makeup in order to get the worked-on effect out of it.

She arrived at Bryce's Cove, a ten-minute walk, as the sun set, and found Abe waiting. Hopping into the Plymouth, she gave him a quick kiss on the lips and placed a hand on his knee. He pulled into a thicket of mountain laurels and turned off the engine, and she nestled her head on his shoulder. The canyons looked pink from a distance, and even the bluffs had dabs of lime and red color.

"It's perfect," she said. "Like nature decorated for our party."

"Spoke like a true woman." He had turned to kiss her when she suddenly pulled back.

"Hon, forgive me, but first I have to know if you've had a chance to call Dr. Humfleet."

He lifted his head and straightened his shoulders.

"I did."

She sat up, her face bright with joy.

"And this time you talked to him personally?"

"I insisted on it. I wouldn't take no for a answer."

"Oh, Abe, I could just burst I'm so happy!" She picked up his hand and kissed the palm.

"Thank you, thank you, thank you!"

"But don't get too excited."

"I can't help it. Tell me quick, when's he coming?"

"He ain't."

She looked up at him as if begging.

"Not coming?"

"Negative."

"Oh, but Abe, he has to, and soon. Tell me word for word what he said."

"He said he's off the case. Recommended some doctor in Jellico. A fellow by the name of Hawkins. "

"But I don't understand. *Off the case?* What's that supposed to mean?"

"Beats me."

"Did you ask him why?"

Abe threw up his hands. His face crinkled with irritation.

"Hey. I'm just the messenger boy here, remember?"

"I'm sorry, hon. But Dr. Humfleet is among the nicest men I've ever known. He's one of mine and Pa's very best friends. What you're saying just doesn't add up."

He lit a cigarette and said with a shrug, "What *does?*"

"But are you sure you remembered to say *Lily Eakins* like I told you?"

"I said General Sherman Siler at Mud Creek had a real sore throat and needed to be looked after, pronto."

"You mean you didn't think to mention my name? Don't you remember me asking you to be sure and say it was Lily Eakins asking?"

"Maybe I did. I don't remember." His breathing picked up. "What is this? The third degree? I handled it, didn't I? I got the answer you needed, didn't I? The doc said to find somebody else so do it. He ain't the only fish in the sea, I guarandamntee it!" He threw open the car door as if to storm off. "And if you don't like the way I do things, then you're by-godly welcome to do them yourself!"

Her voice turned into a slow whisper.

"It's just that I feel Dr. Humfleet would've come if he'd known it was me asking."

"Do you now?" He pitched out the cigarette and turned the ignition. "Then you should've called him yourself. Go ahead. It ain't too late. Do it. Show me who's the new boss of this family."

"I'm sorry, hon." She reached for his arm, and he pulled it away.

"Hell, ain't the first time you've gone and took over. It was you urged us here, knowin'..."

"Knowing what?" she interrupted, panic stricken. Was it possible he'd known all along she had chosen to persuade him here, knowing he was turning down the chance to be foreman and not bothering to consider his loss? "Knowing what?" she repeated.

"Hey, if the shoe fits..."

"But I thought we planned the move together."

"Like I say, if the shoe fits, wear it."

Out of desperation, Lily turned to her pa. On a fair Wednesday afternoon, she and he walked along Buck Creek, over velvet trails of moss and near cattails scattering fuzz. A waterfall babbled in the distance. Crows cawed as they circled low, beheading the sweet corn, in spite of Joe Pat Riley, a rifle-armed scarecrow.

"Honestly, Pa, Abe's changed. He's not the same man I married," she said.

Wade Eakins put forth a well thought-out smile.

"They never are," he answered. "We're actors, Lily, all of us men. Women marry us for our actions, and then they're forced to live with our reactions. The unpredictability has got to be maddening."

"I just don't know how to handle him anymore. His moods are getting worse by the day."

"Start by making him go see a doctor. When he feels better, he needs to find a job to his liking."

"I've tried and he won't see a doctor. And he already has a job working for June."

"I mean a job he can be proud of. Not a favor but something he can enjoy and learn from. June says he's not cut out to build houses. Got no experience."

"But it's just until we get on our feet."

"Then what?"

"Then we'll grow tobacco."

"What if he's not cut out for farming either? What if the sun blinds his eyes?"

"Abe's smart. He can do anything he sets his mind to."

"Not if his heart's not in it, he can't."

"But, Pa, we don't have a choice."

"We always have a choice. That's what we were born for, Lily. To make choices and take chances."

"Speaking of taking chances, I have a favor to ask of you, Pa." Feeling overwhelmed, Lily paused to work up her courage. "Maude wants to hire somebody to finish the barn, and she's asked me to ask you for the name of a good and affordable builder."

With his scythe, Wade Eakins whacked an oak sucker. He took down a spider web crossing their path.

"Take my advice and let Maude handle the matter."

"Oh, she is. She says she'll be glad to take everything on herself—blame, cost, and all. She plans to go ahead with it, Pa, with or without me. All she needs from you is the name of a reliable builder. Nothing else."

"Nothing else?"

"I promise."

"A name, huh?" He removed his felt hat and picked off some beggar's lice.

"Of somebody she can trust. Our family needs a home of our own, Pa. Abe and I have been married over twenty years, and there's never once been a place we could call ours. That Plymouth Roadking is the closest he's ever come to owning anything he can be proud of, and it's ready to break down."

Wade frowned. He put on his hat and pulled the brim over his eyes.

"You know this won't be to his liking."

"It's like Maude says. His having roots is all that will stop him from going back to the mines. You've heard him cough. That coal dust is killing him, Pa!"

"He wants to go back to mining, does he?"

"You know Abe. He never tells anyone his business til after it's done. But I've got a feeling he's making plans to go as we speak. Last week he went to Frankfort and tested for his foreman's papers. I didn't agree to help Maude with the barn til after the letter came saying he'd passed."

"I don't know, Lily. The man's got a right to be part of the decision."

"I know he does. But, Pa, Abe's stubborn. Sometimes he can't see the forest for the trees."

"That's true of us all. Talk to him."

"I've tried. He won't listen."

"Then make him talk and you listen."

"We're beyond that, Pa. Even when we try to be close, it winds up a fight. Now we're next to strangers. It's like there's suddenly a stone wall between us."

"It's not stone, Lily. It's human. Communication between a man and a woman isn't easy. For some it's darn near impossible. But human beings, thank God, are not Humpty Dumpty. They can fall and put themselves back together. Keep trying to reason with him. Don't give up yet."

"What concerns me now is the children. I promised them a home, and Pa, I aim to see they get one. So help me, I will not break that promise!"

The preacher glanced over his head as if seeking out God. He blinked and wrinkled his forehead.

"Tell you what. Talk to the Lord. Talk to Abe if you can. I'll come by on Wednesday and see how you feel then."

"And if she still insists on hiring somebody?"

"Then I'll have you your man."

CHAPTER FOURTEEN

Lily chose her usual Thursday shopping trip with Vi to inform Maude of her pa's offer to help. From the back seat of Vi's Ford convertible, she leaned forward to say his choice was Silas Holmes, a 36-year-old forest ranger at Cumberland Falls State Park. She explained that Silas was a new but close friend of her parents, a widower, and Chairman of Little Wolf Creek's building committee. He had spent many an hour at their supper table and pot-bellied coal stove, reading the Bible, praying, and grieving over Rebecca, his deceased wife. Before Rebecca died, the two had built a log cabin in a niche of Vanderpool Mountain, raised goats, and operated a Christmas-tree farm that employed children from a nearby orphanage.

"He's coming tomorrow at lunchtime to discuss details, and that's it," she said as Vi swung into the parking lot of Wilders' Hardware, cut the engine, and accidentally hopped into an iridescent film of spilled oil.

"You make this Silas Holmes sound so good, maybe I should come check him out," Vi said. "Only I ain't interested in no mealy-mouthed churchgoer with his head stuck in a Bible. I had my fill of them growing up."

"You could do worse," Lily said. Letting Vi in on the Silas Holmes secret made her uncomfortable, but since she didn't drive, a shopping trip seemed to be her best chance for convenience and efficiency. And besides, she felt a girls' outing would do Maude good.

"The man is being paid to work," Maude said. "He'll have to court on his own time."

Lily smiled, knowing Maude would've stayed home had she known Vi would come dressed like a carnival doll on the rearview mirror of some coal miner's pickup. They went inside a spacious room that sold not only hardware but also home-decorations, outdoor furniture, and a limited supply of work clothes. Lily and Maude picked out hammers, tape measures, and work aprons. Lily also bought a mouse trap and fly swatter. Vi chose a pair of blue overalls, a "Lover Girl" cap, red with white letters, and a red bandana scarf.

"Imagine them with my red and white polka-dot blouse and red high-heel shoes," she blurted out. "Would that draw Abe's attention, or what?"

Lily let the moment pass, but Maude squinched her eyes as if to say if looks could kill, Vi had just taken her last breath.

"Not if he don't bother to look, it won't," Maude said.

"Men and bulls are naturally drawn to red is all I meant. Lily here knows I'm pulling her leg, don't you, Lily? Abe's a sweetie pie all right, but me, I got my own man, Clyde."

"Clyde? Does he by any chance rob banks?" Maude asked with high eyebrows and a wiry smile.

"He's a wrestler."

"Cattle?"

"You're thinking of *rustler*. And no, he's no rustler. No kidding. Clyde's been on TV."

Lily decided it was time to step in.

"To answer your question, Vi, I'm hoping Abe won't be anywhere near the barn. I mean, if Silas Holmes works out, we'll tell him, of course, but not until we have reason to. So I'm trusting you to keep all this to yourself, hear? Not that it's a secret or anything." Lily felt a guilty gnawing in her stomach, the same feeling she'd had when explaining the situation to her children.

"Like I said, I was just teasing. But truth be told, the forest ranger sounds kinda sexy. Me, I'm a sucker for a man in a uniform. I don't care if he's a bus driver or a mailman, although a soldier I'd prefer. Silly ain't it?" She leaned back in the seat, took out a nail file, and made long, grating strokes. "Tell me, what does Silas Holmes look like?"

"Like a parrot," Maude, who had never laid eyes on him, commented.

"I only met him briefly at church," Lily said and thought of Silas' thick blond hair and golden skin. She recalled his blue eyes and lemon-lime scent. "He looked nice," she said.

"Nice? What does *nice* mean? That he's got good manners and false teeth? Expensive clothes and a bald head?"

"He's handsome enough," Lily answered. "But didn't you just say you're with Clyde?"

"It's a woman's prerogative to change her mind, now ain't it?"

"I can see off the bat you and him would be unequally yoked," Maude said. "The man's a Christian. According to the Bible, a Christian is to stick with his kind."

"Shoot! It's never too late to change," Vi said.

Maude clicked her tongue and waved a finger.

"*Repent,* you mean!"

"No, I mean *change.* Ain't you ever heard of teaching a old dog new tricks?"

They paid for their goods and continued their conversation in the car. Lily sometimes leaned toward the front seat and forced out an occasional hum to suggest she was following Vi and Maude's new conversation on women's fashions when, in fact, she was thinking about Abe and Bryce's Cove, and how quickly their talk had spun into a quarrel. Just one more injury to the heart she would have to find a way to hide until it healed.

Vi talked about the ridiculousness of wearing a dress when working in construction, and she tried to convince Maude to buy a pair of ladies' jeans or slacks. Maude was set against women wearing men's clothing, but she finally agreed to accompany Vi to Woolworth's to look for some culottes.

They took their time, and she and Maude finally purchased two pairs at Woolworth's without taking the time to try them on. By then it was after three, and Maude was supposed to meet Silas Holmes at 4:30. After an A&P stop for the usual staples, the three headed home.

The subject of food—cornbread, for example—came up, and Maude and Vi disagreed as to which kind—with or without sugar—was better. "Sugar is for cakes, and salt is for cornbread," Lily said when called on, and she sank down in her seat to avoid further questions. Rude perhaps, but she could not shake off the Abe quandary. She considered asking Vi to stop at a phone booth so she could use this opportunity to call Dr. Humfleet. Then she changed her mind and decided to wait until after she and Abe had a proper chance to talk. Her overriding concern was that Sherman, in spite of her care, was not getting better.

"Abe's back in Mud Creek where he belongs and it's all due to Lily! That sister of yourn is a angel if ever there was one," Maude was saying when Lily next lifted her head.

"I've heard that all my life," Vi said, her lips pressing inward. "In Pa's eyes, his precious Lily couldn't do nothing wrong." She laughed, the too loud kind. "Little did he know!"

"Now you know that's not true, Vi," Lily said. "Pa loved all us kids the same. He just had different ways of showing it is all."

"Like hell—heck—he did!" Vi chomped down on her usual wad of Spearmint. She sloshed it in spit and cracked little bubbles.

"If you're free, Vi, why not stay for supper?" Lily asked as a kind of reparation for past injuries, and for the hidden delight she had taken in knowing she, and not Vi or Peony, was her pa's favorite daughter. For Maude's sake, she avoided mentioning her intention to play matchmaker between Vi and Silas. "I'm sure Maude won't mind."

"No, thanks. Tonight I'm cooking supper for Buddy. I'll just stay long enough to catch a glimpse of your man, Silas, and go."

"He's not my man," Lily said with an air of resistance.

Maude took off her plastic wind scarf and folded the pleats.

"Now, Lily, when he comes, you're to do the talking, hear?"

"Oh, no." Lily thought first of her shyness, and then of Abe's disapproval. "Bring Sherman along and the decision will be entirely up to you and him. And I assure you, Pa won't be the least bit offended if you choose to use somebody else."

"I'm sure your pa and brothers have give you some idea as to what's a fair wage. Me, I got no notion."

"I'm sorry," Lily said. "If you're sure this is what you want, the children and I will be glad to help with the work, but you and Pop must be the ones to make all the decisions."

"But surely you'll be there for support."

Maude's suggestion that she go behind Abe's back returned Lily to her more pressing dilemma. The three were nearing home, and her chance to call Dr. Humfleet for Sherman's sake was running out.

She uttered a quick prayer for Abe's sake.

"Vi, stop at the Quickie Market if you don't mind. I need to make a phone call that won't take but a jiffy," she said.

Vi parked and Lily got out with some coins and a small wad of paper. She dialed the number, and the receptionist promptly answered and said the doctor was with a patient. Determined, she identified herself and said the call was urgent. When the doctor came to the phone, he remembered his former student with great pleasure. But as for agreeing to see Sherman, he continued to insist that he'd been dismissed from the case; that he had sent Sherman's test results when received to a Dr. Hawkins, a trusted colleague at nearby Middlesboro Hospital; and that as a personal favor the doctor had contacted the family, but also with no success.

"Do you mind telling me who dismissed you?" she asked.

The doctor hesitated as if considering his professional ethics, and Lily stepped up her plea.

"Because his wife, my mother-in-law, will be at prayer meeting this Wednesday evening, and he's too sick to go. If you could by any chance come see him then, I give you my word you two could be alone." She sighed into the phone so he could hear her. "Please, Dr. Humfleet, he's like a real daddy to me. He needs help now, and we've waited this long—

way too long—because I just couldn't let him be seen by anybody but you."

"Wednesday at seven then," Dr. Humfleet said, "since it's you."

"Thank you. Thank you a million times over!"

"No thanks necessary. Just know I'm presently out of a nurse and might try to recruit you."

Lily laughed to avoid declining, hurried a goodbye, and sprinted back to the car in a mood of elation mixed with sorrow.

"You didn't answer my question," Maude said before she was seated.

"Your question?"

"Will you at least come meet Silas Holmes?"

"Okay...sure," Lily sputtered, mind focused elsewhere, not having the slightest idea of what she had agreed to.

Dr. Humfleet showed up to see Sherman as promised. Lily met him on the front porch, and they hugged like old friends.

"Little Lily Eakins, still pretty as a picture," he said with his old flair for charm.

She noticed how gracefully the doctor, reaching seventy, had aged, in spite of a latticework of wrinkles under his handsome tan. She admired his kind and gentle demeanor and remembered he had always smiled when he taught, even when explaining sex and reproduction before gigglers like her friend, Bunny.

"You're so generous to come at this late hour." She glanced at her watch—two minutes past seven. She had told Abe the doctor would be coming at seven. He had agreed to try his best to be home, and she had prayed he would show up.

"It wasn't generosity on my part," the doctor said. "I've never had a more impressive student. As I said on the telephone, I'd love to recruit you."

Smiling, Lily led the doctor inside. From his recliner, Sherman peered at them with a look of surprise mixed with scorn. Lily cringed, feeling that she had betrayed him, that she should at the very least have shown the consideration of asking for his permission. But at the time she had felt she couldn't take the chance of him refusing to be examined. Even the born-again Sherman could be mule-headed.

"Pop, Abe and I love you too much to watch you lie here and suffer," she said while taking his hands. "Please, will you forgive me and let the doctor check you out?"

Sherman's tension eased, and he reluctantly nodded.

"This won't take long," the doctor said, and clicked his bag open.

Lily placed a gooseneck lamp behind the recliner and called Sweet William to bring in a slat chair. She had meant to set the stage earlier, but had spent the time coaxing the girls off to church with June and Eula. "Feel free to tarry," she had told them, and they had grinned with the compliance of people with secrets.

Sweet William approached with the chair, and Sherman tapped his arm.

"My grandson to be a doctor. Fine boy, he is," he whispered.

Dr. Humfleet shook hands and questioned the lad, who, he said, bore a striking resemblance to Wade Eakins. With Sherman's consent he invited Will to stay and observe while he checked the vital signs. Then he looked inside Sherman's throat with a tiny light at the end of what looked like an ink pen. Both agreed the larynx was red and bumpy, clearly angry.

"Mined coal a long time, did you?" the doctor asked.

"A long time, yes."

He pressure tested Sherman for pain and narrowed his eyes as if to say he'd found it.

"I recently read an article on the hazards of strip mining. It grieves me to think they'll butcher our mountain tops and dump the waste into nearby valleys. The health consequences will be tragic."

Sherman balled his little fist.

"There oughta be laws."

"You're exactly right." The doctor pushed his glasses high on his nose and cleared his throat. "Mr. Siler, I believe the cancer has spread since I last saw you."

Lily's hands flew to her mouth.

"Cancer? What cancer? Pop, what's he talking about?" From behind, Sweet William touched her shoulders.

"I'm sorry, Lily." Tears washed down Sherman's face and onto his pillow.

"Cancer of the larynx," Dr. Humfleet said. "Mr. Siler and the missus came to see me some time ago, him complaining of a sore throat. I spotted some lesions on his vocal cords. Considering the signs and his history of alcohol, tobacco, and coal dust, I recommended radiation."

"How soon can it be arranged?" Lily asked breathlessly. "The radiation?"

Sherman reared up and took a quick sip of water.

"First I'll need eight months to help with the tobacco," he said, and flinched from the pain.

"I'm leaving you a little something for pain," Dr. Humfleet said. "Lily will call when you need more. Feel free to ask."

"Just eight months. Then I'll be ready."

The doctor shook his head and snapped his bag closed.

"Bad thing it is, that strip mining."

That night Lily sat alone on the porch swing, a white knit shawl over her shoulders and a chill over her soul. She was not waiting for Abe as much as escaping from Maude and the heartbreaking possibility that she had lured Abe and her here to learn the process of growing tobacco while knowing Sherman was too sick to help.

Abe showed up shortly after nine, a smoking muffler announcing his arrival.

"The doctor?" he called from the Plymouth.

"Gone."

"I'm sorry, Lily. I really am. I tried my damnedest to get home. But June was short on help and behind on a deadline."

Lily nodded. Even if she'd had the will to argue, her energy for it was spent.

"Daddy?" Abe asked at the steps. "What did the doc say?"

"We'll talk after you have your supper."

"To hell with supper. Is he up to the tobacco or ain't he?"

She motioned for him to sit beside her on the swing. He dropped down on the porch and crossed his legs the length of the steps.

"Abe, Pop has throat cancer. He and Maude went to see Dr. Humfleet in March, and he recommended radiation treatments, which they ignored. Now the cancer seems to have spread."

"Cancer! How bad?"

"Bad."

Abe got up in a spin, his hands whacking the air like paddles through water.

"That means the ole rascal let us move here for nothin'!"

"I'm not sure your daddy understood. I know for a fact he thought he had more time. We should have guessed something was wrong when he didn't plant this year's crop."

"Oh, he knew, all right!"

Lily studied him. What in his past had hardened Abe to this point of hatred? she wondered. And why was he so quick to condemn Sherman while turning a blind eye on his mother?

"Abe, I don't understand why you can't ever give him the benefit of a doubt. He's a good man now, trying to stay alive just so he can help us. Tell me, what could he have done so bad in the past that you can't forgive?"

"He's a loser."

"*Was* a loser, yes, but now he's saved." She paused to work up some courage. "Your mother also knew about the cancer. Why don't you blame her?"

Abe frowned and looked away. A black moth peeled from the night and onto the porch, and he watched it venture too close to the porch light, scorch, and fall on its back. It was such a frail little creature to put out such a stink, he thought, and he pondered it as he had the fly.

"He's a long way from home," he said.

"Who?" Halfway expecting to see a visitor, Lily glanced toward the road.

"That black moth. He drifted here from some mining camp. Over years they changed colors to blend in and be safe. Here he's a goner."

"Abe, where there's a will, there's a way. The good Lord willing, we can still raise the tobacco."

Abe rubbed his eyes. He sat down beside her and placed his arm around her shoulders.

"Now listen here, Lily. This here's the deal. We done it all wrong, see? Me, I won't cut out to build houses and I ain't no farmer. I left the coal mine in too big a hurry, see? Iris' asthma is better now, and you said yourself she might outgrow it. Let's go back to Cordel-Lewis and take Mother and Daddy with us. We'll get him a good doctor in Harlan and fight this thing together."

Lily pulled away and drew in her arms.

"You gave me your word, Abe. You promised there would be no more mining camps. I believed you and promised the children."

"But I don't know the first thing about growin' tobacco. There's no way in hell I can do it without him."

"You've got a book. We can learn. Peony's boys have grown up in tobacco, and so has Buddy. Sweet William…Will…is learning. Pop will be there if we need advice."

"Lily, it's too risky. A man has got to know he can put food on the table."

"I can help. Rosy will be back in school soon and I'll have more time."

He stared down at the spinning black moth and blew out a breath. The moth flicked its charred wings, twisted onto its stomach, and flew an inch or so before falling back down.

"The poor idiot should've stayed where he belonged," he said.

"What? she asked. "What idiot?"

"That black moth. He should've stayed with the coal."

CHAPTER FIFTEEN

Lily still couldn't bring herself to out-and-out hate Maude. She was family, her children's grandmother. Not believing in her would mean the end of everything she and her children had dreamed of. It would question God's seek-and-find promise and suggest that chance, and not faith, rules the world.

She's a strange and zealous old woman, she told herself as she contemplated their second meeting with Silas Holmes. Trusting God and not medicine to heal Sherman would be completely consistent with her Pentecostal faith. And what loving mother wouldn't do everything within her power to keep her son safe? Would she, Lily, not do the very same if it were Sweet William?

And yet Lily knew with the certainty of daylight and dark, sunrise and sunset, that Dr. Humfleet was a man to be trusted; that her relationship with Abe was now tenuous at best; and that now, with Pop so sick, was no time to bring on new problems. She felt tormented, pushed and pulled at the same time, like an open book coming apart at the center. Still, she and Maude had spent a good part of their weekend cleaning out the barn—sweeping, taking down greasy shelves and tool racks, and throwing away more than they kept. Regardless, she'd thought, the job needed doing.

On Monday, Abe left home at seven, and Silas showed up at eight, just as the women were setting out for the barn. Maude was in a good mood, and Lily was glad. The two chatted about family as they passed the hen house and toilet, and she noticed the pink Joe Pye weeds in full bloom. She'd always thought it odd that they, like cosmos, were a summer pink but bloomed in the fall. Nothing made sense to her on this day.

The two were within a few yards of Silas when Lily mustered up the courage to speak frankly.

"Maude, I've been having second thoughts about the barn renovation," she said. "Abe's not himself right now and, well, to be honest, we've not been getting along. I did a lot of thinking and praying last night, and I'm convinced now that hiring Silas Holmes was a big mistake that'll send Abe to the mines for good if he finds out. Please, for all our sakes, I beg you to tell him his service is no longer needed and pay him his due before it's too late."

Maude knit her brow.

"Girl, have you lost your mind?"

"There's also Sherman's health to think about. His throat's not healing as it should, and we can't rule out the possibility of cancer."

"Cancer? The man's got hay fever."

Lily felt a wretched taste in her mouth. She desperately craved the freedom to wallop Maude with the details of Dr. Humfleet's visit.

"Abe and I can't grow the tobacco without Sherman," she said.

"Now you listen here. Losing your gumption is one thing, but blaming it on Sherman is another. It's too late to turn back now and we both of us know it. Why in two, three weeks, the thing will be done."

"But three weeks is a long time, and a lot has happened since we made plans. I didn't want to worry you with it, but

Abe went to Frankfort to test for his mine foreman's paper and passed. You know what that could mean?"

Maude groaned from the back of her throat.

"What we have to do then is talk to Silas and see if he can work faster, say take a week."

"A week? That's impossible!"

"The Lord, I tell you, can work miracles. Maybe Silas has a vacation coming up or a friend what can help. The place is small and Sherman and me don't need much. Silas can just do enough for us to get by and finish once Abe comes to his senses."

"But what good is a house if it breaks up a home?"

"Think, Lily. Think how the girls need a place of their own. They would have beds and be fresh for school. They would have a quiet place to study and space enough for friends." Maude dabbed her eyes. Her voice fell to a whine. "Unless you weren't serious when you made them that promise."

Lily flinched. "They told you?"

"Yes, indeed. So let's be done with this nonsense and go help Silas. Trust me. It's a decision you and your girls won't regret."

"But I haven't made a decision," Lily said as Maude stalked ahead, leaving her to follow.

At the barn, Maude delivered her proposition to Silas, and he agreed to do his best, short of a promise, to meet the rushed deadline. He took measurements that day in both house and barn, made drawings from the women's ideas, and went to buy supplies. Then he built the kitchen cabinets at home in his basement.

On Tuesday morning Lily heard the pound of his hammer. Only minutes before Maude had lost her glasses, and Lily and Rosy had taken up the search. Lily found it most strange that Maude appeared to be dawdling when time was so urgent.

"Maude, Silas is here," she said.

"You go on and see he don't lollygag. I'll be along directly."

"He can wait." Lily felt modesty did not permit her to be alone with a man she didn't really know, even her pa's friend, and she was surprised that Maude, of all people, had suggested it. Sherman had dozed off in his rocker, and Verni and Iris had gone to pick berries. Time and money were slipping away, and Maude was not hurrying.

"I reckon I'd lose my head if it wadn't attached," Maude said, and Lily recalled that she had recently looked for the salt and pepper shakers and found them in the refrigerator, where Maude had to have put them. Common incidents like toast burning, a pot boiling over, one ridiculous question after another, or repeats reminded her that Maude, though not yet sixty, was showing signs of early aging.

"I'll stay and help her, Mama," Rosy volunteered. "You go on."

"All right, I'll go but don't take too long," she finally agreed. "Daisy, you and Tansy come sweep up the attic."

Lily and the girls hurried to the barn while taking in the changing season. A slight breeze swayed the leaves, and the excited girls chased them as though they were coins or candies.

Silas greeted Daisy and Tansy with compliments and questions that made them giggle and blush, but before Lily he seemed reserved, attractively shy.

"Go on now," Lily said while handing each girl a broom, a stack of newspapers, and some paper bags. "There are squirrel and rat droppings up there. Remember to go wash your hands the minute you're finished."

"Well?" Lily asked when the girls disappeared, and she and Silas were almost alone.

"Well...what's your ideas?" he asked, and she liked the fact that he had deferred to her judgment. "Your pa says he taught all his children to build houses."

"That he did. Put hammers and saws in our Christmas stockings." She made a coy smile, and he laughed. "I saw boards in your truck so I imagine we'll start with the perimeter," she continued.

"Great idea! And the boards just happen to be 2 x 12s."

"Just happen?"

"Okay, I made the call, but you can decide what role you want to play. I bought two of every tool just in case."

"Perfect. I want one of each." He left to go carry in the supplies, and she followed to take her part of the load. He observed her at first with a smile and a sense of disbelief. Then each measured, cut, and nailed horizontal boards against the inside walls to make a base for the floor joists and then plywood. They worked fast, stopping only to stretch the cramps from their backs and debate the issue of whether or not they needed to add concrete blocks to reinforce the rock foundation.

Lily couldn't believe how comfortable she felt with this new man, even proud and happy. But still she thought of Maude, and wished she would hurry.

"Grandmother! Grandmother! I found your glasses!" Rosy squealed, and she hopped around with excitement.

"Quick, child. Where are they?"

"They're on your head, see? You must've pushed them back when you were washing your face."

"Well, I swan. If they'd been a snake they'd of bit me!" Maude dropped into her quilting chair and held out her arms. "You sweet thing you, come here and give your grandmother some sugar."

"Can we go now? I want to help Mama."

"I'll need a minute to catch my breath," Maude said and gestured the child closer.

Rosy stooped to give *sugar,* and Maude scooped her onto her lap. She pressed her against her heart and held her down with her arms.

"We'll rest a spell. And then we'll go," she said.

Rosy tried to turn away from the smell of Bruton's snuff and rose camphor.

"Silas and Mama will be worried. Did you forget she's waiting?"

"As a girl, I wanted a houseful of pretty daughters like you," Maude said. "I dreamed of sewing them ruffled pinafores and braiding ribbons through their hair like Mama done mine and Blessie's. But the Lord, he saw fit to give me a son."

"Daddy, you mean?"

"I was only fifteen, you see, and looking to have a home and family. Well, anyway, the baby, your daddy, was born early with bad lungs. Then the little feller got the fever when he was two. Tried his best to choke to death on me just like my mama did with tuberculosis. Sherman had worked hisself tired and said to let the baby cry."

THE TIME TO RUN · 185

"Not if he was sick he shouldn't of."

"I told your daddy, Son Boy, you're all I got and you ain't leaving me, hear? I jammed a spoon down his throat and gagged him til he vomited up the white stuff he was choking on. What he didn't vomit up, I pulled out with a finger."

"Did the doctor give him a shot?"

"Doctor! It was me saved his life. That poor darling, he couldn't get air without me beating it into him. Then he'd squall and go to coughing and whooping that pitiful gasping sound like my mama til he turned blue in the face and soppy wet with fever. It went on like that for weeks, my nerves worn plumb threadbare with little or no sleep atall til he snapped out of it."

"Did Daddy have the measles?"

"No."

"Mumps?"

"It was the coughing disease."

"Miners' asthma?"

"They called it whooping cough. Which ain't no different from miners' asthma except that one is a fast death, and the other ever so slow. The slowest death there ever was, I do believe." Maude wiped her eyes. "Sometimes I will lay awake at night and listen to your daddy gagging and whooping and it takes ever ounce of strength I can muster up not to go grab him up and beat air into him like I did then. But it's no longer my place, only Lily's."

"Don't worry. Mama will take good care of him. Mama's a nurse."

Maude sighed and stared into space.

"It's my lot to worry. Such is God's wrath."

Lily and Silas smiled at Daisy's and Tansy's happy sounds in the loft. Silas suddenly thought of Rosy, whom he'd met on the day of the business meeting.

"Where's your sidekick?" he asked in spite of the nails in his mouth.

"Maude? She lost her glasses." Lily glanced down at her watch. Over an hour had passed and no Maude.

Silas grinned. "No, I mean the little one."

"Rosy? Oh, she stayed to help Maude."

"Such a sweet little girl. Sarah and Wade said she has arthritis. How long has she been...crippled?"

She wiped the sweat from her face and brushed some hair from her eyes.

"Crippled? Why, law, we're so used to that limp, I plumb forgot she has it."

"It's not bad, really."

"Good."

"Arthritis is right painful, I hear."

"Yes, but she's good at coping."

"Definitely. Any chance she'll outgrow it?"

"We sure hope so." *Surely*, she told herself. No need for vernacular.

"Me, too."

Lily had tried to keep the conversation businesslike, in spite of Silas' warm personality and good teeth. She had expected anything private or probing to quiver from her lips like crumbs off a warm biscuit. Instead, she drew a quick breath and rushed ahead.

"I take it you like children?"

"Me? Oh, yes, I love children. Thought we'd have a half dozen, but the wife and I got started late, and, well, she passed young."

"Pa told me about her. I'm so sorry." She felt led to put down her tools and stop to listen.

"She fell off her horse and died of a blood clot. Tough time. I don't know how I'd have made it if it hadn't been for your folks. They're really fine people."

"Oh, the best!" She thought about Abe and how he totally misjudged her pa's good intentions. How he could be so impatient with the children.

"I understand you're a registered nurse. My wife was a nurse."

"And a good one, I hear."

"She was. She really was. Had a passion for it." He smiled. "Wade says he did everything within his power to turn you into a teacher."

She fumbled for a measuring tape but didn't open it.

"And I suppose he also said he paddled me when he found out I'd quit teaching to become a nurse."

"Oh, yes. He's even told that story from the pulpit. Puts all the blame on himself though."

"From the pulpit? You're kidding!"

Silas raised his right hand.

"Scout's honor and I was a troop leader."

"Oh my gosh! I'm so embarrassed."

"Why? Everybody admires a woman with spunk."

"Funny, that's what my father-in-law used to say. Back when nursing as a profession for women was considered an abomination." She felt a tug at her heart and smiled at the memory.

"They do indeed," Silas said. "Wouldn't your husband agree?"

"My husband?" she said weakly, as if she weren't sure.

Lily heard the sound of leaves crunching underfoot and ran to the door, hoping to see Maude.

"How's everybody doing?" Vi prissed inside, sporting her new red and blue outfit and looking like the Fourth of July. She unwrapped a piece of gum, and Lily remembered June saying: "Even if Vi don't make it to heaven, her chewing gum will b'cause she chomps the living hell out of it!"

"Put me to work," Vi said. "That's what I've come for."

Her eyes took in the room, and Lily remembered her real reason for coming. She motioned for her to spit out the gum and raised her voice above the blows of Silas' hammer.

"Vi, thanks for coming! Maude should've been here by now, and I need to go see what's keeping her. Take my place, will you?" They moved toward Silas' work space. When Lily saw she had his attention, she said, "You two haven't met. Violet Horton, my sister, this is Silas Holmes, a friend of the folks." She felt proud of herself for remembering not to say *baby sister*, a tag Vi detested, as did Rosy.

Silas stared as if shocked to see that Sarah and Wade had such a colorful daughter. He laid aside his hammer, and the two shook hands.

"Glad to meet you," he said, his fine teeth gleaming.

"Likewise, I'm sure." Vi removed her "Lover Girl" cap and shook out her pretty curls. "I think I may of seen you from a distance, only up close you're a lot more handsome."

"Why, thank you, ma'am."

The introductions done, Lily turned to Silas.

"Vi's taking my place while I go check on Maude. Trust me, she's a far better carpenter."

"That's hard to imagine," Silas said. "If you don't mind, check on Sherman while you're at it. Tell him with all these women around, I might need backup."

"I won't get my clothes dirty, will I?" Vi asked.

"Use my work apron," Lily said, and Vi made a face that suggested "Yuk!" Before leaving, Lily mixed some mortar and told Tansy and Daisy to go chink logs. "Bye," she called, plain and simple.

Alone on the path, she felt shaky, and she willed strength to her legs. At the back porch, she stopped to deadhead the petunias and clean her face and hands in the washpan. Her cheeks felt flushed, and her heart pounded to the rhythm of clashing impulses. For the life of her she could not have explained why at one minute she hoped Vi and Silas Holmes would fall madly in love, and at the next minute, she hoped they would not.

CHAPTER SIXTEEN

That night Lily tossed in her sleep, and the next morning she avoided the barn altogether. "An open book," Ceola sometimes called her, and she abhorred the possibility that Maude, let alone Silas Holmes, might read her sinful pages. She also hated the fact that she who had always considered herself stable and levelheaded was now feeling weak and uncertain. Like a schoolgirl with a crush.

The next day, Vi returned to the barn with a basket of hot dogs and a cooler of Pepsis. Missing Lily, she left the food with Silas and Maude and went to the house. Lily put aside her mending and followed Vi outside, where they could talk alone, and the two sat down on a rusting iron glider.

"I just came from the barn," Vi said with a child's excitement. "They were so busy there, no one would stop to talk." She placed a stick of gum in her mouth and chomped down. "I can't believe how the place will change. Silas says you plan to let some of the logs show on the inside and plaster over others and use beadboard in the kitchen. I gotta hand it to him, Lily. He sure seems to know what he's doing. Maude and Sherman are gonna love the place, I just know it. And by the way, Maude said to remind you there's a deadline." She tapped Lily's elbow. "Shirking your duties, are you?"

Lily blushed. "What brings you here, Vi? I thought you'd be at work."

"Ruby took over for me. I was aiming to bring you workers a snack. You weren't there so I left everything at the barnhouse and came here."

"They'll love that. Thank you."

"The last time we talked, you said you were about to tell Abe about Silas so I thought I'd come see how it went. I see Silas is still around so I gather Abe was okay with it."

"I tried to tell him but just couldn't. Maude talked to Silas, and he agreed to take a leave from his job and finish the place in close to a week, maybe even get extra help. I figured what difference could a few more days make." Lily's fingers moved from one dress button to another. "And speaking of Silas, how did you and he get along after I left? Any sparks?"

Vi had bunions on her feet. She took off her canvas work shoes and hiked up her legs. Instantly, the air smelled of mildew and sweat.

"Are you kidding? It was great. The man's a cutie pie if ever I saw one. Reminds me so much of Sweet William, I could just eat him up. They've both got those big elephant ears, you know. Pretty boys, they are. Blonde, blue-eyed, pretty boys, sexy as hell."

"Shame on you," Lily teased. "Don't you be calling my boy *sexy*. He's only a kid."

Vi hummed. "I'm not so sure. But anyway, I'm just plumb crazy about Silas. Believe it or not, the two of us have a whole lot in common. He's a widower you know, and I'm a widow, but that's just for starters."

"Don't tell me he likes wrestling and dancing?" Lily said. "Did you tell him you write poetry?" The greeting-card type, Lily might have said.

"No, but we both love to cook."

"I took him to be the type that grows a garden and camps out," Lily said self-consciously.

"Oh, yes, yes, he does! Oh, Lily, I nursed Brody for so long with the cancer, I keep thinking how wonderful it would be, having a strong man like Silas around to take care of me for a change. I have to confess, I just now looked at all he's done, and I imagined a place like that in the woods for him and me, in case we clicked. If I play my cards right, who knows? He might someday build me a little nook like that and then you and me'd both have a home."

"Yes, that would be great. God knows you deserve something better than a wrestler."

"And a cheating one at that!"

Lily winced. "Clyde has been unfaithful?"

"Yep. Louise, my girlfriend, she caught him in the act. And in the back row of the movie theater if you can believe it!" She ran a finger under an eye. "I tell you, I'm ready for a change."

"But what about Silas' religion? Surely you know he's a Christian."

"I forgive him. I might even pay Pa's church a visit."

"Oh, Vi, Ma and Pa have lived for that day!"

"Yeah, well, don't cross any bridges. Maybe he was friendly for Pa's sake. You know he thinks Pa hung the moon."

Lily crossed her knees, making a place for her hands. She twisted her wedding band, now loose on her finger.

"Well, let's pray he comes courting," she said.

"You pray, I'll hope."

"We'll both wish."

Vi sniffed and reached into her pocket for a Kleenex. Her eyes took on a far-away look.

"Speaking of wishing, Lily, do you remember when at night we used to sit outside on a glider like this one only nicer and wish on that star, Venus?"

"Do I? We hooked our little pinkies. You once asked for a gun to blow Pa's brains out."

"And you wished for a dictionary of all things!"

Lily laughed. "I got it, too. Remember? Remember how we looked up Ma's word *wetchy*, thinking we might actually find it."

Vi nodded.

"If Venus was out now I'd wish for Silas to love me," she said with a sigh.

"That's sweet."

"Did you happen to notice his lemon-lime smell?"

"Lemon-lime?"

"Enough about Silas," Vi said with a start. "I've done put you to sleep already."

"Not at all," Lily answered. "But if you're sure you want to move on, I confess I've been waiting for a chance to talk to you about Sweet William."

"What about him?" Vi looked down at her watch as if to say her visiting time had run out. She put on her shoes and tugged on the laces.

"Well, he's been going to Buck Creek of late." Lily paused, choosing her words. Vi could be so defensive where Buddy and Minnie Mo were concerned, especially after Buddy's recent arrest on a drunk-driving charge. "I was wondering if it's got anything to do with Buddy."

Vi smirked. "You think bad Buddy is leading him astray, do you?"

"Oh, no, no, nothing of the sort. But Sweet William's all packed to go off to college, Vi. He's worked hard for this opportunity, and it's an exciting time for us all. I'm determined to see that nothing don't get in his way." She tossed in the double negative for the sake of Vi's pride. It wasn't easy, speaking of her nearly perfect son without sounding uppity. "You know what a good son he is. I've never known him to lie, is all."

"So you think he's lying, do you?"

"I think he's hiding something, yes."

"Like what?"

"Like how he's spending his time when he's not here or working in tobacco."

"Have you asked him?"

"Not yet."

"Maybe you should."

"Maybe, but right now I'm asking you, and I've got a feeling you know something I don't."

"Oh, you do, do you?"

"Remember that time you swore you weren't smoking rabbit tobacco, and then I had to put out the fire? Come on, Vi. As Ma would say, Tell the truth and shame the devil."

"I gave Buddy my word, is all. I don't want him thinking I'm a snitch."

"I promise. Neither Buddy nor Sweet William will ever know we talked." Lily held up a hand. "Promise."

"But you'll tell Abe. You'll consider it your Christian duty and you'll go and blab."

"He's my husband. We don't keep secrets from one another.... Not many. Not unless we have to."

"Then he'll go nuts and beat Sweet William and I'll be to blame."

"Oh, no, he doesn't do that anymore. I'll make him promise."

"Phooey! The day that man listens to you will be the day hell freezes over."

Lily felt offended, but swallowed her pride and plunged on.

"Vi, I need you to tell me if Sweet William is in some kind of trouble so I can help him."

"Not til you promise me you won't tell Abe."

"I promise."

Vi shot her a skeptical look and chomped down on her gum.

"Uncross your legs and say it."

Lily obeyed, frowning at the silliness of it all.

"All right. I promise."

"You promise what?"

"I promise I won't tell Abe."

"Tell Abe what?"

"What you're about to tell me about Sweet William. What you've hinted at in the past."

"You do, and, so help me, Lily, I'll hire a hit man!"

"So help me, I'm losing my patience!"

"Okay then. But you won't like it."

"Just tell me!"

"Buddy says Sweet William's in love."

"In love? In love with who?"

"Fairy Enlow."

"Fairy Enlow from Shackville?"

"I said you wouldn't like it."

For the second Wednesday in a row, Dr. Humfleet traveled the winding dirt road to Mud Creek. The first time he'd come as a favor to Lily. This time he came for himself.

"Just a routine house call," he'd planned to tell Lily, check on Sherman, and leave something for pain. At the door he would draw her aside and tell her his real reason for coming.

The doctor pushed his glasses toward the furrows on his brow and wondered what profession, if he had it all to do over, he might have chosen in the place of medicine. He asked himself how a sheltered lad from Fox Hollow, Kentucky, could possibly have known when starting out that with most patients comes the challenge of reckoning with a family; that one cannot tend to a patient's body without also treating his soul; that human beings are as fragile as the intricate parts they're made of.

He'd put in a full day and was tired, and couldn't bear to think of Maude Siler leaving church early and arriving home to scold him again with her Dame Van Winkle tongue. Even more, he dreaded the pain he was about to inflict on poor Lily.

He turned onto Crab Orchard Lane and parked on the road. The place was as he remembered it, but alive now, with asters and chrysanthemums in plant beds and lights behind windows. He sniffed the smell of pine cones and wet earth.

Lily met him at the front steps, and they embraced like family. Under the porch light he studied her soft features. She was not only a favorite former student but also the spitting image of her mother, the striking midwife he had courted and lost to Wade Eakins.

"Dr. Humfleet, I've got to know," Lily charged. "If Abe and I had contacted you in June, when we first noticed Pop ailing, could we have…"

"No, Lily, no! As I said before, in March Mr. Siler and the missus came to my office. I checked his throat, spotted ulcers that looked malignant, and recommended radiation treatments at once. He seemed open to the idea but wanted time to consider. I cautioned them both on the danger of waiting, and when I didn't hear back, I came here and was blatantly told to leave."

"Most likely Pop was worried about the cost. Sherman can be awfully tight."

Dr. Humfleet reflected. He had traveled some twenty miles to deliver one message. Now that he was here, he was not about to lose courage.

"It was the missus."

Lily clenched her jaw.

"Maude."

"Maude, his wife, yes."

"Maude sent you away?"

"Three times I came. Three times she met me at the gate, saying he was away or asleep and not to be disturbed. I finally pressed her for a convenient time to return, and she said I was no longer needed."

"But are you sure she understood it was cancer?"

"I begged her to understand that without treatment, her husband could die. She said his life was in God's hands."

"Maybe she was simply following his orders. You said yourself you explained everything to him there in the office."

"I thought I had, yes. But now that I think back, he left planning to put in a crop of tobacco."

"Then he was too sick to do it."

"Quite so." Dr. Humfleet envisioned his late wife, Darla, weaving at her loom. Two years ago this November, she had passed from a stroke. "I've seen a lot of grief in my day, Lily, and I can say with some certainty that Maude Siler was not grieving."

"It's true there's no love between them," Lily said, "but to just stand by and let him die? No, no, she didn't. She couldn't. Why, the woman's a Christian."

"As was Judas."

CHAPTER SEVENTEEN

Ceola read such sorrow between the lines of Lily's letters that she decided to pay her a visit. She packed a picnic lunch and a six-pack, and she and Dog set out for Saxton following a Sunday sermon on patience, preached by the Company pastor with the intention of calming angry miners. It was a good day for travel, with sunshine and a blue sky, each so bright they looked glassy.

"Are you gonna tell Abe?" she asked as Dog unwrapped a plug of Red Man tobacco.

"Tell Abe what?"

"That the mine is still looking for a foreman?"

"Stay out of it, Ceola."

Not one to take in the scenery, Ceola thumbed through a magazine of award-winning hairdos. She used hair clips to mark the most impressive ones.

"Just say the foreman job's up for grabs. He can always say no."

"I reckon maybe I will if he asks."

"Dog, dammit. How can he ask if he don't know?"

"They're happy in the country, Ceola. They'll live longer there. I say leave well enough alone."

"And let that bastard Lance Porter take over? No way in hell!" She leaned into his ear, made half-deaf by the continuous roar of coal and equipment. "All you gotta do is tell him the doctor said your ticker's playing out and you've got no choice but to leave mining. I say you owe him that much."

Dog nodded. "I'll chew on it."

"Dog, dammit, either you tell him or I will!"

Dog gripped the steering wheel with both hands. His ears turned as red as the fake ruby beads she was wearing.

"I said I'd chew on it, didn't I? Hell, Ceola, sometimes I wish you'd just mind your own beeswax!"

Ceola flattened him with her eyes.

"Fine and dandy!" She reached into a small wicker basket under her feet and took out the two chicken breasts she'd packed with some loaf bread and boiled eggs. Holding a breast in each hand, she sank her teeth into one and without swallowing bit into the other. "And while you're *chewing on it*," she rumbled, "I'll go ahead and eat!"

The pair drove for over two hours and arrived in Saxton shortly after three. They brought along an ice-cream maker with all the fixings, and Ceola unpacked four different varieties of her special homemade cookies. Sherman was waiting on the porch and offered to help crank the ice cream while Maude took to her bedroom and quilting.

Within minutes the yard had the air of a family reunion. Dog ground the stub of a missing finger into a nostril and pretended to pick his nose. He found a quarter in his right ear and juggled four peaches. Ceola tied a knot in a cherry stem with her tongue. She brought out a bag of letters and keepsakes from camp friends, and the girls took turns reading them aloud.

"If that's not the sweetest thing!" Lily raved. "Of course we'll answer each one."

"Do, and I'll have the preacher read them at church. His sorry, no-good Company ass oughta be good for something!"

"Ceola!" Lily couldn't hide the shine in her eyes.

"Well, it's the truth!"

The girls giggled, and Lily hastened them to the kitchen to cut up some fruit. "Leave a little for the ice cream," she teased.

As if they'd never been apart, Abe and Dog poked each other in the ribs and joked in the raw language of coal miners. They gossiped like women and argued like children. Dog, a Company man and therefore a Republican, accused President Truman of having been soft on Communists; Abe predicted that Truman would go down in history as one of our nation's finest presidents. Dog supported Eisenhower and Nixon; Abe swore loyalty to Adlai Stevenson and the politics of Franklin Delano Roosevelt.

"It's amazing how they can argue and laugh at the same time!" Ceola shook her head. "Why, those two could make the Korean War seem like a poker party!"

Lily laughed. "It's true what they say, that miners act crazy to keep from going insane."

"Sweetie, it ain't just miners!"

In time Dog brought out his banjo, and Ceola took up her fiddle. Abe sang and played his guitar for the first time since he'd left Cordel-Lewis, and Sweet William chimed in with his harmonica. The girls danced arm-in-arm. Lily clapped her hands and sang with such perfect alto harmony that she felt an exciting new sense of belonging and an actual homesickness for the camp. Recently, while watching Abe with her pa and brothers, she'd been embarrassed by his crude manners. Now she celebrated this chance to see him through the eyes of good people who knew him inside and out, and loved him like a brother.

During a break, the men lowered their voices to discuss mine problems, and Ceola delivered the latest camp gossip with her stage sense of humor. Lily burst out laughing when she heard about Palatia Porter's latest hairdo, orange and frizzy to match her miniature poodle, Fifi. She chuckled, too, over Nulty Gatewood's fancy new hats, a different one each Sunday.

"It ain't like the whole congregation don't know that on Monday those hats are boxed up and sent right back to Sears! And did I tell you about Lottie Bowes' upper plate falling lickety-split into a 20-gallon pot of Baptist Brunswick stew?"

"Law, law," Lily said with a huff. "What a waste of good stew!"

"Waste? What waste? Must of been the Efferdent b'cause, girlfriend, that stew ain't never tasted better!"

"You're kidding!"

"Swear to Wod!"

They were chatting on the front porch, near the open front door, when Lily heard the sound of Maude's heavy tie shoes, too close for comfort.

"Come walk with me," she said, and sent Rosy inside with a spoon and the last of the peach ice cream.

"How are things?" Ceola asked as they headed toward the toilet and barn.

"Good," Lily said. "Mostly."

"Don't bullshit me, Lily. That ain't what I come here to hear."

They stopped, and Lily dropped her head onto Ceola's shoulder.

"I'm sorry. It's just that I was always taught a preacher's family should leave their dirty laundry at home, so now it's hard for me to open up, especially at the expense of another's joy."

"I know," Ceola said as if fighting off a cry, her voice so sad that Lily stopped altogether to listen. "That's exactly how I felt when my boy Pup got electrocuted in that mine and Dog shoveled a part of me right into that grave with him. I cussed and cried. I shunned Dog and God and drunk enough liquor to flood the Smoky Mountains. Wouldn't speak to a soul. Poor Dog! He finally had his fill and packed up to leave, which showed me no matter how bad things are, they can always be worse. Every day of my life I think of Pup and shake off the blues. A mother losing a child is not fixable, Lily, but most everything else is." She took Lily's hand. "Come on, girl. Pretend you're playing solitaire and lay it all out."

"I'm so sorry," Lily said with a sigh, and Cela motioned away the pity.

"You're right, but honestly, Ceola, I don't know where to start. I'm so confused I wouldn't know the truth if we butted heads. One minute I understand my mother-in-law wanting her son out of that pit. I want him out, too. The next I'm convinced she's trying to oust me and the children and have him all to herself. Then I wonder if sometimes I'm jumping to conclusions. I think if I lock horns with her, Abe'll take her side, and I'll end up hating them both. What good would that do the children?"

"Lily, whatever happened to that gutsy gal Abe called a *hellion*? The independent, educated one that stood up to her preacher pa?"

"Oh, Ceola I was a foolish, rebellious sinner back then. If the good Lord hadn't saved me, who knows what kind of wife and mother I'd be."

"And so now you feel *safe*?"

"*Saved*, I said. There's a difference."

"You know, when Abe used to brag on you, it was like a whole heaven of stars fell over his eyes, and you, you listened with that admiring look of a woman who's just dying to hop in the sack."

"It's true. We were…connected."

"Now I see a difference and I ain't gonna tell you things will work out because sometimes they don't. You're strong, Lord knows, but you don't seem to know it anymore. Trust yourself like before."

"But there's so much going on, I don't know where to start."

"Start by taking charge."

"Of Maude and Abe? You must be kidding!"

"No. Of yourself."

Lily and Ceola stopped at the toilet on their way home. At the house, Lily reached to hug her again and saw tears in her eyes. For a moment she felt cheated, unable to cry and show proof of her own love.

"You said Abe would never be happy outside a mining camp, and you were right. Thank you, my wise woman, for not saying I told you so," Lily said with warmth in her voice.

Ceola giggled as she squeezed her.

"Trust me, it wadn't easy!"

The men had packed up Ceola's goods and were waiting at Dog's truck. Both smoked cigarettes. Dog leaned a foot on the running board, and Abe squatted on the ground. The grim looks on their faces said they were commiserating over the mine.

While everyone said their final goodbyes, a flood of memories washed over Lily. She imagined her and Abe back at the mining camp, him with his band, laughing and playing music, relaxed and confident, bigger than life. She pictured potlucks, square dances, bingo, and bazaars. She recalled the rewards of nursing injured miners, little children, and Ceola. When Pop dies, Abe and I could move back to the camp, she told herself. His being a foreman would make the job safer, and we could live in one of those pretty two-story houses on Silk Stocking Row. The girls would be disappointed at first, but proud in the end.

Dog's truck pulled away, and the children went their separate ways, all but Rosy. Lily took Abe's arm, leaned her head into his big, muscular shoulder, and drifted inside in a cloud of not-so-awful possibilities.

Ceola and Dog had lifted their spirits to the point that Lily missed church that evening to go with Abe to Bryce's Cove. Willows on each side of the road bowed as if to welcome lovers. It was September, and quiet. The air was cool and tender. They made love like youth with no problems and no burdens, and returned home to make love again.

The next morning her arm was draped around his chest when he woke up, and their heads shared the same pillow. Seeing that he was awake early, she slipped her feet onto his for the usual warming.

"I like spooning," she said.

"So you didn't get enough last night, huh?" he teased her.

"Is it that obvious?"

They cuddled and talked about small matters until Abe sat up to smoke. He spotted his wallet on the bedside table and took out a 5-dollar bill.

"Here. Here's a five. Go buy your ma a little somethin' for her birthday and Sunday I'll take you to Buck Creek. Last night was worth every dime of it."

"Oh, Abe, you remembered!" She reached to kiss his nose with puckered lips, the way she did Rosy's. "You can't imagine how bad I was dreading having to ask Vi to come take us."

"Here. Here's some more." He left the five and whipped out a twenty. "Do a cake and whatever, and we'll celebrate her and Will both. Ain't every day a man's only son goes off to college."

"University," she corrected him and hopped up to get dressed. "What time will we leave?"

"We'll go to church first, which I know will make you happy."

"Oh, you know it will!"

"Will and me'll leave out right after. Don't bother to cook big. We'll grab a burger on the road. He'll like that, don't you think? Just the two of us, father and son, eatin' out and talkin' the man stuff."

Lily stared at the silver drips of fog on the windowpane. She noticed the paint peeling where they dropped into the wood. For weeks she'd imagined the wonderful time she would have touring the campus and seeing Sweet William's dorm room. She had looked forward to helping him unpack his belongings and spread his bed with one of Maude's finest quilts, geometric so it wouldn't look feminine. She couldn't wait to meet his roommate and neighbors. By then the barn-house would be finished, and the trip home would be a perfect opportunity for her to tell Abe that she had gone behind his back to help Maude and Silas Holmes with the project. Surely he would take the news better if she simultaneously offered to move back to the mining camp.

"But I was really looking forward to leaving the kids with Ma and coming, too," she said.

"I've worked such long hours, I've neglected the boy, Lily. This could be our big chance to catch up. Be a good girl and do me this one favor and we'll both go and bring him home for Thanksgiving. You'd like that, wouldn't you? Seeing all them autumn leaves that you say blind your eyes, they're so pretty."

She had to admit that Sweet William was starving for his daddy's attention and in bad need of manly advice. Maybe he would open up and talk about Fairy Enlow, and Abe could actually be of help.

"It's just that I had something important to tell you that would take time, and I was thinking the trip home would be a good chance to talk."

"There'll be plenty more times oncst the boy's gone."

"But that might be too late."

"Too late? You make it sound like a matter of life and death." He left the cigarette smoking in the ashtray and reached for her hands. "Tell you what. We'll set a date for Bryce's Cove just as soon as I get back. Then you can talk all you want."

Lily got up, dressed quickly, and went outside to feel the cool morning air. There she consoled herself for the letdown of missing her son's first trip to college. She thought of Ceola's advice and wished she'd had the courage to stand up for herself. On her way inside she checked the pot of pink petunias. Cool nights had pinched their edges and they were finishing their season. Inside, Abe sat at the table, eating a breakfast prepared by his mother. She forced a smile and took some small degree of comfort from the fact that he had at least agreed to attend church.

Abe finished his breakfast, gave Lily a peck kiss, and raced off to work. Lily, still filled with disappointment, returned to her warm bed to await the sound of the children. The room was chilly. She had pulled the covers up over her head and closed her eyes when Maude knocked on the door.

"Lily?" she whispered, and Lily pretended to be asleep.

"Rise and shine!" Maude called and slightly cracked the door. "Silas will be here soon. Have you forgot?"

"No, it's just that I'm not at my best today. Sweet William is done with the tobacco. Tell him I said will he please go help in my place."

Maude invited herself in and squeezed next to Lily on the edge of the bed. Lily didn't slide over, and Maude shoved for space.

"Dog and Ceola can be a handful. Maybe all that entertaining was too much for you," she said.

"I may be coming down with a cold," Lily said.

"Judging by all the racket, I'd say you and them had a right good time."

"A little rest, and I'll be fine."

"Abe's all perked up like as if Dog sugared him with temptation and now you're slacking off at the barn. I can't help but think you've chickened out."

"I'll do my share, but maybe later in the day. Silas Holmes can leave us instructions, and the children and I will work hard."

"That's not what you agreed to. We agreed to work together and finish fast."

Lily avoided the charge, and Maude leaned in and whispered.

"Tell me, Lily, did Dog talk to Abe about going back to the mine?"

"Not that I know of."

"But you and Ceola went off and left them alone."

"We took a walk, yes."

"So they might've."

"I suppose they could've."

Maude frowned. Her fierce eyes took on the look of a treed coon, glaring into the light of some night hunter's lantern.

"Now see here, Lily, this is starting to feel like a game of sorts and I'm not taking kindly to it. I want you to promise me right here and now that no matter what happens, you won't let Abe go back to that mine. Promise me you'll say if he goes, he goes without you and these younguns."

"But I wouldn't."

"Promise me, I said. I'm done with your hem and hawing."

"I'm sorry, but I can't."

"You will!"

Lily felt the thrust of a threat.

"You said I should follow God's will, and I'm trying to."

"You think I don't know hogwash when I hear it? After all I've done for you, you've got the gall to take him and go back there, leaving Sherman to die and me stuck with a house I don't want."

"No, no, I didn't say that."

"You didn't have to."

CHAPTER EIGHTEEN

"Thank God for parties to take our minds off our troubles,"
Lily said as Vi pushed a cart down A&P's baking goods aisle.
Lily was dressed in her usual gray housedress and carried
coupons in her pocket. Vi wore her once white waitress uniform, now spotted with dabs of mustard and brown gravy.

"You got troubles?" Vi asked.

"Not any more than anybody else." Lily picked up a box of
confectionery sugar. "What's next?" she asked, and Vi looked
down at the list.

"Cocoa."

"A white cake's more practical."

"But boring."

They agreed on coconut, and Lily recommended
delegating the responsibility to the girls, Minnie Mo included.
Vi gave in on the condition that she be in charge of the punch,
orange-sherbet with flakes of canned peaches.

"You won't tell if I spike it, will you?"

"You do and die!"

Vi selected yellow-and-white paper plates and cups and
debated over white or yellow napkins.

"I'm getting the small party ones just so you won't be
tempted to cut them in two," she teased Lily.

Lily glanced down at her brown Oxford shoes, the left heel
so worn she felt a slight dip when walking.

"We can tell Ma the party's for Sweet William, and we'll
tell Sweet William it's for Ma's birthday. That way they
won't suspect a thing," she said.

"Unless Rosy goes and blabs." Vi picked out some plasticware and candles, yellow to match the paper plates. "The whole bunch of you has gone and spoiled that li'l darling something awful."

"I know. But she's been good of late about keeping secrets. Didn't say a word to her daddy about Silas and the barn. Promised me she'd tell only Hairy."

Vi's mouth flew open.

"Lily, do you mean to tell me Abe still don't know about Silas and the renovation?"

"I'll tell him after Sweet William leaves for college. Abe might let go of his temper. The boy's got enough to worry about with his granddaddy so sick and all."

"Girl, you're courting trouble. I can't believe you've got away with it this long!"

"I promised Maude I'd not tell Abe until after Silas finishes, and the job's almost done. It's a promise I regret, but still a promise."

"Honestly! *That woman!* Don't you promise her a thing, Lily. She's got something up her sleeve, and you and me both know it!"

Lily considered the awful scene in the bedroom, when Maude had out-and-out threatened her regarding Abe and the mine. How? she asked herself, had life gotten so complicated. And in spite of her good intentions.

"I admit I have my doubts," she answered.

"I'd sooner trust a peddler going door-to-door with hair tonic. I'm warning you to go ahead and tell Abe before she beats you to it."

"I just can't believe she'd go that far. Think what it might do to her grandchildren."

"If you're afraid, I'll be glad to tell him for you."

Lily flinched. "Don't you dare go behind my back, Vi Horton. Abe needs to hear it from me, and he's going to really soon."

"Do you really think I'd go behind your back?" Vi asked in a pout.

Lily pictured that night Brody died, and Vi turned to Abe for solace. She imagined the seductive way they danced and disappeared in the moonlight. She batted her eyes as if pulling down a screen and imagined Rosy crossing her fingers.

"Not really."

"Well, I should hope not."

Vi put her groceries in the trunk of the car, and Lily added hers to the clutter in the back seat. Then the two set out for home.

"So how are things going between you and Silas?" Lily asked. She had waited for the subject to come up. The fact that it hadn't made her uncomfortable.

Vi took out a stick of gum. She shoved it into her mouth and tossed the wrapper out the window.

"Silas hit the road. I invited him to supper and cooked chicken with gravy and creamed potatoes. I even dusted off the family Bible and put it on the coffee table next to that little picture of Ma and Pa's forty-third wedding anniversary. He came but left shortly after dessert." Vi smirked. "Would you believe he asked me to say grace? *Grace*, I said, and you should of seen the shocked look on his face when he saw I was serious. Honestly, Christians and undertakers, they've both got the personality of a cast-iron skillet!"

Lily touched Vi's hand out of pity. A part of her wanted to comfort her. Another part wanted to whack some sense into her head, as Abe would say.

"Vi, you've simply got to put a zipper on that loose tongue of yours. Silas is a member of Pa's church. What did you expect?"

"That's the point. I never know what to expect. Men— they're every one like those artsy paper fans from over in Japan. Til the heats on, you ain't about to see a one of 'ems true colors."

This time, Lily had to agree.

"I was bored with him anyway," Vi continued. "Thank goodness it wadn't too late to make up with Clyde. Clyde's a hoot. Said he'd marry me in a second if I'd have him."

"Thank goodness you said no."

"Seems you kinda got tired of Silas yourself. Else you'd still be working at the barn."

Lily noticed Vi watching her from the corner of an eye, and she felt a burning blush on her cheeks.

"Me? Tired of Silas? Why, I hardly know him."

"The only reason he came to see me in the first place was to talk about you. Men, they're so obvious—except, of course, when they ain't."

"Why, Vi, I'm practically old enough to be Silas' mother." Lily looked away, as if afraid her eyes might twinkle, her lips curve a certain way, or Vi remind her that she was only forty. The window was cracked, and a flock of squawking geese interrupted the conversation.

"What's wrong? You got quiet all of a sudden. I mentioned Silas, and you clammed up like a fist," Vi said.

"Oh, I was just daydreaming is all. It's silly but...have you ever wished you could spread your wings and fly like those geese? Trade these mountains for a seashore or city for a while and come back with no problems and no price to pay? Not even to God?"

"Are you kidding? All the damn time. That's why I drive a convertible." Vi pointed to a wall of brown bluffs with black horizontal streaks. "I just get in my car and whiz by these ugly coal seams til I come to something pretty like them purple bachelor's buttons there in the ditch. That way, can't nothing or nobody break me 'lessen I let 'em."

"Oh, Vi, I wish I'd learned how to drive like you and Ceola. Pa was too busy teaching the boys, and Abe thought driving wasn't for women. I should have insisted. Think of all the fun I could've had with my girls. It just kills me having to depend on you and June."

"I don't mind helping out but it's a fact you should learn to drive. You drove Pa's tractor, didn't you? There ain't much difference."

"Oh, no, no, I couldn't. In traffic I'd be a nervous wreck. Abe would throw a fit!"

"Sherman's pickup is rusting out back. It's a shame somebody ain't using it."

"Pop would certainly want me to have it." Lily's face lit up. "You may not remember, Vi, but he was proud of me for being a nurse back when Maude agreed with Pa that nurses are to doctors what nuns are to priests—to be used sexually, I mean. But Pop was proud of me. He said I had spunk."

"Say the word and I'll pull off on one of these dirt roads and you can take over."

Lily watched the geese fly in a perfect V, tackling the sky like arrows making war. Like Vi and Ceola, they were Tennyson's Ulysses drinking life to the lees.

For a minute she felt the sting of self-pity.

"Well?" Vi asked.

"Well, maybe this one time—provided you don't tell Abe."

On Friday of that week Lily spent the better part of her day sewing and watching the girls make crafts and party favors for Sweet William. They framed school pictures of themselves inside the golden rings of canning jar lids; they turned a tin can into a pencil holder and assembled a letter tray out of popsicle sticks. For Sarah they made a bouquet of colorful carnation flowers out of pink tissues and a clothespin bag on a coat hanger in the shape of a playsuit.

Lily baked a ham, glazed it with mustard and brown sugar, and topped it with pineapples and cherries. She arranged a platter of mouth-watering treats—deviled eggs, cheese-stuffed celery sticks, watermelon-rind pickles, plump pickled peaches—as if each were a flower in one of Sarah's centerpieces on the Little Wolf Creek altar.

Buck Creek day came, and she was overcome with excitement.

"Almost too pretty to eat, if I do say so myself," she said of the ham as she wrapped it in wax paper and placed it inside a brown paper bag. From the kitchen window, she had seen Abe waxing the Plymouth Roadking. She checked on his progress and saw an argument going on between him and his mother. Instinct said Maude was telling Abe about Silas Holmes and the barn-house, and a sharp pain tremored across her forehead and over her right ear. She stumbled into a chair beside the window and, fighting back the tears, stared out at a recent nightmare: Maude was tongue lashing and whacking the air with both hands. She pointed a finger and grabbed at Abe's shirttail.

Sherman circled the chopping block some seven or eight feet away, collecting pine cones and kindling for a fire. Lily called him inside, and he hobbled but moved fast.

"What's going on?" she asked and served him milk and warm molasses cookies to make sure she didn't leave and him hungry.

"Don't know, but it ain't friendly."

"Try to eat the cookies while they're soft," she encouraged him and served him a dish of apples run through a colander.

"Thank you," he said, but ate little.

The fear of leaving him with Maude in her angry state terrified her. She pushed four fingers against her forehead as if to force away the pain and told herself the squabble was over nothing more than Abe's smoking or cursing, that it was not unusual for mother and son to fall out, especially if Maude resented having to stay away from the party.

In the meantime, her opportunity to nurse was a godsend.

"Now, Pop," she explained, "remember that the trick to taking medication is to stay ahead of the pain. Don't wait until you need it." She showed him his favorite foods she'd left in the fridge and begged him to eat more. She pointed out clean clothes and linens, particularly some extra sheets, should he need them. She was about to prepare his bath when hateful shouts shot through the window.

"Maude's flying off the handle," Sherman said. "Abe needs rescuing." Grabbing at furniture for support, he hurried back outside.

Lily ran to the door and saw Maude yank Abe's arm. Abe pushed her aside, and she launched back at him. When he flung the wax can in her direction, and she aimed before pitching it back at him, Lily couldn't believe Maude could be such a hellcat, the likes of her son when in his black mood.

"Abe, the children!" she cried at the door, and to her surprise, he threw up his hands and stalked inside.

"Can we go now?" she asked.

"Ready, willing, and able!" he said with too much liquid in his eyes. He shoved past her and broke a family rule by drinking water directly from the dipper. "You dodos get you a drink of water and then you go pee," he added. "B'cause once we get on the road, there ain't gonna be no stoppin'," he added.

"Time to load up. Grab a dish," Lily yelled to the girls. She relaxed her voice for their sake and called out, "We're going to a party!" The girls grabbed platters and bowls and then scattered, and Rosy came running with presents and trinkets. Sweet William was waiting at the car trunk to help load when Lily came with her pretty ham.

"Your mama's right. It's a party. What could possibly go wrong?" Abe said when everyone was seated, and Lily detected the sarcasm. Maude had disappeared without saying goodbye, and she rejoiced at the stroke of good luck.

From the road, a ghostly fog dressed the hollow, and ridge trees looked black against the pale palette. While Abe adjusted the wipers and leaned forward to see, Lily made the hush sign with finger on mouth, and the noisy girls fell silent.

"A fine day for travel," he drawled, and Lily handed him a clean handkerchief and a cup of hot coffee.

"It's early," she said. "The sun may come out yet. In these mountains, anything can happen."

"You got that right!"

He swallowed a Goody's Powder and turned up the radio.

"The Lord knows we've had our share of rain," she said. "I pity the farmers who chose the wrong day to cut hay."

"That's the breaks," he said and glared ahead at bar-b-que restaurants, fireworks stands, flea markets, and craft shops stocked with area rocks and minerals. He was cursing coal trucks for shedding retreads and poking along like mules in a mine when Sweet William noticed wisps of steam coming from the radiator.

"She's overheated. Pull over, Boss. We just passed a creek!" Abe cut the engine, and Sweet William nabbed a can from the trunk and took off.

"Avoid the road," Lily called after him.

"What a damn waste of time. I cain't win for losin'," Abe said and didn't stir from his seat in the Plymouth. Lily, half-way expecting him to whack something, sent the girls to follow Sweet William by way of a field. She waited the minutes away, and still he sat as if planted.

As if Maude had told him about Silas Holmes and the barn-house, and she, and not time, was what he had lost.

CHAPTER NINETEEN

Abe pulled up beside Sarah's pink rambling rose bush with shrinking blooms from too much rain, and the kids grabbed their items and hurried toward the kitchen. Lily was trifling with her ham in the trunk when she noticed the engine still running and Abe slumped over the wheel.

"You kids go say hello and come back for more food," she called, slipped in beside him, and cut the engine.

"You kids get lost and don't come back til I say to!" he yelled. He cleared his throat and swiped the sweat from his forehead. His voice was hoarse, as if he, like her, was holding back tears.

"Abe?" she said, pity making a whisper of her voice.

"Lily, I ain't gonna lie. I'm flusterated on account of the barn mess and you know I don't cotton to secrets, most especially my own wife's. So tell me the truth. Did you or didn't you scheme to make a house of the barn behind my back?" He stopped to cough. "I brung you here for a party and a party we're gonna have. No matter what, I promise I won't blow a gasket or do nothin' stupid. But what I need is the truth. I hoped it could maybe wait but I'm bustin' inside, see?"

Her first instinct was to shower him with affection; her second was to feel annoyed. Time was scarce, and she couldn't believe his bad timing. If he'd wanted to talk about the barnhouse, why hadn't he spoken up when the Plymouth overheated and Sweet William and the girls went for water and he sat planted like a rock?

"Abe, have you forgot my brothers will be here any minute, and we're way late as it is. Vi's right now waiting on me to come help her set up."

"No, I ain't forgot. But no way in hell can I go inside that house with the whole fam damily knowin' my business, all but me. Just tell me the truth is all I'm askin'. The details can come later. Did you scheme behind my back or didn't you?"

"It's not a yes or no matter. A question like this takes time. Don't you remember me saying I'd planned to go with you and Will to UK so we'd have a chance to talk on the way home? I meant a good, long talk, one you could ponder on and understand." She placed a hand on his knee. "We've waited this long, hon. Surely we can wait until we're alone."

"A fine celebration it'll be for me if'n I'm made a laughing stock of in front of your family. Just tell me what I heard ain't true about you and we'll go in like nothin' happened."

"But I have no idea what you've heard. I admit I've made mistakes I regret. But you've gotta believe me when I say your mother has lied to us both."

"That won't cut it," he said and bit down on his lower lip. "And who said it was Mother?"

"Who else?" Lily squeezed out of the Plymouth and walked around to his side. The air was damp and nippy, and she shivered. "There's tables to be moved, chairs to be set up. The party was your idea. I was counting on your help."

He held up five fingers.

"Five minutes of your time is all your husband is askin'. Five lousy minutes."

"I'm sorry, but five minutes is not enough time."

"Just five lousy minutes," he said as she turned and walked away, clutching the ham.

Rosy finished her share of party chores and struck out for the creek to find her beloved granny and papaw. A few minutes later she came running back, out of breath and looking struck with confusion.

"Mama, you were wondering where Daddy disappeared to and I saw his car at Aunt Vi's."

"What's he doing there?" Daisy asked. "She's supposed to be here."

"Daddy reminds her of her poor beloved Brody," Verni said with a snigger.

Lily tore outside, cut through the corn field, and made a beeline for Vi's house trailer. She arrived in time to see Vi let go of Abe's arm and him tear off in the Plymouth. The pain-on-pain felt unbearable.

"Pray tell, Violet, when are you gonna get a husband of your own and leave mine alone?" she let go and screamed— screamed, to make up for all those times she'd wanted to and hadn't.

Vi ran to her, and Lily hopped outside her arms' reach. Tears gathered in the corners of her eyes.

"Oh, Lily, sweetie, thank God you're here! I didn't know what to do. Abe's mad as a hornet because he just caught sight of Sweet William with Fairy." She pointed a finger. "Look down at the creek near the waterfall and you'll see." Lily stood stiff-necked, her eyes half-shut to stop the tears."

"You told him about Silas Holmes, didn't you, Vi? I thought surely Maude told him, but it was you, wasn't it? I said not to, and you told him because you want him for yourself! Or is it that you just can't resist a man you can't have?"

"No, no, I didn't! I don't. His mother told him and blamed everything on you and Pa. He came to ask me what I knew of it and I said Maude lied like a rug! He was headed back to the party when we heard laughter coming from the creek and saw Fairy and Sweet William laying on a blanket right near that white water. Then he took off mad as a hornet and now you and me've gotta stop him!"

Vi ran inside for her shoes, and Lily dropped into some weeds beside a heap of empty Schlitz and Coca-Cola cans. Eyes open, mouth in a slant, she prayed that Vi, and not Maude, was the guilty one. Vi she could go on resenting, and life would not change. But not believing in Maude would mean the end of her dreams.

"So how long has Abe been coming here?" she asked when Vi hopped back, wearing one tennis shoe and putting on the other.

"What?"

"I said how long have you and Abe been carrying on behind my back?"

"Shit, Lily! Stop the nonsense and let's get down there before Abe does something he'll regret!" She reached out a hand. "Come on, hon, I know a shortcut!"

"Don't bother." Lily took off her black pumps, caked with garden dirt, and wiped them with a handful of leaves. When they were as clean as they would get, she kept wiping, as though the shoes were the only thing that mattered now. "My poor Sunday shoes," she muttered, "and I wanted to look nice for the party."

"Lily!"

"Don't worry, Vi. Abe's not about to hurt Sweet William in front of the girl. Not with him about to go off to college, he won't." She turned the shoes over to reexamine the soles. "No, he'll say the boy was plucked while still green and is just sowing his wild oats. It's me he'll blame for knowing about Fairy and not telling him. Just one more secret I've kept from the boss man."

Vi lowered herself on her knees and tapped Lily's right shoulder.

"Now you listen here. When Abe asks if you knew about Fairy, you lie your fool head off, hear? You swear you didn't have so much as a clue. You say the same of the barn-house and I'll back you up tooth and nail." She took Lily's hand. "I'm the only one knows the truth and I won't tell a soul, so help me, God!"

Lily chuckled at the irony of Vi calling on God.

"So they come that easy for you, do they?"

"What?"

"Lies."

"Sometimes lies work for the good."

Lily remembered learning from Ceola that Abe had been chosen as mine foreman and keeping the truth to herself. The unspoken lie that she daily had to live with, and now regret.

"Not true. They always find you out."

"Huh?"

"Lies. Your sins. *Beware your sins will find you out.* That's Bible."

Vi shrugged. "I wouldn't know about that."

Lily's mouth tightened, and her eyes glittered with mockery.

"That's right, Vi. You wouldn't!"

Abe was his old self when time came for the party. "Hail, hail the gang's all here!" he sang as Sarah and Wade's children arrived with toddlers and teenagers, in-laws and cousins. Twelve people crowded around the walnut trestle table Wade Eakins had built while others chose to eat in the cool but dry garden. The scene with its wide-open doors gave off the scent of rich foods and the last of the summer flowers.

"T'ain't much, folks, just enough to wetchy bread!" Vi teased as she and Lily set out the ham and turkey, rich gravies and relishes, dumplings and creamed potatoes, an assortment of green and yellow vegetables, and biscuits with crispy crusts. On a nearby buffet, also built by Wade Eakins, sat dishes of cookies, pudding, fruit cobbler, and a colorful, sugar-sequined coconut cake with three layers, soon to have candles.

Guests reached for hands before Wade Eakins said the blessing. It was humble, but poetic, and designed specifically for the occasion.

"M-m-m-m!" some hummed, and there was the usual sounds of clanked forks, scraped plates, and swigged coffee. At the end, nothing was left of the turkey and ham except bones to make soup. The men went outside to smoke and pick their teeth while the women pulled chairs under a walnut tree to gossip while catching a breeze. The school children, led by Minnie Mo and Verni, applied themselves to the task of cleaning up the kitchen while Rosy played games like Ring Around the Roses with children half her age. Stomachs settled, and everyone gathered in the living room to sing "Happy Birthday," eat cake, and watch the honorees open their presents.

Along with handkerchiefs and nightgowns, Sarah received a hand mixer, a wristwatch, and a portable Motorola television—an everybody-pitches-in gift managed by Lily. Sweet William got shirts, ink pens, books, money, and an eight-string Deering banjo, used but in good condition, secretly paid for by Sherman.

The banjo prompted a move to the front porch, where Sweet William attempted to prove he was worthy. Abe had brought along his guitar, and Sarah took out her lap harp. Some joined in with spoons, a washboard, a crock jug, and combs wrapped in wax paper while others sang "Boil 'em Cabbage Down"..."Aunt Rhody"..."Old Time Religion," and such. The sounds flowed like the rich aromas still mingling in Sarah's kitchen. Even the smallest children were in the act of learning that you can't have a party without home-grown music.

Sarah played down her sixty-fifth birthday, claiming she'd stopped counting birthdays the day she got too old to remember hers and Wade's ages. She shifted the attention to Sweet William and dubbed him "the grandson from heaven!" but praised her other grandchildren as well. "They each one fills a special place in Wade's and my life," she pointed out, while everyone knew Sweet William was the favorite.

For Buddy's sake, as well as the Creech boys', Lily had asked Abe not to mention all the awards and scholarships Sweet William had won. But Abe, with Verni's help, had compiled a list, and he was quick on his feet.

"Served as senior-class president and valedictorian from a class of twenty-two, voted "Most Likely to Succeed," offered a basketball scholarship he turned down in order to have more time to study and two others, one for civic responsibility and one for academic achievement, that he accepted."

"A real star you've got there, Abe!" June said, and slapped his back.

Abe smiled through the pain.

"Hell, yeah, he's a star! And they's five more ridin' his coattail!"

CHAPTER TWENTY

Father and son headed north after Little Wolf Creek's church service the following day. Like each other's prisoner, the two sat silent and still, pretending to listen to Billy Graham on the radio. When Sweet William did move, he slowly shifted his weight and winced at the pain. He had college and a new life to look forward to, but could think about nothing except how his daddy had grabbed him by the shoulders in front of Fairy and claimed he would shake some sense into his dead head. He had shaken him so hard with his coal-shoveling hands that Sweet William had gone limp and fallen on the ground, after which Abe told him to stand up like a man.

What a way to say goodbye to one's girl! Sweet William thought, and he mourned the fact that Fairy had run away screaming. What a way to say goodbye to one's daddy! he also thought, and mourned even more.

For a half hour the two traveled on, Abe coughing and wheezing and Sweet William aching and choking on tears he couldn't shed. He was considering dropping his head and pretending to nod off when he remembered a line from a William Wordsworth poem he'd studied in tenth grade.

"The child is father of the man" had struck him as a meaningful line because then as now he, with his mother's keen intuition, had sometimes looked on his daddy as the real child of the family, and everyone else as a kind of emotional caregiver. The line moved him to pity, his usual antidote for anger, and urged him to look on his daddy's bad behavior as a queer and pathetic sign of love, a yearning to see that his one

232 · FAYE SOLOMON KUSHNER

son didn't end up crawling for a living "like did your ole man."

He sat up, wiped his eyes, and told a Polack joke that fell short of funny. Remarks about family and friends like Dog and Ceola also failed. When he felt he'd exhausted every possibility, he brought up the one subject he knew was safe— coal. He showed a keen interest in the new continuous miner—a machine on steel tracks that gnaws and sweeps the coal from the mountain and pulls it onto a conveyer—and he asked if Cordel-Lewis No. 1 mine would ever have such a machine.

"Where's your faith, boy?" Abe answered, but stopped short of making a prediction.

Sweet William then confessed that he and Buddy had once ridden their bicycles down the chute of a closed tipple. While at it, he admitted they'd hopped a train to Harlan and raided a box car, only to find crate after crate of brown canvas shoes.

"You better hope and pray your mama don't find out. That gal would skin you alive!" Abe said with stiffness in his smile.

"You got that right!" Sweet William shifted his head and grimaced at the pain. He remembered the sheer awfulness of his daddy's hands—big, scratchy, coal-shoveling hands, far stronger than his daddy could've known—pressing against his shoulder blades until he thought they would crack. "What we need to do, Daddy, now that I have a banjo, is form a band like you had. The "Cumberland Fox Chasers Reborn" we could call it. So what do you think?"

"Yes, sir-e-e. Them was good times." Abe switched off the radio. "Your mama used to say I strutted like a peacock."

"She said your head was so big you had to reach a good mile to scratch it."

"Yep! That was me all right."

"I'll come home on weekends. Dog can join us, and we'll take our road on the show as you used to say. How about that?"

"No way in hell! You stay on campus. Hit them books and get you a education like your mama. Take it from me, boy, education is the one thing you can't lose once you get it. The one thing."

"But I could..."

"No!"

The boy felt flattened. He pulled up his chest to let out a man's curse.

"Well, I'm for damn sure coming home for Thanksgiving!"

"You bet you are!"

"We'll go surprise that turkey nesting in granddaddy's hay field!"

"You, betchy!"

"Mama can stuff it with dressing and little wieners!"

"Yeah, man! Them was good!"

As Sweet William relaxed, the pain seemed to ease. He wrapped his hands around the nape of his neck and remembered a special autumn morning when he was nine. His mama packed their lunches, and his daddy took him hunting for the Thanksgiving turkey. Granny Eakins had sewed them matching orange vests and put lemon drops in the pockets. Granddaddy Siler had whittled him a small bow with arrows. He could still smell the scent of freshly cut hay and ripe apples, still hear the cornstalks rustling and magpies yapping like women at a quilting bee. Even now he could taste his lemony rush of spit.

He'd been practicing for that hunting day ever since he'd gotten the bow, sometimes targeting a tree stump or a ragged kite nailed to an oak. But nothing, not even the death of a human, could have prepared him for the squalling thud of that bigger-than-life bird, and he had made the mistake of grinding his fists into his eyes and refusing to look at the belly-up thing with crouched claws and bony wings.

"Don't worry, boy. One day you'll get the hang of it," his daddy said and plunked a big forgiving hand on his head. But he had known by the slow, pensive way he rolled his cigarette afterwards that he was grappling with the words *sissy* and *shame*.

"I'll show him. One day I'll be a lung doctor and I will cure him and Iris and a million billion coal miners," he had promised himself that day of the turkey. "Then he will be proud I'm his son and call me a man."

Abe hadn't felt like eating breakfast, but lunch was a different matter. Though Sweet William claimed he was full, they stopped for lunch at Shoney's in Richmond, roughly an hour before reaching Lexington and the University. The restaurant was crowded, and loud with to-be students and their proud parents. Sweet William and Abe ordered hamburgers with fries. They ate while watching a downpour of rain blast the big sheet-glass windows as though they would burst into shards at any minute.

"Might as well have a dessert while we wait til it clears," Abe said when they'd finished the burgers.

"No, thanks," Sweet William said, his mouth watering for the sweet treats featured on the back of the menu.

Abe signaled the waitress and ordered himself a piece of strawberry pie with a whipped-cream topping and the boy a chocolate sundae with nuts. Each ate slowly, savoring the taste and saying little because of the deafening roar of rain. They were at the cash register when a shapely girl with blonde ponytails and full lips smiled flirtatiously at Sweet William, making him blush and turn away.

"That little gal was givin' you the eye back there," Abe said when back at the car.

"I didn't notice."

"When the time's right, you'll find you a pretty gal with smarts like your mama." He paused, hoping he didn't sound like his meddling mother. With men it's different, he told himself. Men have the know when it comes to sons and women. They have a obligation.

"Maybe." Sweet William gazed out at the rolling sky. The rain came suddenly and ended suddenly and came again suddenly and ended in a spurt, as if each cloud dropped its load and moved on to make space for the up-and-coming one. "Right now I ain't studying on it."

"Son, take it from me. Fairy Enlow's kind is a dime a dozen. They get themselves knocked up and trick green fellows like you into marryin'. Then where would you be? Trapped in a coal mine the rest of your life, chokin' to death of silicosis."

"That won't happen to me!"

"Yeah, well, that's what they all say."

"I mean it! I'm gonna be a doctor!"

"You better!"

Abe didn't like the stress of stringing words, even though he couldn't seem to stop once he got started. He had rehearsed a speech a dozen times in his head and planned to explain to the boy that smart sex is one thing and stupid sex another. Maybe he would even admit he knew these things because he himself was the bastard child of some drifter.

"You say you were careful?" he asked, and raked a hand through his hair. He scratched the dark mark behind his right ear as if it were itching. "No chance of a screw up?"

"We're just friends is all."

"Don't bullshit me, boy!"

"I'm not."

"Because one mistake is all it takes."

"Trust me, Daddy!"

"*Trust me*? That's what they all say!" Abe's face shriveled with anger, and he chuckled a throaty sound meant for his meddling mother and backstabbing wife, his fake daddy and the rascal run-away whose gene pool he carried. "*Trust me* won't truck, boy! No sir-e-e, that dog won't hunt!"

Abe cut the silence that followed by yawning into his hand. It was one of those deep, drawn-out yawns that make a loud noise.

"If you're tired of driving, Daddy, I can take over. Uncle June took me for my driver's permit back in July."

Abe snorted. "Oh, he did, did he? Funny that nobody bothered to tell me."

"Wanta pull over? I need the experience."

"Thanks, but this chick is moody, won't behave for just anybody." Abe reached into his shirt pocket and took out a toothpick. "So June taught you, did he?"

"I could try."

"If June wants to play daddy, he should've had a kid of his own."

"He just wanted to help."

"Help, my eye! The man interferes is what he does. Just like his meddlesome daddy."

He knows I'll pay back every red cent of that loan Lily took behind my back and with plenty high interest. A slick businessman he is, and that's not to be confused with being generous, which is what he most definitely is not."

"He's slick, all right," Sweet William felt led to say. "Loves that almighty dollar!"

"Sly like a fox."

"Amen to that!"

When the two arrived at UK, Abe surveyed the campus of red-brick buildings, dormer windows, and wooden columns. He parked the Plymouth at Sweet William's dormitory beside a bed of straw-like flowers he knew Lily would've loved, and he pictured Rosy skating on the wide sidewalks.

"Let me carry that, Daddy," Sweet William said as Abe jumped out and reached for a cardboard box filled with jellies, breads, and Sweet William's favorite candies, all made from scratch.

"Just tell me where to go." Wheezing, Abe reached the dormitory, found the room, and stifled a groan as he bent to place the box on the floor. He wiped his face and neck with his handkerchief and hooked a chair with his foot.

Sweet William emptied his own arms and rushed to open a window. He returned with a smile on his face and eyes like Lily's when she had an occasion to nurse somebody.

"I don't know how to thank you," he said.

Abe was fidgety. He swung his arms to work out the stiffness. Not sure of where to put them, or how hard to press, he attempted to hug his son and make a fast exit. Will felt scrawny to him, too light for hard work. But it was okay, he told himself, since college students build brains and not muscles.

"Stay, Daddy, and I'll show you the campus," the boy said.

Abe leaned against the wall and breathed as if still carrying the box.

"Save it til when I come back with your mother. Today your ole man's got people to do and things to see." He stared at Will's suitcase, the same sissy satchel Lily had carried to Cumberland College. By Christmas he'd be able to buy him luggage fit for a man, he thought, plus the set of encyclopedias he'd promised the girls. "Mind you, stay away from that wild crowd," he said, "and hit them books like your mama. She's real proud, too. Practically hit the roof, she did, when I said this trip was to be just us men. I had to near swear we'd both of us come get you at Thanksgivin'."

"You don't need to go to all that trouble. I can hitch."

"You know how women are once they set their minds to somethin'."

"Speaking of Mama," Sweet William stuttered, "now's a tough time for her, what with Granddaddy so sick and me leaving and all. Try and be patient with her—not that you ain't already—but, I mean, let her talk when she needs to and make a point of listening. Maybe take her out to eat occasionally and buy her a present. Okay, Daddy?"

Abe stood up and nudged Sweet William's shoulder, rocking him sideways.

"Shoot, boy. You've not been gone from home a full day and already you're givin' your ole man advice. The thing is, women feel, men think, get me? Men cain't be bothered by all that whiny emotion crap. That's what women's got sisters and girlfriends for, to run their traps to." He shook his head as if amused by the boy's naïveté.

"Think so?"

"Hell, I don't think, I know. I guarandamntee it!"

Abe replaced the chair and walked toward the door. Before leaving, he checked out the small room with blond bunk beds, built-in desks, and matching dressers. The room was joined to a second room by a bathroom with shower, and he checked it out, too. Lily and the dodos would hit him with all kinds of questions, he thought, and he wanted to be ready.

"Is that it?" he asked. "Is there anything more I can do before I go?"

"I think we're good."

"Now remember what I said. Keep a cool head and don't do nothin' I wouldn't do."

"I will. I won't," the boy teased, and Abe noticed his fine teeth like Lily's. He discovered his long neck and big ears like Wade Eakins' and felt sad that he hadn't noticed them earlier. Hadn't had time to chat with his one son at the supper table, check his homework, attend his baseball and basketball games, and teach him to drive instead of June.

What a crying shame, he thought, and left wishing he could turn back time.

CHAPTER TWENTY-ONE

From the screen door Lily watched Sherman settle into his porch rocker instead of a bed. Hoarse, he talked to himself while staring at his birthplace on Patterson Mountain. He wrung his hands until they were as dry as kindling and shook away the snores from his little cat naps.

"You should come in from the breeze," she said as she joined him. Chilled, she crossed her arms against her chest and tried not to shiver. "It's not good for your throat."

"You're afraid I'll catch my death, are you?" A smile played on his lips. His sense of humor told her the morphine Dr. Humfleet prescribed was working, and she was glad. He nudged a second rocker from against the wall and patted the seat.

Lily was afraid to sit, afraid she might relax with her dear friend to the point of spilling out anguish. The last thing on earth she wanted was to add to his pain.

"I'm afraid if I rest I'll get rusty," she answered.

He gripped her hand, a weak little gesture that vibrated like a heartbeat.

"Lily, I ain't blind as to what's going on between you and Abe."

She saw both kinds of pain on his face and spoke fast to ease both his throat and heart.

"It's just a spat," she said, but the piercing look on his face said he knew she was lying. "Someone told Abe about the barn-house and Silas Holmes, and he left for Lexington mad."

Knowing that dogs go mad and people go angry, she still chose the word *mad* when describing Abe in his black mood.

"It ain't often we get a chance to catch up. Sit with me, why don't you?" he asked.

They agreed to go to the kitchen, where Lily poured him coffee and chamomile tea for herself. She pushed aside her mending, and they sat down facing each other on opposite sides of the table. Out the window, Maude and Rosy started a fire with newspapers, kindling, and old paraffin rings. Over it, a sooty iron pot of wash water dangled from a tripod, and Lily hoped it would warm slowly.

"Lily, I ain't got long here and I need to depart from this world knowing everything's gonna work out between you two," Sherman said.

"It's all my fault. I kept the barn-house a secret from him, as you well know." She paused, hoping he would mention Maude. Now that some time had passed, she wondered if she'd been rash when calling Vi the informer. "A reckoning is coming and, well, quite frankly, Abe and I will need all the prayers we can get." She paused again, thinking of Maude's probable deceit and wondering if she should mention it. "I'm not claiming Abe's an easy man to live with, but I don't know a soul who tries harder, works harder. If good intentions count, he has paved himself a sure path to glory. Me, I'm the one that's fallen short."

"Nobody needs to tell me what a good man he is." Sherman drew a deep breath and exhaled, causing his ribs to poke up from his shirt like the ripples on a washboard. Smoke from outside caused him to cough. "But, the man is too quick to anger."

"And his own worst enemy."

"Maude says he's going back to them mines."

Once again she yearned to hear Sherman speak of Maude's strange hold over Abe. She longed to know if Maude had plotted to keep Abe all to herself, and why she would go to such extremes. But Sherman seemed as anxious to talk about Abe as she was to talk about Maude. Day after day she'd watched his eyes tear up when he thought no one was watching, and she wanted nothing more than to ease his suffering.

"Try not to worry," she said. "Things have a way of working out."

Sherman cast her a look that said he questioned her judgment. He touched his throat with his hand, and she brought him hot coffee.

"You don't know how much I wish I could undo all the wrong I done him, Lily, back before I got saved. I was a sorry drunk then. Thanks to me, he saw bad things he shouldn't of. Maude, she tried to make up for it. She called him *Son Boy* and *My Little Man* and smothered him with love I myself wanted. None of this is your fault. I'm the one took him into that hellhole and left him, thinking it would turn him into a man and punish her to boot. Maude, she thinks he was cursed when the lightning struck, but it was me and that mine that had him sell his soul to the devil."

"No, Pop, no! Abe's soul is not sold. He's free to do whatever he chooses, and you yourself just said he's a good man. Maybe you did force him into that mine pit, but he stayed of his own free will."

Sherman's folded hands were shaky against the table. He reached for the coffee and made a rattle sound.

"I still say Maude's right. Mining coal cast some sort of spell over him, Lily. It's like it's a religion, and him a worshipper. *I look into the hills from whence cometh my strength,* the Bible says. Coal makes steel, and making steel gave Abe the feeling he was somebody big and important." He stopped to clear his throat. "The *black gold,* they call it but to him it's more like the *black god,* something he can put all his faith in, something that won't ever let him down. For too long I've stood by and watched him look to that high tipple like it's a church steeple and me knowing it'll be his tombstone."

"Now Sherman, we can't know that for sure. It's true he puts his faith in coal, but mining coal is all he's ever known. Now that he's finally found the courage to try something new, he might come to like it."

"The man is scairt of his own shadow," Sherman sputtered. "To this day he clings to his mother."

Lily sat up and bent close. Seeing that his throat was giving out, she rushed ahead.

"Pop, there's so much I don't understand about those two, and I've been hoping you could give me some insight. It's like Abe can't live with Maude, and he can't live without her. Please, please, tell me what she's holding over him that makes him so attached?"

"It's his conscience."

"But why? What has he done to feel guilty about?"

"Way back I gave Maude my word. She's proud and I said I'd never tell."

"But surely, you would if you knew it might help save our marriage."

Noises came from out back, and Lily cringed at the sound of Maude and Rosy climbing the porch steps.

Sherman dipped his head into his hands. He looked up wild-eyed, waving a finger.

"Watch out for her, Lily!"

"Don't you worry. Abe and I will always see that she doesn't want for a thing."

"No! No! I mean..." he was saying when one door suddenly opened, and another one closed.

Lily knew Abe was not one to linger. She tensed up that evening when supper was cold, and he had not come home from UK. With all her heart she wanted to trust him, but her intuition said he was hunkered in the shadows of some road joint, drinking liquor with pensioned coal miners and such.

She insisted that the girls go with June and Eula to evening worship while she stayed home to pray. Knowing Abe would be grieving over his son's leaving home and his dying daddy, in addition to the barn conflict, filled her with such remorse that the conflicts with Maude and Vi seemed almost trivial in comparison. She contemplated the harsh way she'd treated him and wished she could go back and redo it. Every fiber of her body hoped her prayers would be answered, and that he would come home to forgive her and start over. Where they would live, even if it meant a mining camp with disillusioned children mattered less at this time. To them she had made a promise. To Him she had made an oath under God.

Thanks to Dr. Humfleet, Sherman was sleeping soundly in his bed. To calm her growing sense of doom, she did small household chores like dusting, straightening, and sorting clothes. She tried mending, but finding the stillness gave her too much time to think, she pulled out the vacuum cleaner in spite of it being Sunday.

Iris will breathe better now, she told herself as she drove the appliance over furniture and floors. It was nine o'clock.

Perhaps Abe had toured the campus and lost track of time or maybe the Plymouth had broken down, and he was stranded. Actually, his absence at so late an hour was not all that unusual, considering the distance he had to travel. And yet, she suspected, knew with the inherited intuition of her wise-woman ma, that he was not coming home.

Not this night for sure, and maybe never.

Lily tidied her hair and rouged her weary face in an attempt to appear hopeful. Maude had ridden to church with a neighbor and arrived home just after the girls. The girls rushed inside, wind and rain at their coattails. They inquired about their daddy and, assured by Lily, went to the loft to do homework. Expecting Maude to make a fuss, Lily ordered Rosy there as well.

"Abe's not home yet?" Maude said at the door. She dropped her Bible and prayer shawl and rushed to the stove to cook him a hot supper.

"No."

"Has anyone heard from him? June, maybe?"

"Not that I know of." The single syllables gave Lily a false sense of control. They masked the quiver in her voice and the intense resentment she felt for this woman who had likely schemed to break up her home. The urge to confront Maude hit her so hard, she felt the usual shaky hands and weak stomach. But she knew better than to act without getting Abe's permission. Hopefully, he would believe her and give his immediate family priority over his conniving mother.

Maude reached for the cast-iron skillet. She took out some lard and russet potatoes and ran the old tin knife over a whetstone. The wind picked up speed. Tree limbs swished before cracking. Porch chairs rocked. A kettle on the back porch skidded off a two-penny nail.

"It's coming up a storm," she told Lily. "Better get out some candles."

"It could blow over."

"They're calling for flash floods."

"Only a slim chance."

Sparks crackled in the cookstove Lily had left to burn out, and Maude kindled a blaze.

"He'll come hungry," she said, "and needing a bath."

"No doubt."

"Any idea what's keeping him?"

"None."

"Could be the weather. The fog's bad tonight."

"Maybe so."

Lily filled a glass with water and counted out Sherman's pills. She was headed to his bedroom when Maude tagged her elbow.

"You know, I could help you with Sherman now that the barn-house is done."

"He'll need all the help he can get," Lily said and pushed on.

"I ain't a nurse and I don't pretend to love him like you do but I've spent near a lifetime coddling that ornery old man. They ain't no reason why I should stop now. No reason excepting that he prefers you."

No reason. No reason! In spite of her resolve to wait for Abe, Lily felt the fire outrunning the firefighter.

"Hypocrite!" spilled from her mouth as pills rolled and a sliding glass tilted the tray she was holding. Luckily she thought of Sherman and the need to lower her voice.

"Lily!"

"Your offer to help came too late, Maude. In case you haven't noticed, your husband is dying."

"I would've offered earlier but I thought you loved nursing. I thought it gave you something to do, a reason to stay here."

Lily put down the tray and held up four fingers.

"March, April, May, June—who took care of Pop then, Maude? Before we came?"

"I did. Night and day."

"Did you?"

"God as my witness, I did."

"That's not what I heard. I heard Dr. Humfleet told you in March that Sherman had cancer and needed radiation, and you would have no part of it."

Maude clutched the back of a table chair.

"Sherman wouldn't spend the money."

"Dr. Humfleet even came to the house to plead, and you sent him away at the gate. You should know he came to us with the truth, but by then it was too late."

"Well, I swan. So you two've been sneaking behind my back and in my own house?"

Lily smirked over the issues of who had been sneaking, and whose house it was. She noticed that Maude's response had completely overlooked the matter of Sherman's impending death.

"We tried to save him."

"I told you, Lily. Sherman put his trust in the Lord. We had laying on of hands at church and healing comes through faith. Sherman and me felt God was saying he needed to hold firm to his faith."

"Sherman needed the care of a doctor!"

"Sherman said he didn't have the money for a doctor. He told me, no doctor! "

"But you had a nest egg, right?"

"Lordy, girl, watch your tongue!"

"I will not watch my tongue! All my life I have watched my tongue. Now I will fight for my family!"

Maude fanned herself with her handkerchief as though she might faint.

"Well, well, so the time has come. Like it was yesterday, I remember making my own stand. But you be prepared, girlie. With them Siler men, there's a price to be paid. You stand up to them and it's like the first time leaving home. Once you pack up and go, they ain't no turning back."

Lily felt a chill and then a sweat come over her, and she reminded herself to back away and wait for Abe. To go give Sherman his medications, stay there, and pray. But the rage in her struck a blow at reason, control, calm—any form of intelligence. The bell tolled, and she met the moment.

"You tricked me. You told Abe about the barn-house and Silas Holmes, and you blamed Pa and me."

Maude stood erect. Her eyes flashed with anger.

"And so I did."

"And I suppose God had you do it?"

"God understood why I had to. You invited those sinners here from Cordel-Lewis to tempt Abe back to the darkness. You were planning to take him and go and you can't say you wadn't. No matter how much I care about you and these younguns, I will not stand by and watch you hand him back to the devil!"

"Dog and Ceola? Sinners? Why, they're church members like us."

"The devil does his finest work while at church."

"And to think I trusted you over my own sister."

"Listen, Lily. Listen to the Bible: *For every one that doeth evil hateth the light, neither cometh to the light, lest his deeds should be reproved.*"

"The Bible again!"

"But he that doeth truth cometh to the light, that his deeds may be made manifest, that they are wrought in God. Read John 3:16-21, Lily. Please! Read the verses and take them to heart. Then you will understand that I done what I had to."

"You tried to lure this family into a hole far blacker than any mine pit. That's what you did!"

"The boy had to be saved twice. Not just from that filthy mine but from hellfire and damnation. You had your chance and made light of it."

"And you were willing to break the hearts of your grand-children to get even."

"No, no. I did it for them. If he don't die in a coal mine— he'll die from one. This way we at least stand a chance."

"And now he's probably drunk and sulking in some sleazy road house. Making plans to get away from us all."

"The good Lord promised to watch over him. Faith heals!"

"Like faith has healed Sherman?"

Lily reached for Sherman's tray, and Maude escaped outside, where she pulled her black dress above her ankles and tore out to the cave. The path rose and fell at steep angles. Thickets loomed under a chalky slice of moon. She gripped her Bible and forged ahead, her feet and one arm feeling the way.

She knew the lay of the land as well as she knew the sag of the cot she slept on at night, but darkness and tearful eyes tested her, and she moved like a cat. Twice she stumbled and fell, once into a patch of stinging nettle and another into a bed of fuzzy clover. She lay there resting and remembering the clover necklace Caleb, her first and last love, had laced her. The sweetness of him who had disappeared made her smile, in spite of the pain, past and present.

Beyond a barbed-wire fence and a creek with a log bridge, she arrived at a clearing where the two had stretched out on a blanket. In a corner rose a hillside, and at its base arched an opening the size of a washtub. Pushing through a stand of red sumacs, she cleared the brush and fieldstones hiding the entrance, shooed away some bats, and crawled inside.

The air was cool and damp. It gave off the smell of mud and feces. From the rear of the cave, rats made scratching sounds; crickets chirped their last songs before winter. The roof rose, and she walked directly to a straw pallet beside half an oil drum used to hold fire. Nearby stood a rusty tricycle, and a whip made out of cowhide. Dropping down on the pallet under the cave's highest point, she lit a candle and opened her Bible.

For a time she read in silence, then mumbled in tongues with increasing fervor. When drunk with the holy spirit, she unbuttoned her dress and let it fall from her shoulders. The candle flickered as she swung the whip toward her flesh and moaned, sometimes screamed, from the anguish. Her right arm gave out, and she resumed with her left. Both arms spent, she dressed, wrapped herself in the shawl, and turned onto her side.

"No turning back," she muttered to the stirring night creatures. "Once you find your tongue, they ain't no-o-o turning
back!"

CHAPTER TWENTY-TWO

The next morning Lily slipped into Sherman's room while he slept and removed the odorous chamber pot that he called a *slop jar*. When he woke, she bathed his upper body, placed a wash pan and soapy cloth nearby, and disappeared while he fumbled the job to its finish. She returned with a pair of clean pajamas and bedroom slippers instead of his usual overalls and farm shoes. He dressed alone, and she came again with buttery oatmeal and hot biscuits.

"Bless me," she heard him say while turning away from the food. His face was red and hot with fever, and his breaths shallow. She felt his pulse and frowned.

"Pop, God blessed you years back when you got saved. Whatever you might've done in the past is bygones. He is all grace and mercy, and you will sit at His throne."

"Bless me," he appeared to say again, more anxious than before, and she sat down close.

"Your house is in order, Pop. You're a good man and ready to meet the Maker. He's prepared a safe and lasting place for you. You can rest now with no more sorrows."

Rosy wandered into the room, bringing her granddaddy a jar of wild butterfly weed in a glass jar with no water.

"Is Granddaddy okay?" she asked.

Lily nodded, placed the flowers on his bedside table, and suggested she sit on the small stool in a corner. She had so little time to give the child, anything, she told herself, was better than no attention at all.

"Do you want me to call the preacher? Should I call Pa?" Lily asked, and tried to make Sherman eat.

"No," his pinched face said, and he seemed to repeat, "Bless me."

She slipped from the room and came back with a pencil and pad of paper that she laid on the table.

"Write down what you mean," she said, and he felt for the pad.

"Why is Granddaddy asking for Auntie Blessie?" Rosy whispered.

Blessie, Maude's younger sister, Lily thought. But why on earth would he be calling for her now?

"Pop, do you want me to call Maude's sister, Blessie? Should I have her come for a visit?"

To her surprise, he dropped the pad, nodded, and closed his eyes as if to say some heavy burden had been lifted.

"I'll do it, of course," she said, and he nodded before drifting off to sleep.

"When's Daddy coming home?" Rosy whined when she heard her granddaddy snoring.

"He's coming soon. Real soon. Go get me a brush, and I'll make you pretty," Lily answered.

Rosy didn't move from the stool.

"But you said that before."

"So I did. But I spoke too soon."

"I'm afraid Daddy got lost in the dark."

Lily had that same fear, but in a different sense.

"Maybe, but he can always stop for directions."

"But places close on Sunday. Maybe I should send Hairy out to find him."

Lily tidied the room, switched off the light, and reached for Rosy's hand.

"Huh? Should I wake up Hairy?"

"You do that, honey."

Abe's joints ached from the travel, and his brain felt fuzzy. Sawdust and sun from the construction job had dried out his lips. He nibbled at some flakes of loose skin and imagined the silky smooth taste of something cool and biting. At a pawnshop near the University, he hocked his old Benrus watch, bought two pints of Kentucky Bourbon, and took to the road. One pint would do the trick, but two gave him a certain safe feeling, like the 10 dollar bill staring up from his wallet. He put one pint in the glove compartment and the other in his jacket pocket. Not because he was one to drink and drive, but because he liked having something to hold on to.

As a rule he loved driving alone, just him and the Plymouth, smoking and humming and listening to each other's gripes, coughs, rattles, and so forth. Only recently he'd discovered a patch of road through a rusted hole in the car's front flooring. The possibility that the two were aging together struck him as both sad and funny, like Lily's clay clown with two different faces.

Lights loomed. The mass of city horns made him jittery. The streets were poorly marked, and curves came out of nowhere. If'n he'd let Lily come along, he wouldn't be feeling so nervous, he admitted. If'n, a word coined for dreamers, and losers like himself and the Plymouth.

Shifting to more practical matters, he thought about the life insurance policy he'd bought the year Will was born. Not one payment had he missed in eighteen years, which hadn't been easy. The possibility of suicide, maybe death by way of a car accident, came and went. That the policy might educate his kids while he slept on the job brought on his usual sarcastic chuckle.

"No, sir. Abe Siler won't be put down til he shuts down!" he said, and he thought of his always jabbering mother. Jabbering and old—exactly where he was headed if he didn't shut off the brain rattle.

He forgot it was Sunday and switched on the radio to find nothing but preaching.

"Not tonight," he said, and turned the dial. But the familiar words of an old hymn, "At the Cross...where I first saw the light, and where the burden of my heart rolled away," touched him, and he felt the hunger, the all-out craving of a sinner for God.

In the town of Richmond, Abe spotted Lucky's Bar and Grill and stopped for a grilled-cheese sandwich and coffee. The log cabin sat within a square of dusty cars and pickups. Inside, chrome bar stools matched a bubbling Wurlitzer jukebox. The smell of onions and French fries made his mouth water. It reminded him that he had not eaten since Shoney's.

He checked out the smoky place and liked its dark and manly mood, its odor of poverty. He ordered and sidled toward a big open area where he played pinball and shot pool with two bearded loggers. Then he drifted into a smaller, more private room and joined three has-been coal miners in a lively game of five-card stud.

"I ain't got long," he said. He called for a second coffee and considered ordering a round of beer for the boys. Then he thought of Will at lunch, swearing he wasn't hungry. He thought of his family, who he knew would be worried sick if he didn't make it home soon. His heart raced. Compared to this heart pain, the pain in his lungs was the mere sting of a splinter.

The miners gave their usual spiel about the safety hazards they'd faced while mining coal. Most accounts started with: "The bosses had us...." They spoke of lying on their sides or crawling with short-handled shovels and picks in coal seams 18-inches thick; of bolting machines that torqued at 400 pounds, when 150-180 was normal; of crooked inspectors who conducted clean dust tests outside the mine; of live wires tickling their backs while their feet stood ankle deep in underground spring water; of striking up to five matches inside a mine without air enough to light one. And still they joked like clowns in a hospital for terminally ill children. Bent, crippled, missing limbs and memory, not one of them, not even Abe, could remember having been injured.

He thought to check the time and remembered he'd pawned his Benrus watch. It was between shifts, and traffic was thinning. If he hurried, he could make it home before the Squirt went to bed and Lily got all fired up. He ordered a cup of hot black coffee to go, collected his meager winnings, and went looking for the Plymouth Roadking and the snaggle-toothed ridge that meant home.

Once on the road, he lit a Camel and dialed a country music station buzzing with static.

"Gees! Wimps! Get a life, will ya?" he barked at Kitty Wells for whining about cheating hearts. "I got my own damn problems, get me?"

Johnny Cash was singing "Hello Stranger" when he reached for the pint bottle in his pocket, and took a big swig.

"Stranger!" he screamed at the no-good rascal that knocked-up his mother and ran out on them both.

"Stranger!" he shouted at Lily, her brother June, Wade Eakins, and Sherman, a wimp like June, who had settled for another man's son because he wasn't man enough to make one of his own. "Sonovabitch!"..."Coward!"..."Two-bit phony!"

Takes one to know one! he imagined Sherman coming back at him, and he swigged again and again.

"Why you god-damned, yellow-bellied, good-for-nothin' shell of a man! Calling yourself *daddy* like that entitles you to beat the livin' crap out of a kid and his mother and expect to be loved for it!"

Look who's talking! Look who run out!

"I never laid a hand on Lily!"

You might as well of.

He took another swig, and another.

"Hell, I can be had but I ain't no pushover!" He tightened the hand on the steering wheel and leaned forward to see the road better. "Tried to pull the wool over my eyes, did you? Well let me tell you, I knew! All along I knew you was a fake daddy."

He spotted a place where a tractor path ran between two fields of tall cornstalks, followed it, and stopped beside a rut wide enough for two foxhole buddies, or a man and his guitar. He had sworn that, come hell or high water, he would see home this very night. But he was not one to endanger others' lives by driving under the influence.

The almost full moon was close and round, so bright he had the feeling of being on a lit stage, and all wired up for a show. Using his jacket for a sleeping bag, his shoes for a pillow, and the young Lily for a companion, he settled into his spot, then sat up and reached for his guitar. "I'm Thinking Tonight of My *Brown* Eyes," followed by "*Brown* Eyes Crying in the Rain," gave him a homey, happy feeling. While Lily teased him into her pa's toolshed and purred like at Bryce's Cove, he played and sang and loved and enjoyed the first vacation he'd had since the day he stopped drinking.

On the road by nine the next morning, Abe had the old hangover, made worse by fatigue and chain smoking. A dirt-and-dew blend smudged the sleeves of his white cotton shirt; his damp pants felt cold against his unsteady legs. A mile down the road he stopped at a creek to wash up and cringed at the sight of his scruffy face in the water. What he wouldn't give for some soap and a razor! He took the time to spot wash his shirt and put it on wet, then set out for Saxton, stopping only for coffee to wash down a Goody's Powder.

Less than two hours later he reached the town of Corbin, wolfed down coffee from Jerry's drive-in, and moved on. He was fifteen miles north of Saxton when Harlan road signs caught his attention like flashing neon lights at nighttime. He pictured a camp band playing music on a crowded front porch. He heard the creaking porch swing and the cries of little kids catching fireflies in Mason jars. Although he wasn't hungry, he had an intense craving for Ceola's fried apple pies, the dough fried fast like bacon to make it brown and crunchy.

Brakes squealed and angry drivers honked horns when he swerved the Plymouth toward the Cumberland Plateau and big Black Mountain. Past leaning shacks and played-out mines he drove until he reached the dusty black shingle that had once read "Cordel-Lewis No.1 Mine."

CHAPTER TWENTY-THREE

The mine manager sat behind a desk strewn with maps, charts, paper coffee cups, and cigarette ashes. His right hand against his mouth held a pencil. When Abe appeared in the doorway, he dropped what he was holding, jumped up, and threw out a hand.

"Why you old son-of-a-gun! I never gave up hoping!" He pointed to a round-back captain's chair and returned to his own swivel chair while Abe continued to stand, his hands in his jacket pockets, fumbling the rabbit's-foot keychain. "What kept you so long?"

"Yeah, well, I got waylaid."

"I'd say! And the family?"

"They're hangin' in."

"Like I said, this place ain't been the same without you."

"Thank ye." Abe looked around at the familiar wall maps, glass-block walls, and concrete floor marbled with dust cracks.

The manager opened his desk drawer, took out a disk—a metal tag with a miner's personal number, taken off a board as the miner enters the mine and returned as he exits safely—and made a perfect toss.

"You ready to get started?"

Abe caught the disk, studied it, and sailed it back to the manager.

"Seriously, you must've heard Dog's heart can't take the dust anymore and we'll soon be needin' a new night foreman. Or, in your case, a day foreman if you want it."

Abe frowned. "You're sayin' Dog's heart's worse now?"

"Apparently. I thought you knew he had a attack. Come to think of it, it might've been a secret."

"Yeah, well, maybe he mentioned it."

"As you know, spirits are low. You may be just what the men need."

"The need for coal fell after the war. That's the problem in a nutshell. Without a miracle, this mine's playing out like all them other ones."

Afraid to open his mouth, afraid *yes* might tumble out, Abe shook his head.

"There's bound to be somebody else." He recalled that during his last visit with Dog, he had asked about his health and Dog had answered with a smile and thumbs up.

"Nope."

"Import somebody."

"The men would raise holy hell."

"Maybe I'll give it some thought but don't count on it."

"Fair enough." The manager bit down on his pencil. When Abe turned to go, he vaulted up and grabbed his right shoulder. "We're talking time here, Abe. Like I said, a good man such as yourself might could save her."

"Roger."

"The better the sooner."

"Yo," Abe said and smiled at the word play. Outside, he waited before letting go of the doorknob. To the east clouds gathered. They swooped low to the ground. If he went now, he might could outrun the rain. But then Ceola wouldn't never forgive him if she learned he was in camp and hadn't stopped by at least long enough to sample one of her blue-ribbon cookies. And what if Dog, his best friend, died before he had a chance to say goodbye?

By godly, he had no choice but to go calling.

Boys playing hooky from school knocked on front doors with a message. Wives turned off the heat under boiling pots and scurried to their gossip stations along back fences. Peddlers screamed from their carts on the street:

"Abe Siler's back!"

The camp rallied as it would for a Fourth of July gala. People showed up at Ceola's dressed for a come-as-you-are party. Men toted infants and toddlers on their shoulders, or pulled them in little red wagons. Women brought leftovers or canned goods or quickie desserts sprinkled with dried fruits and nuts. Young people dropped off their schoolbooks at home and hurried to catch up. Even Palatia Porter came, her rhinestoned miniature poodle, Fifi, looking up from a pocket.

"I ain't got long to stay," Abe said.

"At least stay long enough to dry out," Dog said with his big gap-toothed smile and laugh lines fanning from the corners of his sparkling eyes.

"I'll fix you a plate," Ceola said.

"No thanks, I ain't hungry."

"You will be." She waddled into the kitchen and came back with two paper plates, the second filled with desserts.

Abe reached for his guitar. His band, a group of six including Dog and Ceola, presently four, opened with Bill Monroe's song, "Molly and Tenbrooks," about two old race horses. The clippety-clop rhythm sent cloggers to the front porch in spite of the wind.

"One more and I'll be heading out," he said after four songs, three cups of coffee, and some grabs at his barely touched food.

"Shucks! You just got here!" someone spoke up.

"I know, but the family, they'll be worried."

"Hell, they're coal people. Worry is their middle name!"

"Another time, boys."

The day shift ended, and more miners piled in wearing their work clothes.

"You cain't go now! You'll hurt our feelings!" they complained.

Weakness crawled along Abe's body. His head felt light, and his feet felt heavy. Requests poured in, and more instruments came out, the improvised kind. Even the humor was music to his ears.

Uncle handed him a jug.

"No can do," he said. But after one quick sip for the hell of it, he took another...and another.

What Uncle lacked in youth, he made up for in wit. Age gave him a certain license with vulgarity, especially when in the company of miners and musicians.

"Hey, Dog, is it true what they claim about fat ladies bein' oversexed? I hear tell they got so many of them sex hormones, why, they'll take it in any wrinkle!" he joked between songs.

Dog looked around. The women, all but Ceola, were off gossiping or dancing the combs from their hair. Teenagers played Post Office and Spin the Bottle under a lean-to out back.

"Well, now, fellers, I don't rightly know if fat cells hold hormones but I know for a fact they hold a helluva lot of sugar. Ceola here, she's so fat when she walks her buns clap. But kissin' that gal is like eatin' a juicy ripe watermelon. Ain't no way you gonna stop after just one bite."

"That's my lover boy!" Ceola hooted, and sawed down on her fiddle.

"A-l-l-l right!" Josh Payne whooped.

"I'll drink to that!" another pitched in, followed by others, not in any order but in a rhythm so in tune it sounded rehearsed.

"Now you fellers just hold your durn horses!" Floyd Bowes, rot-gut whiskey boiling in his belly, added. "Me, I got myself a skinny woman and she's right sweet herself. Ever' night we're frisky I tell her, Sugar, don't you worry about them jugs you don't got 'cause more'n a mouthful's too much!"

"Whoa, buddy!"

"I'll drink t' that!"

"Skinny woman, my eye! Hell, I'm hangin' with Dog, here! I like me a woman what's got some meat on her bones. Love handles, I call 'em. My gal's so fat I can roll over her and still be on top. By the time I git off, it's time to get right back on. But do you hear me complainin'? N-u-u-u buddy!"

"Whu e-e-e!"

"I'll drink t' that!"

"My wife's fat and b'damned if I don't love ever' last bite. Babe, you got the makings of one fine automobile, I tell her. More cushion for the pushin', I say! More bounce per ounce! Ain't that right, Honest Abe?"

Abe dropped his jaw and cleared the gravels from his throat.

"Well, boys, I reckon that depends on how you look at it, now don't it? Myself, I'm personally inclined to hang with my ole buddy, Ben Franklin, what claimed all cats are gray in the dark. Meaning if'n I've worked me up a good appetite, hell, I ain't finicky about the pickin's. Just so long as I've got both meat and 'taters on my plate and the right to go back for seconds, why, hell, I'll take fat or skinny, provided it ain't overpriced."

A riot of two-fingered whistles, feet stomping, pop crates rocking, and waving Mason jars or jugs followed.

"Lily would kill him!" someone hooted.

"H'm, H'm, H'm, H'm, H'm!"

"I'll drink t' that!"

"You tell 'em, Honest Abe!"

"That's Honest Abe fer you!"

"When you comin' back for good, Abe?"

While they celebrated him, Abe meandered toward the center of the porch, where he stood inside a circle of worshippers. Under the glare of a naked ceiling bulb, his toothpick wavering between his teeth, he grinned and picked and savored the flavor of those mouth-wateringest of words:

"Take it away, boys!"

Abe had left Buck Creek for UK on Sunday. By Monday night, Lily felt she was back in a mining camp, gulping down herbal tea and slipping the children her ma's sedative made of oat seed and straw. What if Sherman should die before Abe gets home? she asked herself. What if Abe doesn't come home at all? Who, then, would look after his mother? The thoughts filled her with a mixture of both sorrow and horror. She decided that come morning, even without Abe's permission, she would grant Sherman his wish. She would go to the store and call Blessie, Maude's sister. Hopefully Blessie would do them the favor of taking Maude off their hands, just as Sherman had no doubt planned.

"Please don't make us go to bed!" the children pleaded as they sat hunched over their schoolbooks, waiting for their daddy.

"A few minutes longer then," Lily conceded.

In the kitchen Maude stirred pinto beans and fried potatoes and peered out the north window every time a leaf rustled. Finally she saw car lights and flew outside just behind Lily.

"It was my brother June," Lily said as he drove away. "He was in a hurry."

"Did he know anything about Abe?"

"He said Abe's okay and will be home tomorrow." Lily made no reference to Ceola, who had been the one to call June. Nor did she say he was brief because he was so furious at Abe for running out on the job.

"Thank you, Sweet Jesus!" Maude sniffled and took out her damp handkerchief. "Did June say where he was?"

"I gather not far away."

"Let's just pray he's not up to some mischief!"

"Be grateful he's safe."

"My poor fated boy!"

"Maude, I'd rather you not say that before the girls," Lily said and walked away to avoid a discussion.

"Mama, why does Grandmother always claim Daddy's fated?" Rosy asked when Lily returned to the living room. "What does *fated* mean?"

"Because she's a fanatic!" Verni said, and Lily shot her a disapproving look.

"What's a *fanatic*?"

"It's someone who feels strongly," Lily whispered. "She's your daddy's mother. He's late coming home. It's only natural she would worry."

"Verni says she thinks Daddy's gone back to drinking."

Lily's eyes sought out Maude in the kitchen. Relieved to see that she had gone into the pantry, she turned to Verni with a warning look on her face.

"Verni, of all times! Sometimes I just don't understand you!"

"Well, it's true, ain't it?"

"No, it's not true. You and I are due to have a talk, young lady! Or maybe I'll let your daddy do it."

"I'm sorry," Verni said with Daddy fear on her face.

"Now you all go to bed." Lily spooned out some nightly doses of cod liver oil while pretending not to see the disgusted looks on the younger one's faces. "And don't forget to brush teeth."

"But how can we sleep til we know for sure Daddy's safe?" Rosy protested.

"Tell you what. If he's not home when you wake up, I'll go find him."

Verni chuckled. "And just how will you do that? On a magic carpet?"

"I'll drive Pop's truck. Rosy, tonight you can sleep in Sweet William's bed, but not a peep out of you, hear?"

The girls began their nightly climb to the loft, and Verni fell behind.

"Could you really drive Granddaddy's truck or were you just bluffing?" she challenged.

"If June charged the battery, I could."

"I don't believe it. When did you learn how?"

"When I had to."

CHAPTER TWENTY-FOUR

Close to eight o'clock, the party people left, and Abe fell asleep on Ceola's rippled corduroy sofa. Ceola washed his clothes as he slept, and the next morning she woke him early for a tub bath and breakfast. Once he passed her grooming test, she sent him off with cookies for the kids and the tongue lashing he'd expected.

"I swear to Wod, Abe, if I find out you've pulled a stunt like this again, I'll find you and wring your neck myself, hear?"

"I'm sorry," he said from his heart. Still, the words never came easy.

"Don't tell me, tell Lily." She followed him to the Plymouth, all the while nagging.

"I'd just as soon Lily not know I fell off the wagon," he said and dropped his head.

"It won't come from me, so long as you get back on."

The two discussed Dog's health before saying goodbye, and Ceola begged him to consider coming back to the coal mine.

"Lily would have a fit."

"Talk to her. You may find she's more willing than you think."

"Not likely."

"You won't know til you try."

Between failed attempts at starting the engine, Abe dropped his hands and felt a tremor against his lap. Breaths came hard and hurt. He tried to sit up, shoulders high, and found himself sinking. Turning to the Man Upstairs, he asked to be forgiven for the awful way he'd treated his family, and he pleaded for the strength to once again give up liquor. On the road, he glanced toward the mine, looming in the shadow of its skeletal tipple. The yard was deserted now, except for what looked like some workmen laying track. He viewed the new track as a good sign, proof that Cordel-Lewis was in no immediate danger of playing out. Again he turned to the Man, this time with gratitude.

On Route 119-S, he passed ghost camps with only gasoline pumps and a post office to prove they'd existed. Flatbed trucks hauling scrap iron from closed mines hogged the narrow roads. Packs of hungry dogs canvassed ditches, looking for road kill. Riddled with parasites, they dragged their itching hindquarters over road ruts and coals.

At Williamsburg, he stopped for more coffee and pushed on to Saxton. The leaves were bright with color, but he didn't notice. He had never been one to take an interest in nature since both sun and sunset burned his night eyes. He thought only of Lily, and wished he'd at least thought to call and leave June a message. But what if June answered the phone and hit him with words like *fired* and *fed up*. Would he say, "June, don't get your bowels in a uproar?" Would he tell him to take the damn job and shove it? Or would he hang head and kowtow the way he had with Wade Eakins?

Just thinking about June made his breakfast sit bad on his stomach. It occurred to him more than once that June, and not Lily, might have been the reason he'd skipped town. Not just June, but the freakin' job. Wouldn't June have no other choice now but to fire him? Free him, in fact? What could a family man do then but go back to the one trade he knew?

Funny how the mind will play tricks on you, he was thinking when he approached Crab Orchard Lane. His palms sweated, and blood raced through his veins as he felt a run-for-your-life fear of facing not one but two angry women.

"Son Boy! Where have you been?"

Abe wormed out of the Plymouth and into Maude's greedy arms.

"Howdy," he said.

"You should be ashamed of yourself! You had us worried sick!" She felt his ribs. "Why, you're skinny as a rail! How long's it been since you eat?"

"I'm sorry, Mother."

"We thought you was dead!"

"I'm sorry. I really am."

"Whatever possessed you to...?"

"Car trouble." He pushed toward the fatback scent of something cooking and looked around for Lily. He pictured her stealing a last-minute glance at herself in a mirror, maybe brushing her hair over her shoulders the way he liked it.

...Or maybe she was tied up with nursing his daddy.

...Or mad because he'd stayed gone so long without calling.

...Or didn't give a hoot if'n he come home or not.

"How's Daddy?" he asked.

"He took a turn for the worse right after you left. Lily ain't had a free minute. He's been asking for you and Lily says you're the reason he's holding on. Lucky thing you got here when you did."

Abe shuddered, knowing if his daddy had died while he was away, Lily would never forgive him. And besides, his

grieving kids would need him around, in spite of the fact that
he was never around. The chance that he and his pretend daddy might patch things up before he died occurred to him, and
he dismissed the idea with a shrug and a scowl.

"And Lily?" he asked. "Where's Lily?"

"Gone."

He'd tried to avoid looking into her hard face, but his head
snapped around, running a sharp pain down his neck.

"Gone? Gone where?"

"I got no idea."

"She knew I was comin', right?"

"She knew, all right. June come and told us."

Rosy had recognized the Plymouth's rattle and run from
the privy, the hem of her dress hiked inside her panties. She
held out her arms, and he hoisted her up, in spite of his stiffness.

"Hey, Squirt," he said. "How goes it? How's come you're
not at school?"

"I sent Hairy out to find you!" She lay her head on his
shoulder. "Did you see him?"

"Did I? If it hadn't been for him, I'd still be lost."

"Goody, goody gumdrops!"

"Where's your mama?"

"Mama went looking for you."

"Vi took her?"

"She drove Granddaddy's truck."

"Drove Daddy's truck? Lily? Drove?" He imagined Lily as
a little girl, not much bigger than Rosy, steering her iron-
willed daddy out of the mine pit and up to the pulpit. He remembered her shaming her pa by leaving teaching to become
a nurse and, worse, marrying a coal miner. And now she was

driving a truck without asking her husband's permission. It figured.

"Well, I reckon she showed me!" he muttered from the back of his throat.

"You're sweating. Let's get you inside." Maude took hold of his arm. "I made some tapioca pudding just for you and that sweet tooth of yours."

"I ain't hungry."

"Then come have some coffee."

"So June taught her to drive, too?"

"What?"

"Nothin'."

A minute later Lily sped into the driveway and parked at the corn crib. Perched on Sherman's straw seat cushion, she looked tall and confident, like Vi in her convertible. She wore barrettes in her hair that he recognized as Verni's, a birthday gift from John Mason and Phoebe. She was even wearing lipstick and rouge like Vi. Funny, for twenty years he'd been married to this woman and he was just now noticing the family resemblance.

She darted out of the pickup, and they hugged as if overcome with joy. Both, however, let go the second they felt the other stiffen.

"I'm sorry, Lily. Sorry to the bone I've been gone so long. I reckon you think I'm one lousy scoundrel!"

"I'm sorry, too. We both have a lot to explain."

"I needed a chance to clear my head is all."

"And did you?"

"Hell, no!"

"You look exhausted. Come say hello to Pop, and then you should rest."

"Mother says he's worse."

"He is, yes. Critical. Dr. Humfleet says he could go any time."

"Too bad."

"Yes, it is," she said flatly, as if disappointed in his lack of feeling.

"Are you hungry?" she asked on the way to the house. He walked beside her, hurrying to keep up.

"I think Mother's gone to fix a little somethin'."

"Oh, yes, of course."

"I see June's taught you to drive. Congratulations. Great thing it is, independence."

"Vi taught me. Well, actually I taught myself by circling the farm a few hundred times."

"So now I s'pose you'll be getting' a license?"

"I hope so."

He cleared the catch in his throat to keep from coughing.

"I reckon June would be happy to take you the same as he took Will."

"No one blames you. You were busy putting food on the table."

"No, no. Good idea. Great idea, in fact. You never know but what you might be forced to take over a wheel sometime, especially now that Will's away at college."

"That's what June said."

"June was right. June's always right."

They reached the back door, and Lily waited for him to catch up.

"If you don't mind, give me a few minutes to prepare Pop before you go in. Then I'll leave you two alone."

"Cain't you stay on?"

She shook her head to the contrary.

"Promise you'll be kind?"

"Suretainly," he answered, and stood wondering how he could possibly be kind to one of the two bastards he'd spent his life hating.

Abe's feet felt like lead as he moved toward Sherman's room and the hideous stink of rotting flesh. Sherman sat upright on two pillows, his face still pink from the washcloth Lily had just used to give him a fresher look. His hair was parted neatly in a comb-over, and he put out the scent of Listerine and coconut oil. Lily had decided to let Abe's homecoming be a surprise. She left the room as he entered, and Sherman saw him and let out a shrill little cry. Abe stood with one hand on the doorknob. Speechless and needing a drink.

"How do," he said, hiding the shock of seeing the man he'd called *Daddy* look so emaciated, a mere skeleton with onionskin cover. He took three steps closer, removed his cap, and leaned down for a quick hug. Sherman patted a spot on the bed, very close to his face, and Abe hesitated before sitting down.

"You've been gone," Sherman said.

"Yep! Glad to be back."

"Forgive me, Son. I've hid things from you." Sherman rushed as if afraid of not finishing. "Things you should've knowed a long time ago." He sipped water through a straw, and Abe helped him stabilize the glass on the table. "Truth is, another man your mother loved better'n life was your real daddy and my younger brother. He up and died, leaving her poor and with child and, wanting her for myself, I convinced her to marry me so I could take care of them both. I hoped she might come to love me. When she didn't, I tried to make her think he'd run out." He stopped to work up a breath. "I drunk the pain away. I let the devil work through me and I was evil to you both. The note says it and more. I pray to God you'll forgive this old sinner who's loved you like his own since the day he was reborn."

Abe was speechless. The old man's confession, though short, struck him as real, more than something said for the sake of going to heaven. He'd made his own share of mistakes, he figured. Who was he to not forgive? The hand on his knee was so veiny, so smelly, Abe hesitated before touching it. But once he felt the humanness of it, he reached to touch the old man's face as well.

"Abe?" Sherman asked as if about to draw his last breath

"We're good," Abe said as his heart muttered the sorrowful tune of all they had missed.

CHAPTER TWENTY-FIVE

Lily's mind had run wild while she waited for Abe to come home from Lewellyn. During both nights of his absence, she had lain awake crying inwardly and asking herself how she would react when or if he returned. In a nightmare one night, she had watched Silas Holmes making love to Vi on Maude's kitchen floor while she and Abe sat handcuffed together in back-to-back chairs, no sheriff and no jail and no reason for the handcuffs. She awakened rubbing her wrists and wondering if the scene had suggested commitment...or bondage?

Now that he was back home, she tried her best to forget the old anguish. Regardless of the buts and what-ifs, she felt committed to her marriage and wanted nothing more than to resume her role as a dutiful wife. To cocoon herself within her family and celebrate blessings over burdens. Her son's enrollment at UK, for example.

Like everyone else, she cherished every word of Abe's report after his short nap with Sherman, but she longed for more personal details: What did Sweet William's campus and room look like?...Did he like his roommate?...Had father and son patched up their differences? Both she and the girls pestered him with questions while his mother sat smiling, overjoyed that he had come home.

That evening everyone ate a healthy supper and then watched "Gunsmoke" on television until Abe grew restless. He went outside to smoke, and Lily followed.

"How did you and Pop get along?" she asked him.

"It was good, real good."

"Did you two make peace?"

"He explained things that helped to clear the air between us. We both apologized and agreed to forgive."

"Great," she said, and felt led to ask as if teasing, "Then there were no dark family secrets?"

He hesitated before answering, no doubt thinking about the loyalty he owed his mother.

"None that I know of."

Bedtime came at ten. Lily and Abe undressed in opposite corners of the room and lay in bed with a pillow's width of space between them. Minutes passed, him smoking a cigarette and her working the high buttons of her long cotton nightgown. In the lamp-lit silence, she noticed the quiet outdoors, nature's small tenants in the act of hibernating or dying. She wished, as she had so often, that human conditions could be as predictable.

Maude was in the living room, banking the coal stove. Like a stack of unpaid bills, her presence was always there, even when it wasn't.

"I can't wait to hear more about Will," Lily said as an ice breaker. There was so much more she yearned to know, but because he was so exhausted she felt guilty asking. But then, she'd felt so lonely, so drained, during his absence, sleep, turning off the light, was now the last thing she wanted.

"Like I said, he's fine and dandy. We agreed to let bygones be bygones but not before I set him straight on some matters of importance."

"I knew you two would patch everything up. I'm sure you sounded very intelligent."

"Just gave him some pointers is all."

Lily couldn't wait to discuss the matter of Silas Holmes and the barn-house as well. But his eyes were closing, and once again she was not about to rush the matter of him and his mother.

"Thank you for giving Pop permission to die peacefully. It won't be long now," she said, and thought they had reached the end of their evening.

"Better he not suffer."

"I know."

He cocked an ear toward Maude as she slammed the stove handle. "The poor old gal don't ever stop, does she? Works like a trooper."

"I reckon not."

Guess my staying away 'bout killed her."

"She clung to her faith," Lily said.

"Especially at a time when Daddy was dying."

"God told her you were safe," she said and continued. "Abe, I know you're exhausted and with good reason, but I also know Maude told you about Silas Holmes, and I think you would sleep better knowing the whole truth."

The subject of his mother and guilt awakened him like a cup of hot black coffee, and he sat up to smoke while he listened.

"I'm sorry," she said for a start. "Truly sorry that I didn't take the time to explain the matter to you at Buck Creek. Sometimes I'm so focused like Pa, I allow efficiency to get in the way of kindness. I did you wrong, and I couldn't wait for the chance to say I'm sorry."

"No, Lily," he said. "All that don't matter now. The Plymouth didn't break down. It's me. I'm the one broke down. I helped Will settle in and drove straight to a bar. Stayed drunk as a skunk for two days and nights. Now I'm sorry as can be but that don't excuse me one bit. Don't matter what you did or didn't do, I'm the one went back on my promise. Weren't for my mason pledge I could be a drunk."

She touched a sleeve of his pajamas. Tonight, pajamas.

"It's okay. Anybody could've made that mistake considering all the pressure you've been under. The important thing is that you stop now."

"No, it ain't okay. Some kind of husband and daddy I turned out to be. Ain't worth the mud I was made of. You deserve better."

"But, Abe, I'm at fault, too. I knew in Lewellyn—Ceola told me—that you were about to be made mine foreman, and I pretended I didn't and let you come here, knowing you might very well regret it. You promised the children and me a home we didn't seem to get, and I thought that meant you were considering going back to the mine. I wanted a real home for the children so badly I went along with your mother's scheme to hire Silas Holmes. I agreed to keep him a secret and even help with the work. Then I changed my mind, but she had her way of pulling me back into it, which didn't seem to matter at the time because it was her project, and she was going to do it with or without me." She paused. "Maybe I just needed her to love me."

He pushed up for the sake of defense.

"I dragged my feet on the house deal for the same reason I turned down Wade Eakins' offer of a free piece of land some years back." The hard look on his face mellowed. "It ain't right, Lily, takin' somethin' for nothin'. It's a ghost that will always come back to haunt you."

"From the beginning Pa said you had your reasons for holding back and that he would have no part of going behind your back. He gave us the name of a builder because I said Maude would do it with or without me. Honestly, Pa was innocent."

"I suspected as much. Mother told it different but the ole gal has a way of confusin' the truth."

"She lies, you mean!" The words slipped out so suddenly that she threw a hand over her mouth to indicate she was sorry.

"She lies," he conceded and nodded his head.

A hallelujah chorus exploded in her head, and love swept over her as it had in a corn crib way back when they courted. The thrill was not so much that Abe had taken her side against his mother, but that he had believed her, his wife, and was no longer angry. She moved her hand under the covers until she found his warm skin and firm muscles.

"Then you believe me about your mother, and you're not mad?"

"Like I said, I got no beef with you, Lily. I was mad, sure. But while I was gone, I had time to think. You're a good woman, Lily. As good as they come. Mother, she's good too but the ole gal's turned bitter and with good reason."

Lily chose to overlook the question of his mother's goodness and get straight to the point.

"So what happens now?" she asked. "Now that we know her intentions?"

"Whatdoya mean?"

"I mean it's obvious she schemed to break up our family and have you all to herself."

"Whoa, Nellie! Granted she wanted to get me out of them mines but to say…"

"When Pop dies, we could move back to Lewellyn," she said, thinking he would recognize the sacrifice she was making. "Ceola says you could still be foreman."

He shot her a doubtful look.

"What's the catch?"

"Catch? There's no catch. I know now that nothing but mining coal will ever make you happy. You were willing to give up everything to come here for your family, and now it's our turn to give back. The girls would do anything for you. I'll talk to them. They'll understand."

"And what about Mother? Does she come too or do we just leave her behind before the dust will have a chance to settle on Daddy's grave?"

"Not leave her, no. Now that I drive, the kids and I will come check on her weekly. We can all come on Sundays, and she will be welcome to visit." Lily paused. "I was even thinking Vi might want to rent whichever house Maude doesn't choose to live in. That way she could look in on her daily and bring her food from the restaurant."

He squinted his eyes. "I thought you said there wadn't no catch."

"Now see here, Lily," Abe said when he woke up the next morning, after he'd rested and collected his thoughts. "I've give it some thought and like the idea of going back to the camp all right but I say we leave now and take the both of 'em with us. The ole gal can be a worriation, I know, but, hell, that's a part of growin' old. If she pitches a fit, we'll tie her in a gunny sack and toss her in the trunk yelpin'."

"No, Pop has to die in his own home. I couldn't accept anything less."

"Then after? I got no job here, Lily."

Lily sighed. "Abe, there's more about Maude I've not told you. Now I see you won't understand the extent of our problem until you know the whole truth."

"Shoot then," he said with impatience.

"Dr. Humfleet came here while you were away. He told me, as you know, that he'd recommended radiation treatments for Pop way back in March, four months before we got here. He said he explained to both Maude and Pop that the radiation would slow down the cancer, and he encouraged Pop to start the treatments at once. They left his office saying they would think it over. When he didn't hear back, he came here to make sure they understood that the cancer would spread if left untreated. Twice he came, and both times Maude turned him away. He even went as far as to substitute a doctor whom he highly recommended and Maude sent him away, too."

"Daddy's known to pinch a penny til it squeals. Maybe Mother was simply following his orders. And who knows? She's just a ignorant country woman. She probably don't even know the meaning of words like *cancer* and *radiation*."

"I'm sure Dr. Humfleet was very thorough."

"So were the treatments supposed to kill off the cancer?"

"They would prolong his life while improving its quality."

"That's nothing but a fancy way of saying no. Hell, if it was me, I'd wanta die and be done with it."

"Anyway, I tried my best to wait until you came home to confront her, but tension was high, and we ended up quarreling. I accused her of telling you about the barn-house before we left for the Saxtan party and blaming everything on Pa and me. To my surprise, she owned up, and not one sign of regret did she show. In fact, she seemed proud. She said Dog, Ceola, and I were in cahoots to take you back to the devil's pit, and she was prepared to do anything within her power to stop us. I can't remember her exact words, but this much I do know: That woman schemed to take you away from me, and hell will freeze over before I will stand by and let her!"

"So says the bosslady," he murmured, turned away, and buried his head in a pillow.

That night Abe moved his guitar and Will's sleeping bag to the barn-house. For days he canvassed nearby hollows looking for work. Finding none, he applied himself to completing the carpentry details Silas Holmes had been forced to leave undone. He gave backaches as his reason for sleeping on the barn floor, and everyone but Lily seemed to believe him.

One afternoon he and Lily accidentally met on the path to the privy. It was November. Abe had plowed the weedy fields and a glaze of frost sat on the furrows. This was their first time alone since the argument that led to separation, and each moved with care. He kicked at the mixture of stove ashes and gravel, and she looked past him to a neighbor's pasture with black angus cattle bulking for the winter.

"So what's new?" he asked her.

"Beats me," she answered with one of his old expressions, causing nostalgia that helped to ease the tension. He dug his hands into his jacket pockets, and she pressed hers inside the flaps of her Florence Nightingale cape lined with red satin.

"The dodos?" he asked.

"Great. Come back to them."

"So help me, Lily, I get your point about Mother, honestly I do!" he spoke up. "You think the ole bat don't get under my skin too? But I've thought and thought and I just cain't see her with Vi. Vi's too hot to trot for Mother's taste."

"Then forget about Vi." Lily said. "I called your Aunt Blessie in Atlanta, and Earl Ray, her son, has agreed to bring her here for a visit. I'm hoping she'll love the new house and agree to stay longer."

"Blessie?" he asked as if unbelieving.

"Remember I told you Pop asked for her."

He took off his ball cap and exaggerated scratching his head.

"So let me get this straight. Without askin', you took it upon yourself to shift my responsibility for mother over to Aunt Blessie?"

"I took it upon myself to help a dying man I happen to love. It's his house, Abe. He's entitled to invite whoever he wants. I only followed orders."

"*Only?*"

"They love each other. You should be happy for them to be together unless…"

"Unless what?"

She swallowed the cotton-like thickness from her throat and felt her lips trembling.

"Unless you're afraid she'll steal Maude away."

"That's a stinkin' lie and you know it!"

"Then prove it. Ask Blessie to stay on here, and let's move back to the mining camp."

"Negative."

"Abe, Maude and I will never mend, not now. Our marriage simple can't last with her there plotting."

He paused, stuttered, stumbled for the right words. Tears gathered in the brims of his eyes.

"The problem ain't really Mother, Lily. It's us, you and me. Let's face it. You done outgrew me. While I was hittin' rock bottom, you been turnin' into Lily with that college piece of paper. I saw it the day I come home and I ain't mad. It makes sense. A woman such as yourself needs a man she can look up to. A man needs to know he's respected. Me, I cain't afford to put food on the table, much less pay for the girls' college. So I guess June can do that too."

She clutched his arm.

"No, Abe, no! Here we're not close. Here, with her and the poor job possibilities you can't help. But if we moved back to Lewellyn, you'd be foreman, and everybody would look up to you just like before. I'm your wife who loves you, and that won't ever change."

He bit his lower lip and raked a hand through his hair. His foot sent an acorn flying.

"Oh, yeah? I wish."

Sherman died peacefully in his sleep the second week of November. Women attended the funeral in veiled black hats and coats smelling of mothballs. Men wore mail-order suits and carried their hats in their hands. Maude leaned on Abe for support, and Sweet William and the girls supported Lily. Attendance was poor, mostly family and church friends. Aunt Blessie was there with her Georgia family, and she and Maude clung to each other like little girlfriends. Silas Holmes stayed away from the church but paid his respects at the cemetery. Ceola and Dog came and went the same day.

When the occasion ended and everyone returned to their homes, Lily sought consolation in nature, especially the Kentucky warbler, who was no longer a stranger. One late afternoon she slipped away from the girls to go for a walk. A light snow covered the ground; icy tree limbs gleamed in the pale sunlight. When she didn't come home to cook supper, Abe went looking for her and found her near Bryce's Cove.

"The dodos are lookin' for you," he said as he came up behind her.

She turned and smiled.

"I was just thinking about the time we went walking here, and you said you smelled a copperhead, and I thought you were trying to scare me. Later you found and killed it with a tree limb, remember? I've always meant to ask you how you knew it was there."

"Copperheads smell just like cucumbers."

"Really?"

"I found the mate and killed it too, remember?"

"I do. With you, I always felt so safe."

He looked away, fumbling the mark behind his right ear.

"Lily, I been thinking. I finished the last of the painting and stuff at the barn and the farm's good for winter. There ain't work available here and, you know me, I cain't just stick around, doin' nothin'."

"Of course not."

He mined his next breath.

"Cordel-Lewis offered me foreman and I've thought and thought and decided to take it. You know yourself if'n there's a snowball's chance in hell of keepin' that mine up and goin', it'll be Abe Siler."

"Of course it will!" She pictured him in his white foreman's hardhat, his proud eyes smiling under the brim. His dream of being foreman had finally come true, and she pictured God smiling behind His white walls. Overjoyed, she threw herself into his arms and felt his hands go back into his pockets. Behind him, balls of mistletoe and caterpillars' nests snagged with old leaves clung to bare trees. He and the icy creek made no sound.

"And your mother?" she asked after a time.

"I told her. I said, Mother, I'm going to be a foreman in the mines and move the family back to coal country. So make up your mind. You can come or not come, provided you're on your best behavior."

She shifted her weight. Her legs tried to fold, and she willed them to keep going. She even managed to look calm in spite of the heartbreaking fact that he had chosen to share the news with his mother before his wife. Without consulting his wife, he had even invited her to come along.

"And?"

"And the ole gal threw a hissy fit. Then she went and got packed." He stopped to cough. "Honestly, Lily, she wants peace as much as we do and she'll apologize if you'll just give her a chance."

Lily turned toward the house.

"I see your mind's made up, so I suppose she'll be the one to look after you from now on." Sarcasm tempted her to say, "God knows you'll need somebody!"

"Come on, Lily. I'll give her a talkin' to. I'll make her promise. You two've argued before and made up. For my sake, cain't you do it this one last time?"

"No."

"You've been through a whole lot with Will leaving and Daddy dying and maybe this ain't the right time to decide. Maybe you could use some time here to rest and cool off whilst mother and me go on ahead. A vacation without her might be just what the doctor ordered. Til you're ready to go for good, I could come back on weekends and we'll buy you a car. With a car you'll be free as a bird."

"Hardy, har, har, har," came to her from the innocent lips of the children, and she gave in to the humiliation of feeling like a fool. She covered her face and was all set to cry when a visitation of self-respect hit her like a wind at the summit, and she turned, drew in her cape and stalked off so fast he fell behind."

"Wait, Lily, wait! I'll take the hoot-owl shift and commute."

"A foreman can't leave the camp, and we both know it," she called back to him.

"Ain't I always said rules were made to be broke?"

"And hearts too, I guess."

"No. I love you. Just give it a chance, Lily. That's all I'm askin' you for is a chance."

The house was in sight. Wisps of dove-gray smoke drifted from the chimney, and the dusty Plymouth slumped in the driveway. She turned to find that Abe had stayed behind, and already she missed him. She slowed her pace and re-studied her options. Even now she wondered if she should accept her old place for the sake of the family. For the sake of good intentions and deep-seated dreams.

CHAPTER TWENTY-SIX

Abe clocked in as the new day foreman of Cordel-Lewis No. 1 mine and found the situation even worse than he'd expected. Miners showed up for work without knowing who would stay, who would be sent away for the day, and who would be sent away for good. Union supporters turned against those who blamed the Union for increasing demands and driving the smaller mines out of business. Brother turned against brother.

Hard hit by cutbacks, pay cuts, and longer working hours, the miners also faced increasingly poor safety conditions, made worse by the winter dryness that increased the danger of explosions. In order to survive, many of them sought part-time jobs, trapped, hunted, or made bootlegged wine or whiskey, sometimes in their own kitchens.

On a night in early December, a drunk miner fired a volley of shots into Abe's house on Silk Stocking Row from a cove near the river. Windowpanes shattered, and a fluorescent light fell to the floor. He and his mother dropped down and no one was hurt, but word of the incident spread like dandelions on forgotten lawns.

Soon after, arsenic-poisoned cats died under front porches and near water. Dogs pocked with BBs hid in tall grass. Teenage boys formed prankster gangs; pink flamingos and flower pots from Silk Stockings Row disappeared and showed up in church and school yards. Children carrying grudges clashed at school, prompting frustrated parents to join in.

At the time the Harlan County Coal Operations' Association was under contract with the UMWA, but no official vote to strike took place. Just before Christmas, however, a handful of men led by Lance Porter turned over their lunch buckets and walked off the job. During daylight they carried signs demanding the usual changes: better pay, job security, and safer working conditions. In the evenings they formed a picket line and rallied before a barrel fire outside the supply yard. Supportive wives spread blankets on the site and tended their shivering children; others with tin cans begged for money along Route 38. Some sang the songs of the famous Union activist, Aunt Molly Jackson, a Clay County midwife said to have delivered 884 babies.

Mine good coal fast!" Abe preached. No vote to strike meant no negotiations, but he made heartfelt promises. Within a few months most of the miners, and gradually all of them, showed up for work, and the so-called strike came to an end.

"Ole buddy, the battle is lost here," Floyd Bowes tried to warn him. "Go home to your family."

"Not on my watch it ain't!" Abe spewed. Like Abraham in the Bible, he fathered his flock and held firm to his faith.

On Mud Creek, Abe's family, especially Rosy, suffered from his absence. The four older girls, with school and popularity on their minds, carried on as usual, in spite of their crowded conditions and missing daddy. Lily, however, struggled through lifeless days and lonely nights. To fill time, she cooked more but, budget challenged, cut back on ingredients. She learned to use a measuring cup instead of handfuls, and a pinch instead of a tad. Life, like the food she served, seemed tasteless, in spite of her girls. Something was missing that could not be put back.

As caterpillars with thick coats had predicted, heavy snow came early. She wiped frost from kitchen windowpanes and stared out at the ghostly trees, at their ice-laden limbs, some broken and jutting up from the snow like the bones of plowed skeletons. At times the snowflakes appeared pretty, but often they were nothing more than thieves isolating her, stealing her freedom. Sleeping alone in a cold bed with no feet to warm hers, she often lay awake grieving. Communication between her and Abe had been a problem, she believed. Maude had been a problem. But the marriage itself had not. She blamed herself for handling the matter poorly. She even blamed God for giving her prayers the wrong answers. And she blamed Abe.

Often she recalled his letters and promises. He had sworn he'd come home for Thanksgiving. He had not mentioned his mother, but she had assumed he would bring her. This was, after all, her house, and Lily a mere squatter. But just as she had expected, he reneged at the last minute, giving a slack in coal demand and labor problems as reasons. He begged her and the kids to come to Lewellyn, and even sent extra bus money. She declined the invitation on the grounds of crowded conditions. By *crowded conditions* she had meant Maude.

During this bleak Thanksgiving, she made wishes. She wished she'd had the chance to tour Sweet William's campus as promised. She wished the sun would melt the ice so she could see her family on Buck Creek. She wished she had Sherman to nurse. She wished for floors to scrub and cloth to sew with her fingers. She wished Maude would get homesick so that the two could exchange places. She saw no reason for Maude to go on living, and even looked forward to her death. Revenge, rather than children, became her reason for living.

Although hating Abe at times, her keen intelligence recognized that indifference, and not hate, is the other side of the love coin. The end of their marriage still appeared to her as a fate worse than death. Death was final, God's will, perhaps a doctor's mistake, but acceptance in the end. But to win love, own it like a birthmark and let it slip away due to human error seemed like a hideous defeat, a never-ending hunger for what might have been.

She had eaten a bowl of Quaker's oatmeal for breakfast and no lunch. The fire in the cookstove had gone out, and the children would be home from school soon. She stoked it and added newspapers and a measured amount of wood. Sparks crackled as flames whooshed through the ashy pipe. Gone in a flash, she thought, like all her expectations.

The girls came home as she was preparing mackerel cakes and creamed potatoes (with powdered milk) for an early supper. Dressed in caps and mittens knitted by Sarah and hand-me-down coats, they, all but Rosy, grabbed a graham-cracker snack and hurried outside to slide on the ice. Rosy sulked in a chair in a corner.

"Are your legs hurting?" Lily asked her.

"No."

"Lie down, and I'll massage them," she offered when she heard Rosy sniffling and knew she was crying for her daddy.

"My legs don't need massaging."

"Well I need a hug." Lily stepped away from the window and held out her arms.

"I can't."

"Please?"

"My legs are stuck."

"Then come here and I'll unstick them."

To her surprise, Rosy took the bait and came. After a squeeze hug, Lily patted her toward a shoebox of old paper dolls, mainly Betty and Veronica, and wished all conflicts could be as easily resolved.

The other girls came inside and went directly to the cookstove to warm.

"When's Daddy coming home?" they asked.

"I don't know." Lily didn't want to build up their hopes, just to disappoint them.

"Is he coming for Christmas? Will we have a tree?" Iris asked.

"Of course we'll have a tree. Whoever heard of not having a Christmas tree?"

"I bet Fairy Enlow don't have a tree," Rosy said.

"Then we'll pray she gets one."

"And will Daddy bring presents?" Daisy asked.

"Can I write and ask him to bring me a pair of roller skates?" Rosy followed.

"Daddy's awful busy saving the mine," Lily said, her usual way of explaining his absence. "Why don't you write Santa Claus instead?"

"Because Santa's like Jesus. He watches to see if you've been good and if you've not, he brings switches."

Lily didn't have to ask who had filled Rosy's ears with such nonsense.

"But, Rosy, you've been a wonderful girl, and Santa Claus and his elves know it."

"But I drew in Daisy and Tansy's funny books by accident and let Daisy's pencil sharpener fall in a hole. Don't you think the elves saw me?"

"Yeah, you'll get nothing!" the twinsies agreed.

Lily suspected the pencil sharpener was not lost. She felt certain it was hidden in Rosy's get-even stash underneath a corner of Sweet William's mattress.

"If you find and return the sharpener, he might come anyway," she said. *Might*, she had learned to say in the place of *will* because nothing was now certain.

Although coal dust belched from the tipple and coal cars on steel rails thundered northward as usual, the mining camp grew quieter and sadder. Neighbors who had once chatted at clotheslines or pole-and-wire back fences now stayed inside and hung their wash on pulley ropes strung across kitchen ceilings. On boisterous Tipple Row, parties ceased. Women no longer clogged, and men avoided the clownish barnyard shuffle that finished with a heehaw and the pretense of scraping manure from their boots. More school desks and church pews sat empty, and the commissary porch had fewer sitters. Hopeless people without jobs, or some with jobs like Josh Payne, foresaw the mine's future and moved on. Some took up farming.

Neighbors carrying food checked in on Maude daily; they found she cooked little and slept a great deal. In the evenings she and Abe ate light suppers, often a slice of fatback with cheese and crackers. Afterwards Abe tucked her into bed, stayed for her prayers, and slipped off to the mine. When back at home he lay awake thinking of his kids and eventually fell asleep to dream about Lily. She appeared to him as the perfect woman, not the kind of chick men looked up and down, but the lady kind they looked up to. And yet, a wind blew through her, sometimes making her wild as a buck. There was nothing she wouldn't do for the sake of his pleasure.

Back on the job at eight o'clock the next morning, he focused on coal production, and his promises to protect miners' safety. He told himself that if he had the foreman choice to make again, he would do it all over. He saw being foreman as not just a gut-wrenching challenge, but a moral responsibility, a contribution to mankind—far better than the nothingness of pounding nails in Saxton. He convinced himself that the Man Upstairs and fellow masons would not have him turn his back on sick and hungry children and drop-dead-tired miners sold out by their Company.

He vowed he would work hard, bring the mine back to safe conditions and a profit, and leave it in good hands. Then he would go home to Lily and his family. This time he would listen to her. Her plans for his mother weren't so bad, now that he'd had time to think about it. In fact, they were generous, considering how his mother had done her.

Yep, he would wind things up and go home and spend the rest of his life making it all up to Lily and the dodos. If she would only stop being stubborn like her pa, Wade Eakins. If she would just understand the rut he was in, and hold her damn horses.

CHAPTER TWENTY-SEVEN

Lily choked on her food, Rosy screamed, heads jerked, and cries of joy went up as Abe stormed inside on Christmas Eve night, just in time to eat and open presents. Lily hopped up from the table, and he kissed her with such fervor that the children broke out in laughter and relief. Once again she felt swept off her feet and safe in his manliness. With him there, the bitter snow became a seasonal decoration, and the cold house felt warm. Even the loud wind seemed to lay low, avoiding the windows. Everybody hugged in a tight circle, Abe's hands fumbling until they found six bobbing heads. Sweet William also got a pat on the shoulder.

"B'damned if it ain't good to be home!" he exclaimed while Lily ripped off her apron and let down her hair. She had wondered so often if she would ever trust him again, and here he was, husband and father, the Christmas present with bows she'd dreamed of. If anything, absence had made her heart grow fonder. He was even more handsome now for the wear and tear he had taken pains to hide with a fresh shave and haircut, scrubbed fingernails and knuckles, and excitement she'd not seen in ages.

And he had come without his mother!

Not taking the time to remove his jacket, Abe pulled away and whipped out a sack of shiny half dollars, one for every *A* appearing on the girls' report cards. From his jeans pocket he took out a pretty hair comb and a pearl bracelet held together by elastic.

"Ceola said the pearls matched your disposition, Lily," he said proudly. "Sorry they're not wrapped. You deserve a fat ribbon."

"They're wonderful."

The girls chattered as they counted their half dollars. Rosy, the poorest student of all, slipped into a corner, and Lily went to stand beside her.

"Hell, you idiots keep up the good work and one day your old man will die a proud pauper!" he whooped.

"What about that set of encyclopedias you been promising?" Daisy asked before Lily could shush her.

"It won't be long now," he said. "And that's a promise!"

"Why don't we eat, and then we'll open the other presents," Lily suggested for Rosy's sake. "This is just the beginning. Your daddy and I have more surprises."

Believing he would not appear, she had cooked a ham and made potato salad to take to Buck Creek the following day, provided the country roads were clean enough for Vi to provide transportation. Sherman's pickup truck was available, and she had earned her driver's license, but it was too small to seat the entire family. She opened a jar of canned peaches and added them to the ham, potato salad, vegetables and bread fresh out of the oven.

"Take off your coat and stay a while," she said with a touch of humor.

He removed his old ball cap and worn denim jacket, and she saw he was thinner, his shirt dingy and needing ironing. She smiled while thinking about the Christmas shirts she had bought him before the flea market closed down for the winter.

Abe took double helpings of every food and licked his fingers when he finished. The children ate fast. Sweet William was the first to leave the table, followed by a winking Verni. Iris motioned for the younger girls to follow, leaving Lily and Abe alone in the kitchen.

"Where's your guitar?" Sweet William asked as he tapped his dad's shoulder on the way out.

"Hell, I don't need it. I brung a heart full of music!"

The two sat close, held hands, and updated the other—him on the mine and sobriety and her on the children. They kissed briefly before going to the tree.

"Golly Jees Moses!" Rosy cried as Abe and Sweet William brought larger packages from the attic.

Lily had sold her woven baskets and canned goods at the flea market, and she had shopped for bargains, mostly small treats like grooming articles, hats and gloves, school supplies, and costume jewelry. With gift money from her parents, she had also bought Sweet William a man's suitcase; Verni, a baton with tassels; Iris, a bicycle with a basket; Daisy and Tansy, a record player with some 33 1/3 rpm records; Rosy, a pair of roller skates with a key; and Abe, apart from the plaid shirts, a tooled leather wallet, the kind made by convicts in prison workshops, and a brown corduroy jacket with a thick, quilted lining. A red and white afghan waited for Maude under the tree, and Lily held up a pink nightgown and matching robe she'd received from the children. The sheer negligee, with its tiny silk bows and tapered skirt, looked youthful. She couldn't wait for Abe to see it.

"Think the children would forgive us if we sent them to bed early?" she leaned close and whispered.

"Or maybe we could sneak off without them even noticing," he teased.

"Wouldn't that be nice!" she said and pictured the way he had always loved the feel of her long, silky hair sweeping his body. Anticipation filled her with longing. Then she noticed he was no longer smiling.

"Lily, I...we need to talk," he said, and she tensed before pulling away. Slowly she led him into the kitchen.

"Forgive me, Lily, for dreaming, but the God's truth is that I hafta get back to the camp." He placed his arms around her waist and looked into her eyes as if pleading. "Trust me. I'd give my life to stay over but..."

"When?"

"Tonight...now."

She managed a nod. The fingers on her chest found a thimble's worth of flesh to knead.

He took a stack of large bills from his wallet and tossed them on the table.

"I brought you a little somethin' more," he said. "Merry Christmas. It's for the car I been promisin'. It won't buy much but June can help you pick something safe til I can do better."

Lily imagined him rushing home to tuck in his mother— his mother, a subject he'd managed to bypass, and she had chosen to suppress. The pain of their chilling Bryce's Cove goodbye rushed over her as though it had happened only yesterday, and she felt an incredible urge to run from him as she had then. But there was a matter of the children.

"A car? How nice. Thank you, but no," she said as if talking to a salesman.

"Honestly, Lily, I'm goin' plumb nuts without you and the dodos but like I said at Thanksgivin', there's some serious labor disputes and things at the mine are touchous. It might well be spring before..."

"I thought you said things are better," she interrupted.

"It's nothin' I cain't handle provided I get back b'fore somebody notices I'm gone."

"I see."

"But before I go I aim to make sure you're all stocked up. Wood? Coal? Make me a list."

"We're fine. Don't need a thing." She left to get his gifts and placed the money in a pocket of his jacket. "I'll clean up while you go say goodbye to the children."

"Please, Lily, a little more time is all I need and we can be together for good. Then we'll decide what to do about Mother. I've give it a hellova lot of thought and this time I'm ready to listen."

Her hands shook as she placed the dirty plates on the counter near the sink. With her back to him, she threw her palms over her eyes in case they made tears. Twice he had broken her heart, and twice she had not cried. Today would be no exception.

"Goodbye," she said and pointed him toward the children.

"So long, you mean. Hell, you know I ain't leavin' my family. The checks are still comin', ain't they?"

"Then so long," she repeated, the moan of a long O blending with the chill of disappointment, dying embers, and frost on the windows.

While preparing breakfast some days later, Lily glanced down at the toaster and saw the sagging, uncertain face of an aging woman who owned little more than a nurse's cape and uniform, and a now sexy nightgown. Turning to the washstand mirror, she noticed her eyes, red and puffy. In spite of her despair, she smiled as she remembered Ceola recommending Preparation H for Palatia Porter's swollen eyes.

New Year's Day came with the usual hog's jowl and black-eyed peas and cornbread to sop up the juices. Supposedly a time for celebration and change, the holiday made her feel even sadder than Christmas. Today of all days she had no resolutions, no plans except to shovel snow, and no dreams to build on. Of all possible choices, Maude's house was the last place on earth she wanted to be, she thought. *To be*—the words struck her as a perfect description of her bare existence. Simply *to be*, and not *to live.*

Her mind hunted for a way to keep going. "When at the end of your rope, tie a knot and hang on," Ceola had advised her when Abe first left, and now she spent her days and nights wondering if she had hung on too long. Why merely survive, she asked herself, when one is equipped to succeed?

In the living room, Verni, Daisy, and Tansy played Monopoly with Rosy as banker, and Iris scribbled in her diary. The spiffy voice of Patti Page reached Lily like a sudden knock on the door. She hummed first, then broke into a song. Rhythm pulsed through her hips and legs, her shoulders and arms, even her fingers, and she felt like dancing, swinging, twisting, thrusting her body the naughty way she and Vi had done when their Pa was away preaching revivals. The memory made her feel young again, and filled with that same crazy zip Abe had seen in her when they dated. It told her she was not too old, or rusty, or even afraid to start over. Yes, an escape plan had knocked, with opportunity waiting. Abe had opened that door with his neglect, and she, thank goodness, could now see through and beyond it.

"Supper!" she called, and slapped down plates, silverware, and glasses. Then she sashayed over to the new calendar, a collection of landscapes illustrating the weather. With a crayon she put a big red check on the square that said January 1. "Go wash hands," she ordered, and continued with her alto version of "How Much Is That Doggie in the Window?"

The girls took their places at the table, elbows on oilcloth. She poured milk and cut the cornbread into wedges. Then she took out chowchow and butter, but didn't sit down.

"What's up?" Verni said. "You're acting weird."

"*What's up?*" Lily asked, questioning Verni's choice of words.

"I mean, how come you're so frisky?"

"Am I?" She rounded the table, dropping a Hershey kiss in the center of each plate. For dessert there would be banana pudding. "Listen up," she said. "There's something I need to do now while it's fresh on my mind. When you all finish eating, Verni washes the dishes, and Iris dries. Daisy and Tansy will put away, all but the silverware, which is Rosy's. In the meantime, I better not hear any bickering or be interrupted, hear?"

"Ain't you eating first?" Verni asked.

"*Aren't*...Aren't you eating first?" Lily corrected her.

"No, I'm dieting." The twinsies laughed as if Verni were the new Sweet William, and Verni took a bow. "You could at least tell us what you're doing that's so urgent," she continued.

"I need to write a letter."

"Cain't it wait til after we eat? It's a holiday, you know."

"No, I might run out of music."

Verni rolled her eyes and made a loony sign at her ear with a circling finger.

"Who to? What's so important that it can't wait til after supper?"

"It can, Verni, but I can't."

"Is it to Daddy?" Rosy got up from her chair. "Can I write too?"

Lily pointed a discipline finger at Rosy, and she plunked back down. Lily wished she could point that same finger at Verni and have equally good results. Unlike Abe and Maude, she did not believe in disciplining with belts and switches. But with Verni she wasn't so sure.

"Ceola?" the twinsies asked.

"Silas Holmes?" Verni said with a snicker.

"No!" Lily answered and spun around on her heels to avoid any more questions.

Every day before noon, Lily traipsed through the snow to the mailbox out front, hoping to receive news from her old friend and college suitemate, Beulah Lee Phelps, now Director of Nursing at Southeastern Kentucky Baptist Hospital in Corbin, seventeen miles north of Saxton. At night she lay awake fearing that the lapse of time and lack of hospital experience would spoil her chance of getting the position she looked on as salvation.

A week passed.

"Praise the Lord!" she cried as her fingers finally reached into the mailbox and felt the crisp, warm bulk of a fat letter. She ripped open the envelope and read the words aloud, extra loud since wind rippled the pages. Icy snow reached the top of her short rubber boots. It cracked as she deliberately pressed footprints into it to mark the occasion.

"There are always openings for good RNs," Beulah Lee had written, "and I would be overjoyed to recommend my good friend, Lily." Because of Lily's outstanding character and excellent scholastic standing, Beulah Lee said, she could almost guarantee she would be hired once the Board of Directors held its quarterly meeting in March. In the meantime, Lily was to fill out and return the enclosed forms.

"Outstanding character!" Lily repeated and smiled. It was not so outstanding once she'd met Abe, but Beulah Lee had sworn herself to secrecy.

Memories of Beulah Lee and Bunny entertained her during her climb to the house. She remembered when Abe underwent surgery for a crushed ankle at the Middlesboro Hospital, and the two of them unofficially adopted him, in spite of regulations. She recalled the autumn jamboree when they schemed to bring her and him together and the subsequent snickers and sighs, the excitement of a first love imparted in a dormitory.

Beulah Lee and Bunny had stayed together after graduation, and now each nursed at the Corbin hospital. They had visited her on occasions and sent cards at birthdays and Christmas, but the relationship had slacked, and now she couldn't wait for a chance to catch up. But her teeth quaked from more than the cold as she ambled home, wondering how she would tell them about the separation. Without alcohol, adultery, or abuse to report, would she explain that life, in spite of good intentions, sometimes takes wrong turns? That opposites attract, only to repel.

Would she say Abe was *gone*...or simply *away*?

CHAPTER TWENTY-EIGHT

In early April, Beulah Lee met Lily and the girls at the Greyhound bus station and insisted on giving them a tour of the town. Corbin—birthplace of Kentucky Fried Chicken, home of the Corbin Redhounds, and a neighbor of the famous Cumberland Falls—was a friendly but segregated town of some seven thousand people. Before the Louisville and Nashville railroad came through in the 1890s, it was said to have been a booming frontier swampland with slap-dash shacks, shady boarding houses, and gun-smoke saloons. Now the Corbin Chamber of Commerce ranked it as a fourth-class town with ample restaurants, small businesses, recreation, schools, and churches. Mostly crime-free, people said it was a happy town, the perfect place to rear a family.

The seven ate hamburgers and fries at the Lunch Queen on Main Street. Then Beulah Lee's Ford station wagon swung a right onto Fifth Street, toward the painted wood house Lily had rented just before town proper ended and rural Fifth Street Road began. The girls poked their heads out of windows in spite of a wind. Dogwood and Bradford pear trees had just begun to bud, making them likely victims of a frost. Red and green nandina bushes blushed like summer foliage, and sparrows and old brownish-red cardinals sought out their red berries.

"Won't it be just great, having a bathroom and all the hot water we can use?" Lily asked. "Paved streets and a downtown and mail brought to the door? Isn't that cause for a celebration?"

The girls were too busy looking to answer.

"Is that it?" They pointed as Beulah Lee followed the street past gabled brick houses with high-pitched roofs and wide porches.

"Not yet."

They cruised past smaller wood cottages with lantern lights and ornamental shutters, detoured to Fourth to take a look at the hospital, and turned back to Fifth. Daisy spotted a house with a "For Sale" sign in the yard.

"Is that it?"

"It's close."

At a point where a sewage canal cut under the street, cheers turned to silence. Verni and Iris drew in their heads. Rosy pinched her nose with her fingers and cried, "Phew!"

"Are you sure we're in the right place?" Daisy and Tansy were the first ones to ask.

"I bet we went too far!"

Verni blew the curls from her forehead.

"You said we'd have a home of our own we could be proud of."

Lily, burdened by her promise that day in Maude's barn, couldn't bear to scold.

"Keep in mind that it's only temporary," she said. Her eyes aimed low; her hands wadded the handkerchief in her lap.

Ahead, the neighborhood changed from fair green to ugly gray. Cracked sidewalks disappeared under mud holes. Old wrappers and piles of curled leaves hugged street curbs, and bottles and cans peeped out from weedy yards. Houses with peeling paint and broken windowpanes looked ready to collapse onto stretches of Johnson grass and crown vetch. Some had been turned into churches and stores. A sign before a cabinet shop said, "No job *to* large or *to* small."

"Now, girls, settling into a new town takes time and money," Lily said. "First we have to buy a dependable car. Then we'll look for something closer to town."

"But when?" Iris whined.

"When our rich uncle gets out of the poor house," Verni snapped.

"Something with a sidewalk to skate on?" Rosy asked.

"We'll do our best," Lily answered, "and soon."

Beulah Lee veered left and squeezed her woodie station wagon into a driveway so narrow the vehicle practically touched a neighbor's board-and-batten siding. She cut the ignition, slipped down in the seat, and slid her man's felt hat over her face as if napping. Verni shook her head hopelessly and refused to speak. Iris shoved her tongue against her front teeth and overbite; the twinsies teared up; and Rosy clutched Hairy. Lily had never been more embarrassed.

"Come, girls!" She hopped out. "Let's go see what it'll take to make the place pretty."

Not one girl moved. Not one uttered a sound.

"Come on now. Where's your daddy's sense of adventure?"

"I'll die before I'll let a school bus pick me up at this dump!" Verni said when at a distance from Beulah Lee. "And we thought mining camps were bad!"

"Picture it with a fresh coat of paint and some pretty yellow curtains." Lily stepped over a trail of irregular rocks embedded in mud and leading to a squat stoop. She unlocked the door and stepped inside. "You all come on now. We've got loads of work to do before June arrives with the furniture."

"What if Daddy can't find us?" Rosy whimpered.

"Okay, you guys, pray for a tornado!" Verni said as she approached the porch, followed by her flock. From an inside window she glared into the backyard hillside with tree stumps and locust volunteers and a narrow dirt path that disappeared at the crest of a little hill. "Where do you suppose it goes to?" she asked, and pointed a finger.

"What?"

"That path. Maybe there's a road up there. Maybe we could catch the bus from up there."

Lily worked up a smile and added chirp to her voice.

"Just remember, it's only temporary."

In late April of that year, Lily wrote to Ceola. "I have a nursing position in Corbin," she said, without mentioning either Abe or his mother. "I will invite you to visit just as soon as we find a more suitable place to live."

Ceola read the letter in her beauty shop. It was Wednesday, her half-day, and she had shooed away lagging customers. After a second reading, she popped open a bag of potato chips and a Bud and snacked til she felt bloated. Then she dropped into the shampoo chair, threw back her head, and cried to her people in the posters.

"Oh, well," she said after she'd allowed herself a fair amount of grieving. She jumped up to go throw some clothes into a suitcase, then packed scissors, curlers, clips, rods, permanents, and a hair dryer, the portable kind with a tube connected to a plastic bonnet. She also packed a portable sew-

ing machine with fabric scraps, brushes, trays, and paint—
leftovers from decorating her beauty shop.

Early the next morning she blew Dog a kiss, grabbed a
road map, and heavy-footed his pickup toward Corbin. She
arrived before noon. It was a warm day with bright skies.
Bridal veil spirea and Japanese quince were in bloom, their
white and red flowers frail compared to the blooming ropes of
yellow forsythia. She beeped the horn in the driveway to the
rhythm of "Shave and a haircut, two bits," and Lily and the
girls came running. They piled on her, nestling their heads in
her cushy blubber and welcoming the smell of her Evening in
Paris perfume.

"How'd you find us?" everyone exclaimed.

"Will power," Ceola said. "Will power and a address."

Lily glanced at the packed boxes in Ceola's truck bed.

"Why did you bring all this?" she asked, eyebrows arched.
"What's it for?"

"It's for you. Had most of it and stopped at some flea markets along the way."

"Well, I can't accept it unless you let me pay."

Ceola turned away. "Girls, I'll need your help bringing it
all in. Be careful with the paint. It's heavy."

They unpacked the truck, and all went inside to talk, Ceola
laughing when she wanted to cry and refusing to hear excuses
for the shabby house. She asked umpteen questions about the
town, schools, and Lily's job at the hospital. She wanted to
know all about new friends and activities and followed each
answer with a new set of questions. Excitement grew to the
point that Lily and the girls couldn't wait to put forth their
own questions. Even when asked about Dog's health, Ceola
sounded as cheerful as when she'd arrived.

Lily later cooked spaghetti with meatballs. After they ate, Ceola laid out her cookies and plans.

"Okay, girls, now listen up! Early to bed, early to rise!" she said, and had Lily set a five o'clock alarm for the next morning. "We'll begin our day with breakfast and a fresh coat of white paint on bedroom woodwork. Then we'll plunge in, fast but careful. Tonight we'll simply clean, set the stage, and move furniture."

"What about the kitchen and living room?" Rosy asked.

"We don't wanta bite off more than we can chew," Lily said.

"I figure it may take two trips. Maybe I'll bring Dog next time with his tools. Come summer we can redo the floors and paint the outside." Her eyes flashed between rows of thick black mascara. "Then when you sell the place, we'll share the profit," she said and winked.

"We won't be here in the summer," Verni said, and Ceola, rather than answer, handed her a broom with a brush extension for taking down cobwebs.

The girls used measuring sticks to check the size of each window. Ceola estimated the amount of fabric on each roll by measuring a yard from the tip of her nose to the length of her extended arm and hand. She let the older girls decide which fabric belonged where. The wall paint, all antique white, was an easy choice.

"I'm bushed," Ceola said after everyone had finished work and was watching Perry Como on TV, and she proceeded to make her way to Lily's bedroom. "No fartin', hear?" she told Lily.

"Just you stay on your half of the bed."

"I might need three-fourths."

"And I might need the couch."

Ceola was the first to get up the next morning, even before the alarm. A good night's sleep had left her fueled with energy and excitement.

"Arise and shine! Reach for the stars! There goes Mercury! Here comes Mars!" she whooped as she roused each girl with a hug. By noon they had finished painting three rooms of woodwork and walls and went shopping for bedspreads that Lily clutched to her breasts and insisted on buying herself. At the cash register Ceola twirled her barrel buttocks and bumped a shocked Lily out of her way while the girls burst into laughter. Afterwards she insisted on treating everybody to a foot-long hot dog and all the A&W root beer they could drink. The root beer inspired some burps and an eventual burping contest presided over by Ceola.

"Yee gads! Bring it up again and we'll vote on it!" she teased after Iris' rip-roarer earned her victory and the promise of a Lilt perm.

Back at the house, Lily made coffee and hot chocolate, and she served them with Ceola's almond-molasses bars. A second coat of paint was needed. When it had almost dried, the decorating began. The girls turned small amounts of fabric into dresser and table scarves, and they sewed curtains from Ceola's rolls as well as the yellow eyelet Iris had won at bingo. Scraps made lovely pillows and trims.

Lily had not seen so much excitement since Abe came home for Christmas. Some touch up on the walls, and the day's work was close to being finished.

"Gorgeous!" Ceola raved as she shoved through the clutter of furniture in the living room and kitchen. "Just like a brand-spanking new house!"

"It's amazing what a fresh coat of paint can do for a room!" Lily said, her big eyes twinkling for the girls' sake. To Ceola she whispered, "I only wish people could be as easily transformed."

Ceola patted Lily's head.

"Forget about her, honey. She's Abe's problem now."

"It doesn't make any sense. Right now I've got every reason in the world to be happy, and that woman still brings me down."

"Not if you don't let her, she can't. You're the oldest girl in your family, which I take to mean you've got more testosterone in you than the other two put together. Use it."

The two moved to the kitchen for privacy and more coffee. Ceola asked for an update on Abe, and Lily, hearing the girls stirring nearby, chose to be brief.

"I've made clear I would do anything on earth for him and the children but live under the same roof as his mother. I've even offered to move back to the camp. At Christmas of all times he didn't even want to…be together. I'm starting to think he's got reasons for staying away other than just the mine and his mother."

"Another woman? Lily, have you lost your marbles? Did you ever stop to think maybe he's got no time to screw around, what with all the pressure he's under? Imagine having to take on the United States government, the Union, the Company, the scads of angry miners, his mother, and his wife all at once. Why, the man should be eating lightbulbs by now!"

The girls were coming closer, and Lily felt the frustration of unfinished business.

"Ceola," she said and paused, wondering if she had the right to put her friend in the torturous position of taking sides.

"You know I trust you more than any woman on this earth besides Ma. So there's a question I hafta ask, knowing you have the right not to answer."

"Let's have it."

"Loving Abe and that mine as you do, do you think I've been selfish?"

Ceola shook her low head.

"No."

"Foolish?"

"No."

"Are you absolutely sure?"

Spit had dried in the corners of Ceola's mouth. She licked her lips, bent her forehead toward Lily, and spoke with wide-open eyes.

"Swear to Wod."

An hour before the girls left home for their second day of school, Lily set out for her first day at the hospital. The air was chilly. Shivering in her white starched uniform and Florence Nightingale cape, she crossed from Fifth to Fourth Street, a stretch of small crowded houses with cluttered yards and rotting porches, some similar to the one she had rented. From there she tackled Mitchell Hill, where boys on bicycles tested their strength going up and their nerve coming down, and the tired sirens of old ambulances competed with the noise of downtown traffic and trains.

Once she reached the crest, she stopped to catch her breath and look back at the long line of streetlights behind her, a measure of how far she'd come. The three-story brick hospital with a flat roof and covered entrance was to her left. The facility, built in 1951, sat on an isolated plot of ground. Its front overlooked concrete and cars and a circular patch of grass dressed by yard lamps and scrubby shrubs. Lily stepped inside to a small foyer and a wide-open space with the usual humming lights, gray floors waxed yellow, cleansing smells, and personnel trained to smile. She checked in at the front desk, and within minutes Beulah Lee and Bunny came running.

She embraced Beulah Lee who led, and then Bunny, a cute little blonde with her same Doris Day haircut. Bunny was as sparkly and chatty as ever while Beulah Lee appeared more reserved and officious. The Bunny hug was tighter and longer.

"Bunny will give you a tour, and I'll check in with you later," Beulah Lee said. "Now, I'll show you the cafeteria, and we can grab a quick coffee."

Bunny started the training by introducing Lily to the second-floor supplies, equipment, and staff. She also pointed out the lab, X-ray area, nursery, and operating room. They spent time there, Lily asking question after question while recalling her hospital training and taking delight in the medical progress made since that time.

"There's so much to learn, I feel like I'm back in training!" she spilled out. The joy of learning, growing, becoming—how had she managed to live so long without it? How indeed!

"Are you ready to meet your patients?" Bunny asked, and she felt like a long-distance runner tearing through the ribbon.

CHAPTER TWENTY-NINE

Abe slept until noon on Sundays, his one day of rest.

"Breakfast!" Maude called and he stretched out of bed, his swollen joints aching. He made his way to the kitchen and was reaching for the forks she'd forgotten when he spotted the corner of a letter poking from under the silverware tray. The letter was from Lily and postmarked two weeks before. His mother must've put it away and forgot where she put it, he told himself. In her present state of mind, the ole gal had done well not to lose it.

"Don't let it get cold," Maude said, fretting. Each day she seemed to fuss more and understand less.

He folded the letter in a tube shape, stuffed it into his pants pocket, and sat down to have the usual fried baloney and egg breakfast, baloney instead of bacon and toast in the place of biscuits. His mother was chatty today, mixing good sense with tripe. Sundays belonged to her. To please her he sometimes played card games like "Go Fish," read her the newspaper, or sat around the radio, listening to ministers preach hellfire and brimstone before asking for donations. But today he ate fast and slipped outside to be alone with his special letter. Special because Lily was not one to write now without a reason.

"Son Boy! Where are you? You didn't finish your breakfast," Maude called.

"Comin'!"

The possibility that something could be wrong with one of the kids worried him, and he ripped open the letter and scanned it before actually reading. Blood raced to his face, and he cursed loud in spite of his mother. After crumpling the letter inside a fist, he unballed it to read.

Lily's message was short, but complete. He studied it three times before storming off to the Plymouth.

"Dammit to hell, she should've waited!" he yelled. "She knew my hands were tied and she should've waited!" What kind of wife would run out on her husband in a letter? he puzzled. What kind would go and take away his kids when he faced one crisis after another?

"Son Boy!" Maude called and came to the car in her stocking feet. "Is somebody here? I thought I heard talkin'."

"They left," he said. He ran a snappy hand over his face and went inside to play Old Maid and shove down some tapioca pudding.

Abe arrived at work early the next morning with the telephone number Lily had sent in case of an emergency. At his desk he smoked one cigarette after another while working up courage. Then he telephoned her at the hospital and hung up twice before anyone answered. He rehearsed his lines again and succeeded on the third try, but without the patience he'd practiced.

"Cute surprise!" he charged when she answered. "Why in hell didn't you tell me you was movin'?"

His voice was so loud Lily slipped around a corner of the nurses' station before answering.

"Because you would've tried to stop me."

"You damn right I would've. I thought we agreed to ride this thing out together."

"We still can. When the mine shuts down, you might consider coming to Corbin."

"*If'n*, you mean! If'n the mine shuts down!"

"There's a coal-washing plant here, and Beulah Lee says they're hiring. We're less than an hour from Saxton. Think of the possibilities."

"Hell, I got my own possibilities."

"The schools here are good, so much better than the ones in the country. The children have activities to choose from like 4-H Club and Tri-Hi-Y that lets them go help run the government. Just think what that could mean for their futures." She remembered that she had once offered to move back to the mining camp, but even Ceola admitted that the mine was playing out.

He answered with silence and sighs, as if every breath were torn from his body.

"The girls need to see you. Especially Rosy. Any chance you could come home for a short visit?"

He stopped pacing the floor and dropped down at his desk.

"Home? You call Corbin home? Hell, Lily, cut the crap. I ain't got a home thanks to you and neither does Mother."

"Maybe we could have our own home in Saxton, and *I* could commute."

"Fat chance!" he yelled and slammed down the receiver. Alone, he dropped his head onto a stack of pink slips and let out a whimper.

Lily was looking forward to some catch-up reading and was in no mood for more company. But Vi arrived in Corbin unannounced on a Saturday noon to deliver school dresses Sarah had sewn from the girls' measurements and patterns cut out of newspaper. It was a warm spring day, breezy but not windy. Lily prepared a tuna casserole for lunch while the girls led a house tour and modeled their new dresses. Vi had brought some treats of her own, mostly hand-me-down clothes from Minnie Mo and sweets from the restaurant, and the girls, especially Verni and Iris, were ecstatic. But little folks should be seen and not heard, they'd been taught. Knowing the two sisters would want time alone, they drifted toward the outside and attic.

"Love the house!" Vi said as she and Lily settled at the kitchen table. "Update me on Abe, quick, before Rosy comes back. Has he been here?" Vi was quick to ask.

"Not yet. He still can't get away from the mine."

"When, you think?"

"I don't know."

"Soon?"

"I don't know."

Vi leaned forward on her hands with red fingernails to read Lily's upcoming expression.

"I ran into Silas Holmes at Ma and Pa's the other day and I thought you might be pleased to know he asked about you and the girls, especially Rosy."

"That was very nice of him," Lily answered. "Please give him my regards the next time you see him."

"Your *regards*? I swan! Is that how country people talk once they move to the city? Gittin' too big for your britches Abe would say."

Lily got up and checked to see if Rosy was nearby.

"I would hardly say Silas Holmes and I are on familiar terms, Vi. Why, I hardly know the man and vice versa. And you might keep in mind that I'm still a married woman." Lily was aware that she often assumed a strict tone with Vi, not at all like the affectionate one she used when with Ceola. She reflected on the matter and decided that since she'd helped her ma rear Vi, she'd been sensitive to her faults. Or maybe it was because of that night people came to mourn Brody, Vi's deceased husband.

"You know him well enough to know he's got the hots for you. Good Lord, girl! I'm not suggesting you shack up with the man but he's like family to Ma and Pa. Sending a warm hello wouldn't exactly put you at risk."

"Why? Has he said something?"

Vi smiled to say she knew Lily was fishing.

"Naturally he's too much of a gentleman to give himself away. But Silas speaks with his eyes and I know for a fact he's taken with you. He asked me about Abe."

"What about Abe? So help me, Vi, you better not be carrying tales."

"He asked me when Abe's expected back from Harlan County and offered to come help you and the girls with the yard work and such. Ma and Pa must've told him Abe had gone back to the mine." Vi threw up a hand. "Not me, I swear!"

"He's not to know I'm in Corbin, you hear me? You have to tell Ma and Pa not to tell him."

"Why? You afraid he'll come calling? Afraid of maybe what could happen?"

"I just don't want his pity. And anyway, your theory is all wrong, and I want you to forget it. True, he likes nurses, but that just goes to show he's still in love with his wife's memory. And even if he did like me as a friend, he liked the old Lily, the Christian one like her daddy. Silas would take one look into my hard eyes and know the trusting Saxton woman is gone. Not changed, but gone."

Vi raised her eyebrows.

"Gone? Gone where?"

"I don't know. Maybe God gave up on me. Maybe I gave up on Him."

"Well, I still say you're crazy to give up on Silas. I mean, nobody wants you with Abe any more than me and you know it. But a girl's gotta think ahead. She can't wait forever. Wadn't it Abe that said a man that lives on hope dies farting?"

"Actually, he was quoting Benjamin Franklin. Now can we change the subject?"

"Okay, all right, you don't have to bite my head off!" Vi reached for her jacket and car keys. "I'll be back next week and we'll go to Buck Creek. I promised Ma and Pa I wouldn't take no for a answer. You can drive Sherman's pickup back with June if you want to practice and I'll follow with the girls. It's not safe, you not having transportation."

"I appreciate your trying to help, Vi, but a pickup truck is no automobile for a family."

"It beats having nothing. What if there's a emergency? What if Iris needs oxygen?"

"We'll have our own car soon enough. Until then we can walk or take taxis."

Vi shook her head—her long ponytail, curls about her face, and dangling earrings with it.

"I don't get it. The truck's just sitting out back rusting. Abe ain't about to give up that poor sick Plymouth Roadking and you know good and well Sherman would've wanted you to have it."

"I know, but legally it's Maude's, and I don't want a thing that woman's got! Nothing!"

"Lily, she's your kids' grandmother. Eventually you'll have to let her see them."

"Says who?"

"I don't know…God?"

"God? Where was God this winter when I was closed off on Mud Creek, lonely and miserable and praying to a solid white sheet of nothing? I'll tell you where He was. He was in Harlan County, watching over Abe's poor mother. Believe me when I say I would gladly sell my soul to the devil for the right to hate her forever. So don't you of all people, Vi Horton, preach to me about God."

"Oh, honey, what good does all that anger do besides soak up your energy? You think I wadn't furious when Brody died for nothing? You think I like carrying cigarettes over to Buddy at the county jail and wondering what Minnie Mo has traded some jerk for a fake piece of jewelry? Believe you me, I'd cry a ocean of tears if it would save my poor family. But it won't and so I don't." Vi's voice softened. "This meanness just ain't like you, Lily. You've always been so easygoing. So good-natured."

Lily's lips closed tightly. She folded her arms and drew them into her body. The tuna and noodle casserole in the oven sent up a ready smell, and she removed it with a potholder made by Rosy.

"Are you sure you won't stay for lunch?"

"I'm not hungry."

CHAPTER THIRTY

Abe and Cordel-Lewis' final blow came in July when a group of troublemakers led by Lance Porter got drunk one Saturday night and dynamited the tipple. Three days later a local owner called a meeting and reported that because of rising costs, management was shutting down the mine and having it disassembled.

"Other Company properties will be sold at public auction," he said. "Vandalism will be prosecuted, and residents have one month to vacate the premises."

Following the announcement, the commissary handed out free lollipops and stick candy to camp children, many of them with bulging eyes, bowed legs, and swollen bellies. Trucks carrying furniture, cars with old mattresses roped to their roofs, and Harley motorcycles headed north to Detroit and Cincinnati. Some sought government food and refuge with kinfolks; others moved into automobiles, boxcars, barns, and big cardboard boxes. Dog and Ceola moved to Beckley, West Virginia, to take over a farm run by Dog's elderly daddy, Bull Dog; there they could visit Pup at his gravesite and Ceola's ma and two sisters. Abe stayed his month at Cordel-Lewis and worked part-time at a truck mine in nearby Evarts.

One Sunday, while bringing Maude a food tray, a neighbor, Lottie Bowes, found her sweeping the front porch, wearing nothing but a petticoat and cotton slippers. Noticing blue and purple welts on her back and arms, she went home and told her husband, Floyd, who presently commuted with Abe to Evarts.

"Too bad Abe's off to Corbin now without no way to reach him," Floyd said. The next-to-oldest miner at Cordel-Lewis, Floyd was a good man, tall and skinny with a limp that pitched his body forward. He shook his head and sat down for his supper. "Maybe she fell," he said. "I'll talk to Abe."

"I don't think it's from falling." Lottie ran a hand through her thinning bluish-gray hair. It was soft and silky and permed to lay in corkscrew curls the size of coat buttons. "She's a bit absent-minded but not clumsy."

Floyd placed a hand to his right ear to remind Lottie that coal miners are hard of hearing.

"Say what?"

"I said it was like she'd been whipped."

"Whipped? By Abe?"

"Abe Siler wouldn't harm a hair on her head and we both of us know it. No, it had to of been something or somebody else."

"Shouldn't you write and tell Lily?"

"Poor Lily's done washed her hands of the matter and moved to Whitley County to work in a hospital. You and me's about all he's got now."

They held hands as usual while muttering their usual child blessing, the rhyming kind. Then Floyd scooped some vinegary spinach with rounds of boiled egg onto his plate and mixed it with cream of wheat oozing with butter. Lottie picked at her food like a child forced to eat vegetables.

"Are you sayin' Lily's up and left Abe for good?" Floyd asked.

"I'm saying she's moved to Whitley County and it ain't likely he'll join her."

"That don't sound like the Lily I know."

"Sometimes there's more to a thing than what meets the eye so don't let's jump to conclusions. But Ceola wrote and told me and Ceola would be the first one to know. She says she's worried sick about Abe. Asked me to look in on him and I did. The poor dear, I do believe he's near as bad off as his mother. That mine was his heart and soul, you know, not to mention Lily and them sweet younguns."

"Did Ceola say how long it's been since he last seen 'em?" A streak of butter drizzled down Floyd's chin, and he nabbed it with his thumb.

"I believe it was Christmas. This here's August, which would put it at eight months. Stayed near a hour and went back to the mine."

"Funny, Abe and me spend all that time on the road together and he ain't said nary a word about it. It's kinda like the real him's gone into hidin'."

"No, it ain't funny. Talk to him, Floyd. Give him a chance to blow off some steam b'fore he boils over."

"I don't know. Coal miners ain't ones to meddle like you ladies."

"Try anyways."

"And say what?"

"Say we love him and can't help but worry he's not okay."

"Should I tell him about Maude's bruises?"

Lottie kneaded her double chin as she pondered.

"Maybe not."

When his month at the mine ended, Abe canvassed the area and landed a job at a mine in neighboring Bonnie Blue, Virginia, a camp with a population of about a thousand people. Mayflower Hollow, Magazine Hollow, Monitor Hill, Fairview

Hill, and School House Hill had plenty of vacant houses to choose from. But the cost of rent, coal, and electricity was so high he settled on a small ramshackled place outside the camp that was equipped with electricity and a coal stove but no running water.

The weathered shack looked ready to fall in on itself. Rats and squirrels nested in the attic under a tar-paper roof. Sometimes at night their noises frightened Maude, prompting her to go wake up Abe. To persuade her back to her bed, he let her tend to his cough, at which times she spooned out a syrup made of butter, sugar, and vinegar and rubbed his chest with a mixture of turpentine and oil. When she finally went back to bed, he sometimes stayed up to write his children letters.

"The work I got now is sketchy but I ain't worried," he said. "I'm well known in these parts. Once they find out I'm free, hell, they'll roll out the red carpet."…"There's good work out there. It's just a matter of finding it. Somebody like your ole man can afford to be choosy."…"Nothin' yet. But I gotta feelin' tomorrow'll be my lucky day."…"I'm a little low on cash at the moment but will send more next month."

Moved by pity, Lily wrote back with detailed accounts of the children. She begged him to come visit in the place of sending money. He read the letters over and over but never answered.

He was laid off from the Bonnie Blue mine two months later and looked for work at some small gassy mines in Tennessee and West Virginia. A hundred or so younger and more able-bodied men applied for the jobs, were hired, and then fired before working enough hours to earn compensation.

Once *scabbing*—replacing men on strike—became his only option, Abe swore he'd die first. Heartsick, he gave up mining coal altogether and moved to Dayton, Ohio, where Lily's youngest brother, John Mason, offered him a job stocking shelves in his drugstore; thanks to his good business sense, the drugstore had mushroomed out of a corner market. John Mason also offered to provide a home for Abe and his mother.

"Thank you muchly," Abe said when visiting John Mason's big plantation-like house for his first of many dinners. "But we don't want to be a bother."

The dining room was splendid with its French reproduction furniture, silk swag draperies, and chandeliers with glass prisms. He ate fast, licked his fingers, and escaped when he could to a patio furnished with wicker. There he could smoke and cough and keep a close eye on his shawled mother. The autumn air was overcast and chilly, just the way he liked it. Not being afraid of breaking something valuable made him breathe easier.

"Abe, it's only right you let us help," John Mason said. "You and Lily took me in til I could get in the army when I finished high school and Pa sent me packing. You wouldn't take a dime, and turnabout's fair play."

"I done took advantage of one of Lily's brothers and one is enough." Abe twisted the Masonic ring on his finger and proudly recalled the hour, day, and year he had pledged to work for the welfare of mankind by helping the poor and needy. "It's just a matter of time til I pay back every red cent of June's money Lily borrowed and with interest!"

"Then at least let us take care of your mother," John Mason's wife, Phoebe, added as she and Maude returned from collecting a bouquet of pink cosmos and sedum. Phoebe was a slight, pretty woman in her late thirties who helped manage the drug store and treated herself to beauty salons and unlimited shopping. "She can stay here, and you can come take your suppers with us in the kitchen or out here if you prefer. But I warn you, you may be lucky to get a peanut butter and jelly sandwich."

"Thanks, but Mother's my responsibility. She's old and needs a lot of lookin' after. She'd pee on your bed clothes and drive you batty with her jabberin'."

"We could bring somebody in from the store to help look after her, and I think I know just the person," John Mason added.

"Mighty nice but we already rented rooms that'll do us just fine." Abe consciously substituted *rooms* for *room*, a tight space in an area nicknamed Hillbilly Heaven. It had a bar smell, cigarette burns on chipped veneered furniture, and bathrooms at the end of a dark hallway. The cramped space brought back the claustrophobia he'd felt while in the pit, and in some ways felt good.

"Then at least let Phoebe take Maude to see a doctor. Just for a checkup."

"No doctor," Maude squalled. She thrust her hands through her nest of wild hair and rapped her elbows together.

"B'cause of Daddy's attitude, Mother don't believe in doctors. The ole gal would raise Cain," Abe said.

John Mason stared down at the frostbitten sedum and back again at Phoebe.

"I doubt she'd even know."

Abe got a job at a factory that made parts for Lance vending machines, and he and his mother moved into a boarding house close to the work. Cracked plaster walls, chipped paint on sloping floors, and a rusty fire escape leading to a noisy alley made an ugly sight, but he liked the area because it was a haven for railroaders and pensioned coal miners.

A Company man, he received no benefits from the Union but saved what he could and sent small amounts of money to Lily, who returned it to John Mason, who promised to see that it got back to Abe.

"Instead of sending money, come see the kids," Lily continued to write and he, slack-jawed and coughing worse than ever, cringed at the thought of appearing to her as a dropout, a down-and-outer, a graduate of the school of hard knocks, a bad example.

In November he decided to go to Corbin while Will would be home for the Thanksgiving holiday and before the roads froze. Before leaving, he made some trips to the dentist, and Phoebe took him shopping for a new set of clothes, supposedly bought on credit. He admired a pair of spiffy loafers but turned down their offer.

He left his mother with Phoebe, made the trip in five hours, and stayed at the Wilbur Hotel, where Old Joe, Corbin's only visible black resident, shined his shoes and kindly described them as "broke in."

"It ain't easy finding the right fit," he told Old Joe, "and I ain't one to settle."

"Yes, sir, boss, you're smart to wait and stay away from them what cramps the toes," Old Joe answered.

In spite of his new exterior, Abe still refused to see Lily. She agreed to drop the kids at his hotel after school, and he took them for an early Thanksgiving dinner at the Hungry Hound Restaurant, a step-above restaurant on the Cumberland Falls Highway. Sweet William sat up front and was responsible for most of the conversation. He volunteered that he had acquired a part-time job as a science lab instructor and loved helping other students, and he assured Abe he could teach and still have ample time to study. Pressing for more conversation, he asked question after question about his relatives, and about Abe's job, friends, and activities in Dayton. He no doubt prayed that the subject of Fairy Enlow would not surface.

A nervous listener, Abe sat restlessly in his chair and cut his eyes from table to table. The waitress appeared.

"Order up!" he said. "The best steaks in the house!" All chose a hamburger, fries, and a Coca-Cola. They no doubt considered themselves lucky since Lily claimed carbonated drinks were bad for the body and therefore banned.

"So how's the UK playin' field?" Abe asked when time had passed and he could no longer fight the temptation.

"Sports, you mean?"

"Hell, I mean girls!"

"I got my eye on a chick or two," Sweet William answered to please him.

"Atta boy!" Abe patted his shoulder. "At your age, the more the merrier!"

"Well said."

While eating, the girls chatted about school and good friends. Daisy and Tansy said they were making all *A*'s and planned to be teachers. Verni volunteered that she would be graduating a year early from high school and attending the summer term at Eastern Kentucky State College in Richmond. She talked about her plan to major in chemistry, become a pharmacist, and work for Uncle John Mason. Iris said she planned to graduate early as well, one year after Verni, and hopefully attend nearby Berea College to study psychology on a work-study program. She expressed her dream of helping emotionally abused children.

"Hot dog! Didn't I say Abe Siler's kids have got the smarts like their mother? Smart as tacks they are! The pick of the litter! Best of the bunch! God's gift to teachers!"

"We tried to contact you, Daddy, honestly, but Uncle John Mason said your address was unclear at the time, and you didn't have a phone," Verni said.

"True fact. The job kept me hoppin'. And how about you, Squirt? Nothin' short of *A 's*, eh?" he asked Rosy.

She avoided answering by posing her own question.

"How come you're not sleeping at our house?"

"Rosy, you ask too many questions," Verni said and cut her eyes toward Iris and Sweet William.

"When you coming home for good?" Rosy continued.

Abe wiped his forehead with a dingy handkerchief. A train hooted on the tracks, and he smiled painfully through the familiar echo.

"Well, Squirt, I don't rightly know. As it is, your ole man's facing the whoppertunity of a lifetime in Dayton. Hell, who knows? Maybe I'll strike it rich and you all can come live with me in a big fancy house like John Mason's. How'd you dodos like to be buckeyes?"

The waitress returned, and he ordered apple pie and ice cream to go around.

"And Mama too?" Rosy asked. "Would Mama be a buckeye?"

"If she plays her cards right, she might."

"Golly Jees Moses! Then I could quit school and go work in a factory that makes chocolate!"

338 · FAYE SOLOMON KUSHNER

"Like hell you will!" Everybody laughed, especially Abe, who seemed happy to show off his improved teeth. They lapped up the dessert, and he asked for the ticket.

"It's been a funful time," he said and stood up to be seen. Tall and erect, a manly figure in his spiffy new clothes, he opened his wallet to a catalog of small bills, counted out what he owed, and tossed out a tip.

In December Lily got a loan co-signed by Wade Eakins and bought a two-story brick house on the Main Street end of Fifth. The four-bedroom structure had a dressy living room with a fireplace and silk curtains. It also had a large, open kitchen with wood-grain cabinets, vinyl tiles, and pretty papered walls showing green vines climbing a stone wall. There were also three bathrooms, a utility room with a washer and dryer, a small sewing room or office, and a basement, too damp for a den. Wide moldings, shiny hardwood floors, fresh coats of paint, ample windows, and some new furniture gave the place such a handsome appearance that the girls couldn't wait to have parties.

"The best Christmas present in the world!" they agreed while Lily proudly reminded them of the home-of-their-own promise she'd made, and kept. Once settled in, they celebrated with Beulah Lee and Bunny at a beef-brisket dinner prepared by Lily.

Phoebe and John Mason fought the heavy snowfall and showed up for an early Christmas. They brought gifts wrapped in foiled wrapping paper with bows the size of hydrangea blossoms. They also brought a small RCA television for the kitchen.

"It's from your daddy," they said, leaving Lily to wonder.

The two removed their leather shoes and wool coats at the door. They hugged everyone with such merriment you would have thought Christmas had already arrived. Then they sat down for coffee and some Fig Newtons.

"We were hoping Daddy would come, too," the girls agreed when the excitement had worn down, and Phoebe explained that he was looking forward to the trip, but had come down with a last-minute sinus infection. She maintained a consistent smile and seemed to convince everyone but Lily.

A Christmas tree decorated with lights, balls, popcorn, and tinsel and topped with a silk angel blinked before a bay window. A fire crackled from the other side of a big living room with twin sofas. Red plastic boots filled with hard candy dressed tables, and a string of Christmas cards swung between windows.

"Can we open the presents now? Do we have to wait until Christmas?" Rosy pleaded.

"Yes, open them now so we can see if you like them," Phoebe answered.

"Golly Jees Moses!"

A dresser set, locket, and beaded bracelet went to Rosy. But she seemed more interested in the older girls' body lotions, perfumes, and cosmetics, especially the box of lipstick samples, shiny little tubes not much bigger than the head of a pencil.

"Does anybody here want a facial?" Phoebe asked, and five girls jumped at the chance.

"Now all we need is Ceola here to do our hair!" Verni, the first in line, announced with excitement.

John Mason asked for a tour of the house. It began and ended in the kitchen, with more coffee. Windows quivered from the harsh winter wind; some wore fog curtains. Lily was disappointed that her pretty landscaping lay under snow and the play-dead thatch of winter, and that her pots for pretty flowers were garaged for the season.

"Lily, can I speak frankly?" John Mason asked when the tour was over and the two were alone.

"Sure."

"Then I'll get straight to the point. Abe is dying of lung disease and grief for his family. His mother has dementia. I don't think either of them will last through another Ohio winter. Please, for his sake and the children's, let him come home while he still can." Lily held up a hand to protest, and he waved it down. "I mean a trial visit. I know you're busy taking care of the kids and working too, so hire somebody to help out. Phoebe and I would be glad to cover the expenses and come take him back to Ohio if things don't work out."

"Abe would never agree to come live in Corbin."

"His options are limited. Soon he won't have a choice."

She sat up straight in her chair and regarded him with steely eyes.

"Is he drinking liquor?"

"Not a drop. He works every day and still believes his success ship will one day sail him home to his family. It grieves him that you're the one putting his children through college."

"Not really. They're mostly doing it themselves." She switched on the radio to make sure no one was listening.

"I've got nothing against Abe coming, John Mason, and I've made that clear from the start. In fact, I want him to be as close to his children as possible for their sakes and his. But if he came for a stay, he'd insist on bringing her, and I'll not have that woman in my home. Not now, not ever. Nor will I be trapped into being her caretaker. She schemed to have Abe all to herself, and she got him. Now let them suffer the consequences together."

"It was his pride that kept him away. We both know he's proud to a fault."

They talked on, Lily sometimes attempting to change the subject and John Mason pleading all the harder. At times she pretended the radio had drawn her attention.

"I believe if you saw Maude, you'd change your mind. I guarantee she's changed."

"No, I wouldn't."

"Well, he won't leave her, that much is for certain. If he would, Phoebe and I would gladly take her in. We'd take them both, but Abe's proud, as I said. He claims he botched things up with June, and he's not about to depend on another one of your brothers."

"That's true, he did." Her eyes dropped as she remembered the discomfort he had put her and June through that time he took Sweet William to college and didn't bother to call or come back when expected.

"You know he's never stopped loving you," John Mason said.

"Never stopped loving me, huh?" she answered with a snicker. "Tell me, John Mason, what good is love if it's a check you can't cash? He was in Corbin for Thanksgiving and didn't even bother to see me. Does that sound like love?" She rose from the table, rigid, as if to dismiss him.

"I sure wish I'd been able to persuade you," he said.

"Let her die, and then come back asking."

CHAPTER THIRTY-ONE

Spring arrived, calling Lily to Buck Creek, where she helped her ma plant her annual crop of lettuce while watching her pa hook up the mules. It was a warm day with a soft breeze and clear blue sky. Cloud banks, white like angels, parted for a yellow burst of sun. The site rendered an impression of glory and God.

Lily removed her cardigan sweater and shook the winter drowse from her bones. She breathed deep, taking in the earthy smells of sweating animals, plowed earth, bulb flowers, and her sweet-scented folks. The earth seemed electric with spontaneity, color, movement, and music. Nature's shoeshine, she thought as she noticed dogwoods and redtips, their limbs grabbing sun at the edge of a woods.

"Such a pretty day to be outside!" she said and leaned on her hand hoe. "It makes me almost dread going back to the hospital."

"But I thought you loved nursing," Sarah said.

"I do, I really do, but working behind walls on days like this one makes me feel, I don't know, a little trapped. Sometimes I think if it were not for loving my patients so much, I could leave nursing and go back to farm life for good. No starched uniforms or rules or time clocks to punch wouldn't be bad."

Sarah looked up, her eyes probing Lily's for signs of regret.

"Are you sure it's the farm you're missing?"

Lily cocked her head to the side and squinted her eyes as if to say the question had caught her off guard.

"What do you mean?" she asked harmlessly.

"I guess I'm wondering if it could be the past you're really missing. Not the farm exactly but the life you had there."

"With Abe, you mean?"

"With the family all together."

Lily's fingers went to her chest and followed the usual worn path.

"Maybe, but I try not to think about it. What's gone is gone."

Sarah stooped before the different varieties of red and green lettuce. From the same bottle she used to sprinkle clothes for ironing, she doused each plant with soapy water to keep away insects. She sifted light coats of fertilizer through her long, gloveless fingers and worked them into the loamy soil with her arrowhead hoe.

"Tell me about the younguns," she said as if purposely switching to a brighter subject.

"They're great kids, every one of them, as you well know," Lily said and paused. "But, Ma, I have reason to believe Sweet William's still seeing Fairy Enlow. I can't help but worry that she might pressure him into getting married."

"You think it's that serious?"

"It's hard to say. Sweet William's as tightlipped as his daddy. All I know is what Vi tells me. She says he didn't stop seeing Fairy when he went away to college, but I think there's a chance they're just friends. You know Sweet William. He's so filled with compassion, he may think she needs looking after."

Sarah nabbed a handful of bittersweet weed, its tiny yellow flowers wavering on clover-like stems, and dropped them inside a rusty red bucket with an iron handle.

"He's like Rosy."

"Rosy's compassionate all right. Especially toward her daddy. It's funny, you know. Abe's always worked such long hours Rosy was the only one of the girls who really got to know him. But now that he's gone, they talk about him constantly. It's like his trip home for Thanksgiving rekindled love they'd almost forgotten."

"He's their daddy. It's only natural they'd miss him."

Lily stared up at Indian Mountain, purplish blue, like larkspur, her favorite flower.

"John Mason said the Ohio winters are wrecking what's left of his lungs, Ma. He keeps after me to take him and Maude in, but he has no idea what he's asking."

"It would be a giant responsibility."

"He said Abe's lungs are so swollen they poke through his shirts."

"Imagine the pain of it, the poor man."

"Believe me, I have. For the children's sake, I'd let him come back under certain conditions if it weren't for Maude. Her, I'll never forgive."

"I can see why."

"Not after how she did us."

"That's understandable."

"We'd still be a family if it weren't for her."

"She meddled for sure."

Lily wiped the moisture from her eyes. For whatever reason, can't or won't, she had never been one to shed tears.

"You think I'm being too hard on her, don't you?"

"I think you've suffered a good deal of unkindness."

"When does it end, Ma, the bitterness and anger? Sometimes I feel my heart shriveling like earthworms on a hot pavement. Hate is a fungus, I do believe." Lily sighed and shook her head. "The children see I'm not at my best, no matter how hard I pretend. I can't stand to think this new me is how I'll be remembered."

"Healing takes time, Lily. And so does change."

"But what if I don't heal? What if I go on hating?"

"It's still too soon. You're not ready."

"And how will I know when I'm ready?"

Sarah landed a spit of snuff just outside the iceberg lettuce. "You'll know."

After talking with her ma, Lily dwelled on the state of Abe's health, the children's need for a daddy, and the space that could be available once Verni left for college. In July, she threw up her hands in frustration and began the task of writing John Mason a letter saying Abe and his mother were welcome in Corbin. But should she use words like *home? visit? trial run?* she wondered. Should she make her expectations read like a contract? Short and sweet, she decided after an anguishing clash between conscience and common sense, and she issued the invitation without mentioning either conditions or expectations. She sent the same letter to Abe and was neither surprised nor disappointed when he didn't answer. In fact, she felt relieved, thankful for the chance to spend alone time with her children, especially on those wonderful weekends when Sweet William came home from college. What a tiresome life it would be to tend to patients all day long, even the well-loved ones, and come home in the evenings to tend to more patients, she told herself. She even congratulated herself for having acquired a clean conscience, as gratifying as a clean house, but without all the effort.

The peace, however, was short-lived. In the days to come, she suffered from the *mopsies*, as Rosy would say, and couldn't sleep at night or focus during the day. Dull pains in her back reminded her of when she'd been pregnant. Her conscience nagged her to the point that she considered praying and reading her Bible. Finding herself short of faith, she turned to the self-trust teachings of Henry David Thoreau and Ralph Waldo Emerson, New England writers whose works she'd purchased from the flea market at Saxton. She also took consolation from her favorite old novel, Nathaniel Hawthorne's *The Scarlet Letter*, a story about love between a young, thought-to-be widow and her well-meaning minister. During her most wretched winter days without Abe, she had turned to the book for escape and even pretended to be its heroine, Hester Prynne, known for her strength and courage when accused of adultery by a self-righteous New England community. Forced to openly wear the sin's symbol, the letter A, as punishment, she had embroidered it large and in fine gold threads, and had proudly displayed it on her chest like the true love that burned beneath it. What would Hester have done in my place? she had asked herself, and she had vowed to bear her suffering with that same pride and dignity, even compassion. Now she was beginning to wonder if she had been motivated more by stubbornness than by dignity.

The answer came to her one day in August as she noticed her garden flowers dying from the heat and clearing ground for the nurturing leaves of a new season. Daily she recalled John Mason's prediction that Abe would not survive another

Ohio winter. She pictured him shivering in his frayed denim jacket and coughing before the fumes of a gas space heater, and she decided to write once again, this time in a softer, more persuasive tone, consciously admitting that *she*, as well as the children, missed him, and that the children longed to see their grandmother. At the same time she made an arrangement with Jetty Jacobs, a third-shift aide at the hospital, to help care for Maude when and if the time came.

Weeks passed without a reply, and she had practically given up when a scribbled note arrived with the message, "Muchas gracias." In it Abe said he accepted her invitation even though he was leaving his best job ever. He promised to bring a hell of a big surprise.

Crêpe-paper streamers hung from tree branches, and balloons floated over the mailbox the following Sunday afternoon when Abe and his mother sputtered into Corbin in the sick but shiny Plymouth Roadking. Waving a certificate entitling him to sell Globe Life Insurance, he wrestled from the car to announce he'd come to put his family on Easy Street, "right up there with the by-godly best of 'em."

"Surprised, eh?" he whooped, and pulled out his textbook, two big chrome rings holding flip-over pages with the appearance of upholstery samples, only lighter. His eyes at times held the sunlight. His expression and movements were beyond excited; they seemed almost goofy.

Sweet William and the girls showered him with affection while Lily stood as lifeless as the wooden coat rack in her kitchen corner. A dozen emotions toyed with her psyche after close to two years of waiting. Thinner, stooped even more than before, he still had the looks of a man sought by women. And judging by his slicked-back hair, cheap cologne, and hairy chest under an open collar, she figured he'd had his fair share. At what point had he given up tee shirts and creased khakis? Had he also put aside his pride and good character?

She invited them inside, and Abe paused in the foyer to look around. He focused on the carved, natural-wood staircase and the brick fireplace with wooden bookshelves reaching the ceiling.

"Nice place you got here! Thanks for the invite," he said, and turned away as if humiliated by the extravagant sight of it. Every item he and his mother had brought fit inside a battered cardboard suitcase with yellow and brown stripes and a Grand Ole Opry sticker. Lily noticed he carried it with both hands behind his back, and she felt a tinge of sympathy mixed with disappointment.

Earlier, when Beulah Lee and Bunny had teased her about getting her lover boy back, she had scoffed and called the idea ridiculous. And yet she had dared to dream because dreaming was safe and exciting. It added color to a sometimes drab and lonely existence.

She had gone to the beauty shop for the full treatment, and the beautician had cut her long hair in layers to give it body. She had shopped at Maggie J's, the trendiest shop in town, and bought bright, pretty clothes, forgiving clothes that complimented her slender figure. She had sat through a facial at Merle Norman's and purchased the pricey products. She had even attached some heroic motive to his departure, as if he were returning home from a war or expedition. In her dreams she had smelled his old flavors, and drawn him in like a fresh breath of springtime.

But he had returned as an outsider, someone far beneath her heart's expectations.

"I'm here to see that you and the dodos don't want for a thang!" he said and clunked the suitcase on the porcelain floor. He wheezed, coughed, drummed his fingers against his forehead, and announced with a certain proud air, "Any li'l thang your heart desires, just you name it and, by-godly, it's yourn for this askin'."

"That's really good, dear," she answered. *Dear*, she said to keep things impersonal, and because his Bible name now seemed out of character. This slick new man was somebody soiled and spoiled, unfit to be her children's daddy, one step above a beggar. And she had never been one to pity beggars.

"Hell, woman, I mean it! Your lucky day is come! The same goes for you dodos!"

"Golly Jees Moses!" Rosy cried. The twinsies, eyes big with glee, whispered back and forth about crinoline slips, rock-and-roll shoes, and Angora hats fashioned after those of the 1920s.

"Yes, dear," she said, sick of his act.

She turned to study his mother, a slight, smiling woman with gray hair, capsule eyes, and wispy lips that left her looking toothless. When Maude stopped smiling, her eyes receded, and she hid behind Abe like a shy toddler. Remembering that patients in nursing homes are sometimes invited to bring their own furniture, Lily led her to the familiar kitchen table and the smell of chicken and dumplings. She had the girls bring out old photographs and trinkets. Sometimes Maude called the children by their given names and remembered incidents even they had forgotten. At other times she confused them with her childhood family, and she tried to catch elves on the curtains.

"Sweet little things," she said of the elves until Abe lost his temper.

"For Pete's sake, Mother, there's no elves, see? Now straighten up and fly right! Get a grip, will ya?"

Lily's first inclination was to pity the old woman, but a stronger urge was to smile and feel avenged, to look on Maude's unfortunate state as a kind of natural consequence, harsh but well deserved. Such was not a feeling she, a nurse, was at peace with, but peace, she told herself, was a luxury she had learned to live without.

"Where should I put the bag?" Abe asked, a matter Lily had purposely avoided. Earlier she had decided to give him Sweet William's upstairs room near a bath and have Maude sleep in the small bedroom nearby that belonged to Rosy, who would move into the sewing room, small but cozy. Because of his shortness of breath, she had even considered offering him her own bedroom downstairs, with Maude sleeping in the nearby den. But the generosity had been before, when she had fooled herself into overlooking the fact that he was a man who had chosen his mother over his wife.

"Lily, the bag?"

"Oh, yes," she said. Head poised, eyes focused straight ahead, she led the two into a big den. "It's an open room with a television and close to the kitchen and bath so Maude can easily find her way around. The couch converts into a bed, and there's a rollaway in the closet. The girls will bring clean linen, and when you have settled in, you can join us for lunch in the kitchen."

Abe's face turned fire red, and his breath made quick push-and-pull sounds. The thought of him sharing a room with his mother, and in plain sight of his wife and kids, had undoubtedly hit him like a devil's rock from a soft ceiling.

"No problemo," he said, grinning, and dropped the suitcase into a pile of green shag carpet.

"Please let us know if you need anything," Lily said before turning and making a landlady's exit.

The next morning Abe shaved, bathed, and helped his mother dress before going to the kitchen. According to her, he was bright-eyed and bushy-tailed, but the humiliation he'd suffered the night before had left him down-and-out, and wanting to go back to Ohio. In spite of his anger, he managed to make what he considered a manly decision. He had come here knowing it wouldn't be easy, and Abe Siler had never been one to run away from a challenge, or his children. Let alone be driven away by the likes of a cocky woman.

"So what do you think of your ole man?" he asked the girls as he posed before the washstand mirror. His blue suit, shiny with age, needed pressing. The shoulders sagged. The trousers gathered under the belt. He sucked in his barrel chest, pulled back his shoulders, and thrust out his arms for inspection.

"You'll need new clothes." Lily eyed his ashy tie and loose-fitting shirt collar. "I'm sure Verni will be happy to go shopping with you."

"Thanks, but Phoebe took care of it. The suit and tie are just to make a good first impression. Then I'll wear the sporty duds she picked out."

"Daddy, you look like a movie star!" Rosy exclaimed, and his face lit up. The other girls agreed that he was very handsome. Even Iris nodded.

He combed his fingers through his hair that needed cutting and ran half a biscuit over his shoes, leaving crumbs on the floor. They were the same cracked shoes Lily had kept polished for close to twenty years. The ones Old Joe, shoe-shine boy at the Wilbur Hotel, had referred to as *comfortable*.

He sat down with the girls and was glad Lily was at the stove and not there to find fault with his manners. Refusing to eat had occurred to him since she had done the cooking, but he knew he would need his strength for a hard day of work. He would need a hard day of work in order to make enough *moolah* to put food on the table.

He shoved down his food, fed his mother, and reached for a cigarette.

"No smoking in the house," Lily retorted, and he bowed to the boss lady.

"Which one of you nitwits wants to carry my debit book to the car?" he asked. The three youngest girls scrambled, and Daisy and Tansy got there first.

"Tomorrow I get a turn, don't I, Daddy?" Rosy wiped the tears from her eyes.

"Ye damn right you do!"

"Will you be here when I get home from school?" she continued.

"It's a long workday but I'll be back and forth to check on Mother."

Lily left and came back wearing her white starched uniform that aroused a smirk.

"Be sure to take the Plymouth by McCall's service station," she said. "I noticed it's leaking oil."

"Not today. Today I ain't got time." He held up five fingers. "This here's the deal. No medical exams, no waiting period, 30-day money-back guarantee, no federal income tax, and guaranteed for life! A policy only a nincompoop would pass up, am I right?" His face took on the old pride. "You'll see, Lily. This works out and, hell, this family will be done with scrimping forever!"

Lily looked down at her watch.

"Park the Plymouth on the street," she said and walked ahead to rush him along.

Slowly he tackled the porch steps, gripping the rail. Barefoot, Maude slipped onto the porch with a brown paper bag and an RC Cola. The cotton nightgown she wore, washed until it looked knobby and practically see-through, clung to her hips like a cellophane cheese wrapper.

"Son Boy, you forgot your lunch!" she said, eyes dancing. "I packed you a peanut-butter sandwich."

"Hell, Mother, a businessman don't brownbag his first day on the job! He goes and eats out, meets people, makes contacts, builds a image!" He fingered the rabbit's foot on his almost empty key ring and let a hand brush his guitar belt buckle. "Shoot, I'm thinkin' I just might go to the Dixie and have me a foot-long hot dog. B'damned if you can't smell that chili and onions from one end of Main to the other!"

"A hot dog? Oh, yes, a hot dog. Well, don't forget your rubbers. They're calling for rain."

"Put the sandwich in the fridge, Maude. He'll have it later," Lily said and turned to Abe. "This is no time to get sick. If I were you, I'd avoid the spicy foods."

"Sick, hell! When have I ever been sick? Good Lord, woman, you're talkin' to a man about to embark on a new career. Ditch the tongue wagging and wish him good luck, will ya?"

"Children, wish your daddy good luck," she said, and sent them inside to finish dressing for school. "Brush teeth," she added, and hoped Maude would get that same message.

"Good luck Daddy!" the girls exclaimed. "We love you!"

"Knock 'em dead!" Rosy added.

Lily followed him to the Plymouth and watched him curl into the seat.

"You know where you're going, right?"

"Central Street. I figure I'll start out with the houses near the high school." He took out a wrinkled yellow handkerchief and wiped the sweat from his forehead. "It's the math that gets to me, Lily."

"You passed the test, didn't' you?"

"Yes, but John Mason was there to give me some pointers."

"Just relax and take your time."

He perked up and pushed out a laugh.

"Nothing ventured, nothing gained. That's the ticket! Am I right?"

"You should know!" she said with renewed anger, and stalked away, leaving him puzzled.

Lily breathed a lot easier when Jetty Jacobs, Maude's caretaker, showed up early the next morning. Jetty was fortyish, with blue-black hair like Ceola's, ruby red lips like Vi's, and a round buttocks that wobbled like a staggering drunk. She came carrying a basket of dampened clothes, an iron, and some tubed wire hangers. With Lily's permission she planned to iron clothes while Maude napped and deliver them to customers along her way home. Once home, she would tend her six children and mine-disabled husband and grab four hours of sleep before going back to the hospital at eleven.

"I want Maude's bandages changed daily," Lily said, and pointed to different creams and lotions. "She won't agree to let anybody but me do it, so you'll have to win her over. You may find you have to bandage her hands to keep her from clawing." Maude was sleeping soundly on her stomach. Lily raised her pajama top and eased aside a bandage to show some of the bruises and cuts, the different shades of red, green, purple, and even black. Only a few cuts had healed over. The bandage was sticky with blood and drainage, so Lily took her time. "Her moods are unpredictable. Feel free to call Abe for help," she added, "and make sure she wraps up and goes outside to walk daily."

"The poor darlin'. I never seed such a back," Jetty whispered and closed her eyes while shaking her head. "How'd she get 'em?"

"Self-inflicted." Lily replaced the bandage and swept the hair from Maude's face.

"The poor soul. Lord love her heart!"

"Keep telling her that," Lily said. "That God loves her. She's a firm believer."

"She is?"

"She is, yes."

"Then why on earth would she do such a thang?"

"I'm sure she was confused."

"She must be in plain awful pain."

Lily thought back to the day she first met Maude in her mid-thirties. Eyes pinched, mouth drawn, wearing all black, and old already.

"I think Maude stopped feeling pain some time ago."

CHAPTER THIRTY-TWO

Abe woke up one morning as Lily, wearing her white starched uniform and the nurse smile he despised, held out an orange tray of food, the cafeteria kind, one she'd no doubt bought at the Saxton flea market. The color orange as a rule spooked him. It put him in mind of Halloween and autumn, when dry air in a coal mine is most apt to explode and some angry ghosts come out from the rocks to rig machines or shift tracks. It took him back to the mine explosion and the now dead kid he'd held to his heart like a son.

He sat up and felt more fatigued than usual, short of breath, sleep, and patience, and aching as though he'd been tumbled by a washing machine agitator. Mucus clogged his throat, and he yearned for a taste of the steaming hot coffee he pretended not to smell.

"Good morning!" Lily sang as she eased the tray onto a bedside table and reached to plump his pillow. "Are *we* ready to eat something?"

That word *we* got to him. It reminded him of the sugar-sweet but wicked invitation she'd sent, only to stash him in a room with his mother. Damn flusteratin' broad thinks I'm just another one of her poor, pitiful patients, he thought, and he wished he could whack her upside the head.

"I'm ready if you are!" he answered with a sneer.

"You know *we* must eat if we want to stay healthy."

"Hey, knock off the nurse crap!" he said and coughed. It seemed he always coughed when Lily came around in her white starched uniform and the Florence Nightingale pin she wore like a crown. That holier-than-thou cross pin didn't fool him one bit. No way in hell! He'd seen her bullying type in the sonsovabitchin' Bloody Harlan camp dicks that came at Union sympathizers with badges and bats. In those hard-assed Company men that smiled as they sacked hard-working miners from behind big boss desks. In meddling Wade Eakins, flaunting his Bible like Lily her Florence Nightingale pin and preaching hellfire to sinners no different than hisself.

"Drink your coffee while it's hot," she said, and dropped three pills onto the tray: a purplish-colored vitamin, penicillin for inflammation, and Darvon for pain. "It'll help the cough."

"Bull! It's the dust in this house is why I cough! How's come you're here anyways?"

"You asked me to wake you before I left for work so you could clean out the garage. I thought I'd come a little early, and maybe we could talk."

"Talk? Talk about what? Me gettin' well when I ain't sick?"

"About you having a room of your own."

"A room of my own, huh? If that don't beat all! Why would I want a room of my own, now that I've already been made out a lowlife in the eyes of my kids?"

"I took Verni to college. Iris will be leaving soon and you can have their room if..."

"Sorry. Too late."

"Okay. Then I'll let you go back to sleep."

"Great idea!" he grouched, but expected her to stay and play nurse. "Wait, Lily!" he cried when she turned to go out. To soften her, he shoved down a mouthful of oatmeal with warm canned peaches and swallowed the horse-pill vitamin she'd left.

"Yes? Do you need something?" She pretended not to notice the spoon in his mouth.

"Nope."

"You called me."

"I was talkin' to myself."

She reached for his cup.

"I'll freshen your coffee."

"No," he snapped, and when she had gone, he slid forward on his back and lifted his knees to make a tunnel of the covers.

Lily sensed Abe was laboring over more than just his room situation, and she felt the conflict had something to do with his mother, a subject she wished to avoid. Daily she wrestled with her greatest fear—that he had come to Corbin for the sheer purpose of dying and dumping his responsibility on her. To cope, she went on as usual, speaking highly of Maude to the children but overlooking her when possible. But she was, after all, a nurse with a conscience. From a distance she watched over her like a ghost nurse, there but not there. She cooked for her and prepared her medicines and clothes. Noticing that light made a difference in Maude's moods, she had Abe move her rocking chair to a front window, where she could wave at the postman and children going to and from school. Maude spent hours there flipping through pages of her Bible, chatting with her mama, and playing games like "Blind Man's Bluff" with her siblings, Blessie and Clinton. With Sherman she planted corn and tobacco, and helped give birth to piglets she later slaughtered. Regularly she scolded him for taking Abe to the still and coal mine. At such times she might yank the pins from her hair or whack the arms of her rocker.

When Jetty took her outside, Maude plucked leaves as if they were flowers and called them *colors*. Like hummingbirds she seemed to prefer red, a choice Lily attributed to her increasingly poor vision. Everyone saw that Maude's mind was deteriorating with her vision. The girls, who she now referred to as *sweet things*, took pity on her. They read her books, braided her hair, cut and painted her fingernails with clear polish, brought her peppermint candy, the round ones that melt in your mouth, and prepared her for bed like they would a baby.

Abe, too, coddled her. He added locks to the doors and built a banister in case she wandered down the garage steps and into the street. At the foot of the stairway he installed a portable gate and set aside some of Lily's favorite decorations to clear walkways for her. Because of Maude's poor vision, he had the girls make and post signs. For Maude's protection, he seemed to have become master of the house, or created his own new one.

Lily looked on quietly, but she secretly resented her girls giving Maude what had once been her attention. Handing her husband over to Maude had been one thing, but giving up her girls was quite another. Thank goodness, she often thought, for the sense of importance she felt when at work because at home she had no choice but to play second fiddle.

With time, Lily grew bitter. Sarah's saying—"You can change the root of the tree, but you can't change its leaf"—ran through her like a jukebox tune you can't shut off once the coin clicks. Everyone—Abe, Jetty, her girls—seemed to think Maude was an innocent li'l ole granny, a Mrs. Santa Claus stuffing cloth animals for children. Maude appeared harmless, yes. Her voice was softer, and her face was sweeter. But Lily could not shake off the feeling that behind that sweet-smiling luminance lurked that same conniving leaf.

Abe worked long and hard at selling insurance, and even Lily respected his work ethic and patience. Sometimes in the evenings, while knowing he would be met by steely eyes, plastic smiles, and shrugs in the place of words, he imagined the happy company of a jug of corn liquor. *Why?* was still the thorn in his side. Why had Lily pretended to miss him and invited him to Corbin, only to humiliate him by slamming him into a room with his mother?

"Wade Eakins to a T!" he grumbled the evening she refused to let him chip in for household expenses. *Miss Uppity, Boss Lady, Your Heiny, Snoopervisor*, he called her under his breath, and each day he swore he would telephone John Mason and Phoebe to say he wanted to go home to Ohio.

But at night, when lights and whispers went out, and his mother had finally jabbered herself to sleep, he longed for Lily the way he had before she took the hospital job and he found comfort in lesser women. He remembered Saxton and Bryce's Cove and how she had raced breathlessly to him with a flower in her hair and laughter that said she had reached the pot of gold at the end of a rainbow. He recalled her adoring smile and good looks—the dark glossy hair, high cheekbones, skin the color of almonds—and every mark on her perfect body, including the thin white scar on her right knee from when she was eight and wrecked on a bicycle.

There had once been a sense of freedom and adventure in her that at times made him tremble in his boots, afraid she might sprout wings, fly over the mountain, and find the better life she was made for. He'd realized he couldn't live without her that afternoon she'd childishly climbed into a mostly hollow tree, poked her head through a pigeon hole, made paws of her hands, and pretended to be a squirrel munching nuts. It rained that evening and she refused to go inside. They'd made love against the trunk of a birch with knobby white knees and then slept naked on the velvety moss underneath it.

When they woke up, they made love again. She peeled off her clothes with the ease of stripping the paper-like bark from their birch. In a barn loft, tool shed, corn crib, they'd gone at it that same hungry way. Sometimes within a hair of Wade Eakins' breath.

But that was the old passionate Lily, he told himself while knuckling away tears. And come morning he threw himself into selling insurance as if success, and not love, was the winning ticket.

CHAPTER THIRTY-THREE

The autumn weather was damp and gloomy. As usual, Lily left the hospital late, already missing her favorite patients and occupied girls and wishing she had somewhere to go other than home. Her stomach felt queasy; her body ached from stress and fatigue. She didn't make her usual A&P stop, but decided to prepare supper from the freezer.

Once home she noticed a clean concrete driveway, its oil and grease stains invisible in the evening light. Cans, bottles, boxes, and tools sat neatly on garage shelves. The yard was mowed and edged, and the street curb appeared as clean as her kitchen floor. She shook her head in wonder and asked herself how a sick man could accomplish so much work in a single day. No doubt he'd also completed his insurance rounds and hopefully sold a policy. She had to admit she loved the thoughtfulness as well as the help.

Inside, Maude was waiting at her window, giggling as her fingers wove the path of the itsy-bitsy spider. Her gray eyes lit up when she saw Lily, and she waved her hands and babbled something happy. Lily wrapped an afghan around her knees and kept going. Who could have guessed, she asked herself, that this sweet-smiling lady had pitched such a fit the night before that she'd left scratches on Abe's wrists when he'd tried to brush out her tangles?

Maude had gum disease and was losing teeth. Making a mental note to schedule her another dental appointment, Lily hurried toward the kitchen and the old sounds of her girls. All sat down at the table while the girls talked about snooty girls, friendly girls, girls who chased boys, and some who went even further. Iris blushed as she mentioned a cute boy named Ferman who had asked to borrow a pencil while one stuck up from his shirt pocket. Lily noticed a glow, pumped her for more information, and got nothing. The child, she thought, was more like her daddy than she'd realized.

"So will you see him again?" Verni asked.

"We're in Glee Club together, so yes. But we're just friends. He loves to sing just like Daddy."

"By the way, where is Daddy?" The words seemed to pop out, and Lily paused afterwards to consider her intimate use of the word *Daddy* instead of the usual *your daddy*. And why had she even bothered to ask? Was she softening because of the clean garage and his hard work and determination to pay his own way. Or was it the patient she had lost today, leaving her feeling sad and lonely and lusting for child candy, some delicious treat that provoked a simple *gosh*! or *wee*! or *Golly Jees Moses*!

Iris answered by reporting a ukulele lesson. Daisy and Tansy spoke of a jigsaw puzzle he'd help work. Rosy said they'd raked leaves.

"Did he wear a mask?" Lily asked, knowing he had not, in spite of her nagging. She shook her head as if to say he was stubborn and impossible, but smiled over the kindness he'd shown to their girls.

She found him sprawled on his couch in the den, one foot on the floor, no doubt so exhausted he'd not bothered to pull down the mattress. He was sleeping and the den was quiet, except for his labored breathing and the buzz of a stink bug drawn to a window. The room smelled of Vaseline, coffee, and the cigarettes he sneak smoked, as if she wouldn't recognize the smell. She pushed a chair up to the couch and sat squinting at him through a grim hint of light. His face, so long protected from the sun, was smooth, fuller now that he'd begun to eat better. He was one of those men who seemed to become more handsome as he aged. And yet, she knew a sick person when she saw one. The veiled face and pouted lips of someone struggling to breathe stirred her nurse's nature. She reminded herself, as she had so often when sweet memories challenged her judgment, that a realist cannot dwell on the past; that truth lies in the present and future; that he had traded her for his mother.

In time she wondered if, set in her ways like her pa, she had judged him too harshly, and outside the laws of her own nature. Self-evident laws, laws from nature's God, fair laws that make sense. But in spite of the nostalgia, she shook off these remnants of the past and reminded herself that she would not be one of those wronged wives who make martyrs of their husbands once they are sick, or dying. She would not be like her sisters, self-loathing women who lie down to be run over.

"Bad dream?" she asked when he woke up sweating.

"A nightmare." he answered. "I dreamed about Mother."

"Uh-oh," she said and thought he was joking. But seeing the despairing look on his face, she wondered if this conversation would end up like the last one—a *dramedy*, more ridiculous than real.

"What do you think will become of her oncst I'm gone?" he blurted out.

Lily set her jaw and sucked in her lips and was not happy.

"Go see a doctor," she said. "Get better and take care of her yourself."

"The ole gal won't last, you know, in one of them looney bins."

"There are always nursing homes. Some are very well maintained."

"Nothin' doin'! Them places strap patients to beds and commodes and dope them til they ain't nothin' but dummies."

"True, they're not staffed like hospitals. The family is expected to pitch in and help."

"They've got bedbugs and head lice and rats big as possums. And any number of fires. Most of 'em burn to the ground. Which in a way is a godsend." He huffed and puffed, struggled to the point that Lily was tempted to leave and come back at a time when he felt better.

"Let's us talk frank here, Lily. No beatin' around the bush, see? Promise me when I conk out she'll have a home here with you and the dodos and I promise you won't have nary regrets. I didn't know til I brung her here how puny she is. And how much she'd take to you and the girls. I thought she might wanta stay with John Mason and Phoebe. But no. She wouldn't have nothin' to do with nobody 'ceptin' her family." He coughed into his sleeve and slid his arm under a blanket, and she pretended not to see the blood spatter. "Please, Lily, you know I ain't one to take somethin' for nothin'. Take the insurance and farm and two houses and ever red cent her and me's got and tell me you won't dump her in one of them places."

Lily's first reaction was to hate him again, and she overcame the urge by pretending he was a patient she could walk away from and leave at the hospital. But the sound of a person fighting for air came back, and for a minute she was tempted to out-and-out lie by agreeing to keep Maude since he may not live long enough to know the difference.

"Like I said, live and take care of her yourself," she answered.

"Look, Lily, you got it wrong, see? She's different now. In spite of her craziness, and mind you, I ain't excusin' it for a minute I ain't, her idea of a home was never nowhere but with us and the dodos. You should of seen how she suffered when we left here. How she mourned over her bad mistakes and wished she could come back."

"Suffered? Maude suffered?" She, a nurse trained to hide emotion, jumped up from her chair. "Impossible! After all this time, you still think that woman is innocent!"

"Bull! I think she's changed is what I think. By godly, I know it. B'damned if I won't take her with me when I go 'fore I'll let her be sent to one of them places."

Go, meaning *die,* she later realized. But not at that moment.

"You should, yes! Take her and go! Wouldn't be the first time! Silly me to have thought you might have come home to be with me and the children." She pressed her palms against her eyes to seal out the despicable sight of him. "Mama's boy!" she yearned to howl. "Sissy! Wimp! User!"

"I did," he said quietly.

"You did what?"

"I come home hoping I could take care of my family. They's not been a night since we parted I ain't lay and dreamed of how I would do it."

"Then prove it. Send Maude back to the country."

"Lily!" he said with a gasp. "I cain't."

"Sure you can! And while you're at it, tell me the secret you two kept hidden from me all these years. I want to know what power she held over you to cause you to up and leave a loving family. Help me understand the great suffering the two of you brought on me and the children, and then speak of her good intentions."

She had expected him to blow up! To fling curses and rage as though he would hit her. Or beat her with the word *bitch* and then stomp out the door, leaving her feelings, her pride, flat on the floor.

Instead, he dropped his head into a palm and mourned like he had the day Edgar Jarvis, the kid, died in the mine.

"So help me, Lily, I cain't. You deserve the truth and I would give it if I could but I cain't."

"What do you mean, you *cain't*?" she mocked him.

"I promised."

"Promised who?"

"Her."

"Yeah, well, in case you've forgotten, you made promises to me, too. Sacred ones!" she screamed while slamming through two doors and a line of stunned girls.

Abe followed, but Lily moved with an animal swiftness, first through a wooded area out back and then again to the garage. He gave up when her Oldsmobile cleared the driveway and headed toward Main. Then he went toward the children.

A steady stream of coughs and hacks followed. His joints ached. Every breath he drew seemed like a stab in the lungs. Things with Lily had moved fast and crazy and he felt he needed time to think. He sat down on the porch steps and felt the tormented eyes of the dodos questioning him from a front window. He realized they knew their mother to be the peaceful type and were wondering what bad thing he had done to make her act crazy.

He cried so that no one would see and felt old and wasted, like somebody who would do the world a favor by dropping dead. A loser. A failure. A deadbeat. A dog.

In the end he decided that Lily had a right to the truth and once all the fuss wore down, he would tell her, at least part of it. But the shame of giving up what little respect he and his mother had left seemed like a bad way to go out, a sure ticket to one kind of hell or another, and he wished he could find a way around it. He pictured his mother now—a tiny thing catching lint elves, jabbering, half-blind, pissing her pants—living for the purpose of keeping him safe and asking for nothing but that he honor a promise he'd made as a kid. Lily deserved the truth, yes, but hadn't she in all fairness hid truth from him when she let him move to Saxton knowing he could stay in Harlan County and be mine foreman? Wasn't fair for the gander also fair for the goose? Didn't Lily have her own faults? Not that he was superstitious, but didn't that black stripe across her white cap count for something?

"Whew!" He sat upright to breathe easier, stretched, and felt a pain in his back, tough but nothing compared to the pain in his heart. Most all his life he'd suffered from some heartache or nother, he remembered, and it weren't no big deal. It built strength, come with the territory, went down with the drink. But heartbreak like now, that was a bird of a different feather. That kind of heartbreak like methane gas that could maim a person for life. It could screw up his nerves. He knew because he'd experienced both and had the shakes to prove it.

He'd been a chalkeye in the mines when he'd come to know the real meaning of heartbreak. It was that time when his mother said he had no earth daddy. When she prayed on her knees for her fated son without no inkling he was listening. Prayed God would take away her Son Boy's evil curse and make him good enough for heaven.

Autumn's presence made him remember another time when he was ten. Late fall it was because she was cooking soap outside with lye from ashes and meat scraps and he was helping. He could even as yet see her tremble, hear her teeth chatter, smell fear in the white breaths she put out. He remembered the scorched smell of neighbors burning leaves and the fire in his belly while his ole man, liquored up as usual, practically growled his guts out.

"Kick her! Kick her like a man, the meddlin' bitch, your mother!" he had ordered and swung his leg to show what was meant by a good manly blow. Then made him, a mere boy, stand and watch his mother spin off his steel-toed boot and roll like a hog in the bleeding mud of her clothes-lined yard pen. And he had laughed to beat the band, which was the liquor talking.

"Dammit-to-hell, I said kick her!" the ole man howled and rammed a fist in his face to show what would happen if he didn't. Scared witless with his heart pounding twice over, he'd aimed his moccasin shoe at the hem of her dress but felt her flesh cave in like a lump of creamed potatoes. His own leg folded when he tried to stand it back down. His stomach felt queer. It spasmed little sour squirts in his mouth that he swallowed, then dropped his head too fast and barfed til there was nothing left to barf.

"Cookin' soap, huh?" The ole rascal mocked and he had wished him to come closer so to pitch some lye in his eyes. "Whoever heard tell of a boy cookin' soap with his mama? The bitch had it comin'. There ain't gonna be no mama's boy in this family, hear? No yellow-bellied sissy. No, sir! You're gonna be a man like your daddy and his'n before 'im!"

"Ah-h-h," she'd moaned, and he'd near died to stay there with her, to help her up and into her bed, swear to God. But instead he'd give up on the lye, scraped the spew from his jacket, switched off the sound of her pitiful cries, and followed his daddy to the still and the sweet-Jesus relief of a mug of corn liquor.

That same evening, the sky was gray-blue with just enough light to see by when his ole man left home for Red's grease joint on the far end of Clover Fork. He stayed home with his mother and felt all guilty and sorrowful and dead set on making her feel better. She was quick to forgive him and rocked him in her arms like a teensy-tiny baby.

"Oh, fated boy!" she cried as she sung him "At the Cross" and so on and so forth. She pressed his mouth to a tit that he sucked knowing it was of the devil and hell and so on. She called it medicine and it was in a way because it made her all happy and calm-like and because he owed her that much for kicking her and running away to the still to get liquor and because deep down inside he was starved for that talcum powder taste of her that afterwards left him feeling gut sick and all the more hungry.

She'd not took good to shame, his mother. Couldn't stand to think of her dirty laundry being washed in public so everybody would pity her or poke fun. Went to church and nowhere else and at home talked mostly to God only.

"Promise me! Promise me you'll never tell," she'd pleaded with him that one night and most all the others when he'd watched her crawl and cry like some wild animal but run out on her to the still and come back ashamed and giving her the medicine.

"Promise me!" she'd said, but without no cause to worry. Thanks to the manly rush of coal and the magic of sweet liquor, up til Lily started her meddlin', he'd damn near forgot.

CHAPTER THIRTY-FOUR

Lily hunkered inside her Oldsmobile sedan outside the Hippodrome Theater on Main Street. She was not there to see "The African Queen" but to hide in the walls of concrete and cars. It was evening. Steel-gray streaks of cloud raced westward, picking up turquoise and peach splotches. Oaks and maples had managed to hold the last slits of daylight; pines and cedars had a dark, forest look.

A side of her said to go back home and pretend nothing had happened for the sake of the girls, and peace, and a temporary stability. Another side argued for the principle of the thing, a woman's rights, the truth that sets you free, the sweet taste of a scorned woman's vengeance.

"I just can't understand him. What awful thing could he and Maude be hiding, and why?" she asked a Hollywood poster of Katherine Hepburn, but directed her question to her wise ma, at home on Buck Creek. The two were so close, they seemed to have a way of communicating thoughts from one's mind to the other's while being apart.

"Men. Don't try to understand 'em, just love 'em," Ma answered and smiled as if thinking of her own stern and spoiled husband, who even now as a preacher might clear the supper table with an elbow or two. "Your pa got up on the wrong side of the bed," she had said when he'd been a hot-tempered, womanizing coal miner. "The poor man's worn to a frazzle."

"After the storm comes the rainbow," Lily heard as she rammed the gear into reverse and headed toward the voice coming out of Katherine Hepburn.

She arrived unexpected and visited briefly, just long enough to feel her anxiety subside to a bearable, homeward-bound level. Pretending to be back in her girlhood sanctuary helped, especially with Peony and Vi there, Vi entertaining everyone with her tough-broad sense of humor, much like Ceola's, and Peony complaining of a headache.

She felt exhausted. At one point she'd been tempted to fall into her girl bed and wait for the Sandman. But she thought of her girls and how they would worry.

"Goodbye everyone," she said and gave hugs while her sisters insisted that she stay longer.

"Goodbye. I love you...and I love you," Sarah said and Lily was both surprised and amused. Not that the saying was new to her, but because it was something of a secret between the two of them, as if the simple "Goodbye, I love you" for other family members was too generic for this mother-daughter devotion. "I love you as my kin, but I also love you as a person," she had taken the expression to mean, and many times she had echoed the words back, but only when Vi and Peony were well out of listening range. Buttoning up her new tweed coat—long, blue-green, with a high collar—she smiled while realizing that her sad, unspoken situation had not escaped her ma's keen attention.

Lily left Saxton shortly after seven, but instead of going directly home, she drove to Dr. Humfleet's office in neighboring Williamsburg. Her intention was to leave him a brief note explaining her job in Corbin and updating him on Sweet William's progress at UK. She had known the doctor's interest in Sweet William was more than casual since that night he'd treated Sherman at Mud Creek and likely chose the boy to be his replacement.

Dr. Humfleet was working late, as usual. He came out smiling and hugging and inviting her to sit down on a handsome loveseat with carved mahogany woodwork and burgundy tapestry. She stood instead, taking in the scent of a pansy bouquet and staring at art collected from his overseas travels. The office seemed out of place, as if it had been moved from the North and reassembled in one of Eastern Kentucky's poorest regions. To her it spoke of the doctor's trust in his patients, many of whom paid their bills with a pork shoulder or a bushel of Georgia Belle peaches.

"I'm sorry for barging in like this, but I was in the area," she said. "I can stay only for a minute."

"So I hear you chose the Corbin hospital over me," he replied with eyes twinkling. He shook his head and snapped two fingers as if to say, "Rotten luck!" Then he congratulated her with the pride of a good friend and former teacher. "Your pa keeps me informed, but that's not like seeing you in person. I've missed you, Lily."

She blushed. Even to him she was ashamed to admit she had broken her vows by separating from Abe, or vice versa. That she who had always tried to do everything just right had failed in the most important mission of her life, marriage.

"Then you must know Abe and I are...apart."

"I do, yes. And believe me, I have often thought of you and the children."

"Things have a way of working out." She was shocked to learn that she had spoken of her shame, and the earth had not shattered.

"And if you should need anything at all, please know you can ask."

She nodded. "I came here to say how sorry I am about not taking the job you offered, but I think you probably know this place is too close to where it all happened."

"Rest assured I do. And speaking of all that has happened, Lily, something quite important has come up that I was about to come tell you. Can you spare a few minutes?"

"Sure." She made a quick call home and spoke to Verni, who agreed to cook supper.

"I'll get straight to the point," the doctor said when they were seated with coffee. "You cross these mountains enough times, Lily, and sooner or later you're bound to run into somebody who knows everybody."

"That's what Ma says. She's delivered umpteen babies, as you know, not to mention all the colts, calves, puppies, kittens. Once she even sutured a wolf."

"I'm surprised she hasn't put me out of business." He folded his hands in his lap and interlaced his fingers. "Lily, I've met a woman by the name of Flossie Tucker who claims she knew the young Maude. Does that name mean anything to you?"

Afraid he might see the bitterness she harbored, Lily shook her head and looked up, down, sideways, everywhere, anywhere, but into his eyes.

"Not at all."

"It seems she and Maude worked on a tobacco farm for an overseer in his early twenties by the name of Caleb Cash, who was Sherman's brother. She recalled Caleb courting Maude from March of that year up until she was close to six months *gone*, as she put it. She said she had never before seen a couple so much in love. Then Caleb suddenly disappeared, and Sherman, the rightful owner of the farm, returned—some say from jail—to take over. That's when he found Maude and the child."

"Child?" Lily let out a gasp. The color vanished from her face. "But Maude had only the one child, Abe."

"That's quite right."

She threw a hand over her mouth.

"Dear God! You're not saying Sherman's brother, not Sherman, was Abe's real daddy?"

"I'm saying that's what Flossie said. She said Caleb dropped his last name, Siler, in order not to be linked with his bootlegging brothers, and Sherman never forgave him."

"I can't say I'm surprised. Abe and Sherman are as different as night and day and never have gotten along. Abe also had his doubts. Neither he nor his mother ever spoke on the subject that I know of, but I read between the lines, and I loved Sherman so much I chose to leave the question in the closet."

He nodded before continuing.

"Well, anyway, when the tobacco season ended, Flossie went to work at a nearby chicken farm and Maude, alone and quite pregnant, took refuge in a nearby cave."

"A cave? I don't know of any such cave."

"You probably wouldn't. It was on a neighbor's land."

"Come to think of it, Abe once mentioned a cave in a nightmare and woke up panting and sweating so badly I gave him a sponge bath and a sedative. I suppose I thought he was referring to one of the underground mine tunnels."

"Apparently Maude and Flossie were out picking berries one evening when an electrical storm hit, and cloud-to-ground lightning struck Maude before she could get to her shelter. The infant was born prematurely and with a bad case of colic. Flossie said it was cursed. She swore she herself saw the devil appear in a flash and strike a black mark behind the child's right ear. The story is preposterous, but what she might've seen was the lightning voltage entering Maude's body. It makes an electrical burn and smoke is not uncommon."

Lily's coffee cup rattled against the saucer.

"Oh, sweet Jesus! Abe has that mark today!"

"You've seen it?"

"I assumed it was a birthmark or coal scar. Maude has always claimed Abe's extra keen senses, the instincts that made him such a good miner, were the result of her being struck by lightning that brought on his birth. Several times she spoke of it. She even said he was cursed by the devil at that very time, but I never took her seriously because of her weird religion. I guess I was busy quieting her for the sake of the children."

"That's understandable."

"And Sherman? How did he come to marry her?"

"She and the baby needed food, and Sherman caught her stealing from his kitchen. I understand Maude was quite a looker in her day, and I'm assuming he was love struck. At any rate, they married soon after, and Maude moved into the house. That was the last Flossie ever saw of her."

"Whew!" Lily reached into her purse for a Kleenex and worked it like piping between her fingers. Her chest itched. Her fingers traveled the distance. "It's too much to take in."

"The point is, Lily, I've given the matter a good deal of thought, and I'm afraid I may have misjudged Maude. On that day she and Sherman first came to see me, I mentioned cancer, and her face didn't change in the least. Most people will jump out of their skin at the very mention of the word. Even when I explained the seriousness of it, she didn't bat an eye. I took that to mean she didn't care, but now I suspect she wasn't surprised because she had come to expect God's wrath as a punishment for her sin of fornication, or maybe she planned to heal Sherman herself with prayer and faith. I think it's entirely possible she saw Caleb, Sherman, and even Abe as targets of that wrath."

Lily tapped on her face as if to wake herself up.

"The sins of the fathers visited on the children! Oh, how often I've heard her quote that scripture: *He will by no means leave the guilty unpunished, visiting the iniquity of the fathers on their children.*"

"Exactly. Scripture seems to suggest the one who caused the wrath has to be the one to undo it. Assuming Maude saw Abe's so-called curse as the consequence of her fornication, wouldn't she consider it her duty to redeem him? And let's remember, too, that persons struck by lightning can suffer from neurological problems such as loss of memory and cognition."

"Yes, I've considered her Pentecostal Holiness faith but...to just watch Sherman suffer and do nothing. That I will never forgive."

"How do you know she did nothing?"

"Lily looked up, an expression of disbelief on her face.

"I watched her."

"Lily, this is only a hunch, but is there a chance Maude could have inflicted bodily harm on herself?"

Lily threw up her arms.

"Oh, no, don't tell me! *Without the shedding of blood there is no remission.*"

380 · FAYE SOLOMON KUSHNER

"Surely there would've been signs if she had."

"There was a place in the woods where she went when she was troubled. Now that I think of it, it very well could've been that cave. She dressed in black from head to toe, took her Bible and prayer shawl along, and sometimes came home so rattled the children found it amusing. She never stopped to speak but went directly to her room. A time or two I saw cuts on her hands that I attributed to briars or thorns. It's possible they were made by a switch...or something."

Did you ever see her legs?"

"Gracious no! Nobody did, not even Sherman, I'd guess. She wore thick stockings. I suppose I thought it was because of her modesty." Lily placed four fingers on her forehead and pushed the thumb against a temple. "Dear God, I'm a nurse. How could she have been that desperate without my noticing?"

"Again, please understand that I'm only guessing. But in my practice, I've seen many cases of self-flagellation, especially in areas of diverse religious practices. From what you've told me, I gather Maude would have been a classic example. Practically everyone she loved—mama, daddy, Abe's real daddy, Sherman, even Abe—either abused or left her in some way, causing her to feel unworthy of love, even from God, her accuser. When you think of it, why wouldn't she discredit herself? Almost everyone else appeared to."

"I had forgotten until now that you also taught psychology," Lily said.

"In my opinion it's the crucifixion story all over again. She sheds her blood to redeem Abe from the wages of her sin—a coal pit and eventual hell."

"I just can't believe it!" Lily turned toward a window. A breeze brushed against the glass, and she shivered. Only minutes before she'd broken out in a sweat.

The doctor, assuming she was crying, came up behind her and laid a hand on her shoulder.

"I'm sorry, Lily. I didn't mean to upset you. Maybe I should've let the past lie."

"No, no, you did the right thing." She stood gazing into a Bradford pear tree, its head swaying, too heavy for its trunk, apt to snap at any minute.

"You're sure?"

"I am, yes. Thank you."

Dr. Humfleet waited while she thought long and hard. In time he took off his white jacket and headed toward the coat closet.

The sound woke Lily from her stupor, and she whipped around, almost losing her footing.

"Dr. Humfleet, wait! You didn't tell me what happened to Abe's real daddy, Sherman's brother!" she cried breathlessly. "Was he aware Maude was pregnant? Why did he leave?"

The doctor took her hands in his and pressed gently.

"Flossie said he...died."

"Died? Died how?"

"In a mine explosion."

CHAPTER THIRTY-FIVE

Lily returned home, spent some brief time with her girls, faked a headache, and went to bed early. Dr. Humfleet's news about Maude had eased her anger, but not her anxiety. She couldn't sleep and got up at dawn the next morning. Fully dressed, she went into the kitchen, where she sat down with coffee and the Sunday newspaper. Downtown, a train rolled on the tracks, its distant murmur like the lonesome moan of a fog horn during danger.

Abe, no doubt stirred by the tempting smell of hot coffee, rustled, but didn't leave his bed. On Sundays the girls slept until after nine. The usually bustling house, now sighing as it settled, presented itself to her as a compassionate companion, a dog curled fondly at the master's feet, reminding her that she had kept her promise to her girls by providing them a house they could be proud of. "Hats off to Lily!" it seemed to say. "She delivered on her promise!"

Through the window she heard the whisper of rain she couldn't see. She smelled smoke from woodstoves and burned leaves. Earlier in the season, red and gold leaves had appeared to her as autumn's version of flowers, like winter's lights on a tree, little hikes in spirit to carry her until spring. Now piles of lingering leaves, wet and slick like brown patent leather, reminded her that Abe was slacking off as grounds keeper and had given up on selling insurance.

Abe, the man who had sworn he wouldn't be put down til he shut down.

The telephone rang, and he snatched it up as if he'd been waiting. The den door was ajar. Lily cringed while watching him cup a hand over the receiver and turn his back to the kitchen door. All along he'd insisted on contributing to household expenses, and all along she'd been uncooperative because she had silently feared he might leave when his money ran out. This new secret stirred panic in her, and she silently prayed he had not contacted John Mason to say he wanted to go back to Ohio. "Surely not in this cold weather!" she murmured. "Surely not when things were getting better, in spite of the argument."

He hung up shortly, dressed quickly in a dark mining shirt and a pair of old baggy trousers held up by suspenders, and ventured into the kitchen. He had *sick eyes*, as Lily's patients with colds sometimes said, and she knew he hadn't slept. He sneezed and Lily volunteered, "Bless you."

"Good morning," she said, and he nodded. She had him sit at the table and served him coffee, then took a seat facing him, hoping to talk. He took slow sips and coughed more than usual while she pretended to check the coupons in the newspaper. Seeing a chance to be together, she had purposely postponed his breakfast. Now she had the uneasy feeling that he would not eat.

"You're up early," he volunteered.

"I couldn't sleep for thinking about our argument."

"Somethin' sure smells good."

"It's biscuits," she said, knowing he knew already.

"Biscuits," he repeated, and nodded his head.

"If you want to read "Beatle Bailey," she said and slid the comics section across the table, "you better do it before the girls come."

"Lily," he said, eyes squinched, the newspaper untouched. "The Plymouth needs to be drove. Once the dodos get home from church and can see to Mother, I think I'll take her out for a spin."

Lily gazed out the window. She heard the breeze pick up and saw the last of the leaves swirl down like nature's confetti. Her heart beat too fast. Something heavy shoved against the lining of her stomach.

"I'm planning a family dinner. Pot roast," she said. "Will you be back?"

"That's mighty nice." He circled a daisy on the oilcloth with a finger. "If'n I cain't, I'll have some later. Pot roast is at its best, you know, warmed over."

"They're calling for rain. If you're going, you should go soon. I'll see to your mother."

"You'll what?"

"I don't mind keeping her...on occasions."

Daisy and Tansy entered the kitchen in their pajamas and caps of wire curlers. Lily served them scrambled eggs and biscuits with butter and molasses. They pushed away their plates and reached for the box of Kellogg's corn flakes instead. Rosy appeared later and stood staring at the suspenders.

"Where you going, Daddy?"

"To see a dog about a man."

"Will you see Dog?"

He looked at her with a gleam in his eyes.

"What makes you think I'm seein' Dog?" He got up from the table before she could answer and in passing chucked her chin. Then he swung his cap and old jacket off a peg on the wall and headed in the direction of his mother.

"You haven't had your breakfast," Lily said, avoiding the earlier choppiness in her voice. She took out a package of lean bacon and the cast-iron skillet.

"Don't go to no trouble. I'll grab a little something on the road."

"It's no trouble. It'll only take a minute."

"No, thanks, really," he said, and shut the door behind him.

The girls ate and left the kitchen to go dress and study their Sunday school lessons. The glass plates she gathered made high-pitched sounds as they clambered against each other, and she imagined the crashing, smashing thrill of letting go. "Let me know when you're ready for church, and I'll take you," she called. They thanked her but said they preferred to walk with their friends, and she felt relieved. On days like this one, the simplest duty amounted to the energy it had taken to drag the old wringer-type washing machine from the back porch to the kitchen. Sleep struck her as a delicious option.

Abe returned in a hurry, his shoulders stooped like Uncle's. She handed him a sack lunch at the door, pulled his jacket high on his shoulders, and snapped the buttons as if he were one of the children. He'd gnawed his lower lip until it bled, and she handed him a clean handkerchief.

"Try to stay warm and dry," she said pleasantly. "You can't afford to get pneumonia."

"I'm good." He turned and coughed so much air from his lungs that he whistled when inhaling.

"Don't worry about your mother," she forced herself to say, and let a hand graze his back. In a swinging motion he turned and grabbed her in a clasp so tight her feet left the floor, and her elbows cut into her stomach. "I love you!" the hug seemed to say, and her cheeks may have blushed had the embrace not felt so jerky and desperate, equally capable of meaning, "Goodbye forever."

Lily held supper and waited. Abe returned at dusk, coughing and shivering and smelling like coal dust. Shreds of sawdust clung to his denim jacket. His wet cap lay balled like a rag in the pocket. Pearls of rain holed up between the curls of his hair, and some clung to his eyelashes. Cold and dampness had made his cheeks red, as shiny as a boy's.

Lily met him with a cup of hot coffee. She willed herself not to ask questions.

"Drop the wet pants and jacket before you catch pneumonia," she said. She helped him into his robe and had him sit barefoot before the fire. She even took his temperature with a real thermometer and frowned at the reading. This time he didn't scold her for nursing, but she viewed her triumph as a bad sign. She worried less about his health when he cared enough to fight her.

"You need to eat," she said and brought him a plate of hot food from an electric skillet.

"I'm not hungry," he insisted, until the savor of the pot roast—soused in brown gravy with thick slices of potatoes, onions, and carrots—enticed him. Once he had practically cleaned his plate, he sopped a biscuit and sucked the gravy from his fingers.

The girls ate and appeared ready for Baptist Training Union before church, and he hugged each one with an urgency similar to what he'd shown Lily. Meanwhile she made his bed with clean sheets and extra blankets and added a hot-water bottle, the rubber kind.

Then she prepared his bath and helped him undress. Softly, silently, she washed him, and when he stepped away from the usual black towel, she helped him into his pajamas.

"Ah, Lily, my light at the end of the tunnel," he said, and she nodded.

"Shall I lie with you until you fall asleep?" she said when he was under the covers. The words spilled out so naturally, so easily, she didn't realize she was not suggesting, but asking. Not the nurse, but the wife.

"Naw, you might catch something."

"I'm not afraid."

"Well maybe I am."

"Then I'll see you in the morning," she said, kissed his warm forehead, and went to her room. She tried to read but couldn't concentrate on the usual medical journals. She opted for a romance novel, *Jane Eyre*, but found it too plot driven for her drowsy mood and chose a bath and sleep instead.

In the half-light of her bathroom, she pinned up her hair and sank into a tub of hot, bubbly water, its silky white foam swelling and melting around her like an ocean she, since a youth, had dreamed of swimming in. Tonight she felt the downward sway of the big waves, but without the thrill of catching them and flying over.

Curiously, the ocean image took her mind to a painting she'd seen while with Vi in a Williamsburg pizza parlor when Abe first left with his mother. The subject was a hard-mouthed, vacant-eyed, flesh-sagging woman bathing in a tub with no water. The hands covering her old breasts were big and gnarled and glopped with different shades of blue and green slashed with red. She recognized them, the face and hands of someone like Maude or even herself, who had overlooked too many of life's opportunities.

"Where Did All the Bubbles Go?" the painting was called, and Lily had unconsciously held up the serving line to stare at this woman whose tragedy resembled her own. For too long now, she had been lonely and bitter like that empty woman, and although she had not remembered her for some time, she had not forgotten her either. Today she, the woman in the painting, would become Lily's reason for re-living.

The water was cooling to a perfect warm, its bubbles as soft and seductive as the breeze at Bryce's Cove. It swayed her into that gauzy gray zone just before sleep, and she might have dried and gone straight to bed had it not been for the sound of them—Abe and that woman—still whispering.

Jealousy can be a great awakener, she thought, like a sharp pain or loud sound or a light switched on in the dark. She sank into the water, closed her eyes, and waited. When she was certain that Maude was asleep and the curtain between her and Abe drawn for the night, she stepped outside the tub and into her flannel housecoat without bothering to dry or tie sashes.

Bubbles squished between her toes as she tiptoed into Abe's bed and fixed her head on his shoulder.

CHAPTER THIRTY-SIX

Making love like old-timers and new, with a gentle blend of both passion and compassion, Lily and Abe reached the ultimate joy of knowing they still belonged. Together they created a keepsake, a dream come true, what might have been the perfect ending to an imperfect story.

"Will it always be this good?" she had teased him before he fell asleep in her arms, and he had delighted her by recalling the specific occasion to which she referred. It was just after their honeymoon over twenty years earlier, on a night spent behind paper-thin walls and the hoot-owl ears of Wade Eakins. She had posed the question in regard to marriage, and he had misunderstood.

"Will it always be this good?" she had asked then.

"Better!" he had sputtered. A boy of eighteen, he grinned sheepishly while assuming *it* meant sex, the great fixer, a revelry for which he had acquired a super talent.

"Promise me?" she pushed on.

"Hell, I can do better than promise! I can guarandamntee it!" he'd boasted, and cocked his head as if sold on the notion that good intentions win battles, and love conquers all.

But on a Saturday, only a week after their lovemaking, the honeymoon came to an end. In the den Abe rattled papers and slammed drawers. He kicked an armchair, the impact so light that Maude slept on as usual.

"Dammit, woman, I want my car key!" he shouted, but his voice was hoarse and without the fierceness he had intended.

He moved in a stagger and cupped his hands over his blood-red face as if to shut out the drama he himself was creating.

Lily braced herself against the kitchen counter. Since his return, he had been eating just enough food to survive on. His voice was weak and his movements shaky. He napped more, coughed more, and paid less attention to his grooming. After convincing him that he could spread the bacteria to his mother, she had finally persuaded him to sleep in her bed; nurses, she said, have a strong immune system. Then, watching his restlessness get worse by the hour and fearing he might try to leave again, she had taken away his car key and hidden it between the pages of Iris' first diary.

"You hear me? I said I want my car key!"

"You can't have it," she said bravely.

He barged into the kitchen, one hand clutching a chair back, his free fingers gesturing *gimme.*

"Fork it over!"

"No."

"Me drivin' my car ain't none of your business!"

"I care about you. That makes it my business."

"Bull malarkey! Forget that love crap and get me my key!"

"Not until you agree to go see a doctor." She raised a hand to stop him from balking. "I know it sounds ridiculous, but, Abe, you coughed and wheezed and sweated all night long, and there's medicines that could help you get better. I should have insisted. Long ago, I should have made the doctor a provision."

"A *provision?*" He coughed until tears filled his eyes, then spit some red and black mucus into a napkin. "If that ain't a kicker! A wife givin' her husband a *provision!*"

"Then at least let the doctor come here. He can check you and Maude at the same time."

"Over my dead body!"

"Well, I hope not." They heard a murmuring sound coming from the den. "Please, let's not wake up Maude," she said, and motioned him out of the kitchen.

In the living room, he dropped onto a chair and held out his hand for the keys.

"This hurts me worse than it hurts you," she said. "Remember when we used to say that to the children just before a punishment? Well, it's killing me, making you so unhappy."

He took a deep breath, wrung his hands, and popped his knuckles.

"Look, Lily. I been in the dark damn near all my life. I got up in the dark, went to work in the dark, worked all day long in the dark, and come home at night in the dark. I laid on my back in coffins so damn black you couldn't see a foot ahead with your light on. But there ain't no coffin like a bed you cain't leave and I'll suffocate if'n you try and make me your prisoner."

She shook her head and pulled back the tears.

"Hon, you won't last out there."

"Maybe I don't want to last."

It was just as she had suspected, but hearing the words from his own lips made it final.

"I've been thinking you could go see a doctor, build up your strength, and we could maybe leave the kids with Jetty and take a real vacation. You always wanted to go to Renfro Valley and Nashville. At one time you dreamed of performing at the Grand Ole Opry. We could take it slow and stop whenever..."

"Don't make me have to hitchhike," he threatened, then coughed and choked and spit and hacked until he tried but couldn't push up from the chair.

"You most likely caught pneumonia when you were out in the rain. Will you at least stay until you're better? Will you let me make you better?"

"What for?"

"For the children," she said, which was at least a part of the truth.

On one of Abe's better days, Rosy stood before him with a small paperback book, another one of Lily's flea-market treasures. The book was held together by a rubber band. Its pages were yellowed, curled, and nibbled by silverfish with appetites for starch.

"Shakespeare?" Abe whispered, his sunken eyes more shut than open. "Ain't you too young to be readin' Shakespeare?"

"Yes, but I got a book report due and I needed something short. My teacher said it was too hard for a fourth grader. She only approved it because I said my brother read it and would help me."

"It's naughty to fib. Even to teachers."

"But it was only a white lie. White lies are okay."

"So long as you know the difference."

"I do. White lies can't hurt anybody."

He smiled and studied the ceiling.

"I always wanted to read Shakespeare," he said. "So I could conversate with Lily. Your mama, you know, was quite a reader. The smartest gal you ever saw."

"I got a idea! How about I read it to you? Then you can show her you're smart too!"

"Ha! Fat chance of that."

"No, I mean it. You can tell me when you're tired and I'll stop that very second, I mean it. So help me, I'll stop!"

His wiry smile said yes, so Rosy began to read about Othello, the Moorish commander of the armed forces of Venice, who married Desdemona, beautiful daughter of a Venetian senator, and then murdered her in a fit of jealous rage. Rosy grew more excited as she read, and occasionally he, though hard of hearing, signaled for her to lower her voice. The outside air was murky and the room so dark she stumbled over words, even ones she knew. Afraid to ask for light, afraid he would change his mind, she persevered. Every afternoon thereafter she read a scene or two, sometimes skipping pages, depending on how long it took him to lose interest or drift off to sleep.

One day at Cottengem's Drugs on Main Street, where she sometimes went to twirl on a bar stool and crunch a cup of free ice, a shopping idea popped into her head. At J.J. Newberry's, a department store like Woolworths, she would buy two goldfish, a black and a white one, and she would name them Othello and Desdemona, after the characters in the play. She hoped they would keep him good company when she was at school and calm him when he threw one of his fits.

Options limited, she decided to borrow the money from Aunt Jemima and leave a teensy note promising to pay it back just as soon as she launched her spring seed-selling business backed by Granny Eakins. She would work the note through coins until it reached the very bottom. Then she would apologize to Granddaddy Siler, just in case he was looking down.

She chose a Saturday, when her mother had gone to A&P to buy groceries. On Fifth Street, little children waved from front windows. Boys in tee-shirts and shorts bounced basketballs on the street and rode bikes with red, white, and blue tassels on handle grips and baseball cards clipped to the spokes. On Main, women dressed in car coats plugged coins into parking meters and rushed in from the cold.

With Aunt Jemima's money and the help of a kind saleslady, she bought a white and a black fish, a bowl, and a box of food, all of which came to a total of $3.48. On her way home, a five-minute walk, she stopped to gather pebbles.

In the kitchen, she washed and filled the bowl with pebbles and tap water, and she downed a jelly biscuit while waiting for the water to reach what she considered room temperature. Then she cut slits in the bag and dropped it into the bowl so the waters could mingle. Finally, she spilled out the fish and carried the bowl to her daddy.

"Ta da!" she sang as if announcing a birthday cake with lit candles. He looked up, bewildered. Quilts framed his face, and still he shivered. "They're for you!" She eased the bowl onto a table. "Guess what I named them!"

She had her mouth framed in an *O* to say Othello when he surprised her.

"They're Abe and Lily. See, Lily's the fast one."

"Wrong! They're Othello and Desdemona. Remember? Othello was from Africa and black and Desdemona was from Italy and white. Get it? One black and one white!"

"The black one's played out," he rasped. "The white one swims circles around him.

They're coal miner and nurse, like me and Lily."

Rosy looked into the bowl and noticed Othello hovering near the bottom, his gills barely stirring. Desdemona flitted toward the surface in playful, zigzag turns.

"He's adjusting to the change in temperature is all. Maybe I didn't let the water set long enough. Negroes, you know, are from Africa and like hot weather. The saleslady said…"

"Adjusting, hell! He's sick."

"Maybe he's hungry." She ran to get the food, remembering she had been warned against overfeeding.

"Othello, are you hungry?" she asked while sprinkling a few oatmeal-like flakes on top of the water. Desdemona snatched what pieces she could and gobbled them down as if she'd never eaten. Othello waited for crumbs at the bottom.

Abe watched them as if trying to figure out his next move at checkers.

"Maybe I should read now, okay?" she said and took her place without waiting for an answer. Breathlessly, she started with that scene where Iago, the bad guy, plants Desdemona's handkerchief, a token of Othello's love for her, in rival Cassio's room to give a false impression of her infidelity.

As the climax of the story built, Othello was barely breathing. His color had faded; his fins had separated like the teeth of a comb.

Abe took note of the difference.

"It's time I change the water is all!" She tossed aside the book and hurried the fish to the kitchen. "The saleslady said fish like clean water," she called behind her.

Under the window light, she saw that Othello was coated with a fine slippery film that wouldn't wash off. To save him, she would have to act fast. She tucked her grandmother's Christmas afghan around her knees and left a Bible in her lap. Then she raided Aunt Jemima a second time and set out for Main Street.

Inside J.J. Newberry's, early shoppers pushed carts with school clothes for Christmas. Mothers smacked reaching fingers, and toddlers howled over toys they couldn't have.

"I need fish medicine!" she cried to the saleslady who had helped her.

"Beg your pardon?"

"Fish medicine. I need it bad."

"But we don't sell fish medicine. Sick fish usually die."

"But it can't die! It just can't! See, my daddy's a coal miner and sick with dust in his lungs. Somehow he sees himself as the sick black fish and Mama, a nurse, as the healthy white one, get it? If it dies, I'm afraid he'll give up and die too. Maybe I should go to the drugstore."

The saleslady stared at her as if trying to figure out what made the child tick.

"Oh, that's too bad. Did you by any chance bring the fish with you?"

Rosy's eyes filled with tears.

"I didn't know to."

"Do you have your receipt?"

"Somewhere." She prowled through her mostly torn pockets and found it, and the saleslady nodded.

"I'll be glad to give you a new one."

"You will? Black? Just like the other one?"

"Close. But not sick, let's hope. I'll take it from the other tank."

"Golly Jees Moses!"

"Excuse me?"

"Oh, that's just something I say when I'm happy."

"Well, good."

The transaction completed, Rosy raced home with the second Othello. She put together a fresh bowl, and she flushed the old Othello, still alive, down the commode. She regretted that there was no time for a funeral, not even a scripture, but consoled herself with the fact that at least there was water.

She had headed back to the bedroom when Abe stumbled into the kitchen. He jerked lids off canisters and dumped out the breadbox.

"Look, Daddy!" she shouted and proudly pointed toward the bowl. Othello zigzagged playfully toward the surface, while Desdemona swam below him. "Othello made a miraculous recovery!" She put her nose to the bowl. "Othello, are you feeling better? Are you happy now?"

Abe dropped into a table chair and motioned for her to come closer. She set down the fish and came, and he grabbed her wrists.

"Squirt," he whispered, eyes wet, mouth begging like the palm of an orphan. "I got somewhere important to go and I need my car key."

She tried to back away and felt his hands tighten.

"I can't, Daddy. Honest, I don't know where it is."

"Here's two dollars. Find the key and go to Wilder's Hardware and make me a copy. Then put it back where you found it. Trust me. Won't nobody know but us two."

"Tell you what, we're just at the good part. I'll read and you…"

He jerked her closer. His eyes were big and bloodshot. Hers had the look of Lily when she nursed.

"Honey, I need that key. You'll be doin' ever'body a favor, including your mama."

Honey! He had pronounced the word so soft it seemed to melt on his tongue. *Honey,* the kiss she'd never got, the love word he'd never said, the promise that she, not Daisy or Tansy, was his favorite daughter, his one and only rose among the thorns. Golly Jees Moses!

Fingers quivering, heart pounding, she let out a breath and took the two dollars.

CHAPTER THIRTY-SEVEN

Lily arranged for Sweet William—now a third-year, pre-med student—to come help her take Abe to a doctor. He had surprised her by finally agreeing to go, probably for the sake of striking another bargain. But she preferred to think of his decision as a gift, a kind of truce, perhaps a love gesture.

Sweet William arrived the Wednesday before Thanksgiving, just in time to eat a macaroni-salad lunch with his young sisters. They went back to school, and he undertook the job of manhandling his daddy.

"As a favor to Mama, a very good doctor has agreed to see you today at two," he told Abe, who, dressed in his khakis, had spread a towel on his den couch and was clipping his toenails with difficulty. "Mama is right now running your bath water, so you need to hustle."

"Ain't nobody here to look after Mother. No way I will leave her here alone."

"Jetty Jacobs is on her way. Verni and Iris are not far behind."

"Verni and Iris?"

"Tomorrow's Thanksgiving, remember?"

"Oh, yes, Thanksgiving. I knew that."

Lily gave him some minutes to be alone and then found him watching television. Elbows on knees, he bent forward as if entranced.

"Bath's getting cold," she said.

"Sh-h-h." He pointed to "The Young and the Restless," a soap opera for women. "The show's about to wrap up and I need to see if Vanessa and Bruce get their act together."

A thin grin escaped her lips, but Sweet William stood firm.

"Not today, buddy!" Abe had lost weight. Though still a slender boy, Sweet William scooped him up and carried him, kicking, toward the bathroom and bath.

"Put me down, you young whippersnapper!"

"You wanted a doctor for a son, and you're about to have one. The flip side is, I'm the boss when it comes to your health. You got that Mister Hot Shot?"

"But this is my favorite show!"

"First you bathe."

"What for? It ain't Saturday!"

Sweet William plunked him down in the bathroom and met Lily in the hallway.

"I thought you said he'd agreed to go," he said.

"He did. But you know your daddy. Bullying disguises the fear."

She brought in Abe's underwear and starched clothes and shaved him at the sink. She left him to bathe and then smiled at the fuss he made when she blew his hair with Daisy and Tansy's hand-held hair dryer. In the kitchen, she served him a cup of steaming black coffee spiked with a sedative and a grilled cheese sandwich he didn't eat. Instead of his quilted coat and a touring cap from John Mason, he reached for his baseball cap and faded denim jacket.

"We're takin' the Plymouth and I'm drivin'!" he snapped as Sweet William maneuvered him into the passenger seat of Lily's Oldsmobile and got behind the wheel. The motor was already running, and melting the snow crystals. Lily sat in the

back seat. She closed her eyes and prayed to the god of rain-
bows and sunsets.

"You'll drive next time. Today the roads may be slick,"
Sweet William said.

"That's why you need a experienced driver behind the
wheel."

Sweet William smiled. He tapped Abe's knee and said,
"We don't mean to be cruel, Daddy, honestly. It's just that
we'd like to keep you around a while longer."

"Because you cain't stand to see a guy rest in peace is
what you mean."

"Because we love you."

"Bull! You love to abuse me is what you love."

Sweet William stopped the car before a gray brick building
on Poplar Street, just behind Main, and Lily hopped out first.
She hurried Abe inside the building and out of the cold. A
light coat of snow glazed the ground but was too wet to stick.

The office was crowded with coughing, wheezing, sneezing people. She checked in at the front desk and chose three
empty chairs in a far corner under a stairway. Mauve paint on
the walls appeared pretty and bright. On window shades,
splashes of mauve and purple blended to make a flower bed of
what looked like wild orchids.

Abe sat down with his head against the wall, gradually letting it slide onto Lily's shoulder. On a far television, Jack
Bailey crowned a queen for the day. Waiting women clutched
copies of *Reader's Digest* while croupy infants slapped at the
pages, and Lily stared into the purse on her lap. When Sweet
William came inside, Abe was asleep and snoring, and he
took the seat next to Lily so they could *make arrangements*.
"If it comes to that...," he said. "Just in case...."

Lily touched Abe's face and gently removed his toothpick.

"He has always asked for a simple pine box and no preacher," she said. "A short memorial service would do, and hopefully you and the girls would be the ones to conduct it." She paused, "But, please, let's not jump to any conclusions until we hear what the doctor has to say."

Sweet William, spotting her tension, reverted to his usual sense of humor.

"No preacher? Grandmother will have a conniption!"

"When the time does come, he's to be buried on Mud Creek beside his mother and daddy. The plot was purchased well before we met."

"No way!" Sweet William protested. "Daddy will be buried with his wife."

"But we have been...apart. He was with his mother."

"Not so. There's never been a day in his life he didn't yearn for you and us kids, and we all know it. I'll make sure that you and he are together."

"We'll see," she said tersely, her way of changing the subject. She nudged Abe's arm to see if he was still sleeping. When he didn't stir, she lapsed into another of her long, soulful pauses.

"Sweet William," she said. "So much has happened of late that you and I haven't had much time to talk, and we'll have even less once Verni and Iris get here. So forgive me if I'm blunt, but Vi has given me reason to believe you're still seeing Fairy Enlow. At a time like this, I need to think you and I can be truthful, and I'd like to know if the relationship is serious."

Sweet William glanced toward Abe, and Lily nodded to give him assurance.

"I see Fairy when I come home. But that's all because I have to study so much. She needs more attention than what I have time to give her. We fight, and sometimes it keeps me too upset to study. I know she's needy and wouldn't make a good doctor's wife, and I've tried to break up with her, Mama, honestly I have. But she turns to Buddy, who would marry her in a split second. Buddy's my cousin and I love him, but we both know he'd make one lousy husband."

"So you're simply protecting her?" Lily asked, hope ringing in her voice.

"Not just that, no. There's something about her I can't explain. I know we don't have much in common, but I love her, Mama. I always have, even when we called her a beggar."

"But is what you're describing *love*?" She measured her words. "Or the simple need to nurture?"

"All I know is, I've tried over and over to break up because all she talks about is getting married, and I'm in no way ready. But, Mama, she's not strong like Verni. She cries and begs, and, well, I end up going back. She's so sweet and helpless, I can't help myself."

Lily cocked her head. Her wise eyes narrowed.

"You can't help yourself?"

"I've tried and so help me I can't."

She brushed a hand over her heart to calm the beating.

"Sweet William, I've never felt Fairy is the right girl for you, and I think you surely know it." She thought about Maude and how she must have suffered when believing Abe, her one son, was about to make the mistake of marrying the wrong girl. "So I'm begging you to take your time and not let her get in the way of your education."

He gasped before remembering to lower his voice.

"Mama! You know I have to be a doctor."

Her eyes receded slightly, and she shook her head.

"You don't *have* to be, no."

"But I want to!"

"Well, in that case, you have some growing up to do." She yearned to remove the stiffness from her voice, smile into his eyes, and touch his sweet, boyish face, a picture of innocence. When they were alone like this, away from family commotion, she, and only she, could still make out his baby lisp. "Being a doctor requires quick decisions and the confidence to make them. It takes unbelievable strength and courage. You're telling me you know Fairy Enlow is not the right girl for you, and you want to break up, but can't. So my question is: If you don't have the strength to save yourself, how can you expect to save others?"

"But that's different."

"Is it?" She wondered if she should continue. Today he had superbly managed his sick and stubborn daddy. Hadn't his manhood been tested enough for one day? "There are all kinds of healing, Sweet William," she continued. "There's Ma's kind done with herbs and Pa's with faith. There's Vi's roses-are-red poetry. Then there's the healing you and I have been taught with a microscope and textbooks. But the greatest one of all is the gift of self-healing."

Sweet William lifted his eyes to where they met hers.

"Mama, I understand, and you're right as usual. But I get the feeling we're talking about somebody other than just Fairy and me?"

"We're healers, you and I. Sometimes our need to nurture gets in the way."

"In the way of love?"

"Of good judgement."

"Like with you and daddy?" The words had popped out, and he paused as if to ask himself if he should continue. "Everybody says you were one of the prettiest and smartest girls to come out of Whitley County. You could've married anybody, and you chose a big-mouthed, temperamental coal miner. I've always wondered, if you had it all to do over, knowing what you know now, would you have reconsidered?"

She raised her head to a winter window and felt her tired eyes reaching. In the distance she saw Abe in the glittering lights of a jamboree stage, looking like Gregory Peck and sounding like Merle Haggard. She heard him lulling the soft and soothing words of *"Brown* Eyes Crying in the Rain" and remembered the veil over his youthful eyes that she, a student nurse, had seen under.

"Mama?" he said to nudge her. "I need to know."

"Yes," she said, and had another of her long pauses.

"There were always things about your daddy I wanted to change, and vice versa. We've certainly made our fair share of mistakes, and paid dearly." She leaned into Abe's head on her shoulder. How could she express doubt to the hopeful son of his making? "But, believe me," she continued, "being with your daddy and mothering his six masterpiece children was not one of them."

"Abe Siler," a nurse called from a far door. Lily woke him, and the three followed her into an open room with scales, bathrooms, and a long hallway. The nurse, young and pretty with sweeping red hair and bold freckles, weighed him and took him into an examination room, where she checked his vital signs, asked questions, and wrote down the answers. She struck Abe as being so friendly, so peppy, that he attempted to play Cupid between her and Sweet William.

"My son's gonna be a doctor. How's about that?" he said. His enthusiasm vanished, however, when the doctor came in, asked a few questions, nodded at the familiar story, and ordered x-rays, and the nurse handed him a robe and said to get dressed.

When done with the x-rays, Abe drew his arms over his chest and returned to the examination room, so cold the nurse brought him a blanket. The doctor reappeared with the x-rays. He was a serious but friendly young man with long legs, a high waistline, and teeth that suggested braces.

"So you feel like you're drowning all the time, Mr. Siler?"

Abe chuckled. "You got a float you can toss me?"

"Smoker?" he asked, knowing.

"Damn near all my life."

"Alcohol?"

"Done that too."

"He quit," Lily interrupted. "Twelve years ago."

"Coal miner?"

"You bet."

"He was a foreman," Lily said, "one of a kind."

The doctor placed the x-rays before a lit box and pointed to Abe's lungs.

"You see they're black instead of white," he said. "The air sacks are enlarged, causing your trouble breathing."

"Don't look so good," Abe said.

"No, it sure doesn't."

"Then give it to me straight and let me outa here. No pussyfootin,' see?"

"Straight is that you're a very sick man, so sick it's a miracle you're still alive. You're coughing up black carbon mucus mixed with blood. Normally cancer or tuberculosis with similar symptoms can be treated, but you have severe emphysema and bronchitis. I'm sorry to say there's no cure. All I can do is give you something for the discomfort."

Lily sighed. Sweet William wiped his eye and came to stand beside her.

"I should have made him come sooner," she murmured.

"I doubt it would've made a difference."

"How long do I got?"

"I'm thinking a month, maybe sooner. Get dressed and I'll be back with your prescriptions."

"Thanksgiving better hurry. We got a celebration comin'!" Abe called after him. With a half-smile he hopped off the examination table as if to say he'd known the prognosis already. Sweet William shared some private words with the doctor and went for the car. He rushed and quickly returned, and Lily and Abe went directly to the back seat. With both hands she held his head in her lap, up close to her heart, as she'd done with her young children, and he let her. He was calmer than she'd seen him since the day he arrived home from Ohio. At one point he even slept.

"Hon," she said when they reached home and turned into the driveway, "do you think you might should check in with the Man Upstairs?"

"I told you, the two of us, we got a understandin'. Like the Bible says, I knocked on the door and He had me come in. Nice fellow."

"You prayed?"

"Damn straight."

She watched her words and held her breath to draw back the tears.

"What exactly did He say? Did you feel rewarded?"

"The same ole rigmarole. I thanked him muchly for lettin' me be with my family for Thanksgivin'. Told him to keep a eye out for 'em and warned Him it wouldn't be easy."

"So you're at peace now?"

"Damn well better be."

"And your mother, you know she'll be...in good hands?"

"I gotta hunch, yeah."

CHAPTER THIRTY-EIGHT

Lily and the girls cooked their own version of Thanksgiving dinner. Much of the menu came from Sarah, but each sibling chose a favorite food and set about preparing it. Pickled peaches and fried apples were a must, as were shuck beans, creamed potatoes, yellow dumplings, cornbread dressing, and turkey stuffed with little smoked sausages. Shoofly and lemon ice-box pie were preferred, but other desserts like fruit cobbler and tapioca pudding were also available. Lily considered the occasion a perfect opportunity to teach. "You want it, you cook it," she told her girls.

The three o'clock dinner was held at Lily and Abe's house for the first time ever and included the immediate family only, with Abe sitting at the head of the table beside his mother and saying the blessing. There were laughter and love, and everyone said it was the best Thanksgiving dinner ever.

Abe took small helpings and ate almost nothing. He breathed with difficulty and at times left the table. He tired before dessert, and Lily, promising to save his share, had him go down for a nap. He hugged everyone before leaving the room and paused to help his mother into her rocker. His gait was clumsy, and Lily stood close for their safety. The others finished eating and proceeded to wash dishes, and Lily closed the kitchen door to his room to keep down the noise.

"Where's Abe?" Maude called when shadows and drafts crossed her window, backed by a smoky yellow sunset.

"He went down for a nap," Lily said. She adjusted Maude's afghan to cover her support stockings and feet and placed her restless hands in her lap.

"Gone to that mine?"

"Gone to nap."

Maude nodded her head and clicked her tongue.

"Oh, yes," she said. "Gone to that mine."

The girls finished the dishes and set on Maude like a class of student nurses. They bathed and dressed her, brushed her hair, rubbed lotions on her skin, clipped her nails, brushed her teeth, and read her the Beatitudes, the beginning of what would come to be known as the "Sermon on the Mount."

Lily chatted with Sweet William and when he picked up his banjo, she went to look in on Abe. She was sure now that his agreeing to see a doctor was a thank you, an attempt at peace and reconciliation, even a love concession, and she couldn't wait to lie down and place her head on his shoulder.

"Lord in Heaven!" she cried out when she saw he was missing. "Quick! Everyone!"

They all came running. While the girls searched outside, she went through the house calling. Sweet William sprinted to the garage and found the Plymouth missing. He ran to Lily's car and drove off in a hurry.

Lily and the girls waited on the front porch. As if she were the celebrated pole in a May Day festival, they wrapped themselves around her and each other.

"You don't suppose he's gone back to Ohio do you?" Verni asked.

"You know he wouldn't leave his mother," Iris answered.

"Maybe he went to get us ice cream," Tansy said.

"Maybe, but we've had dessert already," Daisy said.

"It's cold. Let's go inside," Lily said. In the living room, she and Rosy sat down on the sofa, and the other girls circled them on the floor. They wiped their eyes and sniffled back the tears.

"How on earth did he get away without anybody knowing?" they asked.

"He went out a window."

"But why?"

"What I want to know is, how did he get the car key?" Verni asked. "Only three of us—Mama, Iris, and me—knew it was hidden in Iris' diary."

Iris went to her room and came back with her old diary, the key missing.

"Somebody took it," Daisy said and looked at Rosy.

"Yeah, somebody nosy," Tansy agreed.

"I didn't!" Rosy spewed. She dropped her head into Lily's lap, and Lily smoothed her cowlick.

"This is no time to turn on each other," Lily said. "That's the last thing on earth your daddy would've wanted. Sweet William's gone looking for him. Maybe he just slipped off to smoke or shoot pool or find a coal miner. In the meantime, let's not jump to conclusions."

"But who gave him the key?"

In spite of her encouragement, the girls cried. They placed their heads on each other's shoulder and uttered the consoling words of sweet children.

Sweet William returned an hour later, his palms outstretched and his eyes wide with wonder. He dropped down on the sofa, the expression on his face indicating failure.

"No sign of him!" he said. "I checked all the places he might've gone to find a coal miner, and they're all closed."

"I still think Rosy knows more than she's telling us," Daisy said.

"Me too," echoed Tansy.

"You shut up!" Rosy shouted.

Lily put out a heavy sigh. The telephone rang. She answered it from her seat and hung up quickly.

"It was Ceola," she said. "You all should know that yesterday the doctor said your daddy is very ill and within weeks, days, of dying. He worked up until his legs and lungs wouldn't let him, and now he's gone off, maybe preferring an early death of his choosing to suffering and wasting away in bed as a burden. Ceola said he's with Dog. She wanted us to know he's not alone."

"Call Ceola and let's go find him!"

"But why would he want to ruin our Thanksgiving?"

"I think he chose this time because he knew we would all be together to give each other love and comfort. Just think of the consolation he must have taken from knowing that."

"He always said he wanted to go out with his boots on," Iris said with a half-smile.

"Yes, he was a proud man. He deserves to die with dignity," Sweet William added.

"But where? Where is he?" Daisy asked.

"A place of his choice," Verni said. "Maybe Lewellyn."

"That's exactly what I decided," Lily said. "Thanks to all your kind hearts, he re-found his place in our family and gave what he had left to give. When he felt useless and knew his kids were headed toward a successful future, he begged Rosy to slip him the car key."

"Uh huh," Daisy said.

"I knew it!" Tansy accused.

"And Rosy was wise enough to come tell me," Lily continued. "I made the very painful decision of having her give it to him. If you need to blame someone, and perhaps you should, blame me and not Rosy. She was a very brave girl. She is what saved him."

That day in Lewellyn, a farmer on a tractor heard banging noises. He followed tire tracks to the place where he saw someone had sawed into a boarded-up portal of an abandoned mine and left it reboarded. The farmer went home and called the county sheriff.

Pansies bloomed in terracotta pots and strutted bright, pretty faces the morning the sheriff knocked on Lily's front door, hat in hand, to deliver the bad news. He motioned her outside to say Abe's car had been left outside a drift mine in Harlan County, but without a driver. He handed her a car key, and she choked at the sight of the rabbit's-foot keychain Abe had no doubt brought along for luck.

"I take it you recognize it," the sheriff said.

In the living-room window appeared a stack of faces, the older girls with their hands clasped around the youngers' shoulders. Sweet William came running outside with Lily's new winter coat. She seemed unaware of it, and he wrapped it around her shoulders, leaving the sleeves hanging.

"What's happened?" he asked, and the sheriff repeated the story.

"Funny thing is, somebody with him replaced the boards and got away in a hurry. You wouldn't happen to know who, would you?"

Both stared at him with astonished looks on their faces. Sweet William shook his head in disbelief.

"With all that methane gas built up, I doubt the rescue team will search but just so far, lessen the family raises a stink."

"No," Sweet William said. "No search is needed."

"There were tools." The sheriff opened his car trunk. They were the same tools Lily had watched Abe load the day she'd cooked pot roast, and he'd come home sick and smelling of coal dust. No doubt he'd tried that day but changed his mind.

"Yes," she answered. "Will will want them."

"Folks that know coal say he was a fine fellow," the sheriff said. "One helluva good foreman!"

"That he was," Lily agreed. "I'll have someone pick up the car."

Her head ached. A cold wind cut through her body and left her shuddering. She expressed gratitude, shook hands, and turned to go to the girls.

"I suppose there could be some sort of investigation, but right now I'm seeing it as a clear case of suicide," the sheriff said.

Lily turned around in a spin. Her grieving voice took on volume.

"No! Oh, no! It was *not* suicide. Abe left something important in that mine, and he went back to find it."

The sheriff, an old friend of Wade Eakins, scratched his whiskers and smiled with his eyes. He gestured a respectable wink.

"And you think he would've found it, Miss Lily, in all that dark?"

"I do, yes, of course. In fact, I know that he did."

"Where's Abe?" Maude asked as she sat at her window, her distant eyes blinking past the crepe myrtle tree Silas Holmes had planted as a tribute to Abe. Rosy had cleaned the bowl and placed the fish on the table beside her rocker. From time to time, Maude talked to the fish instead of elves on the curtains.

"Where's Abe?" she asked some seconds later, her fingers digging through the fringe of her wool afghan.

The twinsies sniffled and looked toward their mother. Rosy ruffled the water to make Abe swim faster. Lily pulled up a chair, sat down, and reached for Maude's hands. They were cold in spite of the afghan, and she warmed them against her face.

"He's gone," she said softly. "Abe's gone."

Maude shook her head and clicked her tongue.

"Gone to that mine?"

"Gone to that mine," Lily said, and turned her head so no one would see that she was sobbing like her pa, that night at tent revival, when he got saved.

75057997R00251

Made in the USA
Columbia, SC
14 August 2017